CURIOUS FLUTTERINGS

Gabriel crooked a finger beneath her chin and lifted her face to his regard. It would have been so easy to escape him, but his surprisingly gentle touch held her motionless.

"A day does not pass," he said, "when I do not wonder if there was something I could have done to turn Bernart from his course, but always it comes to naught."

He felt guilt? Never would she have guessed Gabriel De Vere capable of such emotion.

Regret grooved his mouth. "I am sorry, Juliana."

Was he?

He swept a tear from beneath her eye. So gentle, like the brush of an angel's wing. "If I could change what happened, I would."

Would he?

His breath mingled with hers, warmed her lips. "Though as a young man I scorned your silly notions of love, never did I wish to see you hurt."

Curious flutterings stirred her breast, drew her gaze to his mouth. What would it feel like to press her lips to his? To come to him in the light of day? Imagining it, she closed her eyes. It would be so different from the night past.

BLACKHEART

TAMARA LEIGH

LEISURE BOOKS NEW YORK CITY

At last, a story for Maxen, my littlest love.
May your path be built upon lessons learned
and laid with dreams come true.

A LEISURE BOOK®

April 2001

Published by

Dorchester Publishing Co., Inc.
276 Fifth Avenue
New York, NY 10001

ISBN 0-8439-4855-8

Visit us on the web at www.dorchesterpub.com.

BLACKHEART

Prologue

Son of a whore. Over and over the words resounded through Gabriel. Consumed his being. Inflamed his soul. Beginning to tremble, he turned from his father and pressed his fists to the sill of the window embrasure.

In the bailey below, the garrison stood silent at their posts, castle folk went about their tasks with heads bowed, and a large cat stalked its next meal. As befitting the burial that had taken place two days past, the mood was solemn, and as different from that which seethed through Gabriel as the sun was from the moon.

Son of a whore. Whoreson. How he ached to bloody his knuckles on something! Were he alone, he would turn on the first thing that came to hand.

"I am sorry, Gabriel," his father said. "All these years you have been like a son to me."

Gabriel swung around. "I *am* your son!"

The mighty Arnault De Vere's gaze wavered. "I wish it were so."

"It is!"

"Perhaps, but 'tis Giles who will succeed me."

The third son, whose strong De Vere looks could not be questioned. It was the same for the fourth son, nine-year-old Conard. In contrast, Gabriel and Blase favored their mother's family—tall, big-boned, dark-haired, and possessing faces so plain as to defy description. But Gabriel had one thing Blase did not: their father's gray eyes. Not that it had any bearing on his claim to legitimacy, for the baron seemed willing to overlook it.

"Did Mother . . ." How bitter that his veins strained with her blood. "Did she say I was of another's seed?"

The sunlight slanting through the window spun silver through his father's thick hair and beard. "She did not. On her deathbed she confessed only to"—a muscle jerked in his jaw—"to having cuckolded me before your conception. And, of course, afterward."

Of course. It was no secret that the lady of Wyverly had engaged in adulterous behavior throughout the latter years of her marriage. Gabriel himself had once come upon her in the arms of a man not his father. That had been the summer of his tenth year.

He glanced at the canopied bed in the center of the lord's solar and vividly recalled bodies meshing one with the other, glistening flesh, moans and grunts of pleasure, the trenchant odor of slaked lust. How he had hated Constance De Vere! And now that it was revealed her indiscretions went further back, giving rise to the question of whether or not he and Blase were De Veres, Gabriel was gripped with something so deep and tearing it bore little resemblance to the enmity he had nurtured all these years.

"Then she did not know if 'twas you or another who sired me?"

"I did not ask."

Gabriel's angry stride scattered the herbed rushes underfoot, stirred the air with the scent of mint. He halted before his father. "Why would you not ask?"

The baron held his gaze. "Her confession was made to the priest. She did not know I heard."

Gabriel's fists quaked with the effort to keep them at his sides. "And for this you set me aside?"

The baron's mouth tightened. "When I die, I shall be secure in the knowledge Wyverly is in the hands of a De Vere, as it has been for one hundred twenty years."

Gabriel wanted to rage, but the self-control his father had demanded of him all these years contained the tempest. Silently, he cursed the woman who had borne him. Because of her, he was set aside like a dog that had outworn its welcome at table. Everything that should have been his was gone—his title, lands, betrothal, the son who would one day succeed him. Gone!

He had to leave. Gabriel stepped past his father.

"You will be provided for," the baron said.

Gabriel halted. "On the chance you are wrong?"

Arnault De Vere was not a man who revealed his emotions, but they slipped in, grooved his mouth and brow with regret. "You are a son any man would be proud of, and though you may not be of my body, it does not change my feelings for you."

Gabriel was unmoved. "You are wrong. It changes all."

"Not if you allow me to provide for you."

Although Gabriel had no intention of taking whatever his father offered—and by all that was unholy, Arnault De Vere *was* his father—he asked, "What do you propose?"

Hope entered the baron's eyes. "When your training for knighthood is complete a year hence, I will place Shard Castle in your care."

The greater of Wyverly's lesser castles. Only one whose future had once held all of the barony might not be tempted. Pride was a powerful thing. "What would you have me say to those who ask why I am reduced to a vassal? That my father suspects me of being a whoreson?"

Arnault De Vere's eyes flickered. "None need know the truth. Simply tell them you do not wish the responsibilities of ruling so vast a barony."

"That all who know me will then know me for a liar?"

The baron's jaw quivered with suppressed emotions. "I wish it could be otherwise. You know that."

As deeply as Gabriel wanted to renounce his father's sincerity, he could not. The baron had always demanded more from his eldest son than the others, but never was there any question he loved Gabriel as best he could with a heart scarred by his wife's infidelities.

"Why did you not send her away?" Gabriel asked. "Why did you allow her to dishonor you time and again?"

The baron averted his gaze.

Though Gabriel was racked with pain, he was not alone. Beyond all foolishness, Arnault De Vere had loved his wife. A worse mistake a man could not make.

"Take what I offer," the baron said. "Still you will be lord."

And vassal to his younger brother. Gabriel's gut twisted. "Do you not fear I might seek Giles's death?"

His father appeared momentarily taken aback, then shook his head. "You forget, Gabriel, I know you. You are angry now, but in time . . ."

Gabriel almost laughed. "You do not know me, *Father*. Did you, you would not squander your breath. Keep Shard

10

Castle. I want naught from you." He swung toward the door.

His father caught his arm. "Think! You are near twenty years old. What else is there for you?"

Gabriel looked down. Though the baron was not a small man, Gabriel was taller and broader. Perhaps another *was* responsible for sowing the seed that had begotten him. Instantly he rejected the thought. He was a De Vere, and his father was turning his back on him. Denying him.

Gabriel pulled his arm from the older man's grasp. "I shall return to the service of Baron Sumner"—with whom he had spent the past twelve years training for knighthood—"and when I am knighted, I shall live the life you have dealt me." He strode to the door and paused. "What of Blase? Will you also tell him he is a bastard?"

The baron looked suddenly old where he stood in the middle of the solar. "There is no need. He is destined for the church, and so shall it be."

Except, of course, that Blase was no more fond of the teachings of the church than Gabriel was of treacherous women. Regardless of how hard Friar Jerome tried to fashion his pupil into his own image, it was the sword Blase clasped to his heart, not the Bible.

It was on Gabriel's tongue to inquire into his sister's fate, but he caught himself. Five-year-old Avice no more resembled the baron than Gabriel and Blase, but unlike them, she was blessed with a pleasing combination of Constance De Vere's looks and those of the man who had sired her—whoever that might be. No reason to put more speculation upon her than there already was.

Gabriel threw open the door, strode down the corridor, and descended the spiral stairs. As he stepped into the great hall, he was struck by its warmth, but it had little to do with the blazing fire. What caused him to pause were the splendid tapestries hung ceiling to floor, the plastered walls with their bold, colorful patterns, the dais with its carefully worked table and chairs, the fresh rushes strewn with sweet herbs. He had always accepted that one day all this would be his, had never looked at it through the eyes of one who could never hope to attain such wealth. Now, for the sins of his mother, all was lost.

He started across the hall.

"What is it, Gabriel?" Blase called to him.

He turned and saw that his three brothers were gathered before the hearth. Upon the death of Constance De Vere a sennight past, Giles and Conard had also been summoned from the households of the nobles whom they served. Blase was the only son who resided at Wyverly. If not for Arnault De Vere's determination that he commit his life to the church, he would now be a squire.

Giles stood. "What did Father say?"

Gabriel looked from his younger brother's golden hair to his distinctive forehead, from his high cheekbones to his generous mouth. There was no doubt from whose seed he sprang. But as much as Gabriel wanted to hate Giles for displacing him, he could not. The boy was barely twelve—an innocent. Constance De Vere was to blame. He silently cursed her, and all women. They were a dangerous lot.

"Tell us," young Conard said, worry reflected in eyes the color of Gabriel's.

What was he to say? That their mother was more of a whore than previously thought? Make them despise her as much as he did? Nay, let Arnault De Vere do the telling.

Though it was two years since all four brothers had been together, and thus far Gabriel had been unable to

12

spend much time with them, he could not bear to pass another moment at Wyverly. "I must leave," he said.

Blase gained his feet. "This day?"

"Now."

"Now? But you do not have to return to Falkhead for another sennight."

"That has changed."

Blase, followed by Giles and Conard, crossed to Gabriel's side. "Why?" Blase asked.

Gabriel stared at them. No matter how many times Constance De Vere had strayed outside her marriage, these were his brothers. No matter how deep his anger, he had to shield them from it. "I shall leave it to Father to explain," he said, and turned on his heel.

He strode from the donjon, retrieved his horse from the stables, and shortly sped over the land beyond the castle walls. He did not look back. Not once. Only when a league separated him from all he had lost did he dismount and unburden his emotions. Loathsome tears burned the backs of his eyes, fiery blood pounded in his ears, curses tore from his throat, and every muscle in his body strained as he shook his fists at the heavens.

The sun had sunk low and the land was swept with cool shadows when Gabriel finally regained control. Weary, he knelt beside a stream and splashed frigid water over his face, then sat back on his heels.

Never would he be made a fool as his father had been. Never would he fawn over a woman as his friend, Bernart Kinthorpe, fawned over his betrothed, Juliana. Never!

Unbidden, a vision of the fair Juliana rose to mind, she of fanciful notions of love and chivalry that her mother had learned at Queen Eleanor's Court of Love. Based on the pure and noble love of a man for a woman who was unattainable, be she wed, of higher rank, or physically

13

distanced, the concept of unconsummated love was something silly women sighed over. But some went beyond the bounds of bittersweet suffering. Women like Constance De Vere.

Gabriel's hatred burrowed deeper. Doubtless when Juliana grew into her woman's body she would prove no better than the one who had borne him. Selfish. Deceitful. A whore.

God help Bernart Kinthorpe.

Chapter One

England, March 1195

"I want a son."

The terse words fell into Juliana's consciousness. Thinking she could not have heard right, she looked up from the ledger she'd been poring over.

Bernart stood before the dais upon which the lord's table was raised, his eyes alive with such hunger it sent foreboding coursing through her.

"A son?" she asked.

"A son."

Knowing he would not jest about something so sensitive, Juliana glanced past him. Where minutes earlier servants had bustled about clearing the remains of the evening meal, now the hall stood empty—excepting the young woman who sat unaware before the hearth. As usual, Bernart had overlooked Juliana's sister, as if Alaiz did not exist.

Juliana moistened her lips. "Forgive me, husband, but I do not understand what you speak of."

He stepped up to the dais, pressed his bloated hands to the table, then leaned forward. "I want a son."

Of course he did. Didn't every man? But for Bernart it was not possible. Cautious lest she goad him into one of his grim moods, she pushed the ledger back and folded her hands atop the table. "You know better than I it can never be."

Pain flickered across his features. "But it can be."

Though he was careful to avoid alcohol, Juliana wondered if he'd been drinking. She drew in a breath of air. There was no such scent upon it. "Tell me," she said quietly.

The harsh lines of his fleshly face eased, allowing a glimpse of the handsome man he'd once been. "The child would not be of my blood, but I would raise him as if he were."

Juliana shook her head. "You propose to bring another man's child into our home?"

"Aye. Through you."

"Through me?"

Hunger grew in his eyes. "He would be your son. Born of your body. Of your blood."

His words struck Juliana with the force of a blow. "What are you saying?"

Bernart's limp was more pronounced than usual as he walked around the table. He lowered himself beside her and took her hands in his. "I love you, Juliana. We were meant to be together. We are one."

She had once thought so herself. "What are you saying?" she asked again.

"If you . . ." His voice cracked as it did when he was not careful to modulate it. "If you lie with another man, you could give me a son."

She could not move, could not speak, could only stare at this man who asked the unthinkable. Surely this was but a horrid dream. It had to be. *Wake up. Juliana,* she bade herself. *Wake up clinging to your side of the bed as you do every morning.*

Bernart pressed his brow to the backs of her hands. "Do this for me and no more will I ask of you. I swear it."

She jumped to her feet. Out of the corner of her eye, she caught her sister's start of surprise, but was too roused to pay her heed. "I am your wife! You would have me give myself to another man? Commit adultery?"

Slowly, Bernart stood. "I would not ask it were my need not great."

Grasping for a sliver of sanity in a world gone mad, Juliana drew a deep breath. "Even were a child born of such an unholy union, it would not be yours. Not of you."

"But he would be of you. That is enough for me." He reached to take her hands again.

She sidestepped. "Why do you ask this of me?"

Bernart's struggle to control his temper showed in his tightening fists. "I am without an heir."

"You have an heir. Your brother, Osbern—"

"Is not my brother!"

Juliana shook her head. "Deny him though you do, he is of your blood. This child you ask me to bear would be a bastard. He would never be recognized as your heir."

Bernart took a step toward her. "No one but you and I need know the circumstances of his birth."

She blinked. If not drunk, then he was mad. There was no other explanation.

17

"I have thought long about it," he said. " 'Tis what I want."

So badly that he was holding onto his terrible temper. She swallowed the bitter lump in her throat. "What you want? What of me? You would have me whore myself!"

A tic started at one corner of Bernart's mouth. "You have always wanted children. A dozen, you once said. Remember?"

Juliana remembered. She swung away and stared at the tapestry that scaled the wall behind the table. "I wish children, but not like this. *Never* like this."

A long silence followed; then Bernart's hands fell to her shoulders. "There is no other way."

She closed her eyes. "Then I shall be childless." Just as she had long ago accepted.

With a sharp oath, Bernart dragged her around. "You think I do not know what is said of me?"

Of course she did, just as she knew what was said of her—that she was barren or frigid. Servants talked, and what other conclusion was to be drawn from three years of marriage that had begotten naught but indifference between their lord and lady?

Bernart's fingers dug into her shoulders. " 'Tis said my seed is bad. Worse, that you are without child because I prefer . . . men!"

All the more reason for him to hate his brother. Not that Osbern dared flaunt what he was. He simply did not deny it. Thus Bernart thought to prove his lost manhood by asking this heinous thing of her.

"I can withstand it no more." Tears quavered in his voice. "I beseech you, Juliana, give me a son."

Not since their wedding night, following his return from the Holy Crusade, had his eyes shined so brightly. It was then he'd revealed the injury done him by the in-

fidel, that she would be his wife in name only. Never to
know his touch. Never to bear him children. Through her
sorrow Juliana had told him it did not matter and tried to
comfort him, but he'd rejected her. It did matter. To him.
With each passing day, his bitterness had pushed them
further and further apart. A sob catching in her throat,
Juliana laid a hand alongside his face—so smooth, so
hopelessly devoid of beard. "I am sorry, Bernart, but what
you ask I cannot do."

He squeezed his eyes closed. "Do you love me, Juliana?"

She *had* loved him, had thought she would die if he
did not return from the crusade. But then, she'd been
barely thirteen when he had set off for the Holy Land,
and he a man worthy and capable of love. No more. "You
know 'tis so," she lied.

A long moment passed. "Had I not been faithful to you
before we wed, just as you asked of me, 'tis likely I would
now have a son. True, a bastard, but a son."

She dropped her hand to her side. "Mayhap you do
have one." After all, it was only when she had come upon
him trysting with a wench from her father's hall that she'd
demanded his vow of celibacy—only months before he
had left for the Crusade.

"You think I have not searched?" Bernart demanded.

Had he? "I . . . did not know."

His nostrils flared. "For you, Juliana, I am denied a
child made of my loins. And for what? I cannot even hold
you."

"That is your choice!"

"I have no other."

Nay, he did not. He couldn't stand to touch her when
there was naught he could do to slake his desire. He clung
to his side of the bed and she to hers.

"Please," Juliana said, "let us speak no more of this. I know you are hurting—"

"You know naught!" He shook her so hard her head snapped back. "I ask only that you give back some of what I have given you, and you deny me."

She strained away, but he held tight. "Have I not been a good wife?" she cried. "I keep your household in order, your accounts—"

"You think that is enough?"

" 'Tis all I have to give."

"Nay, you can give me a son."

Her throat so tight she could hardly breathe, she shook her head.

In his eyes she saw that he wished to strike her, but he thrust her from him. With higher-pitched curses that belied his earlier attempt to lower his voice, he knocked over her chair, swept the ledger from the table, sent the ink pot soaring. The latter missed the tapestry by inches and dashed its dark contents against the wall.

"Juli . . . ana."

The timid voice reminded Juliana she was not the only witness to Bernart's fury. Regretting that she had not sent her sister from the hall, she turned.

Alaiz stood before the dais, hands clasped at her waist and bottom lip caught between her teeth as she peered at Juliana from beneath sweeping lashes.

Fearing Alaiz might become an object of Bernart's wrath, Juliana hurried around the table and stepped from the dais. She laid an urgent hand to her sister's shoulder. Not surprisingly, Alaiz radiated heat and smoke. She always sat too near the fire.

" 'Tis all right," Juliana spoke amid the din. "Go abovestairs."

"B-Bernart . . . angry."

"Not with you. Now go." Juliana gave her a nudge.

"You will come . . . soon?"

"Aye. Hurry along."

With Alaiz's retreat, silence descended upon the hall. Fearing it, Juliana looked around.

Bernart's gaze was fixed past her to where Alaiz mounted the stairs.

What was he thinking? Embarrassed as he was by Alaiz, he quickly looked away anytime she fell under his regard. Now he followed her progress with something in his eyes that twisted Juliana's insides.

"What of Alaiz?" he asked.

Dear God. Though Alaiz had been schooled for the church and destined to one day take her place among the great abbesses, a fall from her horse a year ago had impaired her mind. The nobleman who'd bought wardship of Alaiz, their mother, and younger brother upon the death of Juliana's father six months earlier had refused to pay the enormous sum the church demanded to care for Alaiz. Thus, had Bernart not grudgingly agreed to allow her to live with them, she would have been turned out to wander the countryside. He had been more than generous, Juliana conceded, but must she pay for that generosity with so cruel a fouling of her body?

Looking the predator in spite of his flaccid figure and limp, he traversed the dais and stepped down beside her. "When there was no one who wanted her, I allowed her into my home."

Juliana lifted her chin. "She serves me well."

His laughter was harsh. Mean. " 'Tis you who dresses her. A lady in waiting, indeed! She is an imbecile."

Juliana gasped, swept a hand up to strike him.

Bernart caught her wrist. "She is of no use to anyone. An embarrassment."

21

Juliana began to tremble. "Do not speak so of her."

" 'Tis the truth. For the love of you I took her in."

She nearly laughed. Though she could have sought an annulment on the grounds that Bernart was incapable of consummating their marriage, for the love of *him* she had not done it. Only when he had refused to allow Alaiz to come to Tremoral two years later had she threatened to reveal his terrible secret. Thus he had agreed, but not for love of her, as he claimed.

"Juliana?"

She met his gaze. Now he was the one with power. "You are cruel," she said.

"I am what you make me." He thrust his face near hers. "Give me a son. If not for me, then for Alaiz."

As much as she wanted to cry at the injustice, she would not. "Truly you would send her away?"

The man her child's heart had once loved flickered and died in his eyes. "I would."

Could he do it? Not Bernart Kinthorpe who'd set out on that fateful Crusade six years ago, but the man he had become . . . Juliana drew herself to her full five feet, two inches. "I shall never forgive you for this."

"You will do it?"

"Have I another choice?"

Relief dropped his rigid shoulders. "I thank you."

She jerked her wrist out of his hold. "Whose seed will you plant in my belly?"

He averted his gaze. "I have not decided."

But he would, and soon. "And if this man whom you choose tells?"

He skirted her. "Fear not; I will see to all."

"Would you kill him?"

He halted, was slow to answer. "Nay," he said, keeping his back to her.

Did he lie? His eyes—she had to see them. She came around him, but he dropped his lids. Emotion was cleared from his eyes when he gave his gaze back to her.

Juliana filled her chest with breath, took a step back. "Then if 'tis not by death he will hold your foul secret, how? You will pay him?"

A muscle convulsed his jaw. "No payment will be necessary, for he will not know 'tis you who comes to him."

"Not know . . . ?" She shook her head. "Pray, how will you arrange that?"

"Enough!" He backhanded the air between them, missing her by a breath. "There is naught more to be said."

She was dismissed. "I shall pray for your soul," she said, and started for the stairs. She'd taken only a few steps when another question came hard to her. She swung around. "If he does not get me with child, what then?"

Bernart's answer came without hesitation. "When is your next monthly flux?"

He had thought of everything. Though she was tempted to lie so he would not know her time of fertility, she realized it would not turn him from this terrible course. God willing, it would take only once to sow a babe. "A fortnight hence," she begrudged.

He nodded. "The seed will take."

Nausea rolled, burned. "And if 'tis a daughter I birth, would you ask it of me again?"

As if this were an eventuality he'd not considered, his eyes shifted and his brow doubled on itself. "I will not."

Though it was a son he longed for, a daughter would as well prove his manhood. "I will have your word," Juliana said.

"You have it."

Now to put distance between herself and this man

23

who'd once fed her foolish dreams of love. She turned away.

Halfway across the hall, Bernart's voice reached to her. "Forgive me."

She faltered, but ascended the stairs without a backward glance. She found Alaiz in the small chamber her sister occupied next to the lord's solar.

Looking forlorn where she sat cross-legged on the bed, Alaiz glanced up as Juliana stepped inside. "Bernart is still angry?"

Juliana lowered herself to the mattress edge. "No more." He had what he wanted. He ought to be pleased.

"He does not . . ." Alaiz looked to her clasped hands. "He does not l-like me."

Though Juliana hated lying, she put an arm around Alaiz. "Of course he likes you."

Alaiz looked up. "Nay."

Juliana was struck by the lucidity reflected in her sister's eyes. It reminded her of that which, prior to her marriage to Bernart, had shone from Alaiz when she'd disdained her older sister's eagerly embraced notion of long-suffering love. For perhaps the hundredth time, Juliana was haunted by Alaiz's warning that were she not careful she might be granted such a love. How wise she'd been for one so young, and how foolish Juliana.

A moment later, the lucidity retreated to wherever it hid itself behind Alaiz's eyes. It was not the first time Juliana had glimpsed the young woman her sister had been ere the head injury had impaired her faculties, but such clarity was ever fleeting.

Alaiz cocked her head. "You are going to have a . . ." In her search for the elusive word, she tensed, eyelids fluttering, lips trying once—twice—to form the word. Finally she expelled her breath and smiled. "You are going to have a baby, Juliana?"

What she'd witnessed in the hall had not escaped her. She was childlike, but not an imbecile as Bernart believed. Juliana forced breath past her tight throat. "Aye."

Alaiz sighed and settled her head onto Juliana's shoulder. "You always . . . take care of me."

Juliana squeezed her eyes closed. "And I always shall."

Bernart felt as if he would retch. He pulled the back of his hand across his mouth, hating himself more than Juliana could ever hate him. But if she gave him a son, all would be worth the pain. It would silence the cruel gossip and ensure that Osbern never held Kinthorpe lands. Osbern, whose very existence fueled the rumors of Bernart's lack of an heir.

Bitterness in his mouth, Bernart lifted his goblet. It was empty. He rose from the lord's chair and limped to the sideboard that had escaped his earlier raging. Remains of the evening meal were set there, along with pitchers of wine, ale, and honeyed milk. He reached for the latter, pausing midair to consider the ale. It was a long time since he'd succumbed to his yearning for real drink. He could almost taste it. Perhaps just one . . .

Nay, the consequences were too dire, his intolerance for alcohol so great that small amounts depleted his strength and made urination painful. His hand trembled as he poured honeyed milk into a goblet, and more violently when he lifted the vessel and choked down its impotent contents.

He slammed the goblet to the sideboard, stood unmoving a long moment, then splayed a hand over his thigh and crept inward to touch the emptiness between his legs. A whimper broke his lips, rushed revulsion through his gut. The deep voice that had once been his had taken on a feminine quality. He disguised it, at the cost of painfully strained throat muscles, but other effects of his emasculation were not so easily overcome. Much of his body hair was lost or thinned, he carried excess weight he could not shed, suffered from chronic sleeplessness, and had such difficulty holding his urine that the possibility of soiling himself was ever present. His was a hell none would ever understand.

His thigh began to ache, further reminding him of the clash with Muslim soldiers that had not only cost him his manhood, but had smitten him with a limp he could not conceal.

Would a son end his pain? Quiet the voices that taunted him long into the night? It was what he longed for, but the thought of another man touching Juliana, especially the one he intended to father his son, pitched the contents of his belly. Juliana was his, had been his from the moment she'd wailed her way into the world, had made him the envy of every man who gazed upon her beauty. If not for the one whose betrayal had cost him the ability to father children, none of this would be necessary.

Nearly upping the bile that seared his throat, Bernart swallowed hard, coughed, swallowed again. He had to do it. Had to. Now to lure his prey to Tremoral.

France, April 1195

A challenge.

Gabriel stared at the tournament field from which he'd retreated with the breaking of his lance. So Kinthorpe wished to meet him in tournament. Why now? It was—how many years? Four? Aye, four since Bernart had gathered a hundred men to him to take the city of Acre from

26

the Muslims. The memory of it was nearly as clear as the day it had been set in Gabriel's mind. Desperate from months of siege, slaughter, and a stark shortage of food, Bernart and his followers had presented a pitiful image of Christianity knocked to its knees. Destined for death.

At the age of twenty-three, Gabriel had already earned the reputation of being a knight of goodly skill and courage, but he was also endowed with enough wits to know the difference between courage and stupidity. He'd tried to turn his friend from an undertaking foreordained to failure, had confronted Bernart and the others with the reminder that previous attempts by the Christian army to go over the wall had resulted in mass slaughter. Though Bernart had stood against such reasoning, a score of men had not—had walked away. Desperate to reach his friend, Gabriel had assured him the forces of King Richard would soon arrive to give them victory over the infidels—though he was not certain of it himself. In response, another score of men had withdrawn from the ranks of those soon to die. Enraged by what he perceived to be betrayal, Bernart had accused Gabriel of cowardice and, cursing him, had set off for the walled city.

In the darkening of day, the coming of night, Gabriel had stared after Bernart and his diminished band of soldiers, had sworn he would not follow, had told himself again and again that his friend had the right to choose his own path. But what a bloody path it had been, just as Gabriel had known it would be. And Bernart was not the only one to bear its scars. Indeed.

Gabriel ground his teeth. Though he knew he'd saved the lives of those he'd dissuaded from following Bernart, he was burdened by guilt that he had not tried harder to deter a man with whom he'd been friends since boyhood. Then there was the thought that had he not persuaded so many to turn from the foolish quest, Bernart might have succeeded in breaking through the city's defenses. Impossible, though Gabriel could not put it from him. But he yet would.

Abruptly he turned his attention to the melee. On the field, countless knights and foot soldiers engaged in the mock battle of tournament, the purpose of which was to capture and ransom as many opposing knights as possible, preferably without killing them. During the past two hours, Gabriel had taken three. Providing his good fortune held, he would take as many more before the day was done, and by nightfall his purse would be heavy with the coin of their ransom.

A wry smile twitched his mouth. France's tournaments were lucrative. Given a few more years, the siege-ravaged demesne King Richard had awarded him here, on the continent, would rival the great baronies on either side of the channel.

Gabriel searched the battlefield for sight of the knight with whom he'd entered into a partnership upon their return from the crusade. Fighting as a team, dividing their winnings between them, they'd captured more than eighty knights in the past nine months without once being ransomed themselves. But it looked as if their luck was about to turn. Sir Erec was in the midst of a struggle to hold back three knights.

"Damn!" Gabriel thrust his helm onto his head, seized the lance his squire held, and started for his destrier.

"Your reply, Lord De Vere?" an urgent voice called.

He glanced over his shoulder. He had forgotten about the messenger who'd crossed the channel to deliver Bernart's challenge and who had taken the opportunity of Gabriel's need to rearm himself to deliver it.

Fleetingly, Gabriel considered the generous purse Bernart would award the knight who took the most ransoms at Tremoral—enough to complete restoration of the inner wall of his castle. Tempting, but that was all. "No reply," he tossed back.

The messenger hurried forward. "Be it yea or nay, my lord?"

Gabriel put a foot in the stirrup and swung his mail-laden body into the saddle.

The messenger stepped into the destrier's path. "I am not to return without your reply."

Gabriel jerked the reins left and put heels to the destrier. "Then you will be a long time in France," he shouted as he swept past the man. Once more upon the field, he sighted Sir Erec where he held against his opponents. Determining the best approach, he couched his lance under his right arm, taking the rhythm of the horse beneath him.

Was it revenge Bernart sought? The question rent his concentration. It was no secret that he blamed Gabriel for his failure at Acre, the deaths of those who'd followed him, his being lamed, and whatever abuses he'd suffered during his imprisonment. But if revenge, why now?

Nay! Gabriel jerked his head in his helm. He would think no more on it, not when there were more important matters, namely Sir Erec and the three knights who did not know there would soon be ransom to pay. However, try as Gabriel did to ignore it, the air rushing past him whispered of one he'd not allowed himself to think upon for a long time: Juliana the fair.

He cast back to the year 1189, two years following his father's disavowal. He saw again Juliana's tearful flight into the garden where he'd awaited a tryst with a chambermaid. Oblivious to all but her pain, the lovely woman-child hadn't noticed him where he leaned against a wall. Breasts heaving, sobs quaking her shoulders, she'd dropped to a bench and clapped her hands to her face.

Gabriel had needed none to tell him the cause of her misery, for he knew Bernart well. Too, a half hour earlier he'd lost the toss to be the first to lie with a lusty maid who'd been intent on having them both at once.

In spite of a thousand warning voices sounding between his ears, he'd yielded to the strange desire to comfort Juliana and had gone to her. He had lowered himself beside her, spoken her name, and all of him had stopped when she'd looked up.

As he stared into her dark eyes, something had moved through him, something he'd never thought to feel and that would ever haunt him. It had forced him to acknowledge that she was not the foolish child he'd often scorned, but a girl on the edge of womanhood, a gem ready to be put to polish. And soon to be his friend's wife.

"Gabriel," she had choked, and he'd been struck by his name on her lips when she had only ever called him "squire" and, since receiving knighthood, "Sir Knight"— both spoken with disdain. Then she had leaned toward him as if to come into his arms. And he might have let her had Bernart not called her name. For a moment longer he'd held her gaze, which had never before considered him with such intensity, then risen. A tugging inside him, he'd turned and traversed the path to the donjon. As he neared the entrance, Bernart burst into the garden and thrust past him as if he did not see him. Tunic dragged on backward, hose rent from the haste with which he'd dressed, he dropped to his knees before Juliana. Amid his pleas for forgiveness, Gabriel had slipped away.

After that, everything changed. Bernart cleaved to the vow of chastity extracted from him, Juliana crossed the threshold into womanhood, and the scorn Gabriel had felt for her turned to an ache—though he was careful to keep hidden that which her anguish had drawn from his cold depths. Juliana, of auburn hair that tempted a man's hands and brown eyes warm enough to send the chill from the coldest night, was a woman he could never have. Should never have.

Did her eyes still sparkle with delight? Did her easy laughter put light to the air? Or had the years matured her into one of those treacherous creatures who were good only for bedding?

Naturally, Gabriel's thoughts turned to the one whose faithless body had pushed him into the world and the lies she had woven around her like a spider weaves its mortal web. He gripped his lance tighter. Did Juliana tread the same path as Constance De Vere? Following three years of marriage, had the sweet glow of wedlock waned such that she forsook her vows to pursue the senseless ideas of love she'd espoused as a girl? Likely. She was a woman, and no better than any other. But she was not his problem. She belonged to Bernart.

Gabriel settled his gaze on the knight most likely to unseat Sir Erec, loosed a war cry, and positioned himself. Unwavering, he held until the iron tip of his lance met chain mail.

Chapter Two

England, May 1195

He was not coming.

Beneath the table, Bernart clenched his hands so tightly they trembled. Though Gabriel had refused to answer the challenge, Bernart had convinced himself his enemy would come. Now, with all the knights gathered in the hall following a day of practice and tomorrow the opening day of the tournament, he was proven wrong.

He glanced at Juliana. She sat silent beside him, in one hand a wine goblet, in the other a spoon, but not once had she drunk from the vessel, nor eaten from the trencher between them. The only movement about her the gentle rise and fall of her breasts, she stared across the hall.

Although it was two months since Bernart had forced her to his plan, and nothing more had been spoken of it, she assuredly knew the time had come. And she waited to be led to bed like a lamb to gutting.

What was he to do? All was in place, from Juliana's time of breeding, to the chamber in which the deed would be done, to the rumor he had imparted that if she did not soon ripen with child he would rid himself of her and take another wife. So should he choose another to lie with her? Could he?

As with every time he imagined any man enjoying what should have been his, self-loathing filled him. In spite of the resentment Juliana exuded, regardless of her unsmiling face, there was no woman more beautiful. And every man in the hall agreed. They struggled to keep their eyes from her, quickly looked elsewhere when they found Bernart watching them, but ever their gaze returned to her.

Perhaps he ought abandon the idea, Bernart considered. At least then he might regain what little he'd had of Juliana before he'd demanded a son from her. Perhaps the hatred would disappear from her eyes.

Nay, though he was not to have the satisfaction of taking a child from one whose betrayal had cost him the ability to father children, he needed a son to silence the speculation about his manhood. So who was it to be? He studied the knights seated around him. Sir Kenelm, too old. Sir Arnold, a lecher. Sir Morris, too handsome. Sir Simon, a cruel man. He was about to dismiss Sir Henry when the great doors across the hall swung open.

The eyes of the man who strode within were colder than the night air he brought with him. They pinned Bernart where he sat in the lord's high seat and calmed the din to a murmur. He had come.

Relief, darkened by disquiet, rippled through Bernart. Gabriel De Vere was nearly as he remembered him. Tall, broad, unkempt from his long brown hair down to his well-worn boots. In all, he presented little for a woman to gaze upon, but as Bernart knew, it would take no more than a flash of pale eyes to draw women to him like birds to flight.

Bernart glanced at Juliana.

Her face reflected disbelief, then anger. Though it was no secret that Bernart and Gabriel's friendship had been severed years ago, only she knew the true depth of her husband's feelings—and shared his enmity. So how long until she realized the reason for Gabriel's attendance? How long until the hatred she bore Bernart trebled?

Bernart rose from his chair. "Lord De Vere," he called.

Gabriel, followed by another knight whose exemplary grooming differed considerably from his own, traversed the remainder of the hall. He halted before the dais. "Lord Kinthorpe."

His hair had begun to silver at the temples, and there were fine lines around his eyes, nose, and mouth that had not been there when he'd come before Bernart in the dungeon at Acre.

With so many watching, Bernart summoned a smile that could not have been falser had it been cut from the devil's mouth. "You come to tourney?"

Gabriel inclined his head. "By invitation."

Bernart heard Juliana's sharply indrawn breath. She knew. Avoiding her gaze, he said, "You are late."

"We are," Gabriel said without apology.

The knight beside him stepped forward. "Sir Erec Sinward, my lord. Regretfully, during the crossing from France our ship was blown off course. We have ridden hard these past days to make your tournament."

Considering their renown on the battlefield, Bernart knew there would be protests against their late entry.

34

"You are welcome at Tremoral, Lord De Vere and Sir Erec." He swept a hand before him. "Join us. There is food and drink aplenty, entertainment, and willing wenches."

Sir Erec bowed curtly. "You are gracious, my lord." He turned away.

Gabriel regarded Bernart a moment longer, then lowered his gaze to Juliana.

Bernart had wondered whether or not his enemy, the only man he had known to be impervious to Juliana's beauty, intended to acknowledge her. From the day Bernart had introduced his friend to the girl who was to be his bride, their mutual dislike had been more tangible than the chill in winter. Gabriel had named Juliana's notions of love and chivalry foolish, and she had declared him ill-mannered and dishonorable. When Bernart had tried to convince her otherwise, she'd pointed out that Gabriel's own father had set him aside. Bernart had been unable to argue that, for Gabriel had never explained the reason that his future as Baron of Wyverly was past.

"Lady Juliana," Gabriel said.

"Lord De Vere." Her tone was frigid enough to cause a man to sink more deeply into the folds of his mantle.

Just as it should be, Bernart told himself. Juliana would do what was required of her and hate every moment of it—no possibility she would feel anything for Gabriel.

With a curt nod, Gabriel turned and strode after Sir Erec.

The commotion in the hall resumed. Servants returned to their tasks, squires to their excited chatter, lords and knights to their boasting, and the ladies who'd accompanied their husbands to the tournament resumed their idle talk.

Try though Bernart did to ignore the gaze that seemed

to bore through him, he looked down. The hatred that shone from Juliana's eyes wounded him as no words could. She would never forgive him for what he did.

He'd had enough. He wanted music to deafen the voices in his head that spoke against him, jongleurs to make him laugh, tales of the troubadour to wash away his pain. He signaled an end to the meal and stepped from behind the lord's table. "Minstrels!" he shouted.

Slowly Juliana gained her feet. She felt cold, as if she might never know warmth again. Holding her arms at her sides to keep from hugging them to her, she watched as Bernart and his guests surged toward the hearth. As lady of Tremoral, her place was there, but she could not bring herself to join them. Not on a night such as this—a night made tenfold worse by the arrival of the one with whom Bernart intended her to lie.

She swallowed hard. Why had De Vere come? Greed? Vainglory? Or did he truly believe Bernart had forgiven him his betrayal? Was it renewed friendship he sought? If the latter, he was a fool. But then, he did not know the extent of Bernart's anger. That ignorance could mean the death of him. Not that she cared. It was through De Vere's resentment and cowardice that Bernart had been rendered impotent. He was as much her enemy as her husband's. Pained by her years of marriage to a man who would not even touch her, she looked across the hall to where the dark knight and his fair-haired companion stood apart from the others.

Although De Vere had matured and seemed broader of shoulders, he was not much changed from the young man who'd accompanied Bernart to Castle Gloswell all those years past. He exuded the same darkness he had then and, doubtless, was no more chivalrous. A hard man. Incapable of loving and being loved. And if not this night, then the next, she would be forced to submit to him.

Desperation gripped her. How could Bernart ask it of her? What possessed him to choose his enemy? If she refused him, would he truly turn Alaiz out? Alaiz, whom he had ordered to remain abovestairs until after the tournament?

Suddenly Gabriel's pale gaze pierced her.

As badly as Juliana wanted to look away, she held her eyes to his. She was not frightened of him. He was a man, like any other. Not that she was intimately familiar with any other.

In the end, it was she who broke the stare. Uncaring that she might be missed, she lifted her skirts clear of the debris that littered the rushes, crossed the hall, and ascended the stairs.

He was not accustomed to losing. But then, neither was he in the habit of ignoring every instinct that had warned him against accepting Bernart Kinthorpe's challenge. He should not be here.

Wondering what had possessed him, Gabriel folded his arms over his chest and waited to see if Erec fared any better in the treacherous game of dice. Hardly had the next round begun when he was struck with the sensation of being watched. He knew who it was without looking around. During the past hours he'd become inured to the man's scrutiny.

Bernart was laying his plans, whatever they might be.

Hips swaying, a serving wench approached—the same who had thrice attended to Gabriel's thirst, whose dark eyes spoke of another thirst she'd willingly quench. Nesta, she called herself. Not that it mattered. Names were of little import when two people came together for pleasure.

"More ale, Lord De Vere?" she invited.

He nodded.

The wench leaned forward and settled her pitcher against the rim of his tankard.

His loins stirred at the sight of twin globes pushing up from the neckline of her gown. Though he was only a sennight without a woman, he was feeling strangely deprived. True, he had an appetite for the cradle of a woman's thighs, her panting breath in his ear, the rake of her nails down his back, but this night his need was stronger than usual.

The wench drew back. "Is there aught else ye require, Lord De Vere?" Her voice was a husky purr that gave promise of the moans he would wring from her.

Gabriel trailed his gaze to her somewhat thick waist, then to flared hips thrust forward beneath her gown. Was there a darkened corner within the donjon where he might sample her? Behind a tapestry? The storeroom? Mayhap his tent—providing his squire had finished pitching it.

She brushed against him. "Sire?"

Gabriel was about to suggest the gardens when a movement to his left drew his regard. Bernart. His limp more obvious than it had been earlier that evening, he advanced. The man had not lost his talent for picking the most inopportune time to appear. Gabriel looked back at the wench. "Perhaps later."

Disappointment pouted her thin lips. "Mayhap." With a toss of her head, she sauntered to those gathered around the dice.

A smile found Gabriel's mouth. She would wait for him. She had not gone to the trouble of turning other wenches from his path only to cast her eyes elsewhere.

Bernart halted a stride from Gabriel.

"Try a few casts, Lord Kinthorpe," one of the knights invited.

38

Bernart shook his head. "I prefer to watch you lose *your* money, Sir Tarrant."

Several rounds later, with the silence between Bernart and Gabriel grown heavy, Bernart asked, "Is fortune not with you this eve?"

Gabriel met his gaze. "I cannot say it has looked kindly upon me." For proof, his purse hung lighter from his belt.

Bernart cocked his head. "What of the morrow? Think you fortune will look kindly upon you then?"

Gabriel considered him. Though Bernart had once been among the strongest, not to mention most handsome of men, it was obvious he'd fallen victim to excess and lack of discipline. There was spare flesh around his eyes and jowls, the dark hair visible beneath his embroidered cap was thin and dull, his hands were slightly bloated, and his belted waist was by no means trim. A worthy opponent? Though they had once been fairly matched in arms, it appeared those days were gone. "I assure you," Gabriel said, "you will not find me lacking."

Bernart pursed and unpursed his lips. "Nay, I do not think I will."

An exultant shout, answered by groans and the clatter of coins, proclaimed the winner of the latest throw of dice. Sir Erec.

Flashing big teeth, the knight turned to where Nesta hovered over his shoulder, pulled her against him. He kissed her loudly, then set her from him.

Nesta swept her gaze to Gabriel. With a seductive dip of her lashes, she slid her tongue over her flushed lips.

Though she thought to make him jealous, it was an emotion to which Gabriel was immune. No woman was worth such destructive feelings. Still, he wouldn't mind satisfying himself with her.

Bernart stepped to Gabriel's side. "I see some things have not changed."

Gabriel knew what Bernart referred to—his ability to find favor with women when he stood in the midst of men far more handsome and moneyed. "Some things," he agreed.

Bernart looked away, but not before Gabriel glimpsed the darkness that flashed in his old friend's eyes. The hairs on the back of Gabriel's neck prickled.

Several minutes passed. "A chamber has been prepared for you," Bernart said. "I would be pleased if you would stay in the donjon as my guest."

Now the hairs on the backs of Gabriel's hands stood erect. Though Tremoral's castle was more grand than most, its private accommodations were limited, and those few chambers were surely reserved for the great lords and their ladies. All other participants would be expected to pitch tents outside the walls or bed down in the hall. "Forgive me if I am surprised by your invitation."

Bernart shrugged. "We were once great friends."

"Once."

The words Bernart summoned must have been more bitter than the meanest ale. "And now, again, I would be your friend. If you will allow it."

What gain did he seek in having the one he blamed for his capture at Acre beneath his roof? Did he think to sneak up on Gabriel while he slept and slip a knife in his back? Nay, too obvious. Likely he wished to establish goodwill so that whatever he planned for the battlefield would appear innocent—an accident. But Gabriel had no intention of accommodating him. He returned his gaze to Nesta.

She smiled, then turned away.

Ah, but she tempted him. A sennight without a woman—

"Gabriel?" Bernart prompted.

He snatched his mind out of his braies. Friends? The man must think him a fool. "I come to tourney," he said, staring after the wench, "and that is all."

Silence rushed in to fill the void. Finally Bernart asked, "You desire her?" He jutted his chin to where Nesta poured ale for the men at the hearth. "I remember how you like your women. For certain, she will please you."

Obviously Bernart had not forgotten their younger days when they had sought and enjoyed the pleasures of women—before Juliana had demanded his vow of chastity.

"If you like her, you may have her," Bernart said.

The words wrenched Gabriel back to the reality of the woman offered him. So different from Juliana. Dark against light. Though he'd told himself it was only for the winnings he came to Tremoral, it was a lie. But now that he had seen Juliana and felt the force of her hatred, perhaps he could finally put her from him.

"She scratches and bites," Bernart said, "but I do not think you will mind."

So, though he had remained true to Juliana throughout the Crusade, now that they were wed he freely scattered his seed. Strange he had no children running about, legitimate or otherwise.

"I tell you, though," Bernart continued, "she is particular about where she makes love and will not allow you to take her against a wall."

Gabriel doubted that. From what he'd seen in Nesta's eyes, where she opened her thighs was of no matter. Wondering how she fit with Bernart's scheme, Gabriel studied his old friend's face.

Bernart looked across the hall. "Your chamber is on the second floor at the top of the stairs."

It *would* be nice to sleep in a bed, as he had not done so for some time. And to satisfy this need. Knowing Bernart had previously enjoyed Nesta caused her to lose much of her appeal, though it usually did not bother him to bed a woman known to other men, but she would do. "I accept your offer."

"I am pleased."

Bernart staggered beneath the sting of Juliana's palm. He clapped a hand to his fiery cheek and met her accusing stare.

"How could you?" She trembled with anger.

She had been waiting for him, just as he had known she would, but had prayed she would not. He glanced at where Alaiz slept on a pallet at the foot of the bed, dismissed her presence, then stepped into the lord's solar. "You are acting the shrew, Juliana." He closed the door behind him. "What does it matter whom I choose?"

"What does it matter?" As if it was all she could do to keep from striking him a second time, she clenched her hands. "After what he did to you? He abandoned you, turned others from your cause—"

"You think I do not know that?" he roared.

She flinched. "Then why would you give me to such a man? Why Gabriel De Vere?"

Bernart stepped to the bed, keeping his back to her. "We are both dark."

"There are others as dark."

He cursed himself for offering so feeble an explanation. "As one of four sons, the male line is strong in him."

" 'Tis as strong in others."

Curse her! Why couldn't she simply do as told? *Very well.* "As it was Gabriel who took my sons from me, so

42

shall I take one from him. 'Tis the least he owes me."
There, it was said.

"It is more than that. Tell me."

Damn her for pushing so hard! Bernart swung around.
"You hate him."

Her eyes widened. "Of course I do. 'Tis all the more
reason—"

"Quiet!" He closed the distance between them. "You
think I wish you to like the man for whom you lie down?
Nay, I want you to despise him and everything he does
to you—to come back to me without ridiculous notions
of love lightening your head."

Juliana stared at him, searching his face. "I see," she
said quietly.

At least she did not press him further—wring from him
that which he could hardly admit to himself: for all of
Gabriel's betrayal, Bernart admired his enemy. There was
no man worthier of fathering his son.

"You will hate any child he makes upon me," Juliana
said.

Would he? "I will not."

"The child's veins will run with the blood of your enemy. Every time you look—"

"I have decided!" Bernart started toward the door.

Juliana put a staying hand to his arm. "Pray, Bernart,
if you must ask this of me, choose another."

Her expression tore him open. He swallowed. "Nay."
Given a push, he thought he could drown in the tears
flooding her eyes.

She looked away. "You would have me go to him
now?"

Although it was as he'd planned, he shook his head.
"Tomorrow eve."

Her shoulders slumped. "How will you arrange it?"

43

"I have given him Alaiz's chamber. Each night, until the conclusion of the tournament, you will go to him in darkness when all have taken to their beds."

As simple as that, Juliana thought bitterly. Bernart would have her steal into Gabriel's bed in the dark of night. "And if he discovers 'tis me?"

"He will not."

"But if he does?"

"Never will he guess it is you. He will think you merely an eager wench."

A whore. Although Juliana was not inclined to vindictiveness, she found herself wanting to hurt Bernart as he hurt her. "And when Gabriel comes to me, what if I cry out and he recognizes my voice? What then, Bernart?"

Angry color rushed his neck. "I trust you will control yourself."

"I will try, but 'tis not as if I know what to expect, is it?"

With an angry snarl, Bernart swept an arm back to strike her. He stopped his hand inches from her face.

Juliana looked from his quaking palm to pained eyes. "I pray that what you gain will be worth the grief you cause us both," she said.

He pushed past her and flung open the door.

She stared at his retreating back. A sennight from now, all this would be in the past. But what of the future? Would it hold the son Bernart so badly wanted? A child whose very being would never allow her to forget what she had done to get him?

She stood a long time pondering the years before her, then drew a deep breath. Whatever happened, she would endure it. As she reached to close the door, she heard footsteps. Knowing they were not the booted feet of a man

44

and that it was too late for servants to be about, she peered into the corridor.

Nesta. Reaching for the door to Gabriel's chamber.

The implications curdled Juliana's stomach. It was terrible enough that tomorrow eve she must go to him, but so soon after he lay with another? Especially one as lewd as that wench? She stepped into the corridor. "What do you abovestairs?" she demanded.

Nesta snatched her arm to her side. "M'lady! I . . ." She slid her gaze to Gabriel's chamber. "Just wanted to make certain yer guest was comfortable."

As only Nesta could make him. Juliana had many times come upon the wench as she boasted to others of her lascivious trysts with men. Thus Juliana had learned of those things that happened between men and women, things she would have preferred not to know. "How kind of you. However, I am sure Lord De Vere is resting well—as you should be. There is much work to be done on the morrow."

Resentment leaped in Nesta's eyes. "But of course, m'lady." She sauntered toward the stairs.

When she was gone, Juliana let her tense shoulders fall. Nesta was not content with her place at Tremoral and never would be. The illegitimate daughter of a neighboring baron, she believed herself better than the other servants and let them know it at every turn. Thus, since being sent to serve at Tremoral two years ago, she'd proved herself a constant source of unrest. She complained incessantly, instigated quarrels, and was comfortably wanton. Not for the first time, Juliana considered sending Nesta to serve at one of the barony's lesser castles.

As she turned in to her chamber, a thought struck her. She looked to the door behind which Gabriel De Vere slept. Had her husband provided for the possibility that there might be another woman in Gabriel's bed? That Nesta or some other wench might come to Gabriel when Juliana was with him? In the next instant she reminded herself that Bernart knew his old friend well. He was too determined to have a son to overlook such an obstacle. The only question was whether or not she could do what he demanded. Could she surrender her virtue to a man she detested? Could she lie beneath him and knowingly steal a child from his loins? Though she blamed Gabriel for Bernart's inability to father children, what they planned was wrong. Very wrong.

She stepped into the lord's solar and closed the door. The torch, flickering its last breath, cast an eerie glow over the chamber and made beasts of shadows and movement from the stillness. Chill bumps rose across her skin. She rubbed her hands over her arms and glanced at the pallet where her sister's fair head shone against the dark blanket pulled over her.

Alaiz had been asleep when Juliana had come above-stairs and, fortunately, had not awakened during the confrontation with Bernart. How had she whiled away the day? How had she filled the slow minutes that must have seemed hours? Resenting Bernart for refusing to allow Alaiz to attend the festivities for fear her infirmity would reflect ill on him, Juliana crossed to the bed and lay down.

She fought the overwhelming need to vent her emotions, but in the end tears would not be denied. Just this once, she promised herself, then nevermore. As she turned her face into the pillow, the mattress gave on the opposite side of the bed. Realizing her restlessness had awakened Alaiz, she clenched her jaw, but it was no use. A convulsive sob escaped.

Alaiz's arm came around her. "Do not cry, Juliana. All will be . . . well."

Nay, it would not. "I know. You should return to your pallet." Although she would have liked for Alaiz to remain, if Bernart returned this eve he would be angered to discover her sister abed.

Alaiz stroked Juliana's hair. "We could . . . leave."

"Leave?" In that muddled world of Alaiz's, did she grasp Juliana's terrible predicament?

"Aye, r-run away."

For a moment, Juliana considered it, but they had nowhere to go. Though she might find a way to survive outside Tremoral's walls, it would be far too dangerous for Alaiz. Nay, she would give Bernart the child he demanded and, hopefully, life would resume its tedious pace. She wiped her eyes. "Surely you know we would not get far."

Life flickered deep in Alaiz's eyes, revealed something of her lost self. "I . . . I have thought on it some."

That, Juliana did not doubt.

"If we c-cut our hair and don men's clothes, none would r-recognize us and we could . . . go from Tremoral forever."

Whence had she conjured such an idea? Juliana forced a smile. "Such fantastic imagining, little sister." She patted Alaiz's hand. "Tremoral is our home—the only one we have. Here we shall stay."

It was a long time ere Alaiz spoke again, and when she did it was as if Juliana had not rejected her solution to Bernart. "When you . . . leave, will you take me with you?"

Though Juliana did not think it likely she would ever leave, she said, "Of course." She sat up and held her hand out to Alaiz. "Now come."

Alaiz grasped Juliana's fingers, slid off the mattress, and lowered herself to the pallet.

Although Juliana had every intention of returning to the great bed, she yielded to the need to be near another and lay down beside her sister.

"You should not," Alaiz said. "B-Bernart will be angry if he finds you with me."

Let him rage, Juliana decided. *Let him curse and stomp his feet.* If he wished her to do as he demanded, he must also pay a price. She pulled the covers over them. "Do not worry."

"But—"

"Go to sleep."

Alaiz pillowed her head on Juliana's outstretched arm. Shortly, her breathing deepened.

An hour later, Juliana was no nearer sleep.

Chapter Three

The early afternoon sun glinted off shirts of polished mail, made halos of helms settled upon warriors' heads, flashed across sword blades and the tips of lances, and lit the battlefield so brightly it was as if God had turned His face to it.

A fantastic sight, even at a distance, but not without its dark side, Juliana thought as she traversed the edge of the wood. She'd attended several tournaments before her marriage and vividly remembered those who had fallen, never to rise again. Accidents were to blame for a number of their deaths, but there were also the personal vendettas fought under the guise of mock battle. If it were not that Bernart needed Gabriel for the son he believed would restore his manhood, this day he would likely seek his old friend's death. At least there was some good that might come—

Nay! No good would come of what he demanded of her. None.

"Slow down, Juliana," Alaiz said, gasping.

Juliana looked around.

Eyes bright, skin flushed, fair hair loosed from the braids Juliana had woven, Alaiz darted past a group of merchants bringing their wares to tournament. She was having difficulty keeping up, but not because the pace was too brisk. Rather, she kept pausing to stare at the spectacle, then had to run to catch up.

She drew alongside Juliana. "You walk too . . . fast."

"Else you pause too often," Juliana teased. She lifted the hood that had fallen to her sister's shoulders and draped it over her head. Although she no longer cared whether or not she angered Bernart—and for certain he would be furious to discover she'd brought Alaiz to the field—neither did she wish her sister to suffer the brunt of that anger. Better he did not see Alaiz or herself.

Alaiz buried her nose in the flowers she had gathered along the way. Though they were wilted and their petals bruised from careless handling, she seemed not to notice. "They s-smell good," she said, and thrust them forward.

Juliana breathed their fragrance. Aye, like the last of spring. When she looked up, she saw that the battlefield had once more captured Alaiz's regard. The ribbon of meadowland grass was dappled with cowslips that tossed their golden heads in the gentle breeze, but by the end of the day all that would remain would be muddied and trampled petals and stems.

"Is it not . . ." Alaiz's brow creased with thought. "Woeful?" She shook her head. "Wonderful. Aye, 'tis wonderful!"

The truth of this day that would too soon bring the night denied Juliana any happiness. Trying to put it from her, she looked to the knights, who were busy aligning themselves into opposing teams comprised of more than fifty men each. It would not be long before they clashed. As the tournament would become more brutal with each passing moment, Juliana decided they would not stay long. "Come," she said.

As they started forward, one of the participants broke from the team on the north side of the field and spurred his mount toward the bordering wood.

Juliana did not need to see the face beneath the helm to know it was Bernart. He must have recognized Alaiz when her hood had fallen. She pulled her sister against her side. "Say naught," she instructed.

Twenty feet from where they stood, Bernart dragged on the reins. A clod of grass kicked up by his destrier struck Juliana's skirts. Alaiz took a step back, her fear of horses understandable.

Reassuringly, Juliana squeezed her sister's arm.

Around the nasal guard of his helm, Bernart glared at Juliana.

She glared back. It was the first time she'd seen him since their angry exchange last eve. He had not returned during the night and had left the castle ere she had risen this morn.

His breathing heavy, though more from emotion than exertion, she guessed, he leaned down from the saddle. "You defy me, Juliana."

She pushed the hood off her head. "You are surprised?"

"You know my feelings about this."

"This" meaning Alaiz, whom he would not spare a sideways glance. "I do. Just as you know my feelings about what you ask of me."

He flinched. "Damn you!"

Feeling a tremor go through Alaiz, Juliana gripped her

51

sister more tightly. "We will watch with the others." She nodded to the three ladies who were gathered upon their horses to observe the melee. Normally Juliana would also have ridden to the field, but it would have proven futile to try to coax Alaiz into mounting a horse. Thus they had walked more than a mile to witness the tournament.

"You will return to Tremoral," Bernart said. "Now."

Juliana shook her head. "Nay, but do you fear we shall cause you grief, I give you my word we will not."

Albeit his face was shadowed by his helm, his florid color shone past it. "I could have you removed."

"Aye, but 'twould appear quite unseemly, would it not?" Perhaps his anger would serve him well in battle, Juliana thought as it transformed his face further. "Your war games await you, husband."

"You have not won, Juliana."

She inclined her head. "For certain."

His lids narrowed. "We will speak more on this tonight."

Again, she dared. "Lest you forget, I shall be otherwise occupied."

Whatever harsh words he intended to loose were arrested by the sound of approaching riders.

Juliana turned. Two knights rode toward them, at the fore one whose proportions easily identified him, not to mention the hair spilling from beneath his helm. Gabriel De Vere had grown impatient.

"God's blood!" Bernart cursed.

Juliana's heart tripped with fear. She should never have left the castle. She should have spent these last hours on her knees praying Bernart would turn from his ungodly course.

Gabriel and Sir Erec reined in.

Outfitted in magnificent mail, and over that a bright

yellow surcoat, Gabriel contrasted sharply with the unkempt man who had come into the hall last eve. He
pinned Bernart with his pale gaze. "Are we here to do
battle or chat, Lord Kinthorpe?"

Bernart sat straighter in the saddle. "Careful lest your
impatience spoils your aim, old friend."

"I assure you, my aim is as true as ever."

Bernart's mount snickered and pranced sideways. A
cruel pull of the reins brought the animal under control.

Did Gabriel sense Bernart's ire as strongly as did the
destrier? Juliana wondered. Did Sir Erec? She glanced at
the knight and found his gaze upon Alaiz. To her astonishment, he winked.

Alaiz stiffened, as if surprised.

"Let us tourney!" Bernart shouted. He spurred his
mount across the battlefield.

A look passed between Gabriel and Sir Erec as they
guided their destriers around.

"W-wait," Alaiz cried. In her haste to extricate herself
from Juliana's side, the hood slipped from her head. She
pulled a flower from the bunch and took a step toward
Sir Erec, but that was all. She would go no nearer his
horse. "F-for you."

The knight reached forward and accepted the forlorn
flower from her outstretched hand. "I thank you."

She beamed, dragged another flower free, then turned
to Gabriel. "And you."

He stared at the young woman who offered it; then
something flashed in his eyes. Recognition. He remembered the ten-year-old girl who had once been far older
than her years. Alaiz had shunned her mother's attempts
to impress the notion of courtly love upon her, had fo-
cused on reading, writing, reckoning, and discourse on the
affairs of government upon which their father had thrived.

That young girl would have extended a word of sage advice ere she would have proffered a flower. Now, however, it was Juliana who spent her days among books and the like, Alaiz who whiled away the hours singing songs of love to herself. It was as if they had traded lives.

"You do not w-want it?" Alaiz asked in a small, sad voice.

Not realizing she held her breath, Juliana waited to see if the wretch would reject her sister's offer. If he did, he would suffer.

The links of Gabriel's chain mail made music upon the air as he leaned out of the saddle to accept the flower.

Juliana sighed. Though he did not thank Alaiz, it was more than she expected. As he straightened, her gaze was drawn to the flower. How pitiful it looked between his big fingers. How feeble against his strong, tanned hand. A hand that would this night touch her. A man who would know her as no man had ever known her. There were mere hours until she went to him and he covered her. Would he kiss her?

Abruptly she threw out the thought. Kissing was an intimacy reserved for those whose hearts were bound one to the other. Not merely for the making of a child, especially an illegitimate one. Did Gabriel try to kiss her, she would turn away. She swallowed. Hopefully it would be over with quickly, that she might return to her own bed. Of course, on the following night, she would be forced to go to him again.

Distaste shuddered through her as she swept her gaze to eyes too pale to be called blue. Gabriel De Vere was watching her.

He urged his destrier alongside her. "Any words of encouragement, Lady Juliana?"

His strong, masculine scent swayed her senses. It was

not entirely unpleasant, but he would benefit from a good, long soak. "Take thee a bath, Lord De Vere." She turned away. "Come, Alaiz."

Laughter she had not heard in a long time rumbled from Gabriel's chest, but was soon trampled by his thundering retreat.

Minutes later, the teams swept toward one another with raised weapons and war cries.

The first knight to fall fell hard, the one who felled him none other than Gabriel De Vere. Looking more the fierce warrior than the coward Bernart named him, he spun his destrier around, traded lance for sword, and leaped to the ground. A short while later, he had the knight's ransom. Then, as if death were a mere consequence of warfare, he hurtled toward his next opponent.

Gabriel a coward? A man who'd abandoned his best friend for fear of losing life or limb? It did not seem possible. But this was not real battle, Juliana reminded herself. Fighting for ransom was not the same as fighting for blood.

Deciding they had seen enough, she turned a reluctant Alaiz from the violent spectacle and started back toward Tremoral.

The dirt and sweat of hard-won victory would not be easily washed away in the chill waters of the wooded pool. Nor the thought of the one whose delicate senses Gabriel had offended.

He scrubbed harder. Though the filth finally succumbed to his efforts, Juliana Kinthorpe did not. She lingered like a long-lost memory come suddenly to light.

She had changed. When he had looked into her eyes last eve, and again this afternoon, the life with which she had once shone had been absent. And Gabriel did not believe it was because it was him she looked upon—the man who she believed had wronged her husband. As he knew well, such sorrow and bitterness took years to root so deep. Had Juliana's fanciful expectations of love, which were too exalted for any man to rise to, been the ruin of her and Bernart? Was she repulsed by her husband's limp? His diminished physique? Did she turn him away? Perhaps this was the reason Bernart sought other women.

A harsh sound tore from Gabriel's throat. He did not care. His friendship with Bernart was deep in the past, and Juliana . . . she was a woman. With that thought, he dove beneath the water. He surfaced on the opposite side of the pool and saw that his destrier, which had been grazing only moments earlier, had assumed a watchful stance. They were no longer alone.

"Gabriel!"

He looked up.

Sir Erec stood on an outcropping of rock. "Come on, man," he shouted, "we've bellies to fill."

Supper in Bernart's hall was not something Gabriel looked forward to, but a necessity; however, as the sun would light the land for another hour and the meal would not be served until its setting, he did not hasten from the pool. "I will join you shortly," he called back.

Sir Erec turned away.

Gabriel caught his reflection in the water lapping at his waist. He rubbed a hand over his jaw and considered scraping the stubbled beard from it, but in the next instant abandoned the idea. He had come to Tremoral to tourney, not to please a woman who had never more than glanced his way. A woman who would one day bear another's children.

He emerged from the water and, at leisure, donned the

fresh clothes he'd brought to the pool. As he tugged on his boots, he promised himself he would have new ones made following the tournament. Although the majority of ransom money gained this day would be put toward the restoration of Mergot—the barony in France that King Richard had awarded him for his aid in reclaiming lands seized by France's King Philip—he could certainly afford to keep his feet better than he had of late. Perhaps he would even have some new tunics sewn.

He mounted his destrier and guided it out of the ravine to where Sir Erec awaited him.

"Never have I seen you so clean," the knight said. He grinned. "Did that wench you had last eve complain?"

Had he had her, he doubted she would have. The only reason Nesta had smelled any better than he did was that she bathed herself in perfume. " 'Twas Lady Juliana who informed me I reeked."

Erec's eyebrows jumped. "Is that so?"

Gabriel guided his destrier through the trees.

"Since when have you cared what any thought of you?" Erec asked, drawing alongside.

Gabriel looked at him. Erec had cleaned his hands and face and donned a clean tunic, but that was all. As concerned as he was with appearance, not until the conclusion of the tournament would he bathe. Wise, for it was a waste of time, considering the morrow would only dirty him once again. If not for Juliana, neither would Gabriel have gone near the water until the end of the tournament. The admission made him scowl. "I do not care what any think."

Erec chuckled. "Except Lady Juliana."

He was too observant—an asset in tournament, but not outside of it.

"Ah, but she is a beautiful woman," Erec murmured.

57

"Pity to waste her on one such as Bernart Kinthorpe."

Gabriel glanced sharply at him.

Erec's mouth twitched. "What?" He feigned innocence. "What rumors have you been listening to?"

Erec shrugged. "There are several, but the one most spoken is that Lord Kinthorpe is the same as his brother."

Bernart the same as Osbern? Gabriel fleetingly considered the possibility. Nay, not even Acre could have changed him so.

"Three years of marriage and no children," Erec murmured.

"There are other reasons children are not born of wedlock."

"Which brings us to another rumor. The women servants say Lady Juliana is frigid."

Juliana, who had been trained in the art of courtly love? Gabriel remembered her oft-repeated profession of love for Bernart. Indeed, he could not forget it. Still, that did not mean she was as passionate in bed as she was out of it.

"What think you?" Erec asked.

Gabriel glanced sideways at him. "I do not." Whatever the truth of Bernart and Juliana's relationship, it was of no concern to him.

Ahead, the castle stood against a cloudless sky. It was white, from the donjon rising at its center to the outer wall and towers. Painted against this stark backdrop were the many-colored tents of those knights who did not avail themselves of the donjon's accommodations. Even from a distance, the bustle of activity was visible—servants hurrying about, squires cleaning and polishing their lord's armor, knights reliving the day's battles, merchants calling tourneyers to sample their offerings, women enticing men to sample their wares. . . .

An hour until eating, Gabriel reflected. Enough time to cool the fires of his loins? With a nudge of his spurs, he set his destrier to a gallop.

Chapter Four

"You think I have not prayed?"

Juliana lifted her bowed head, but did not look at the one who trespassed upon her sanctuary. She knew why Bernart came to the chapel. What she must now do.

"When my manhood was stolen," he said as he advanced, "I prayed it all a terrible dream, pleaded with God to deliver me from the infidels, but He was not listening, Juliana. He did not care."

She didn't wish to feel for him or his pain, but his words wounded her as they had the night he had told her of the atrocity done him.

"Afterward, as I lay bleeding, I prayed for death, but again I was denied. Do you know the tears I shed? Tears that I could never hold you in my arms and love you as you ought be loved?"

Emotion clawed at her, made it difficult to breathe.

Bernart lowered himself beside her where she knelt before the altar. "Ours is a cruel God, Juliana." He unclasped her prayerful hands. "He does not hear you, just as He did not hear me."

She stared at the altar with its gold cross and candles on either side. " 'Tis men who are cruel," she said. "Men who make themselves God."

Bernart's hands tightened on hers. "You think that is what I do?"

"Do you not?"

He expelled a harsh sigh. "I know what I ask of you—"

"Ask?" She wrenched her hands free. "Surely you mean what you demand of me?"

"I do not wish to do it, Juliana."

"Then do not!"

"I must. Though I did not die at Acre, 'tis as if I am dead. A son would give me something to live for. To love."

As he could never love her. "Then I should not keep Gabriel waiting." She stood and turned toward the door.

Bernart caught her back against him. "He will not hurt you."

There were many ways to hurt a person. Though Juliana did not think Gabriel would abuse her, she knew she would be wounded. Deeply. She tried to turn to Bernart, but he held her fast, as if he could not endure her gaze.

"The wine dispensed this eve was not watered," he said.

She had not known. Tempted as she'd been to seek strength in drink, she had not taken a sip, certain she would need her full reserve of wits if she was to keep her identity hidden from the man who would this night claim her virtue.

"Gabriel drank his fill and is well sated," Bernart said. "I assure you he will not remember much on the morrow."

61

That was of small comfort. "You are certain he is alone?"

"Aye, his squire keeps his tent outside the walls."

"Does he expect a woman this eve?" It would not do for her to surprise him and end up with a knife to her throat.

" 'Tis Nesta he believes will come to him, but she is otherwise occupied."

Juliana pulled out of Bernart's hold, drew the hood of her mantle over her head, and walked to the door.

"Three nights and—" His voice cracked. "And 'twill be over."

Providing that a babe took. Juliana opened the door and walked from the chapel. Any hope Bernart might call her back died when he closed the door behind her. He could not bear to watch her go to his enemy.

Feeling as if it were the executioner's block she was about to lay her head upon, she traversed the corridor. It was normally lit by four torches, but this night there was only one. Enough light to guide her, but too little to creep within the chamber and reveal that it was she who came to Gabriel. Bernart had thought of everything.

She swallowed, eyeing the dark line between door and floor that proved no light shone from within Gabriel's chamber. Three nights. An eternity. She halted and pressed a hand to the door. Her heart raced, breath caught, palms turned moist. She must go to him. But how? How was she to give herself to a man not her husband? Especially the one responsible for Bernart's loss of manhood?

The idea of love espoused by her mother returned to her, but try as she did to convince herself it was her lover who awaited her, that in his arms she would finally know the passion and adoration denied her, it was no use. The man within was Gabriel De Vere, and his heart was as black as a dreamless night. No lover he.

But the sooner she went to him, the sooner she could leave. She opened the door and stepped inside. By the light that strained into the chamber, she located Gabriel. He sat in the chair before the brazier, the coals of which had long ago yielded the last of their warming glow.

Chilled more by fear than the lack of heat, Juliana closed the door and barred it. As her eyes adjusted to the dark that was diminished slightly by the moon's penetration of the oilcloth over the window, the silence stretched. Did Gabriel sleep? If so, perhaps—

Nay, Bernart would send her back. She stepped forward. The half dozen steps seemed a long way, but finally she stood before Gabriel.

He was still, likely more from the potent wine pressed upon him than fatigue. How was she to awaken him? Her heart pounded painfully. She could not call to him, for to speak would reveal her as surely as the light of day. There was only one way, which was something to which she must become accustomed. She would have to touch him.

She released her mantle to the floor, uncovering the homespun gown she'd donned in place of her lady's finery. It had chafed her through the fine chemise worn next to her skin—the latter being the only comfort she allowed herself for fear Gabriel might discover her garments were not the stuff of servants.

Juliana sent a prayer heavenward, then began loosening her laces. An instant later, she was seized and dragged forward.

She gasped and strained away, but her strength was no match for Gabriel's. She landed hard against his chest. Although instinct urged her to struggle, she suppressed it with the reminder that she was here to get Bernart an heir.

Ere the night was over, she was going to come even nearer to Gabriel.

"Who might you be?" he asked, his voice thick and slurred.

He was drunk, though not so much that he mistook her for Nesta. Juliana had hoped he would simply do the deed and be done with it, but it seemed he had no intention of making this less difficult for her. How was she to answer him? As she searched for some way that would not reveal her, he settled a hand to her buttocks and pulled her fully onto his lap.

His scent was entirely different from that which had assailed her ere the commencement of the tournament. Never would she have guessed he smelled of pine needles, grass, a warm breeze—

"Have you no tongue?" he asked, his breath fanning her cheek.

—and wine. Hopefully enough that, come the morn, he would remember little of her visit.

"Wench?" He drew a hand from her buttocks to her waist.

At least he believed her to be a serving girl, Juliana consoled herself. However, there was no consolation in his touch. She felt it as surely as if it were his bare skin against hers—strangely disturbing, though not repulsive as expected.

Reminding herself that Gabriel awaited a response, that if she did not give one he might drag her into the light, Juliana did something she would never have believed herself capable of. She pressed a hand to that place to which she would soon submit. Beneath his tunic, Gabriel surged against her palm. As much as she wanted to wrench her hand away, she held it there, praying he would not pursue her identity.

He groaned and cupped her breast.

She tensed, but in the next instant forced herself to relax. This was neither the time nor place for maidenly outrage. True, Gabriel was drunk, but that did not mean he was senseless.

He kneaded her breast, coursed his other hand down her leg, caught up the hem of her skirts, splayed his fingers over her calf.

A peculiar sensation rippled through Juliana. She told herself it was revulsion. His fingers feathered higher and played at the back of her knee. Fear. Only fear. Through the material of her bodice, he pressed her nipple between thumb and forefinger and roused it rigid. Still, she denied the awakening of her senses, told herself she loathed his touch. Beneath her skirts, his hand turned inward and caressed the sensitive flesh of her inner thigh. Juliana struggled to suppress her response, but could not. As the shudder escaped her, Gabriel's male member surged beneath her hand.

"Ah, wench," he murmured, "you are a sweet one."

His voice was more resonant than she remembered, as if it rose from the depths of him. Had it always been thus? Was it simply that she'd never been so near him?

He lingered over her thigh, then strayed inward and grazed her secret place.

Juliana whimpered. Strange things were happening to her. Things that were not supposed to happen. Her stomach ought to be roiling with nausea, and yet—

He parted her and touched her secret place. A deep ache uncoiled within her. Frightened by its intensity, she squeezed her thighs together, but it did not deter him. He delved deeper.

"You are ready," he said.

65

She hated him. Loathed him. But at the moment, she could not remember why.

He pulled his hand from beneath her skirt and set her to her feet.

He did not want her? Had he changed his mind?

He stood, lifting her against his chest.

Nay, he wanted her and would soon take that which she had come to give. In exchange, he would sow the son Bernart needed. That last reminded Juliana of the reason she hated Gabriel De Vere. But her treacherous body seemed immune. Though she had heard whispered what a man's touch could do to a woman's resolve, never would she have believed it could be so strong.

For as much as Gabriel had imbibed, his stride was sure as he carried her to the bed. He laid her upon the mattress.

She could barely make out his shadow alongside the bed, but she knew he was undressing. Once more, fear burrowed beneath her skin. Now he would come to her and take the gift that should have been another's.

He lowered a knee on either side of her and leaned over. The brush of his hair against her cheek and his wine-laced breath mixing with hers were all the warning she had that he intended to kiss her. And he would have had she not turned her head sharply right. He settled, instead, for her ear. His breath, then his tongue, rekindled the desire he'd evoked minutes earlier.

Heat swept Juliana's breasts, tugged through her belly, quivered in her innermost place. She fought it, tried not to feel the sensations, but to no avail. Gabriel knew her woman's body as if he had lain with her many times.

As he trailed his mouth to her throat, his hands began their assault anew. He eased her skirts up. Touched. Caressed. Pleasured her as she had only ever dreamed of being pleasured. And in that moment, she let herself believe he was her lover. A man who adored her and defied all that conspired to keep them apart.

"Touch me," he said in a groan.

She knew what he wanted. Years of denial guiding her, she closed her hand around his hard length. Surprisingly, he was as smooth as down, but very large.

"Aye," he said under his breath, "now put me to you."

With sudden disquiet, she wondered how she was to take him inside. Surely he would hurt her, perhaps rend her flesh.

At her hesitation, he lowered himself between her thighs and pressed his manhood to her.

Juliana's hand between them prevented him from breaching her. Though she ached to finally cross the threshold that separated girls from women, her arousal was tempered by fear.

He closed his hand over hers and loosened her fingers. The barrier to his pleasure removed, he pressed into her.

Radiant pain shattered her desire, but she refused to cry out. Gabriel must not know she was other than what she pretended to be. If she shed virgin blood and he later noticed it upon his sheets, she could do naught about that, but he must not know now. However, it seemed her reaction was not lost on his drunken senses. Though he did not withdraw, neither did he proceed.

"Have I hurt you?" he asked, his voice strained as if he bore a great weight.

What had betrayed her? In the next instant, Juliana realized it was her body again. She was as tense as a board. Somehow she must relax. If only the pain were not so great.

Gabriel began to pull back.

God, no! She had not come this far to be denied. Would not! She wrapped her arms around him, arched her body

67

against his, surrendered the last of her maidenhood. Though she had not thought it could hurt more, it did. Tears swimming in her eyes, she sank her teeth into her bottom lip and rocked her hips back. A moment later she came to him again, and twice more before Gabriel responded.

He wrested control of Juliana's clumsy attempts from her, slid a hand beneath her, and guided her to meet his thrusts. Gradually her pain receded until all that remained was a dull ache. Though she found no pleasure in their coupling, she moved with him until his breathing turned harsh. Then he drove so hard and fast between her thighs it was all she could do to receive him.

Very soon he would give her his seed, she was certain; then she could return to the solar and brave the interminable hours until dawn, wondering whether or not a babe had taken.

One moment Gabriel was deep inside her, the next, outside. Shouting his release, he gave the stuff of children to the flat of her belly.

For a long moment, Juliana could not draw breath past her disbelief. Dear God, it could not be!

Gabriel issued a harsh sigh and rolled onto his back.

Knowing it was so, that she had naught to show for her sacrifice, she squeezed her eyes closed. She wanted to scream, to rail, to beat her fists against Gabriel for what he had cheated her of, but she forced herself to lie perfectly still.

A short while later, his hand touched her shoulder. "Forgive me. I have had too much drink."

Yet he was lucid enough to take from her without getting her with a child he did not want. Juliana had heard of such means of ensuring against impregnating women, but she'd never considered that Gabriel might practice it himself. Under different circumstances, she would have thought it noble that he should be so responsible. *Curse him! Curse Bernart!*

Gabriel brushed her cheek with the backs of his fingers. "Next time I shall pleasure you first."

Next time. For what? An empty womb? Wishing to be as far from him as possible, she pushed onto her elbows.

He pressed her down. "Stay. There are yet hours before dawn."

Which would see him increasingly sober. However, as much as Juliana longed to leave, she knew that to oppose him might draw his suspicion. Maybe he would fall asleep and she could steal back to the solar.

He settled his arm across her chest and caressed her shoulder. "Sweet," he murmured.

She tried to think of anything other than the man beside her and the not entirely unpleasant sensations aroused by his touch, but it proved futile. His presence was too strong, her skin too sensitive. Fortunately it was not long before his breathing deepened.

Juliana forced herself to be patient a few minutes longer, then slipped from beneath his arm and off the bed. She hurried to where she had left her mantle, donned it, and fled the chamber.

She was not surprised to find the solar empty but for Alaiz on her pallet. For certain Bernart would not be clinging to his side of the bed this night. Was he still in the chapel? Or in the hall drinking away his guilt? No matter. It was done, though certainly not with the result he expected.

Feeling wound tight as the thread on a spindle, Juliana crossed to the washbasin, shed her clothes, reached for the hand towel. The water was chill, but she hardly noticed as she bathed away the evidence of Bernart's quest for a son. Though there was very little blood upon her, it was only passing solace. She prayed she had left even less behind and that it would escape Gabriel's notice. She prayed that when she told Bernart that Gabriel had withheld his seed he would not send her to him again.

She stilled. Bernart would be angered to learn this night's tryst had proven fruitless, but he would surely seek another to do what Gabriel would not.

She closed her eyes. It was horrid she'd had to go to Gabriel, but to be passed from one man to another as if she were more of a whore than Bernart had already made her? She could not stand the thought. But what choice had she? She must protect Alaiz.

Juliana lowered herself to the edge of the mattress. As much as she wished to put from her mind memories of this night, she opened them, relived the scent of Gabriel, his touch, the words he'd spoken. Although the only pleasure she had known had been before he'd entered her, at least he hadn't hurt her as she had heard some men did women. Aye, she would prefer him to an unknown, but only if there was some way to ensure he gave her his seed when next they came together.

Her head began to ache. How was she to steal a child from a man who did not wish one? Unfortunately, there was no one she could turn to. No one to answer her questions. In the next instant, Nesta came to mind. Although Juliana could not approach the woman, the things of which she'd overheard Nesta speak, which had made her blush, returned to her—specifically, how the wench had seduced and pleasured a visiting bishop.

Once again Juliana's skin flushed. Could she do those things to Gabriel that only women of ill-repute did? She swallowed. She would have to touch him as he had touched her, arouse him so he did not withdraw until it was too late. Somehow she would make it work.

Feeling more alone than she'd ever felt, Juliana thrust back the coverlet, slid beneath, and hugged her knees to her chest. She would not cry. She was stronger than that. Two more nights and it would be done.

God, let it be done.

The dream came to Bernart as it did nearly every night. Stealthily it crept upon him. He reached to Juliana, but found only emptiness. Brazenly it covered him. "Nay!" he cried, but Juliana did not rise up to awaken him. Viciously it wrenched him into the past.

More blood than he had ever seen. More fear than he had ever known. Carnage —just as Gabriel had warned. Gabriel, who was always right.

Bernart ran. The shouts formed by infidel tongues carried upon the night air words he had never heard, but understood. If he were caught, his fate would be the same as that of the men he'd persuaded to follow him over the wall.

God, what have I done? Knowing his only hope was to lose himself in the city, he veered right, then left. With each turn, the sound of his pursuers grew more distant.

How he hurt! His sides ached; his lungs strained. He had to stop. He stumbled into an alleyway and flattened himself against a wall. Trembling with the effort to control his labored breathing, he strained to catch the sound of the Muslim soldiers.

Brisk footsteps and voices warned of their approach.

He pushed off the wall and staggered deeper into the alley, praying it did not dead-end. It did. Heart pounding so hard it hurt, he swept his sword around and surged forward. As he exited the alleyway, above the clink and clatter of his mail hauberk he heard them. Then they were before and behind him, swords flashing torchlight.

He was in the hands of the heathens, those who had bled the life from the men who'd followed him into the devil's lair. *What have I done? I should have listened to Gabriel.* Though fear demanded he throw down his sword and surrender, honor said not. He was a knight, not a coward. To the death, then, and with him as many as could be taken. "For God and King Richard!" he cried, and launched himself at the nearest Muslim.

Flesh! He had the man's flesh. The infidel's howl of pain stirring with his companions' shouts of anger, Bernart swept his sword again. He fought them, however many there were, but proved no match.

A blade landed to the mail of his shoulder, next to the muscle. He tried to hold the cry, to keep it from his lips, but the next slice of the sword loosed it. But the blade did not pause at his thigh; it went deeper—to that place wherein man differed from woman.

The pain! He screamed—piercing sounds that sounded as if they'd sprung from a woman's lips. Then, slowly, darkness, his last thought of sweet Juliana, who awaited his to return to England to make her his wife.

With a hoarse shout, Bernart sat straight up. Where was he? The street in Acre that he had made crimson with the spilled blood of his manhood? The stinking cell where he had prayed every hour of every day for death? At last his eyes adjusted to the darkness, revealing the familiar corners of the chapel.

He shuddered and collapsed back upon the bench. He should have died at Acre. If not that he was of the landed nobility, valued for ransom or trade, he would have bled to death. Instead, physicians had tended him and, after long, agonizing weeks, had pronounced him healed. During the long days and nights that followed, his only companion had been his tortured thoughts, which had brought him to the realization that Gabriel was to blame. For everything.

Bernart sat up and wiped the perspiration from his brow. It was a long time since he'd had to endure the dream in its entirety. Always Juliana awakened him. But not this night. This night she was with Gabriel. He stilled. Was the deed done? Had she returned to the solar? He hurried from the chapel and flung open the door of their chamber.

A flickering torch revealed her auburn head upon the pillow. It was done.

He closed his eyes. Though he ought to be pleased with the prospect that a son might be planted in her womb, it was anger that rose in him. He closed the door, strode past the chamber where Gabriel had pleasured himself between Juliana's thighs, and descended the stairs to the dimly lit hall. Here, tournament guests, household knights, and servants littered the floors and benches, their slumber marked by snores, grunts, and mutterings.

Bernart crossed to the sideboard. He shouldn't drink. . . . He lifted a pitcher of warm ale, filled a tankard, drained it, filled it again, then ascended the dais and dropped into the lord's high seat. Though it was rest his sleep-deprived body needed, anger held his eyes wide and turned his thoughts to tomorrow's battle. And the revenge that would be his.

Chapter Five

The chamber was beginning to lighten when Gabriel opened his eyes. Although he usually rose in advance of the dawn, he did not hasten from bed. Something playing about the back passages of his mind, he looked beside him. He was alone. Naught unusual about that, but still there was a vague sense of loss.

Like an elusive dream, remembrance of the night past teased his consciousness—advancing, receding, advancing again. He grasped at the memories, tried to hold them long enough to make sense of them.

Silken thighs. Full breasts. Quivering flesh. Something very . . . sweet. Merely a dream? Conjured by his drunken mind? Nay, a woman had come to him last eve, but not Nesta, as she'd promised. Who, then? Which of the wenches in Bernart's hall had taken the other woman's place? When Gabriel could not put a face to his night visitor, he concluded it must have been dark when she'd come to him. What had she called herself? Again, naught, for she had not spoken a word—leastwise, none he could recall. Not that it mattered. He reminded himself of the distance he put between himself and the women with whom he lay. Still, there had been something about her. . . .

He lifted his head. Though the movement made his teeth ache, he dismissed the discomfort and looked down the naked length of his body. He stared at his loins, then abruptly sat up and searched the coverlet beneath. Telltale spots of crimson verified that which was upon himself.

A virgin? Indistinctly, he recalled the wench's response when first he'd entered her. He had thought he'd hurt her, but then she had wantonly thrust against him. Nay, she had been no maiden come to him. It was her woman's blood. Had to be. So what was it that made her memory linger? Certainly not a dousing of perfume to mask an unclean body. She had smelled . . . feminine. *That* he recalled.

With a snarl of disgust, Gabriel rejected such useless pondering. She was a whore, like any other. He dropped his feet to the floor and stood. The throbbing in his head trebled.

"Damn!" he muttered. He'd been foolish to drink so much, especially as the wine had not been watered. Although he was usually mindful of how much he imbibed the night before a melee, the drink had flowed so freely last eve that no sooner had he taken a swallow than his goblet was filled again. He would not be surprised if it had been arranged by Bernart to gain an advantage over him in tournament. An advantage he would have if Gabriel did not soon shake the effects of the alcohol.

He thrust a hand through his hair and massaged the

75

back of his neck. Food would make him see straight again.

Knowing that as soon as the morning mass was said, the breaking of fast would commence in the hall, he strode to the basin. He splashed chill water over his face, retrieved his garments from the rushes, and donned them as quickly as his clumsy fingers would allow.

He would not even look at her. His gaze fixed on the chaplain, Bernart sat silent beside Juliana as the morning mass was recited to those who'd gathered in hopes God would look kindly upon them in tournament.

During the past half hour, Juliana had endured the tension and anger Bernart exuded. She knew it arose from her having come to the chapel and forcing her presence on him, but it was not out of spite she'd come. Not really. It was for the solace she found within the walls of this holy place. More than ever, she needed to be here, to repent for the night past, to plead strength for the nights to come. Sacrilegious though it might be.

As if sensing her turmoil, Alaiz slipped her hand into her sister's lap and intertwined their fingers.

Juliana had known that to allow her sister to accompany her would further rouse Bernart's displeasure, but she had brought her anyway. After all, it was the only thing she had to show for her sacrifice. Now her sister's place at Tremoral was secure and, though Bernart had not agreed to it, no more would she be hidden.

At the conclusion of the mass, Bernart was the first to rise. Without a glance in Juliana's direction, he stepped around her and strode down the aisle. He would go belowstairs to break his fast, providing he could stomach it, and afterward ride to the battlefield. Juliana would not be surprised if this day he gained the ransom of several knights, perhaps even that of Gabriel De Vere. Of course, did she reveal to him Gabriel had taken her virtue and given nothing in return, it might be Gabriel's death Bernart sought. Another reason to say naught.

"I am . . . hungry," Alaiz whispered.

Juliana dragged her gaze from the altar. "Then we should eat." Her smile felt terribly stiff.

Alaiz beamed most beautifully. In fact, at that moment Juliana doubted there was any woman lovelier than her sister. Unfortunately, beauty was not enough in this world that regarded those who were different with suspicion, as if another's loss of faculties might somehow affect their own.

Juliana stood and was instantly reminded of the tenderness between her thighs. She could not bear to think what pain would be put upon her this eve.

From the back of the throng exiting the chapel, Juliana glimpsed Sir Erec ahead. She was thankful there was no sight of Gabriel, but considering his drunken state last eve, she had not expected he would attend mass. Had prayed he would not.

"After meal," Alaiz said, "may we go to the . . . ?" Her brow crumpled.

Tempted as Juliana was to supply the word, she waited to see if her sister could summon it. She could not. "You wish to go to the tournament?"

Alaiz sighed. "Aye, the tournament."

Juliana laid a hand on her sister's shoulder. "We must first tend to your lessons." It was true, but more of an excuse to distance Juliana from Gabriel.

"Not today," Alaiz beseeched. "I wish to see the b-battle."

"You do not think it violent?"

"Ah, nay! 'Tis . . . exciting. The smell"—Alaiz sniffed

the air—"the colors, the noise." She threw her palms up. "I-I wish to go again."

For all her fear of horses, it seemed her passion for the tournament remained intact. It had been the same before the accident. Still, Juliana needed this day to prepare for the night. "Mayhap tomorrow."

Disappointment fell across Alaiz's face.

Juliana felt a pang of remorse. "Tomorrow. I promise."

Alaiz nodded.

If only there were another who could accompany her to the tournament, Juliana wished. Someone whom she could trust. But there was no one, for she feared a woman servant might say spiteful things to Alaiz, that one of Bernart's knights might take advantage of her innocence. To that last, Sir Randal Rievaulx rose to mind. Though the young knight had rarely spoken a word to Alaiz, too often his eyes followed her, making Juliana uneasy. Whatever the cost, she must protect her sister.

Juliana and Alaiz stepped through the doorway and traversed the corridor behind those eager to reach the meal awaiting them belowstairs.

A chill pricked Juliana's skin as she neared the chamber she must twice more enter. Was he within? In the hall? Departed for the battlefield? If the latter, she would return abovestairs and strip the bedclothes before a maid discovered the evidence of her lost virtue. God, she prayed, let Gabriel be gone from the castle.

But, as Bernart had warned her, God was not listening. The door opened and Gabriel stepped into her path. If not for his quick reflexes, they would have collided. He caught her shoulders and steadied her.

She felt as if touched by fire. Worse, staggered by lightning, as if she might split and fall where she stood. Though she longed to shrink from him, she looked up at the man for whom she had bled last eve. A man who knew her more intimately than any other, yet did not know her—she prayed.

"My apologies, Lady Juliana," Gabriel said. "I fear my head is not right this morn."

The light of morning made him no less menacing than on the night past. In fact, with his shadowed eyes and stubbled jaw, he appeared more so. But at least his eyes were not the eyes of a man who knew her terrible secret. He thought it a whore who had come to him last eve.

His brow lowered. "Are you well, my lady?"

"Quite." She slipped from beneath his hands and stepped to her sister's side.

"Good morn, Lady Alaiz," Gabriel said.

Alaiz smiled. "Lord De Vere."

Damn him! Why could he not simply ignore Alaiz as others did? Why did he have to show a heart he could not possibly possess?

Juliana took her sister's arm and hastened her toward the stairs.

"Something is w-wrong?" Alaiz asked.

"Naught," Juliana whispered. "Let us break our fast."

A moment later, she heard Sir Morris call to Gabriel, "You no longer attend mass?"

Juliana did not wish to hear Gabriel's response, tried desperately to drown it in the discourse of those before her, but it followed her onto the stairs.

"No more," he said as he and the other knight came behind her and Alaiz.

"Your soul is not in need of saving?" Sir Morris asked.

"Not when 'tis already lost." Gabriel's breath stirred the veil atop Juliana's head.

He was near. Too near. Only a step above her, she

guessed. Lord, she could almost feel the brush of his fingertips.

"You have been excommunicated?" Sir Morris asked.

"That is what the church calls it. I can think of other words more suited."

The disturbing sensations that beset Juliana gave way to dismay. What evil had Gabriel done to bring the church's wrath upon him? Though she did not consider herself devout, especially after the church's rejection of Alaiz following her head injury, she held a steadfast belief in God. Thus she was disturbed by the revelation. Lord, that such an ungodly man been chosen to make a child on her!

"For tourneying, no doubt," Sir Morris said.

"The church thought to make an example of Sir Erec and me."

His only sin was tourneying? The church's decree of excommunication and refusal of ecclesiastical burial to those killed at tournament was well known, but rather than enforce their prohibitions against tourney victims, they preferred, instead, to excommunicate living tourneyers. Like Gabriel, it seemed.

"Sir Erec was also excommunicated?"

"Had he not put coin to a certain bishop's palm he would have been."

How familiar that sounded, Juliana mused bitterly. The church considered tourneying an evil pursuit, yet pardoned a knight of past and future sins providing he had enough coin to pay for absolution. And it was not as if the money went to the poor or financed the construction of a house of God. More likely it added to the bishop's personal coffers.

"Your soul is not worth a few coins, Lord De Vere?" Sir Morris asked.

"If coin is all it takes to buy my soul out of perdition, then it can hardly be worth holding on to."

"I see your point," Sir Morris conceded.

Gabriel had had enough of idle talk, something he disliked intensely. He stepped into the hall behind Juliana. As she hastened toward the dais, he followed her with his gaze and watched as she lowered herself into the chair beside the lord's high seat—a seat conspicuously vacant. Bernart must have gone directly to the battlefield. Would that he could do the same. But he needed food to counter the effects of too much drink. He strode to the table where Sir Erec was seated and lowered himself to the bench.

One look at Gabriel and Erec winced. "I take it you did not sleep well."

Gabriel pulled the platter of viands to him, chose a chunk of cheese, and broke a piece of bread. "I did not." Though he had slept after sating himself with the wench, his rest had been fitful. Too much accursed wine. " 'Twas a most unsettled night."

"And I am to pity you?" Erec's mouth quirked. "You who had not only a bed to warm you, but a wench?"

A wench. Gabriel looked around the hall. None of the serving wenches seemed to fit the impression he'd gained of the woman who'd come to him last eve. His remembering hands touched skin as silken as the finest cloth, turned around full breasts, slid over a narrow waist, carried gently flared hips to his. A kitchen wench, then? A chambermaid?

A tankard of ale appeared before him. He looked up and saw it was Nesta who brought it to him. Though she was undoubtedly more experienced than the one who had come to him last eve, he suddenly found her far less appealing. Perhaps she knew who the other woman was, mayhap had sent her to him. He immediately dismissed that last thought. Even had another man enticed Nesta to his bed, he could not imagine her sending someone in her stead.

She leaned forward. "This eve, sire?" Her husky whisper feigned privacy.

"You did not come last night," he reminded her, hoping she might shed light on who had come.

Regret clouded her face. "I could not, but I promise ye will not be alone again this eve. I should come?"

It was that other wench Gabriel hoped would return. "Mayhap." He lifted his tankard.

Nesta blinked. Then, eyes flashing, she turned and flounced across the hall.

"Best watch what she pours you in future," Erec murmured.

The other knights, eager to begin the preparations for the day's melee, quickly finished their simple meals and rose from the benches.

Knowing it would be hours before the first clash, Gabriel was in no hurry himself, especially as his head was a league from being right. He washed down his bread with ale.

"Careful lest you addle your senses further," Erec warned. He nodded to the tankard. " 'Tis a tourney day. I would not wish to be relieved of my horse and armor."

Gabriel looked sideways at him. "I shall watch your back. Just be sure you have a care for mine."

Erec grinned. "Of course."

Gabriel's face was streaked with rust where the sweat wrung of battle had come into contact with his helm. "Methinks 'tis my death you seek, *old friend*," he said between clenched teeth.

Flat on his back, harsh breath echoing inside his skewed

helm, Bernart stared up at him. At that moment, Gabriel looked like the devil himself. "Your death?" he repeated. "Why would I wish to kill you?"

Gabriel bent and retrieved Bernart's long sword that had missed its mark by inches. He fingered the sharp blade. "Why, indeed." He thrust the weapon to the ground beside Bernart.

Beneath the chain mail that suddenly seemed tenfold heavier, Bernart struggled to a sitting position. He straightened his helm, then turned his hand around the hilt of his honed sword. Though he had decreed that only arms of peace were to be used during the tournament—blunted weapons that could scarcely cut butter—it was an instrument of death he'd brought onto the battlefield. If not for Sir Erec's shout of warning and Gabriel's quick reflexes, Gabriel would now be gasping his last. Instead, he had countered with a blow that had knocked Bernart from his horse. As during their younger years when Gabriel had more often than not bettered Bernart, he'd won again.

Damn him to hell! Bernart trembled with anger and self-loathing as he gained his feet. "What price my horse and armor?"

Gabriel swept his gaze over Bernart's fine hauberk, then turned and strode to the lathered destrier that grazed nearby. He ran a hand over the horse's veined neck. "A worthy animal," he pronounced, and named a price that made Bernart swallow hard.

"Done," Bernart said, suddenly and violently pained by a burning need to urinate.

"And your armor . . ." Gabriel named a price no less fantastic.

Bernart snapped his teeth. "I shall pay it."

With a nod, Gabriel strode to where he'd thrown off

his helm. He retrieved it, settled it on his head, continued to where his destrier awaited him.

"Next time 'twill be you paying me," Bernart called after him.

Gabriel swung into the saddle. Though he gave no reply, his eyes glittered dangerously. He would yield naught to Bernart.

Naught but a son—a malevolent voice reminded him of that of which he had lost sight.

With a snap of the reins, Gabriel turned his mount toward the melee.

Bernart berated himself for being a thousand times a fool. He had let what had happened last eve gnaw at him until the only thing that mattered was Gabriel's blood upon his sword. But it was not. He needed a son, one made of Gabriel's loins.

He gripped the hilt so tightly all blood fled his hand. He had to control his emotions, put aside this jealousy that had no place in what he required of Juliana. Forget his passion for a woman he could never possess as Gabriel had possessed her. A son. *That* was all that mattered.

Telling himself the moisture that stung his eyes was only sweat rolling off his brow, he strode toward the wood, where he could relieve himself without fear of being seen.

"See if you can figure this," Juliana said. "Had I sixteen apples and ate four, how many would I have left?"

Alaiz's brow furrowed. "But if you ate so m-many, you would be sick."

Inwardly, Juliana sighed. Though it was a struggle to reteach Alaiz those things lost in her fall, and all said it was a waste of time, she persisted. The rewards were few, but she was certain it made a difference. "All right, then.

If I had sixteen apples and *lost* four, how many would I have?"

Alaiz's eyes strayed to the sticks she'd earlier used for computing.

"Uh-uh," Juliana reproved. "In your head."

"Sixteen . . . less four." After a long struggle, Alaiz's face lit. "Twelve apples! You would have twelve!"

"I knew you could do it!"

Alaiz beamed, but only for a moment before sorrow took the light from her eyes. "But I shall never be as I was."

Once more afforded a glimpse of the sister lost to her—lucid and thoughtful—Juliana could only stare.

Alaiz pressed a hand to her temple. " 'Tis as if . . . as if I have all the keys but know not which locks to fit them to." The hand alongside her head curled into a fist. "I know my letters and numbers and so much more! I just do not know where I have put them."

Juliana lowered her eyes so her sister would not see her tears. "We will find them."

"Will we? I do not think so."

When Juliana looked up, she saw the mist in Alaiz's eyes. Though they seldom discussed the years previous to her accident, from time to time a light came on inside Alaiz, reminding her of all she'd lost. But always she slid back inside her child's mind, just as she did now.

Juliana glanced at the sky. It was beginning to darken. Though commotion beyond the garden walls had earlier announced the return of the tourneyers, she'd ignored it. But she could no longer. She had duties to attend to before the evening festivities began. Fortunately Cook had the meal in hand. " 'Tis time to go abovestairs and change," she said.

Alaiz plucked at her soiled gown. "B-Bernart does not wish me in the hall. He is angry."

"With me, not you." Juliana patted her sister's arm. "Now hurry along."

Alaiz stood and hastened toward the donjon.

Only when she was gone from sight did Juliana let her shoulders sink. Why Alaiz? Why one as kind and sharp-witted as she? She would have made a wonderful abbess, could have given so much to this angry world. Instead she was the pawn by which Bernart would get a child.

A tear, then another, slipped from beneath Juliana's lashes. How cruel life was. It was almost enough to make one question God's existence. She tried to hold the sob that rose in her throat, but it escaped. At least there was no one to—

"The last time we were in a garden together, the tears you shed were for yourself."

Certain her heart had stopped, fearing it might never beat again, Juliana swept her gaze down the path Alaiz had taken. Twenty feet out—now fifteen—Gabriel De Vere advanced. The seams of his tunic straining against his muscular build, his dark hair bound at his nape, and a livid bruise coloring his cheekbone, he looked danger-ous.

When had he come into the garden? Did he know it was she who'd visited him on the night past? He must. For what other reason would he seek her out? If he sought her out. *Lord, let it be only chance that brought him here.*

"The . . . the last time?" She dashed away her tears and averted her gaze for fear he might glimpse something in her eyes that would reveal her.

He halted. " 'Twas in the gardens of your father's cas-tle."

Of course she remembered—and not for the first time.

There were moments, few though they were, when she stole inside herself to a quiet place untouched by the world around her. And sometimes that day in the garden returned to her. Amid the tears had been Gabriel, a young man she'd only ever looked upon with disdain and fear of his influence upon her beloved Bernart. That day he'd spoken her name as he'd never spoken it, looked at her as he'd never looked at her. In that moment she'd longed to go into his arms and to find comfort from the pain curling inside her, but Bernart had called to her. Without another word, Gabriel had withdrawn, leaving Bernart to plead forgiveness for his faithlessness.

"Surely you have not forgotten," Gabriel prompted.

She blinked, feeling embarrassment heat her cheeks. "I fear I know not what you speak of, Lord De Vere. Surely you have me confused with another." She stood.

He laid a staying hand to her arm. "It was you."

Her heart pounded more fiercely as she stared at the strong, tanned fingers that warmed her through the sleeve of her gown, the same fingers that would touch her again this eve. *Dear God.* She jerked her arm free. "I must tend to my duties." She tried to step around Gabriel. Unfortunately there was not enough room between him and the rosebushes that lined the pathway.

"How did it happen?" he asked.

Juliana did not like being so near him. It was much too hard to breathe. She took a step back. "What?"

"I speak of Alaiz. Were not your tears for her?"

Indignation shot through Juliana. "You were keeping watch on us?"

"I was on my way to the kitchens when I heard voices."

Then he had not sought her out, did not know it was she who had come to his bed. Though she was relieved, the knowledge that she'd been beneath Gabriel's regard deepened her embarrassment. "A man of honor always makes his presence known to others."

"I am a long time without honor."

And excommunicated, earning his living in a manner forbidden by the church. "As I said, I have duties—"

"You have not answered my question. What happened to Alaiz?"

Why did he care? No one else did. They stared, or else pretended Alaiz did not exist, but never inquired about her. Why Gabriel? Why this man who was not supposed to possess a heart? Though Juliana owed him no explanation, she found herself offering one. "A year ago, she was thrown from a horse. She struck her head on a rock and has not been the same since."

"I am sorry. I remember her as being wise for one so young."

He sounded as if he truly regretted Alaiz's loss. Why that should sting Juliana's eyes with tears, she didn't care to know. She looked away. " 'Tis the reason she is so wary of horses."

"And the reason you did not ride to the tournament yesterday. You care much for your sister."

Care? The word did not begin to touch the feelings she had for Alaiz, who was all Juliana had in this world. Forgetting herself, she said, "I love her. Know you anything of that emotion, Lord De Vere?"

He arched an eyebrow.

"I thought not. I would do anything for my sister. Anything." As she had done last eve and would do twice more until her debt to Bernart was paid.

"What of Bernart?" Gabriel asked. "Well I remember a girl whose eyes could not touch upon him without her heart bounding from them, but no longer. Is that the emotion of which you speak, Lady Juliana? That which you vowed would endure a hundred lifetimes, but has died?"

His words cut more sharply than the finest blade. How she longed to proclaim her love for Bernart, but she'd never been good at lying or concealing her emotions—ever putting her heart out for all to criticize. She lifted her chin. "You expected otherwise? You who laughed at me, scorned my notions of love and chivalry? How pleased you must be now that you are proven right."

Something flickered in his eyes. "What comes between you and him?"

Bitter laughter parted her lips. "Surely you have not forgotten Acre? Or perhaps you have."

His voice tightened. "Bernart is not enough of a man for you?"

He knew? Juliana's heart jammed in her throat a moment before realization dislodged it. It was Bernart's limp he referred to, and he implied it was the reason for the state of her marriage. That the fault was hers. Anger flooded her. How she wished she could set Gabriel right, put the blame where it belonged, but it was not her place. " 'Tis true Bernart came back a changed man"—more than Gabriel would ever know—"but it was not the injury done his leg that changed him. It was betrayal. *That* is something you understand, do you not?"

The only evidence her words had an impact was a slight flush of color that rose up his neck and darkened the bruise on his cheekbone. How had he come by it? He must have been felled in tournament. "Will you step aside," she asked, "or shall I go through the rosebushes?"

He let her pass.

Juliana was halfway down the path when he called to her. Though she knew she ought to continue on, she turned.

His pale eyes captured hers. "I am not the devil you

think I am, Juliana." He omitted her title as if they were intimates—and they were. "I did not easily surrender my friendship with Bernart."

Something in his voice slipped past her defenses and tested the strength of her enmity. She remembered the sight of him on the battlefield yesterday, as removed from a coward as the earth was from the stars. She wavered between the desire to flee and that which longed for an answer. "Why did you not go with him?" she finally asked. "Why did you turn the others away? You were his friend."

Though Gabriel had always guarded his emotions too well to allow any to see beyond his hard heart, there was no denying the pain she glimpsed across the distance.

" 'Twas an undertaking doomed to failure. It had been attempted before and always with the result of mass slaughter. A foolish quest, especially as King Richard was soon to arrive."

"If 'twas foolish, why did you not stop him?"

Gabriel's brow lowered. "You think I did not try? Bernart, like those he persuaded to follow him—like myself— was tired, hungry, desperate. 'Tis true I turned some from his cause, made them see reason, but Bernart and the others would not be deterred."

Juliana raised her palms. "But had you joined him . . . had there been a hundred instead of—"

"Then one hundred would have died rather than fifty." Gabriel strode to where she stood. "Not even five hundred would have made a difference, Juliana."

Was it true? Had Gabriel and those he'd convinced to stand down joined Bernart, would they now be dead? It was not what Bernart believed.

"The only reason Bernart survived was because of his nobility," Gabriel said. "Had he been a common soldier like so many of the others, he would also be dead."

But he *was* dead. Emasculated. Embittered. Incapable of love. Tears welled in Juliana's eyes, threatened to spill. She cast her gaze down.

Gabriel crooked a finger beneath her chin and lifted her face to his regard.

It would have been so easy to escape him, but his surprisingly gentle touch held her motionless.

"A day does not pass when I do not wonder if there was something I could have done to turn Bernart from his course, but always it comes to naught."

He felt guilt? Never would she have guessed Gabriel De Vere capable of such emotion.

Regret grooved his mouth. "I am sorry, Juliana."

Was he?

He swept a tear from beneath her eye. So gentle, like the brush of an angel's wings. "If I could change what happened, I would."

Would he?

His breath mingled with hers, warmed her lips. "Though as a young man I scorned your silly notions of love, never did I wish to see you hurt."

Curious flutterings stirred her breast, drew her gaze to his mouth. What would it feel like to press her lips to his? To come to him in the light of day? Imagining it, she closed her eyes. So different from the night past.

"Juliana?"

Gabriel's sharp utterance flung her eyes wide. His face was before hers, his eyes questioning, their mouths nearly touching. But it was not he who had come to her. She had raised herself to her toes and leaned toward him.

With a small cry, she stumbled back. Shame heated her face and begot the false accusation that sprang to her lips. "You think to seduce me, Lord De Vere?"

His gaze hardened, frightening her.

"Tell your tales to someone more fool than I!" Juliana fled the garden. She swept past servants who called to her for guidance, skirted knights who stared after her with trenched brows, sidestepped two ladies who sought to draw her into idle conversation. By the time she gained the passageway outside the lord's solar, she was trembling violently. Lest she alarm her sister, she leaned back against the wall and struggled to regain her composure.

What had possessed her? She was not attracted to Gabriel De Vere. Did not desire his touch. She wanted him gone from Tremoral, could not stand that two more nights stood between her and his absence. So what had drawn her to him? Certainly not that he was comely. He possessed a fine build, and that was all. Even Bernart, in his present state of waste, was more handsome. What was it? She closed her eyes. It had naught to do with the outside, and everything to do with the inside. The unexpected tenderness Gabriel had shown, which was too long denied her, had compelled her to do the unthinkable.

She groaned. As great as her humiliation, the real threat was to her identity. When she sought Gabriel's bed this night, would he suspect? Providing Bernart filled him with as much drink as he had on the night past, it was not likely. She straightened from the wall. Hopefully, all she needed to overcome was her own fear. She pushed the door inward. So where was she to find courage? There, in the smile Alaiz turned on her.

Long after Juliana had gone, Gabriel stood unmoving beneath the weight of puzzlement and anger. Had Juliana, a woman who bore him such enmity, offered her mouth to him as if to take him as a lover? Had he imagined it? He reflected on the ale of which he had partaken previous to coming to the garden. Only one tankard. As unbelievable as it was, she had come to him—then accused *him* of being the seducer!

His anger surged. Had he taken what she'd offered, he might have had her right here, might this moment be beneath her skirts. So what had stayed him? Not honor, not that she was forbidden him by the laws of Church and God and a friendship that no longer was. As with everything to do with women, it came back to Constance De Vere. Gabriel did not lie with women who were wed. No matter how tempting.

The faint scent Juliana left behind teased his nostrils. He clenched his jaw. Why had he defended himself to her? He owed her no explanation for what he'd done at Acre, did not care what she thought of him. However, an old longing wended through him, made of him a liar.

"Damn!" he barked. Had he sought out the wench who had come to him last eve, he could have eased this need. Instead he'd been drawn to the garden by the sound of Juliana's voice. But at least now he knew her for what she was, had confirmation of what he'd believed all along. Like all women, she was treacherous.

Chapter Six

He was not drinking.

Unease cramped Juliana's belly as she stared at Gabriel. In the hour following the conclusion of the evening meal, she had seen him take no more than half a dozen swallows of ale and turn away the serving wenches who sought to press more upon him. Obviously he had no intention of repeating the excesses of the night before.

Did Bernart not see what was happening—rather, what was not happening? She sought him out where he stood distant from Gabriel. He looked tense, his smile forced as he conversed with a neighboring baron. The day had gone poorly for him.

During supper, Juliana had overheard what had passed between Bernart and Gabriel on the tournament field. Though the others viewed it as merely another ransom to be gained, she knew it went deeper. It was retribution Bernart had sought and lost. Perhaps even death. For it, he'd paid the high price of his horse and armor. And his pride. He had naught to show for it but the bruise discoloring Gabriel's face.

Did Gabriel have any notion of what might have happened had he not bettered Bernart? Juliana shook off her pondering. What mattered was the night ahead. Not only must she find some way to coax Gabriel's seed from him without revealing herself, but it seemed she must do so with him sober. It did not bear thinking about.

Suddenly his gaze met hers.

Breath rushing from her, she turned her attention to a game of chess two knights played. Though Gabriel refused the wenches who tried to fill his tankard, she'd seen him watching them closely, as if speculating on who had come to him last eve. After what had happened in the garden, did it occur to him it might be she?

Juliana rubbed her hands over her forearms. Perhaps he remembered naught of the night past. Perhaps he had not noticed her virgin's blood upon the sheets she'd stripped from his bed this morn.

"Ooh!" Alaiz cried.

The knight who lost his queen to a bishop looked sharply over his shoulder to where Juliana's sister stood on tiptoe. He was not pleased.

Fearful he might say something unkind, Juliana took a step toward Alaiz, but in the next instant a hand fell upon her arm. Bernart. Considering he'd avoided her since this morn, she was surprised he would seek her out now. Had he changed his mind? A flutter of hope spread through her. She met his gaze.

Angry. Accusing. Something else had brought him across the hall. The flutter turned to stone and settled in her belly.

"I must needs speak with you," he said in a hiss.

Tempted as she was to resist, she allowed him to draw her into a shadowed alcove.

"Send your sister abovestairs."

She glanced at Alaiz. Having escaped unscathed following her outburst, she watched with knitted brow as the knights studied the chessboard. "She is enjoying herself."

"She is making sounds."

Juliana cocked her head. "Sounds?"

"Like a child."

It was true Alaiz's expressions of awe and delight were not something a properly reared lady of six and ten would utter, but she was . . . different. "And what harm is there in that?"

"What harm? Do you not see how they stare at her?"

Juliana lifted her chin. "Aye, and do you not think it rude of them?"

For a long moment he gave no reply; then he snapped, "You spend too much time with her at the neglect of our guests!"

She looked to the ladies who sat tittering amongst themselves before the hearth. They seemed content enough, but it was true she had paid them little regard. "I fear my mind is elsewhere, but I am certain you understand."

Anger coursed a bruising path from his hand to her arm. "You are the lady of Tremoral. I demand you conduct yourself accordingly!"

She glared at him. "Indulge your guests during the day and lie with them at night? You ask much, husband."

She could not have struck harder had she used her fists. Bernart released her. "Do not speak to me of it. I cannot bear it."

Still he would send her to his enemy a second time, a third. " 'Tis Gabriel you ought to concern yourself with, not Alaiz. He does not drink, or have you not noticed?"

Concern wiped the misery from Bernart's face. He hadn't noticed, likely because he could no more stand to be near Gabriel than could his wife.

"If he did not remember last eve," Juliana said, "he will surely remember this eve."

Bernart looked past her. "I will take care of it."

Though she wanted to ask how he intended to do that, she stepped out of the alcove and crossed to her sister. "You are enjoying yourself?"

Alaiz turned sparkling eyes on her. "Ever so!"

Juliana nodded. Her sacrifice was worth the gain.

The night was growing old, and still Bernart could not get more drink into Gabriel. He had sent wench after wench to his old friend in an attempt to press more ale upon him, then wine, but though Gabriel took measure of the women and said things that made them smile and giggle, he would allow none to tip their pitcher to his tankard. Not even Nesta, whose voluptuous curves should have distracted Gabriel long enough to get one or more cups of drink into him. It was as if he knew what was planned.

Now, with Juliana abovestairs, and his guests readying to bed down for the night, Bernart found he had no choice but to deal with Gabriel himself. He ordered a wench to fetch him a pitcher of his finest wine, then strode toward the hearth.

At his approach, Gabriel and Sir Erec looked up.

"Plotting tomorrow's ransoms?" Bernart asked. He nearly choked on the drollery.

Hands empty of a drinking vessel, Gabriel stared at him.

"Of course," Sir Erec said.

Bernart ignored the knight and took the chair opposite

Gabriel. "You ought to be pleased with yourself."

Gabriel's eyebrows rose. "Ought I?"

Bernart smiled. "Of course. Do your ransoms not exceed all others?" Idle talk, but perhaps it would keep Gabriel seated long enough for the wench to return with the wine.

"I have you to thank for that," Gabriel said.

Although Bernart had unwittingly opened himself to the remark, he did not need to be reminded of the foolishness that had cost him dearly. *Damn Gabriel! And damn that lazy wench!* Where was she? He glanced over his shoulder as she emerged from the cellar. He looked back at Gabriel. "Ah, but as I said, next time it will be you paying me."

Gabriel started to rise, Sir Erec with him.

But it was Bernart who was first to his feet. "Join me." He motioned to where the wench poured the wine at a nearby sideboard.

Gabriel eyed him. "Hoping to get me drunk again?"

"Again?"

"As on the night past."

Pretending humor he had not felt in years, Bernart chuckled. "Then that would explain why your reflexes were so poor in tournament today." The moment he said it, he knew he had once more made a mistake. Mother of Christ, he must be losing his mind!

Gabriel's wry smile spoke the words he denied his tongue: even drunk he could better Bernart.

Perspiration beaded Bernart's brow as he fought emotions that had been his undoing on the battlefield. "The wine is from Gascony," he said. "You will have some?" He knew how much Gabriel enjoyed French wine. If this could not tempt him, naught could.

"There is something you wish to speak to me about?" Gabriel asked.

Bernart glanced at Sir Erec. "It has been many years since Acre," he said, hoping Gabriel's partner would take that as his cue to leave. However, the man seemed in no hurry to quit the hall.

"Not enough," Gabriel replied.

As if his own wounds went deeper, Bernart thought bitterly. He accepted a goblet from the wench and nodded for Gabriel and Sir Erec to do the same. When they did, he lowered himself back to the chair. To his discomfort, the two remained standing.

Over the next few minutes, Bernart asked about France's tourney circuit, and Gabriel answered with as few words as possible, revealing very little about his life following the Crusade. Not that Bernart needed to be told, for he would have to be deaf not to know of Gabriel's exploits—that when he was not helping King Richard regain lands seized by France's King Philip, he was taking ransoms in tourney.

Although Sir Erec sampled the wine and commented on its superiority, Gabriel did not so much as peer into his goblet.

Drink! "The chamber is to your liking?"

Gabriel inclined his head.

Bernart took a sip of the fine wine, fully aware that more than a swallow or two would lead to intense discomfort, the same as that which had plagued him throughout the day. "You are sleeping well?"

Gabriel was slow to answer. "Well enough. You sent a wench to my chamber last eve?"

A wench. A woman who'd given her innocence to him without his knowing it. At least, Bernart prayed he did not know. He swallowed. "I do not recall your ever needing help to entice a woman into your bed."

99

Gabriel thumbed the rim of his goblet. " 'Tis just that I was expecting one and another came."

"Ah, Nesta. Regrets, but she was . . . otherwise occupied." Let him interpret that however he wished.

"And you do not know who came in her place?" Gabriel lifted the goblet toward his mouth.

Why did Gabriel care? One woman was much the same for him as the next. Jealousy bunched Bernart's shoulders. "I do not concern myself with the comings and goings of servants."

"Indeed." Finally Gabriel tasted the wine.

More. "One of the wenches must have come upon a liking for you," Bernart said. "But tell, what does it matter who shared your bed last eve?" He shouldn't ask, ought to leave it be, but could not.

Gabriel tipped the goblet once more before answering. "She was different."

Agitated, fearing it showed, Bernart swept his hand toward the half dozen wenches who pushed benches against the walls for the guests who would avail themselves of the comforts of the hall. "Who do you think 'twas?"

"None of these."

"You are certain?" Bernart's voice cracked betrayingly. Had Gabriel heard it?

A frown drew Gabriel's eyebrows. "I am certain." He stared at Bernart a moment, then took a long swallow of wine.

Perspiring more heavily, Bernart motioned to the serving wench.

She refilled Gabriel's goblet, then Sir Erec's. Bernart waved her away when she turned to him. " 'Tis likely one of the chambermaids, Gabriel," he said.

"Possibly."

Bernart abandoned the subject for one less distressing.

"Will you return to France following the tournament?"

" 'Tis where the money is."

"And your lands." Months ago, Bernart had heard that King Richard had awarded Gabriel a demesne. Finally he was a lord, though he would never be as great and powerful a lord as Wyverly would have made him. "Who keeps the barony in your absence?"

"My brother, Blase."

"The priest?"

"Aye." Gabriel stepped from the hearth and set his goblet on the sideboard.

Bernart's insides coiled so tightly he felt he might burst. He stood. "Will you not stay a while longer?"

" 'Tis time I seek my bed. I thank you for the wine."

To argue with him would only rouse his suspicions further. "Good eve, then."

Gabriel strode past him to the stairs.

Bernart turned and found Sir Erec watching him. "And good eve to you, Sir Erec."

The knight dipped his head and strode from the hall.

Bernart raised his goblet. Without thinking, he tossed the wine to the back of his throat. Then, as if death settled in his bones, he rigidly stepped to the sideboard and lifted the pitcher. As he did so, he peered into Gabriel's vessel. Half-full. The man could not have drunk more than a goblet of wine. Bernart squeezed his eyes closed, then opened them a moment later. If not wine, then sleep. He would give Gabriel an hour, then send Juliana to him. Though not as sure as alcohol, sleep ought to find him addled.

An hour and three refills of wine later, Bernart tested his footing on the stairs. Somehow he made it to the landing without mishap.

* * *

Bernart said naught. He simply opened the door, nodded, and left Juliana to gather her courage.

Now, once again, she stood in Gabriel's darkened chamber. When she'd slipped within, she had seen he was in bed, and from his stillness known he was asleep.

Aware that this night would require far more than simply taking him into her body, she fumbled with her mantle, freed the knot she had made of the ties, and dropped the garment atop the chest at the foot of the bed. Her coarse bliaut followed, but as she lifted the hem of her chemise, Gabriel's deep voice melted across the stillness.

"I had hoped you would come again."

Considering her reception on the night past, Juliana should not have been surprised he'd awakened, but she was. Hand to her throat, she searched the inky darkness and picked out his shadow. Doubtless he would never fall victim to one who sought to plant a knife in his back.

She had barely regained her breath when realization struck. There was no slur to his voice as there ought to be, as Bernart had assured her there would be. He was not drunk, then? Or merely not as drunk as last eve? How did he know she was the same woman who had come to him on the night past?

The creak of the bed forced her to abandon her pondering. Fearing Gabriel intended to rise, she hurried forward.

A moment later, his hands closed around her arms. "Eager, eh?" He pulled her between his thighs where he sat on the mattress edge.

She smelled wine on his breath, but it was faint. *Curse Bernart!* She would have fled the chamber if not for the hands that held her firm. Then those hands began to touch her.

Gabriel caressed his fingers up her side to the under-curve of her breast. Through her chemise, he stroked her fullness, causing spikes of sensation to draw her nipple erect. His other hand explored her buttocks.

Juliana closed her eyes. Why did he have to touch her like this, as if she were a lover and not some whore who had once more stolen to his chamber? Rather than being aroused, she ought to be repulsed. Rather than filled with sweet flutterings, she ought to be rolling with nausea. Desperately, she wanted to resist the feelings Gabriel awakened, but they were too pleasurable.

"We do not need this," he said, and drew her chemise upward.

Only when the fine material began its ascent, gliding sensually over her skin as she could not remember it ever having done, did Juliana realize her mistake. In her haste to prevent Gabriel from rising, she'd forgotten about the garment. Had he noticed its texture? That it was markedly different from that worn by commoners?

He pulled the chemise over her head and tossed it aside.

Praying his man's need was too great for him to question the reason a whore wore a lady's garment, Juliana swept her hair from her eyes and lowered her gaze. Though it was too dark to make out his face, she saw his head bend forward.

"This time I pleasure you first," he said, his voice winding through her. Then his mouth was on her breast.

Juliana gasped. What was he doing to her? Why didn't he just . . . She leaned forward, silently beseeching him to feed her desire.

His unshaven face rasped the tender flesh of her breast as he tugged at her nipple, causing small, panting sounds to escape her throat. He nipped and swirled his tongue around her, then moved to the other breast.

Forgetting who she was, who this man was who'd

thrust her into womanhood, the pain of that initiation, Juliana grasped his head to her breasts and clenched her fingers in his thick hair. This was how it was supposed to be between a man and woman. These were the things a woman ought to feel. The things she had only ever heard spoken of and days ago thought never to experience.

Gabriel trailed his mouth to her belly, melting warmth across her flesh.

Juliana dropped her head back, parted her lips on a moan.

"You like that," he said. Or was it a question?

Though she knew he couldn't see her, she nodded.

One moment she was standing, the next on her back, flesh to flesh.

"Who are you?" he asked, his breath stirring the hair across her brow.

She quivered. She was Juliana Kinthorpe, lady of Tremoral. But last night, this night, and the night to come, she was another, a faceless woman come to steal a child from him. *That* she must not forget.

"Surely you have a name," he prompted.

She swallowed. He was likely too sober to allow her to distract him as she had when he'd questioned her last eve. Could she disguise her voice? If so, what to call herself? Remembering from the games she'd played as a child how difficult it was to identify another's voice when it was whispered, she ventured, "I am . . . Isolde."

Gabriel's silence turned her palms clammy and caused her heart to speed. Did he know?

"Isolde," he said. "A beautiful name."

But a poor choice. The oft-told love story of Tristan and Isolde having once been dear to Juliana, it was the first name that came to her. In Gabriel's silence, had he

104

recalled the tale himself, that which had many times been recounted in her father's hall?

"You work in the donjon?"

"The . . . the kitchens," she whispered.

"Hmm." He moved his hands over her again.

She was relieved that he seemed to have made no connection between the woman who came to him in the night and the girl who'd sighed over the troubadour's tale and unabashedly named Bernart Kinthorpe her Tristan. Slowly she allowed herself to be coaxed to an awareness of Gabriel, but when his mouth sought hers she once more turned her head. As in the garden, she longed to taste him, but she feared such a joining. Feared its tenderness.

Why Gabriel wanted to kiss her, he couldn't say, for it was not something he usually gave thought to when he was with a woman. If it happened, fine. If not, it was hardly missed. But he wanted to kiss this wench, to press his tongue inside her mouth and taste her sweetness. He cupped her chin and pulled her face to his, but before he could possess her lips, she jerked her head opposite.

Though the details of her first visit were indistinct, he remembered having tried to kiss her, that she'd also refused him. Strange. Never had he known a woman to give of her body and yet guard her mouth. What did she fear?

He breathed the faint scent that had wafted to him when she had entered his chamber. Familiar, yet he could not name it. "Isolde"—somehow the name didn't fit—"let me taste your sweet mouth." He brushed his lips over her ear.

She stiffened, but in the next instant pushed a hand between them and curled her fingers around his rigid shaft. She meant to distract him and was doing a fine job of it. Still, he wanted what she denied him, and would have sought it had she not drawn her hand up and down again. *Wanton*. He strained beneath her fingers. Lord, he wanted her!

Though she refused to take his mouth upon hers, she surprised him by putting her lips to the flesh between his neck and shoulder. He groaned. He wanted to drive into her depths as her hand upon him imitated.

She drew her other hand down his spine, splayed her fingers over his buttocks, pressed him between her thighs.

Feeling her heat, Gabriel was aroused as he had not been in a long time. Yet for all this wench's familiarity with his body, there was something about her touch that was innocent. Seeking, rather than knowing. Uncertain, rather than wanton. It stirred him beyond all thought. He pushed toward her woman's place.

She held him a long moment, denying him entrance. Then, with a shudder, she loosed her fingers and eased her thighs apart.

Gabriel pressed inside. She was tight. He sank deep, settled against her womb, and withdrew. Through the passion that urged him to take her quickly, he felt her tense. He knew women well, and her reaction was not of desire. Was it that she was too small, or simply less versed in lovemaking than her brazen hands would have him believe? Vague memories of last eve returned. She had reacted similarly when he'd entered her that first time, then eagerly come to him. Small, he decided. Her discomfort would pass.

Slowly he began to thrust. As he did so, he caressed one breast, then the other, then ventured lower and lingered over her thigh, which was more silken than any he had ever touched. She was soft, beautiful beneath his hands. He felt her tension drain, but still he held back. First her, then him.

Shortly, small sounds escaped her throat; then her nails

sank into his buttocks and a whimper parted her silent lips. "Aye. Aye." A moment later, she flung her arms around him, buried her face in his neck, and convulsed.

Now him. Gabriel drove hard, and was nearing release when the wench rasped into his ear, "Let me."

He stilled. As much as he ached for the pinnacle he had been near attaining, he allowed her to press him onto his back. When she lowered herself onto him, he thought he would explode.

Her silken hair skimming his flesh, she pressed her palms to his abdomen and lingeringly slid her hands upward—as if learning every muscle and sinew of him. Then she bent and trailed her lips over his chest. When her tongue flicked his areola, Gabriel jerked inside her. When she drew his nipple into her mouth, he began to thrust.

It was pleasurable. Though such ministrations were not new to him, he had never cared to be suckled. In fact, he'd always found it more of an annoyance than a stimulant.

The moment before climax, he strained into the mattress in an attempt to withdraw, but she sat back, clamped her knees against his sides, and held him inside. With a shout, he spilled his seed into her. Again and again he spasmed until he could give no more. Finally he opened his eyes.

The woman straddling him was still, the only movement about her the slight rise and fall of her breasts. What did she look like? Was her face as beautiful as that which his hands had learned? "You have pleased me greatly," he said.

She said naught.

Gabriel pulled her to him. As her breasts settled against his chest, she turned her face into his neck. She felt like no woman he had ever been with. Draped in hair he imagined to be auburn color, he fondled her hip, the small of her back, her ribs, her nape. "I thank you, Isolde."

She nodded.

He turned onto his side and levered up. "I wish to see you."

Were fear capable of being held, it would be as ponderous as that which leaped from her. She grasped his arm. "Nay, I . . ." It was a long moment ere she found the words. "I am disfigured."

Disfigured? That was the reason she hid herself in night? He reached to lay fingers to her cheek.

She captured his hand. "Pray, do not shame me."

Her scared, husky voice stilled him. Though it was hard to believe this woman whose body was shaped by divine hands did not possess the face of a temptress, it would account for the darkness in which she came to him and her refusal to allow his mouth upon hers. What had happened to her? Had she been born disfigured? Maimed later in life? He wanted to ask, to know more about her, but sensed it would frighten her away.

"I am sorry," she whispered, and started to rise. "I will leave you now."

Did she think him repulsed? Angered? Gabriel pulled her back. "Do not."

He sensed her surprise. "You wish me to stay?"

He slid a hand up from her ribs and cupped her breast. "I do." He bent his head and caught her nipple between his teeth.

She was slower to respond than before, but finally they joined again. Straining with ache, Gabriel once more allowed Isolde her pleasure, then moved in search of his own. As he neared climax, her hands on his hips urged him onto his side. She wanted to mount him again, he realized, but he was too near to stop now.

Withdraw, his conscience shouted. Too late. The spasms were more satiating than any he had known, Isolde's body holding him warm and tight. It felt good to quake inside her.

Supported on outstretched arms, Gabriel drew a deep breath. It was several minutes before he calmed enough to think clearly, but when he did, he was pricked with regret. Though it was too dark to make out more than the curve of Isolde's jaw, he felt her gaze.

He hoped it wasn't her time of breeding, that nine months from now a nameless child would not be born of their union. "Damn," he muttered, and fell onto his side.

He had never been with a woman who could so easily make him forget the vow that had served him well all these years. Now, twice in one night, he'd chanced impregnating her. In future, he would have to be more careful. He would—

There was no future for them, he reminded himself. He was little more than a knight errant, living tourney to tourney to raise the funds to rebuild Mergot, she a kitchen maid in the household of Bernart Kinthorpe. That aside, he did not want a woman in his life. To ease his man's need, aye, but for the moment only.

Isolde touched his shoulder, the brush of her fingertips stirring his lax manhood. They had what was left of the night. He pulled her against him.

An hour later, he slept.

Juliana stared into the dark, every pore of her aware of the man beside her and the things he had made her feel. She trembled. This night she had made herself into Nesta and taken from Gabriel what he'd previously denied her.

109

If a child took, she would have to live with the terrible wrong she had done him. Of course, though he was careful where he scattered his seed, that did not mean he would care if a child were born of his unions. Bastards were more than common, few acknowledged or provided for by their fathers. Still, that did not make what she did right.

She turned her thoughts elsewhere. Why hadn't Gabriel sent her away when she'd told him she was disfigured? What kind of blackheart was he? *The kind who made her feel the impossible,* her heart whispered. *The kind who had not easily given up his friendship with Bernart...*

Knowing the dawn was soon to come, she eased off the bed and gathered her bliaut, mantle, and slippers. However, her chemise was nowhere to be found. She rose from searching the floor. The bed? A few moments later, she grasped the familiar material and pulled it toward her. It resisted. Inwardly she groaned. What else could go awry? If she attempted to free the garment from beneath Gabriel, it would likely awaken him, and she could ill afford to spend this last hour ere dawn with him. She had to leave the chemise. Would he notice it come morn? She prayed not.

She donned her clothes, drew the hood of her mantle over her head, unbarred the door, and slipped from Gabriel's chamber. As she pushed the door of the solar inward, she caught a movement out of the corner of her eye. Fearing what she might see, she peered into the shadows.

Bernart. He stood in the doorway of the chapel, face drawn, shoulders stooped, looking as if he'd not slept.

Though she knew there was no reason for it, Juliana was flooded with guilt, as if caught trysting with a lover, as if she were responsible for Bernart's pain. She wasn't.

All she had done was what he demanded of her. If he wanted, he could stop it.

He withdrew into the chapel and closed the door.

In the solar, Juliana let her clothes lie where they fell and, after completing her ablutions, sank down upon her cold bed. She lay there a long time seeking sleep, but the memories of this night were not easily put away. They filled her nostrils with the masculine scent of Gabriel, her mouth with the salty taste of him, her breast with emotions she dared not delve into.

She hugged her arms to her, turning her thoughts to those things she must tend to with the new day's rising. But it was useless. Her fingertips and palms tingled with remembrances of Gabriel's powerful chest, shoulders, arms. Worse, sensations coursed through her as if she were still joined with him.

There was no denying it. This night she had experienced something she had only ever dreamed of. In Gabriel's arms she'd finally discovered what it was like to be a woman to a man, to scale passion and return to earth more satisfied than she would have believed possible. Such pleasure. Such rapture. She wanted more.

With the admission came the guilt she had denied was her due. It sliced through her. She ought not feel what she had in Gabriel's arms. Ought to be sickened by what had happened. Ought to loathe the thought of going to him again. She didn't. God forgive her.

Chapter Seven

"I know not whether I ought envy you or pity you," Sir Erec said.

Gabriel lowered himself to the bench, lifted his tankard of morning mead. "What speak you of?"

The knight exaggerated a scowl. "You look as if you've not slept in days."

Except for an hour or two before Isolde came to him and after her departure, he had not.

"Was it the same wench?" Erec asked.

The clamor of the hall nettled Gabriel's nerves—loud voices and laughter, the clink and clatter of utensils, the scrape of benches, the yap and growl of two dogs battling over one bone. " 'Twas," he said, and speared a chunk of cheese on his dagger.

"Still you do not know who she is?"

"I do not." Though Gabriel told himself he shouldn't care, it bothered him that when he left Tremoral on the morrow all he would take with him was the name of the woman who'd once more been gone from his bed upon his awakening.

"You are certain 'tis none of them?" Erec jutted his chin to the expanse of hall where women servants bustled amid calls for food and drink.

Gabriel dismissed them with a glance. For certain, Isolde was in the kitchens where few could look upon her disfigurement. This eve, would she come to him one last time?

Laughter pulled his regard to the lord's table. It was without its lord. Once again, Bernart had departed early for the battlefield.

Cheeks flushed prettily, lips bowed wide, Alaiz leaned near her sister and uttered something that made her laugh anew. For the first time since coming to Tremoral, Gabriel saw Juliana smile. The gesture grooved her right cheek and brought a sparkle to her eyes, enhancing her beauty tenfold.

"Come, Gabriel, I did not ask whom you wish it to be," Sir Erec teased.

Gabriel looked around.

The knight grinned and popped a piece of bread into his mouth.

The man was a menace, always seeing more than he should, more than what was there. Still, something niggled at Gabriel. He returned his gaze to the dais and saw that Juliana had risen. She patted her sister's shoulder and stepped from behind the table.

Alaiz looked suddenly lost. Though Gabriel wasted little of his emotions on others, he felt for her. The life she'd been destined for was gone, and as no landed noble would take her to wife, neither had she the hope of marriage. Never would she know the touch of a man—

A thought struck Gabriel. Was it possible? He remembered the silken strands that had slid through his fingers, the figure his hands had learned, the husky voice the wench had all but kept to herself, the fine chemise he had found among the bedclothes. . . .

Perhaps the one who'd come again last eve was not a wench, not disfigured. Perhaps she was Lady Alaiz wishing to be the woman her accident denied her. It fit, but did not. Was Alaiz, yet was not. Chest constricting, Gabriel jerked his head around.

Auburn hair confined to a plait that ran the length of her back, full breasts swelling the bodice of her gown, snug waist accentuated by an embroidered belt, Juliana directed the women servants with an efficiency that bespoke the lady of the castle. Not a wench. Never a wench. But could it be?

Sir Erec's words of minutes earlier echoed through him: *I did not ask whom you wish it to be.* Was that all this was? Wishing for one who belonged to another? Gabriel summoned memories of yesterday, when Juliana had sought his kiss, memories of the night past, the night before. The scent of her, feminine. The feel, silken. Her touch, tentative one moment, urgent the next. Her whispered voice, sweetly husky. Her name, Isolde.

Realizing that if he inquired, there would be no kitchen maid in Bernart's household by that name, he tightened his hold on his meat dagger. Isolde existed only in the person of one who, as a child, had been surrounded by tales of love, her favorite being that of Tristan and Isolde. He had been blind—as if his eyes were put out!

"Gabriel?" Erec said.

Why had she given herself to her husband's enemy? In retaliation for Bernart's infidelities with Nesta and whomever else he took beneath him? Anger tightened every muscle in his body. Juliana had used him. She was a whore the same as his mother.

"What is it, Gabriel?"

He leashed his emotions. "Naught." He finished his mead.

Juliana felt him. His eyes followed her, bore through her. Did he know? Had he discovered the chemise she'd left behind and realized it was hers? Perhaps not. Perhaps it was something else that caused him to look so heavily upon her.

She had to know. Praying she did not appear anxious, she summoned a servant and instructed the woman to strew fresh herbs over the rushes, then lifted her skirts and crossed to the stairs. Shortly, she entered Gabriel's chamber.

Excepting the dust motes that stirred in the shaft of light bridging the space between window and rumpled bed, all was still.

She hurried across the room, put her knees to the mattress, and began searching the bedclothes. Naught. "Please, God," she implored, and tossed a pillow aside.

"You will not find it there." A deep voice shattered her prayer.

Juliana's heart hurtled into her throat. *Dear Lord, let this be but a terrible dream.* She closed her eyes, but when she opened them, the mattress she'd twice shared with Gabriel was beneath her knees. She swallowed hard. "Have you not a tournament to attend, Lord De Vere?"

The crush of rushes announced his advance. "Why?" he demanded.

She would deny it to her dying breath. Keeping her back to him, she lowered her feet to the floor, swept the covers from the bed, gathered them to her chest. When she turned, he stood three feet distant. "The bed must needs be stripped," she said, refusing him her gaze.

"But first rifled?"

She looked beyond him and saw he'd closed the door. Fear pounded at her temples. She must get away. Clutching the bedclothes more tightly, she started past him.

He caught her arm and pulled her against him. "Why?"

She was grateful for the covers between them, but it was not enough. Summoning indignation, she snapped, "You forget your place, Lord De Vere. Unhand me!"

He grasped her chin, forced it up. "And where is my place?"

Her breath was much too labored. "Release me."

A caustic smile touched his lips. Combined with the unsightly bruise upon his cheekbone, it made him appear sinister. "You look tired, Juliana. Have you not slept well?"

She strained backward. "Let me go!"

"When you have answered me. For what reason did you seek my bed?"

"You think . . . How dare—"

"No more than you. Now tell me."

A dangerous man, "I know not what you speak of."

"Mayhap this will help you remember." He lowered his mouth toward hers.

With a cry, she jerked her head to the side.

Gabriel's lips landed on her jaw. Laughter rumbled from his chest as he moved to her ear. "Should we make love by the light of day, *Isolde?*" He swept his tongue over her ear.

She shuddered. "I shall scream. I swear it!"

"You will not." He thrust the bedclothes to the floor and dragged her against him. "Do you remember now?" His hard length surged against her belly.

A mixture of fear and excitement shot through her as

she looked into his intense eyes, their paleness engulfed by the dark of his pupils. Knowing she'd be lost if she didn't stop him, she put her hands to his chest and pushed with all her strength. He was like a rock.

Gabriel cupped her breast, captured her nipple through her gown. "Do you remember?"

She tried to twist free, but he held tight. "You are wrong. Pray, do not do this."

He hitched up her skirts and glided a hand over her thigh. "You liked the things I did to you." His voice lowered to a sensuous throb. "Didn't you, Juliana?"

So much she wanted him to do them again. "Please . . ."

His fingers brushed her inner flesh and found her heat. "Tell me."

She whimpered.

"Tell me you liked it."

Her body harkened to the hunger he roused, moved her against her will. She was drowning.

"Say it."

That she desired him? That more than anything else she wished him to lay her back and cover her again? No greater lie could be told if she denied it. She nodded. "Aye, Gabriel. Aye."

He pulled his hand from beneath her skirt, thrust rough fingers through her hair, and forced her head back. "You used me!"

He knew of the child she hoped to steal from him? As she stared into his wrathful face, panic stole her passion. Chilled her. *To my dying breath.* Though from her response to Gabriel it would be futile to continue to deny she was Isolde, never would she admit to Bernart's plan. " 'Tis not true."

Gabriel pulled her head back, further exposing her throat. "You did not come to my bed for revenge? To lie with your husband's enemy that you might injure Bernart as he injures you each time he takes Nesta or another beneath him?"

Revenge? Bernart and Nesta? Juliana felt adrift. What was Gabriel talking about?

"When did you mean to tell him? Before I leave Tremoral or after I am gone?"

Finally she made sense of him. He thought vengeance had reduced her to a whore, not a quest for a son. Though Juliana knew she ought to be grateful the truth evaded him, it stung that he thought her so ignoble—that mere revenge could cause her to set aside her beliefs, her honor, her pride. If only she could tell him the truth, that she was as much a pawn as he, but if she did, Bernart would retaliate against Alaiz. So how was she to salvage the mess she had made of her nights with Gabriel? How was she to calm the beast?

With a snort of disgust, he released her hair. "Let us have done with it now." He grasped her wrist and dragged her toward the door.

He meant to tell Bernart? There would be bloodshed. "Nay!" She wrenched backward. Her slender wrist slipped through Gabriel's fingers. Though she threw out her arms to break her fall, the bed did it for her. She pushed up from it and met Gabriel's gaze. "Listen to me. Do you tell Bernart, he will kill you."

The smile that touched his lips did naught to ease his harsh features. "As he tried to do yesterday—and failed?"

So it was true. "He will try again."

"And fail again."

"Perhaps."

He cocked his head. "Would you care, Juliana *Kinthorpe?*"

In that moment, she knew what she must do to prevent

a deadly confrontation. Even so, the words that passed her lips were no lie. "I would."

His lids narrowed. He did not believe her.

Juliana drew all of her courage about her and stepped forward. "I am alone, Gabriel. My marriage is . . . hardly a marriage. I do not love Bernart. He does not—"

" 'Tis obvious you do not love him. Is it because he no longer fits your silly image of a lover? That he is lame? Uncomely?"

If only he knew the reason behind Bernart's wasting. As if Gabriel had not spoken, she continued. "Neither does Bernart love me." Now the lie. "He takes his pleasure in other women and I try not to see it. But I do."

"So you avenge yourself with me."

" 'Tis true that revenge brought me to your chamber the first night, but yesterday in the garden, I felt . . ." She halted before him. "I felt something I have not in a long time."

Her declaration appeared to have no effect on him. "What did you feel?"

"Like a woman."

"Not a whore?"

How vicious his words. She swept her gaze to her feet and commanded them to remain still. No matter how cruel he was, she would not flee. " 'Twas more than the flesh that brought me to you last eve."

"Then you profess to have feelings for me?"

Was it true? "I do," she said, uncertain whether or not it was another lie she told. Though she felt the beckoning of his hard gaze, she did not look up for fear her eyes would reveal her.

"Have you forgotten I am your enemy? The man whom you believe betrayed your husband at Acre?"

Had he betrayed Bernart? Doubt settled over her as she

recalled the words he'd spoken in the garden. "You told me you did not easily give up your friendship with Bernart."

"I did not."

She looked up. "I believe you." It was true, though she did not realize it until she said it. All these years she'd allowed Bernart's anger to blind her to the man Gabriel had been before the two had set off for the Holy Land. True, she had never cared for him and his coarse manners that boded no respect for women, but he had been no coward. "I now know you could not have betrayed Bernart."

He laughed, a harsh sound. "Because I pleasured you, Juliana? Is that all it took? A salving of the flesh?"

"I tell you 'twas more than that!"

"How many before me?"

She shook her head. "What speak you of?"

"How many times have you cuckolded Bernart? Or is it too many to put upon one hand?"

She could not fault him for believing he wasn't the first, but it wounded her. "There have been no others."

"I am to believe you? A woman who dons night and whispers lies?"

She was not reaching him. Any moment now he would drag her before Bernart. She stepped nearer. "I do not lie, Gabriel. You are the first. I beseech you, do not go to Bernart."

He turned and strode toward the door.

"Gabriel!"

He looked over his shoulder.

"Will you tell him?"

An excruciatingly long moment passed before he answered. "I will not."

Relief poured into her. "I thank you."

He pulled the door open. "Come no more to me." He stepped into the corridor.

Juliana stared at the empty doorway. Why this ache? Merely guilt? Why this terrible sense of having lost something dear? Only desire? It had to be.

She crossed to the window and pulled back the oilcloth. A short while later, Gabriel appeared amongst the castle folk in the bailey below. With long strides, he crossed the inner drawbridge and passed from sight. Now he would go to the battlefield and face the man whose wife he had lain with, neither knowing that the other was aware of her sin.

She dropped the oilcloth and leaned back against the wall. What was she to do when Bernart ordered her to Gabriel's chamber one last time? As his guilt would not allow him to watch her go to his enemy, she could make a pretense of doing so, but he might await her return to the solar, as he'd done last eve. Could she tell him two nights were enough, that she was certain she was breeding?

Juliana touched her belly. Nine months from now, would she push forth Gabriel's son for Bernart to claim? The thought caused her stomach to heave. If not that she'd eaten little this morn, she would have retched.

Nay, Bernart would not risk the past two nights of pain and jealousy for the gain of one. And what of her? If Gabriel's seed did not take, she would have to lie down for another, and perhaps another. She *was* going to retch.

Juliana hastened to the washbasin and bent over it. When her stomach finally settled, she wiped her face with a hand towel that smelled faintly of Gabriel. What was she to do?

*   *   *

Juliana's heart pounded fiercely as Gabriel ascended the dais. She should have known he would be the one to gain the most ransoms, that she would have to face him beneath Bernart's watchful gaze. She glanced at her husband. He stood silent beside her, his face drawn hard as he stared across the hall. He had little pretense left, could not even look at Gabriel.

With a hand that quivered betrayingly, Juliana pushed back a wisp of hair that the draft in the hall had loosed from her veil.

Gabriel halted before her.

Neither could she look at him. Still, she knew he had bathed following this last day of tournament, for the scent that wafted to her was fresh, yet masculine—the same as that first night when she had gone to him. She lifted the purse of silver from the table beside her. "To the knight who has proven himself above all others," she spoke to the multitude gathered before the dais, "I give thee this reward, Lord De Vere." She extended it.

He did not take it.

The silence was too uncomfortable to ignore. Juliana looked up.

He stared at her, her secret in his eyes.

Did Bernart see it? Was he looking? She swallowed hard. "Lord De Vere?"

He accepted the purse.

The onlookers cheered. It took some minutes for the din to subside, and for each one of them Juliana felt the sharpening of Bernart's enmity. When the roar finally fell to a murmur, she turned to the table again. There lay a jeweled dagger. Its gems caught the last light of day that filtered through the lofty windows. "And that all may know of your valor, I present this dagger"—she placed it in his familiar, callused palm—"and proclaim thee Knight Victorious."

His fingers turned around the hilt, brushing hers as she withdrew, stealing her breath. "I thank you, my lady," he said, "for everything."

Everything. Did any other hear his mockery?

He turned to Bernart. "Lord Kinthorpe."

Stiffly, Bernart inclined his head.

Gabriel turned. Amid renewed applause, he stepped from the platform.

Juliana stared after him, her mouth dry. Only hours until Bernart sent her to him and still she did not know what to do. Surely Gabriel would reject her, deepen her humiliation.

Knights gathered around him, clapped him on the back, hoisted slopping tankards of ale to acknowledge his prowess. Nesta handed him a tankard brimming with ale. Gabriel turned it bottom up, and a moment later thrust it forward to be refilled.

Would drink be enough? Juliana wondered. Would it make him forget what he believed of her?

Bernart shouldered past Juliana. "Let us feast!"

A fanfare of trumpets sounded from the minstrels' gallery. In anticipation, all turned their attention to the corridor that led to the kitchens. They would not be disappointed, for all day Juliana had labored to ensure the banquet was lavish as befitted the Baron Kinthorpe.

As the trumpets reverberated their last note, a procession of squires and upper servants filed into the hall, each carrying shoulder-high a platter of some viand: herbed boar's head, stuffed breast of veal, roast goose, leg of goat, lampreys, beef pastries. And this was only the first of four courses.

Eagerly, the guests hastened to the tables. Before they

took their seats, each was tended by a pair of varlets who poured water over their hands and promptly dried them. Then the food was set before them.

Realizing she stood alone, Juliana looked behind her. Bernart was seated beneath the orange-and-gold-striped canopy. Though he should have led her to table and seen her into her chair before taking his own, he'd overlooked her—as if she had done him a grave wrong. But had she not? Among the reasons he'd chosen his enemy was the hate Juliana bore Gabriel. He had been certain she would despise his touch, that he need not fear she would return to him with her head full of notions of love. Was it love? No more had the thought slipped in than she rejected it. She felt for the wrong she did Gabriel, and it was true she desired him, but that was all. Still, perhaps Bernart sensed the change in her. . . .

She walked around the table and lowered herself into the chair between Bernart and Alaiz.

Her sister put a hand to her arm. "Are you well, Juliana?"

She nodded and lifted her goblet. Though she tried to ignore the sensation of being watched—knew better than to search out the source—she glanced to the table below the lord's. Before Gabriel could harden his eyes, she glimpsed something other than loathing there. Then it was gone. Though she could not name what it was, it revealed that he was less indifferent to her than he wished her to believe. Perhaps that was the reason he was so angry. That black heart of his was not supposed to include shades of gray.

"Juliana," Bernart snapped.

She was surprised to find his meat dagger hovering near, a morsel of roast goose perched on its tip. Though they usually shared a trencher between them, it was a long time since he had fed her—it being an intimacy he shunned nearly as much as physical contact.

"Take it," he said in a growl.

She picked off the meat with her teeth.

"Does he know?" he rasped low.

Her mouth was too full to offer the vehement denial fear demanded. Regardless, the lie was more easily told with a shake of her head.

"Do not fail me, Juliana." He darted his gaze to where Alaiz sat oblivious to their exchange.

His meaning was clear. Juliana swallowed the flavorless meat. "You know I will not."

He reached for his goblet of wine.

She laid a staying hand to his arm. "You have been drinking too much."

Bernart clenched a hand over hers, shoved his face near. "You are surprised?" There was fury in his veined eyes.

Though his grip was cruel, she didn't flinch. "You know what it does to you. 'Twill keep you awake all night."

"Not if I drink enough."

Surely he did not mean to drink himself into unconsciousness. The last time he'd done so was shortly after Alaiz's arrival at Tremoral. The following morning, the agonizing pain of making water had driven him to such anger that Juliana had barred herself and her sister in the solar. Never would she forget Bernart's raging, his pounding on the door, his sword slashing at the thick planks. Though his outburst had not lasted long and afterward he'd been repentant, it had been a frightening experience, especially for Alaiz. "Have you forgotten the last time—"

"When he is gone"—Bernart jutted his chin toward the

lower tables—"and your whoring is done, I shall leave off drink."

Her whoring. Tears spurted to her eyes. She drew a deep breath to prevent them from spilling over. "As you will. Unhand me."

He released her.

She yanked her hand into her lap, then opened and closed it to determine if anything was damaged. Only sore. What would Bernart do if he knew the pleasure Gabriel had given her? That the hate she had once borne his enemy was no more? That he made her feel the woman Bernart could not make her feel? He must never know.

Affecting poise she was far from feeling, she turned her attention to the trencher.

Gabriel pondered what he'd witnessed. The tension between Juliana and Bernart had been palpable as they conversed quietly between themselves, and grown more so when she had laid a hand to his sleeve. Gabriel had glimpsed her tears and Bernart's fury, and against his will had been moved by Juliana's plight—whatever it might be.

Did Bernart know his wife betrayed him the same as he did her? Perhaps. Did he know with whom she betrayed him? Nay. If he did, this moment he would be drawing his sword over a treacherous woman.

But was she treacherous? The unbidden thought crept in before Gabriel could close his mind to it. *Was* he the first lover Juliana had taken? Had she spoken true when she'd professed to have feelings for him? He wanted it to be so. Though he named her a whore, he was pained by the thought he might be one of many she lay down for, wanted to believe that what they'd shared last eve went beyond a quest for revenge, that when he left Tremoral no others would come after him, that none would know her touch, her sweet cries—

God's blood! Juliana and Bernart might be estranged, but that did not mean they didn't seek pleasure in the other. When Gabriel was long gone from this place, Juliana would once more lie down for her husband.

The acknowledgment filled Gabriel with the strength of an emotion he'd never felt, one that forced him to admit something he had spent all day denying: in spite of his contempt for all Juliana embodied, he wanted her. He was even more of a fool than his father.

He growled low. Any other woman would serve just as well. He searched the multitude of servants for the one who had more than once promised to come to him, but had yet to keep her word. It was no great difficulty to distinguish the lascivious wench from the others. Hips rolling, generous breasts swelling her neckline, Nesta plied her pitcher for those seated at the next table. As Gabriel watched, a knight pinched her buttocks. She squealed merrily and leaned forward, inviting the man to test the ripeness of her breasts. He squeezed each in turn, then slid a coin between them.

Aye, she would do.

Chapter Eight

All had imbibed too much, as witnessed by the fervor with which they took to the floor when the dancing commenced. Knights and ladies set aside pretensions, squires and men-at-arms abandoned their posts, and servants forgot their duties to join in what could best be called a violent sport. Couples, be they of the opposite sex or the same, took hold of one another's hands and whirled themselves around, and more furiously as the tempo of the music increased.

Juliana had also had more to drink than usual. Thus Alaiz was able to coax her onto the dance floor. Hand in hand they swung themselves around. Though they were jostled by others, Juliana hardly noticed as she hearkened back to a time when such things had not been unknown to them. As girls they'd often attended celebrations their father held for visiting nobles—far happier times than these.

She closed her eyes and remembered the last time she had danced thus—days prior to Bernart's departure for the Crusade. She recalled the strong hands that had held hers as they whirled around, Bernart's smile, the sparkle in his eyes, the words of love he mouthed amid the din. How sweet her suffering had been, secure as she was in the knowledge that it would end upon his return from the Holy Land, when they would wed. Unlike other women who were forced to marry men they did not love, who were destined to worship their lover from afar, Juliana would one day attain her true love, know his kiss and touch, bear his son. . . .

She opened her eyes. It was not Bernart's face before her, but Alaiz's. It was not the year 1189, but 1195. It was not Bernart's son she would bear, but Gabriel's. Perhaps.

The blur beyond her sister—faces, bodies, tables, tapestries—was suddenly too much for her. She stumbled, tried to right herself, stumbled again. A moment later, she and Alaiz toppled on the floor.

The whirling sensation, coupled with the drink Juliana had consumed, was heady. How long she teetered on all fours, she didn't know, but when she looked up, Alaiz's wavering face was before her.

"Shall we do it again?" Alaiz said with an expectant smile.

Juliana looked around. Past swirling skirts and hosed legs, she saw that others shared their fate—and were even more at risk of being trampled by the dancers than were she and Alaiz, who'd gone down near the outside of the throng. "Methinks I have had enough," she said.

"Once more," Alaiz pleaded.

Juliana shook her head. "Do I, I fear I shall not rise again." She sat back on her heels, but it was too soon.

She pressed her palms back to the rushes and drew a deep breath.

Alaiz sighed. "Very well."

"You could ask another to partner you," Juliana suggested. As long as she was present to watch over her sister, there could be no harm in it. In fact, it would be good for her.

Alaiz colored. "Me?"

"Aye."

Alaiz worried her teeth over her bottom lip. "Who would I ask?"

Juliana turned her head to peer through the dancers. Sir Randal, the knight who was ever watching Alaiz, was the first her gaze fell upon. She dismissed him, for in that direction lay danger. She looked beyond to where several knights were gathered before the hearth, among them Gabriel. He sat back from the others, and at his side stood Nesta. As Juliana watched, he pulled the wench onto his lap, said something that made him grin and her laugh, and nuzzled her neck.

Emotion stole Juliana's breath—jealousy, and deeper than that which she'd felt the day she had come upon Bernart beneath the skirts of another woman.

"Sir Erec, perhaps?" Alaiz suggested.

Juliana silently repented for the wickedness of her soul, then followed her sister's gaze to the knight who stood at the edge of the dance floor. As Sir Erec watched the frenzied spectacle, a half smile played on his lips, a smile that begged to be whole.

"Aye," Juliana said, "he will do."

Alaiz stood and swiped the rushes from her skirts, then offered Juliana her hand.

How odd, Juliana mused. As simple a gesture as it was,

she did not expect it. Always it was she helping Alaiz. She accepted her sister's hand and stood.

Carefully avoiding feet, elbows, flung-back heads, they wove among the dancers. When a knight and his lady went down in their wake, sending the woman's skirts over her head, Juliana and Alaiz paused to exchange grins.

"What if Sir Erec s-says no?" Alaiz asked as they stepped from the dance floor.

Would he? Juliana hoped the knight would not be so cold. "If he declines, simply take his arm and pull him onto the floor."

Alaiz beamed. "I will hold on tight and not let go till he . . . he turns me 'round a hundred times!"

Finally they were clear of the dancers. "Go on," Juliana said. "I will watch."

Alaiz pushed her shoulders back and crossed to Sir Erec's side. A few moments later, the knight led her onto the dance floor.

Juliana sighed. Never must she forget that out of every ill came some good.

He had yet to have her and already he was weary of her. Gabriel slid his gaze over the half of Nesta's breasts exposed by her low neckline. She smelled, talked and laughed too loudly, and groped him as if they were alone. Naught subtle about her. Naught sweet.

"Let us go abovestairs," she suggested again, and rubbed her outer thigh against his manhood.

"What of he who has kept you from my bed these past nights?"

She wriggled on his lap, seeking his hardening. " 'Tis not of my doing, but Lord Kinthorpe's. He makes most generous with me." There was resentment in her tone. Obviously she did not like servicing Bernart.

131

Was he cruel? The thought of him doing Juliana harm burned Gabriel. Mayhap it was simply that Bernart did not pleasure women, that he quickly took his ease in them and turned away. Gabriel sometimes did the same himself, though not last eve, when the dark had once more brought Juliana to him in the guise of a kitchen wench. More than himself he had wanted to pleasure her.

"Son of a sow!" Nesta said in a his.

Gabriel looked up. Contempt curled the wench's lips as she stared across the hall. He followed her gaze to Bernart. Seated in the lord's chair, from which he had not moved since the great feast was served, he motioned Nesta to him.

Was this Bernart's revenge—taking what he thought Gabriel wanted? Never knowing that in doing so it freed his wife to work her own revenge?

"He will have me on my back again!" Nesta spat. "What does he think me? A whore?"

Gabriel was grateful his mouth was not full of ale.

Nesta spun her gaze to him. "Ye ought to have taken me when you had the moment."

Why hadn't he? There had been plenty of opportunity. Instead he had sat with her perched on his lap this past hour so that Juliana might see how unaffected he was by what had happened between them. But it was she who had taken to the dance floor as if the night past, and this day, had not been.

" 'Tis yer own fault," Nesta accused.

"So 'tis."

She heaved a fetid sigh. "And this yer last night at Tremoral."

He nodded.

Suddenly she smiled. "I shall finish as soon as I can

and come to ye then." She traced his jaw with a sharp fingernail. "No matter the hour."

How unappealing. Gabriel withdrew his arm and lifted her off his lap.

Nesta turned toward the dais.

Though Gabriel told himself he wanted naught more to do with Juliana Kinthorpe, he searched her out. She stood back from the dance floor. Alone. Beautiful in spite of the sorrow that had returned to her face. Had he not confronted her, would she have risked coming to him a third time? In that moment, Gabriel wished he'd been blind a bit longer. *Damn!* He ought to have left Tremoral the moment he'd gained his reward.

It was well past midnight when the feasting drew to a close, and only then because the revelers could hold no more drink. Stretched out where they had taken their last swig, they snored noisily and grumbled at the dreams racing behind their spasming lids.

By the dim light of exhausted torches, Juliana picked her way amongst the sprawled bodies toward the lord's table. Was Bernart there? She stepped up to the dais and saw he was slumped in his chair. Before she and Alaiz had earlier gone abovestairs, she had watched him consume enough wine and ale to satisfy two men half again his size. How much he had drunk after she left, she did not know, but it had reduced him to the state of unconsciousness he'd sought. Though it meant she no longer need worry about going to Gabriel, it boded no good for the morrow, when any who crossed Bernart's path would know his wrath. Perhaps he would not regain consciousness until after the tourneyers left Tremoral, but if he did . . .

If he did, it was Gabriel he would turn on. Juliana

looked to the stairs. She had kept to the solar until she'd heard Gabriel enter his chamber a quarter hour earlier. Could she convince him to leave Tremoral this night? What reason could she offer him for doing so? She must try.

Dreading the encounter, she crossed the hall and climbed the stairs with weighted feet. At the landing, she paused. As when she had left the solar, a light shone from beneath Gabriel's door. She crossed the corridor, pushed the door inward, and stepped inside.

He stood before the glowing brazier with his back to her and his dark head crowned by the light of a torch. "I told you not to come again," he said gruffly.

She closed the door. "I come only to ask you to leave Tremoral."

He turned. His face was drawn with nearly as much anger as when they had last stood in this chamber. "This night?"

"Aye."

"Why?"

She moistened her lips. "Methinks Bernart knows."

His eyebrows clipped. "If he does, then surely 'twould be him come to me."

"He has drunk himself into unconsciousness. When he awakens on the morrow, I fear he will—"

"Do me harm?"

The derision in his voice wound Juliana's fear tighter. "He will seek retribution."

"Then you do not intend to tell him the truth about our tryst."

She averted her gaze. " 'Tis my sin, and I shall tell him so if need be."

Silence slipped in and grew heavy.

Gabriel strode across the chamber to where she stood. "What would he do to you?"

Was it concern in his voice? She looked up. It was also in his eyes. Why? Did he not hate her? Should he not be pleased with the thought of Bernart's punishment?

Gabriel lowered his hands to her shoulders. "Does he hurt you?"

His unexpected touch unnerved her, sent feeling coursing through her. "He does not strike me."

"But you fear him."

Almost as much as she feared Gabriel's nearness. "Only when he has had too much to drink."

Gabriel's brow lowered. "Bernart never had trouble holding his drink."

Disturbed by the stirring of her senses, Juliana took a step back, but Gabriel did not release her. "As I told you, he is changed from the man who accompanied you to Acre. His demons bind him hand and foot."

Once more, regret rose on Gabriel's face. "And you are made to suffer for the wrong he believes I did him."

It was true, but if he did not leave Tremoral this night, come morn he might be the one made to suffer. "Pray, Gabriel, leave now. You know not what Bernart is capable of."

He stared at her, searched her face, lingered upon her mouth. "What is it you feel for me?" he asked softly.

Though his hands warmed her through the material of her gown, chill bumps rose across her skin. *Ah, God.* She stepped back. Gabriel followed. Another step and she came up against the door.

He lowered his face near hers. "Tell me, Juliana."

Across the breath that separated them, she felt his awareness of her as a woman. Was he trifling with her?

135

Hoping to degrade her? In his gaze she sought the pain he meant to visit upon her.

"Juliana?"

Though she could not be certain in so little light, it seemed the blackheart was gone from his eyes. Still, she fought desire, told herself she did not want this.

"Show me," he rasped.

An ache spread from her nether regions to her belly, then to her breasts. With a whimper, she breached the last space between them, slid a hand around his neck, and surrendered the one thing she'd denied him: her mouth. She touched her lips to his, gasped at the brief contact, then more boldly joined with him. Though he stood unmoving, she reveled in the curve of his upper lip, the fullness of his bottom lip, his shallow breath upon her face.

Gabriel loosed a tormented groan, gathered her close, and crushed his mouth to hers. He drank from her, leaving her breathless. "I knew you would taste like this," he murmured.

Juliana clung to him as if he were all there was to hold to in the awakening storm. When he thrust his tongue between her lips and swept the sensitive tissue inside, she thrilled. When he drew her tongue into his mouth that she might do the same to him, she eagerly explored that hidden place.

Vaguely, she heard the scrape of the bar as he lowered it across the door. Then, mouths joined, Gabriel lifted her and carried her to the bed. He laid her back, but rather than push up her skirts and take her there, he began undressing her.

He wished to see her, to look upon her nakedness as he had wanted to do last eve. The realization wrenched Juliana back to earth. A protest rose to her lips, but before she could voice it, Gabriel silenced it with his mouth. He roused her again, made her forget all but the feel of him. As he loosened her side laces, he kissed her neck. As he drew the bliaut and chemise over her head, he roused her nipple rigid between his teeth. As he slid the hose from her legs, he trailed his mouth across her thigh to the arch of her foot.

He straightened and, in the soft glow of the torch, slid his gaze over her. "So beautiful," he said.

No man before him had looked upon her nakedness, and Juliana was glad.

Gabriel lifted his tunic up over an abdomen that rippled with strength, past the thickly muscled chest her hands had known, off broad shoulders she'd held to last eve as pleasure shook her. True, he was not comely of face, but he was fiercely masculine. A warrior. A man accustomed to arms and battle—and conquest.

He removed his hose.

Juliana's breath caught as she looked upon his man's root. Though she had handled him the past two nights, she was overwhelmed by the sight.

Gabriel put a knee to the mattress and slid his body up over hers. He pressed his maleness to her belly, claimed her mouth again.

He filled her to overflowing with his masculine smell, the taste of his skin, his resonant breath, the feel of his muscled body, the sight of him as he straddled her. She closed her eyes and arched her lower body toward him.

"Look at me," he said, voice hoarse.

She met his intense gaze.

"Aye." He entered her.

Pleasure rippled through her like moonlight gilding water. She moaned and met his next thrust, and each thereafter.

Throughout, Gabriel watched her, and she him—until the moment was upon her. With a cry, she flung her head back and surrendered to the violent tremors that coursed through her woman's place.

Shortly, she heard Gabriel's answering shout; then he spilled himself into her.

Juliana quaked as she lay beneath him, thrilled as his breath warmed the cradle of her neck. She didn't wish to open her eyes, didn't want this moment to end. Though he could never love her, he was the lover she'd dreamed of long ago. How she yearned to sit with him awhile, to talk, to laugh over silly things, to hold hands, to ease whatever pain blackened his heart.

Minutes later, he levered up from her.

She felt his searching gaze. Though she dreaded what she might see when she looked into his face, she opened her eyes.

Regret. It was in the draw of his eyebrows, the flat of his mouth, the set of his jaw. He rolled onto his back. "God, what have I done?"

Her heart constricted. *If only things could be different . . .*

In silence, Gabriel cursed his weakness. All these years he had believed there to be no woman who could tempt him from his path, but that was what Juliana had done. As much as his conscience had demanded he send her away, he'd wanted her more. Was it the same for the numerous men Constance De Vere had taken into her bed? Gabriel had hated her lovers for stealing from his father, for making his mother a whore, but now he was among their foul ranks.

Juliana leaned over him. "Forgive me. I did not intend this to happen."

138

He shifted his gaze from the ceiling to her flushed face. "Did you not?"

Hurt flickered between her eyes. "Why are you so willing to believe the worst of me?"

The answer was simple. "You are a woman."

She sat up and dragged the coverlet around her. "Who taught you to hate women so?"

He had been asked the question before, but had never answered it. And still he shouldn't. He ought to send Juliana away. Were his defenses not in dire need of repair, he would have. "That honor goes to my mother. A man's best tutor where women are concerned."

"What did she do?"

He sat up. "She stole from me."

Juliana shook her head. "What did she steal?"

Bitterness seeped into his every pore. "Everything."

He could see Juliana's mind working, searching for meaning in his words; then, suddenly, understanding swept the confusion from her face. "She is the reason for your lost title and lands?"

He should have said nothing. Should have sent her away. "She is."

"How did it happen?"

Should he tell her that his mother had whored herself the same as she? Nay, it would hurt her, and he had said too much already. "It does not matter. 'Tis done." Now Juliana would press him as women were wont to do, but it was just as well. Anger would drive out the damning desire he felt just looking at her: her auburn hair spilled around her shoulders, her face aglow with spent passion, her mouth soft.

"I am sorry," she said, and averted her gaze.

Gabriel waited, but she said no more.

* * *

Juliana wondered at what Gabriel had revealed, but she knew she had no right to ask more of him, nor did she think he would enlighten her further. He had told her more than he wanted to. So how had it happened? Had his mother favored another of her sons over Gabriel? Had she somehow convinced her husband their firstborn was unworthy? Juliana had heard tales of such things. Still, even before Gabriel had been set aside he'd shown little liking or respect for women.

A rattling sped Juliana's gaze across the chamber to the door. Was it Bernart? Her heart straining her ribs, she looked to Gabriel.

Though he was still, his muscles were bunched and ready to spring.

"Lord De Vere?" a voice hissed through the door.

His shoulders eased. " 'Tis only Nesta," he said low.

Only Nesta. Juliana was grateful, but hardly relieved. Though Gabriel had had the blessed foresight to bar the door, soon she must venture forth from the chamber, and do so without Bernart to ensure she made it to the solar with their secret intact. Their terrible, treacherous secret. Juliana met Gabriel's gaze.

Over and over Nesta rattled the door and called to be let in. Finally the noise ceased and was followed by the sound of retreating footsteps.

Juliana dropped her chin to her chest and sent a silent prayer of gratitude heavenward, then lowered her legs over the side of the mattress.

"You are leaving?" Gabriel asked.

She nodded. "I must." The coverlet slipped from her shoulder. As she reached to retrieve it, Gabriel caught her hand.

"Stay."

140

Struck by the depth of his voice, she looked up. His eyes were dark again. "Gabriel?"

"She is gone." Without further word, he pushed her back and covered her. This time he was not gentle, but neither did he hurt her. He introduced her to a depth of passion that appealed to a side of her she would have denied possessing. They mated—there was no other word for it.

Afterward, with the beat of Gabriel's heart matching hers, Juliana pushed her hands through his hair, slid them over his muscled shoulders, down his back. There were things she wanted to do to him, things she wished to experience before he was gone from her forever. . . .

When she stole from his bed an hour later, she felt a rending sense of loss. Though previously she'd retreated from the chamber as quickly as possible, this night she lingered, moving slowly as he slept.

Remembering Gabriel's caresses, she pressed her hands to her throat, dropped her head back, slid her palms down her breasts to her hips. Never again. Never again. But always she would have the memories of these past nights when she had been made to feel a woman. Through her tears, she smiled.

Gabriel stirred, murmured something, then turned.

Quickly Juliana donned her clothes and crossed to the door. She stood there a long time, listening for sounds beyond the chamber to alert her to the presence of another. Naught. She lifted the bar and eased the door open. The corridor was empty. Heart heavy, she left Gabriel for the last time.

Never again, the voice in her head whispered as she pulled the door closed. Even if a child did not take in her, no more would she know Gabriel. Bernart would have to find another. The vile thought gripping her, she turned to

141

the solar. It was then that she remembered the reason she had sought out Gabriel this night. In his arms she'd forgotten what the morrow would bring.

How was she to keep Bernart from his raging? Come the morn, the commotion in the hall would surely awaken him from his stupor, but if he were in the solar . . . Aye, that might do it. She would bathe herself, then enlist a man-at-arms to carry Bernart abovestairs. God willing, he would not awaken until the tourneyers were gone from Tremoral.

Chapter Nine

A greater fool had not been born, Gabriel acknowledged as he resolved to do the unthinkable. Consequences be damned, he would take Juliana with him when he returned to France. And they were dire consequences, indeed. He did not fear excommunication, for his tourneying had seen to that. Nay, if it were discovered he'd taken another man's wife he could lose everything he had labored for these past years—specifically, Mergot. God knew, he ought to care, but for some reason he did not. That reason was Juliana.

He raked a hand through his hair. *Fool, you are thinking with that which is between your legs, not that which is between your ears!* Cursing his weakness, he leaned over the basin and splashed frigid water over his face, but it did naught to cool his desire for the one woman forbidden him.

Desire. That was all it was. He did not love Juliana—

knew the true nature of women too well to waste a moment on so senseless an emotion. But to have her at his side, to taste her sweet mouth and be one with her again, he would risk all.

He wiped the moisture from his face and turned to the bed. Not surprisingly he'd awakened alone, but soon that would change. Within a sennight Juliana would be his, in *his* bed only.

In the morning light that penetrated the window's oil-cloth, Gabriel donned the garments that would see him from Tremoral, then gathered the few items he'd brought with him and put them in his leather pack. At the door, he swept his gaze over the room in which he and Juliana had come together, recalled the sight of her beneath him. He stirred. It was a long time since he'd wanted anything as badly as he wanted this woman who bore another's name. He truly was without honor.

Gabriel flung the door open. Commotion in the hall wended up the stairs—raised voices, the scrape of benches, booted feet pounding the floorboards, a woman's squeal of laughter. The guests were readying to depart, but though this day was yet newly born, it would be well past the nooning hour before Tremoral saw the backside of the last tourneyer—if then.

When Gabriel stepped into the hall he was greeted by the familiar sight of disorder that always came with the conclusion of a tournament. Some sat at tables, others sat upon them, some wandered about, others congregated to relive recent victories. Among them moved beleaguered servants and the occasional tourneyer eager to begin the long journey home.

Though the lord's table was without its lord and lady, Gabriel knew Juliana was somewhere among the throng. Unfortunately, she lacked the height needed to distinguish her. He would have to search her out. Intending to do just that, he stepped forward.

"Lord De Vere!" Nesta's hand closed over his arm.

With an inward groan, he looked into the wench's upturned face.

She affected a pout. "Ye barred yer door last eve."

Luckily, else she would have come upon her lady in a most dishonorable state. "Did I?"

"Aye, surely ye heard me call to you."

He touched his brow. "Too much drink."

Nesta's pout lingered a moment longer before stretching into a seductive smile. "There is always now, sire." She pressed nearer, sliding her palm up his manhood.

Gabriel pulled her hand away. "Regrets, but I cannot linger."

She was not deterred. "I would not keep ye long, Lord De Vere."

He looked past her. "Where is your lady?"

"What would ye be wanting with that shrew?"

"Shrew?" Gabriel repeated. It was hardly a word he would use to describe Tremoral's lady. But then, women were a jealous lot, and doubtless Nesta envied her mistress.

"Aye, shrew." The wench made a closer fit against Gabriel and slid her palms over his chest. "M'lady may be fine to look upon, but she is as cold as the night wind. A most harsh mistress. It cannot be soon enough that she is gone from here."

Alarm shot through Gabriel, but there was no way Nesta could know of his plans to take Juliana with him. What did she speak of? "Lady Juliana is leaving Tremoral?"

Nesta rubbed her breasts against him, causing her nipples to pebble the bodice of her homespun gown. "Aye.

145

Does her belly not soon ripen with child, Lord Kinthorpe vows come the autumn he will commit her to a convent and take another to wife."

Bernart intended to cast Juliana aside? Though it could be taken as justification for stealing her from Tremoral, something festered at the back of his mind.

" 'Tis sure to happen," Nesta continued, "fer m'lady is frigid and most certainly barren. No son will she give Lord Kinthorpe."

Frigid? Hardly. Barren? Perhaps. Else the blame lay with Bernart . . . The festering at the back of Gabriel's mind sprang forward. He recalled the second night when Juliana had come to him and determinedly coaxed his seed from him, and last eve when she would have again had he not lost himself in her and freely given it. It was a child she sought. A child whom she would claim as Bernart's to secure her place at Tremoral.

Once more, anger opened a place in him. Juliana had used him, had professed to have feelings for him when all she wanted was for him to sire a child on her. But why him? Why not another? Revenge as he'd first believed? That she might present her faithless husband with a child whose veins coursed with the blood of his enemy? There could be no other explanation.

Gabriel turned his hands into fists. For a deceitful whore he would have risked everything. Would have bared himself as he had done for no other woman. What excuse would Juliana have given for refusing to return to France with him? Honor? Fear of excommunication? How she would have laughed when he was gone from Tremoral!

Gabriel pushed Nesta aside and, amid her sputtering, forced a path through the crowd. Ahead, Juliana stood before the great doors, her back to him as she conversed with a neighboring baron.

"My lord husband sends his regrets, Lord Payne," Gabriel heard her say. "I fear he took ill during the night and is unable to leave his bed."

The baron, who looked as if he ought to have remained in bed himself, thanked Juliana for the fine festivities, took his wife's arm, and guided the graceless woman toward the doors.

Juliana turned as Gabriel reached her. She looked momentarily surprised, but in the next moment wary. She had cause to fear him.

It being all Gabriel could do to keep his arms at his sides, he said in a hiss, "We must needs speak."

She moistened her lips, then glanced left and right. "I have guests, Lord De Vere."

"So you do. Would you like them to hear what I have to say?"

She swallowed, then looked again to see if they'd fallen beneath the regard of others. "The garden," she said low. "I will meet you there."

"Do not keep me waiting." He turned on his heel.

Juliana's heart pained her as she watched Gabriel's long strides carry him across the hall, his pack over his arm. What had happened between last eve and this morn? What wrath must she now suffer and for what reason? Dreading the answer, she began to make her way toward the corridor that led to the gardens. Lest she was watched, she paused to direct servants and chat briefly with one of the ladies, then slipped into the corridor. The door at the end was ajar. She braced herself and stepped through it.

Gabriel's pale gaze went through her.

Braving it, she closed the door. "Of what do you wish to speak?"

"Come nearer."

Barely ten feet separated them and he wished her to come nearer? To look more closely upon his seething anger? "I must return to the—"

"Nearer!"

In that instant, she realized he knew her secret. Dear God, what had revealed her? Though instincts urged her to flee, she knew there would be no escaping his wrath. Somehow she must convince him he was wrong. Her insides trembling like leaves in autumn, she lifted her skirts and stepped onto the path.

"What is it?" she asked, halting before him.

His nostrils flared as he lowered his gaze to her belly. "I know the truth."

She swallowed hard. "The truth?"

He swept his unforgiving gaze back to hers. "That you are a liar, Juliana Kinthorpe. A whore. A thief."

It was true. She was all of those things, as Bernart had made her. She clasped her hands at her waist. "I have already apologized for last eve," she feigned misunderstanding. "Truly, I did not come to your chamber that I might lie with you."

His hands fell to her arms and gripped them so fiercely she had to bite her lip to keep from crying out. "Of course you did. Now the only question is whether you gained that for which you came."

She shook her head. "I do not understand."

"Aye, you do. You came to steal a child from my loins!"

Did he feel her trembling? "A child? Whatever do you speak of?"

"I know, Juliana. I know that Bernart intends to rid

himself of you do you not soon provide him with an heir."

Where had he heard that? Was it Bernart's doing? In the two months prior to the tournament, he'd talked openly of his quest for a son so that all would know he was attempting to get a child on her and would not be surprised when she swelled. But that he intended to send her away if she did not conceive was something she had not heard. Not that he would truly send her away. If Gabriel's seed did not take, he would simply find another to prove his stolen manhood.

"Who told you that?" Juliana asked past a tightening throat.

Gabriel lowered his face near hers. "As 'tis the truth, it matters not. You have no feelings for me as you claimed to have, Juliana. You feel only for yourself."

How she hated that he thought so ill of her. How she wished she could tell him everything. But, as always, there was Alaiz. The two sisters had only each other, and that was more important than this man who so readily condemned her. She raised her chin. "You are wrong, Gabriel De Vere."

The corners of his mouth turned up into what could hardly be called a smile. "I was not drunk the second night. I remember how you mounted me, clung to me, held me inside."

Shame warmed her face. She lowered her eyes to his chest. How she remembered! Like the whore and thief Gabriel named her, she had sought and taken what he had not wanted to give. She was a poor liar. No matter how she denied his accusation, never would he believe her, but neither could she confess to seeking to steal a child from him. What was she to do? As she frantically searched for an answer, a voice resounded above the commotion in the bailey beyond.

"Juliana!" Bernart bellowed.

With a gasp, she looked up. Though the lord's solar was not visible from the gardens, she knew it was from there the shout issued. If she did not answer it, Bernart would come looking for her. And he would be wrathful, suffering from such ale-passion that any who crossed his path would regret it. Dreading the spectacle he would make of himself and fearing the confrontation sure to ensue if he found her with Gabriel, she looked back at the man whose anger was his due. "I beg you, Gabriel, leave Tremoral. Now."

His anger no less palpable, he stared at her, searching her face. "Leave without thanking my old friend for his hospitality? For the gainful sport, the food and drink, the warm bed, for sharing his wife?"

Tears touched her eyes. He could have no idea how near the truth he was. "Have you any heart, Gabriel, you will go."

"Heart," he repeated with a sardonic grin. "I fear not, but I will leave." He dropped his hands from her. "However, this I vow: I shall be back."

She did not have to be told. Gabriel De Vere was not a man to be made a fool of and then simply walk away. For certain, one day she would pay for her sins. Fortunately, Gabriel was without influence. Though he had been awarded a demesne in France, he was not the great baron Wyverly would have made him—he lacked the power Bernart enjoyed in England. Thus he had no recourse. To accuse a noblewoman of Juliana's rank of having lain with him would only see him the worse for it. Still, he *would* return, God willing many many years from now. It was a day for which she would have to prepare. Feeling suddenly cold, she hugged her arms about her.

Gabriel retrieved his pack from the ground and slung it over his shoulder. "And when I come," he continued, "I will take whatever you have stolen from me."

Heaven have mercy on her.

He strode to the gate. There, he looked over his shoulder and stared at her as if to forever impress the moment upon his mind. "Pray 'tis you who are barren, not Bernart," he said. He threw the gate open and stepped into the bailey.

Juliana felt her knees begin to buckle, but as much as she yearned to sink to the ground and surrender to her emotions, she refused herself the weakness. In the days, months, years to come, there would be much time to agonize over the ill she'd done Gabriel and its consequences.

With trembling hands, she pushed back the tendrils of hair that had escaped her plait, then smoothed her skirts.

"Wife!" Bernart shouted.

Silently praying he would not see her fear, Juliana hastened into the donjon.

Gabriel issued Sir Erec and the accompanying squires no warning. With a sharp pull of the reins, he drew his destrier to a halt atop the hill and turned the animal around. In the far distance, the towers of Tremoral pierced the morning mist that overlay the castle walls. Within those walls, Juliana Kinthorpe thought herself safe. She was not.

Soon he would return, and when he did she would discover he never made a vow he did not keep. And what of Bernart? His fury mounted as he recalled the honed sword his old friend had nearly put through him. He would not be spared the truth. He would know of his wife's treachery, drown in it for all Gabriel cared. It was something to look forward to. Something to fill his angry days and nights.

Chapter Ten

England, September 1195

The priest reminded her of Gabriel, though only his dark looks. Father Hermanus was younger, light of heart, and easy to rouse to laughter. Did his vestments not proclaim him a member of the clergy, he could pass as one of the knightly class. Even Tremoral's chaplain, a man who rarely smiled, could not help but be affected by the traveling priest who'd arrived at the castle late this afternoon to request lodging for the night. In fact, if Father Daniel was not more mindful, he was going to break a smile.

Juliana turned her attention from the table, where her guest sat amongst Tremoral's men-at-arms, and looked at the scrap of embroidered linen in her lap. She ran a finger over the stitches she'd painstakingly worked these past nights. Though she had not begun it with the thought of fashioning the material into an infant's gown, there was little else it could be used for. It was so very small.

She resisted the impulse to touch her belly and turned her gaze to the fire before which she sat. It beat warm upon her face, but could not touch the chill fear in her breast that grew with each passing day, nor the pain.

The desire was too great. Surrendering to it, she touched the gentle swell that evidenced her nights with Gabriel. Though four months pregnant, she had only begun to show a fortnight past. It was then that Bernart had gathered his household knights and left for London and the court of the ever-absent King Richard. How he hated her for giving him what he so badly wanted. Though, in the presence of others, his boasting of imminent fatherhood was without end, when he and Juliana lay in bed at night his true feelings strained the space between them. It was as she'd warned him: he would loathe another man's child born of her body. What would it be like when the babe arrived? Would she fear for its life?

Laughter, so out of place in the depths of her despair, reverberated through the hall. She looked around.

The young priest's head was flung back as he and the others heartily enjoyed whatever mischief he'd imparted. Even Father Daniel chuckled.

To be born a man, Juliana reflected, to do as one pleased and control one's life. Absently she stroked her belly, prayed the babe was a boy. Not only would his life be easier, but Bernart would be more accepting, though that did not mean he would be kind to Gabriel's son. As Juliana fought to protect Alaiz, she would have to do the same for her little one.

She pulled herself back to the present and, in doing so, realized she'd fallen beneath the regard of the man her gaze was fixed upon.

Father Hermanus inclined his head and shifted his attention to her hand upon her belly.

As if it were a sin to touch her unborn child, she snatched it away and hurriedly looked at Alaiz, who lay with her head pillowed upon the hearth and eyes closed.

Why this sudden disquiet? Juliana wondered. She had nothing to fear from the priest. Though he was unlike any clergy she'd previously encountered, he seemed kind and sincere. Indeed, rather than expect to be waited upon as many visitors did, Father Hermanus had offered his assistance in the preparation of the evening meal. Then, at the urging of Tremoral's chaplain, he'd said grace before supper. His impassioned words had moved Juliana as she had not been moved in a long time.

There was naught to fear, she assured herself. She was tired, that was all. She suppressed a yawn behind her hand. Darkness was not long upon Tremoral, yet she felt more fatigued than usual. It must be the baby. She laid her embroidery aside and stood. Though it was usually difficult to rouse Alaiz from sleep, it proved even more so this eve. Finally she peeled back her lids.

"We should go abovestairs," Juliana said.

Alaiz levered herself up, rubbed her eyes. "M-may I sleep with you again?" Her voice was thick and slurred.

"Of course." As Bernart had not returned from London and had yet to send word as to how long he intended to remain absent, there could be no harm in it. Juliana put a hand to her sister's elbow to assist her to stand. With Alaiz leaning against her, she turned to the tables, bid all good eve, and started toward the stairs. Minutes later, still fully clothed, she lay down beside Alaiz and slept.

Voices. Wondering whence they issued and to whom they belonged, Juliana tried to open her eyes, but her lids felt as if weighted by stone. The voices drew nearer: men's voices, the words of which she could make no sense. Had Bernart returned? She tried to form his name, but her tongue filled her mouth. She attempted to turn toward the sound, but her body was as if one with the mattress. What was wrong with her? Was it the babe?

Anxiety quickened her breath. Seeking the swollen evidence of her child, she uncurled her fingers, but that was all. Her arm would not lift from alongside her head. She whimpered.

Large hands touched her, turned her. "Do not fight it," a harsh voice said near her ear.

Gabriel? Fear shuddered through her. It could not be. This must be another of her tormented dreams in which he returned to make good his threat to reclaim what she'd stolen. But unlike those previous dreams, this time he came whilst the child was yet in her womb.

Strong arms lifted her from the mattress, settled her against a hard chest.

She breathed in the masculine scent that pervaded the weave of Gabriel's tunic. How real he seemed, but he was only a dream—one that would soon fly away on dark wings and leave her to face sleepless hours till dawn. Convinced of it, she eased against him.

From elsewhere in the chamber, another spoke. She recognized the voice, but could not have said to whom it belonged.

"Nay," Gabriel answered, "leave them." He turned and strode from the warmth of the chamber into the chill corridor.

Juliana shivered.

His arms tightened around her. "Bring her mantle," he ordered the other man.

A few moments later, warmth settled over her.

Effortlessly, Gabriel carried her down the winding stairs, over the rushes strewn about the hall, and outside. The beat of his heart beneath her ear lulled her, drifted her out of the dream and onto a winged horse that sped her through the long, dark night.

She felt nauseated. With a groan, she pressed a hand to her abdomen. It seemed the sickness that had plagued her first two months of pregnancy had returned. Knowing that if she did not soon rise she would soil the bedclothes, she levered herself up. Hardly had she done so when she lurched sideways. She threw out an arm to steady herself, but the bed continued to move beneath her.

Thinking she must be very ill to be so faint, she slowly opened her eyes. It was several moments before she was able to focus, but finally she looked upon her surroundings. And they were not at all as expected. As she moved her gaze from the pallet she lay upon to the planked floor to the awning that enveloped her in shadow, she struggled to make sense of this place. Where was she?

Sounds beyond the awning reached her—the creak and groan of timber, the clank of metal on metal, the shout of men. There was more, but she was unable to place the distant sounds. She turned back the blanket. Though she expected to be clothed in only her chemise, she was surprised to discover she still wore her bliaut. She had lain down without first disrobing? She could not remember doing so. For that matter, she could not remember having withdrawn to her chamber for the night.

Cautiously she gained her feet, and only then realized that the swaying motion she'd mistaken for faintness was not of her but of the floor beneath. Was she on a boat? It did not seem possible, but when she drew back the flap of the awning she saw it was so.

A crisp salt breeze upon her face, the new-risen sun in her eyes, she squinted as she swept her gaze across the deck to towering masts and billowing sails, running ropes and the pulleys that controlled them, gruff-looking men who labored to keep the sails filled with air, the English coast that lay to the left.

Like a tightly wound spindle suddenly loosed, fear rolled through her, put before her an image of one who would be lost without her. Dear, sweet Alaiz . . .

A sudden movement caught her eye. One of the men, using naught but his hands and feet, scaled the great mast to a platform overhead. Just looking up at him made her reel and her stomach lurch. She pressed a hand to her abdomen and lowered her gaze to a man who stood center and aft. Legs braced wide apart, arms akimbo, he barked orders to the two men who handled the steering oars. Was he the captain?

Mindful of her footing, Juliana stepped from beneath the awning and began making her way across the deck. Though it was no easy feat to remain upright, the slightest list threatening to upend her, she finally drew alongside the thickset man. "You are the captain?" she asked.

He turned his regard upon her. "That I am, my lady."

"What is this ship's destination?"

"France, of course. We put in at Bayeux come the morrow."

Foreboding clenched her stomach, swept bile up her throat. She swallowed hard. "How did I come to be aboard?"

The captain eyed her a moment, then jutted his chin toward the bow. "He can answer your questions better than I, my lady."

She looked past a group of men who worked the ropes middeck to the lone figure alongside the starboard railing whose back was to her. In the next instant she forgot to breathe. She did not need to see his face to recognize him, for there was only one with stature so great, shoulders so broad, vengeance so deep.

Death could not be more frightening than the feeling that crept over Juliana. It was then she remembered the dream of the night past. It had not been a dream. This was not a dream. Gabriel had come for her, just as he'd vowed he would.

Grasping at a faith that had not been so firmly shaken since Bernart demanded the unthinkable of her, she clenched her hands. As much as she wanted to cry, to scream, to rail to the heavens, she controlled herself.

"My lady?" the captain asked.

Was that concern in his voice? It did not matter. There was naught he, nor anyone else, could do to help her. Grown strangely numb, she stepped past the captain and slowly negotiated the rolling deck. She halted in back of Gabriel and waited for him to acknowledge her.

His dark brown hair bound at the nape of his neck, the wind beating his tunic against his torso, one leg raised to the railing, he stared out to sea as if unaware he was no longer alone.

She took a step nearer, but still he did not respond. She drew a deep breath. "What have you done, Gabriel?"

It was a long moment before he turned, but when he did his eyes were heavy with contempt. "What have I done? But kept a promise and returned for that which you stole from me."

It was all she could do to keep from curving an arm around her waist. She shook her head. "I have naught that belongs to you."

He lowered his gaze to the modest swell beneath her gown. "You would deny you are with child?"

She could not. So how was she to turn him from his course? There was only one thing she could think of. " 'Tis true. I am three months with child." Ever deeper her lies grew.

His eyebrows soared. "Three months. That is all?"

She drew herself to her full height, pushed her shoulders back, and raised her chin. " 'Tis not your child, if that is what you think."

As if accustomed to the deck of a ship, Gabriel smoothly stepped toward her.

She would not back away, she vowed. No matter how near he came, she would stand her ground. He came near enough that she had to tip her head back to hold his gaze, near enough that the scent of him pressed upon her.

"What I am thinking is that you do not speak the truth, Juliana Kinthorpe. Three years of marriage and your womb lies empty; then you come to my bed and suddenly a child ripens?"

She did not flinch, did not permit her gaze to waver from his. "*My* child—and Bernart's."

"Nay, mine." He said it with such conviction that it left her no hope. "And so shall it be proven when the babe wails from your body five months hence."

As it was not likely God in His heavens would allow the babe to linger a month longer in her womb, Juliana was gripped with despair. "Do not do this, Gabriel. I beg you."

" 'Tis done."

She held herself together with all the strength she possessed. "Do you know what you risk in taking me from Tremoral—in stealing another's wife?"

Scorn curled his lips. "Excommunication?"

Something his tourneying had already seen to, but there

was more. "You could lose everything—your lordship, your lands. . . ."

" 'Tis a risk I am willing to take."

Such was revenge. It made fools of men, victims of their lessers—the latter of which Juliana knew only too well. Had she not paid the price of Bernart's revenge against Gabriel? Did she not continue to pay it? "When Bernart returns to Tremoral and discovers you have stolen me, he will gather an army and come against you. Is that what you want?"

His nostrils flared. "I want what belongs to me, and I will have it."

Knowing it would be futile to continue to assert that the babe was not his, she demanded, "At what cost? Bloodshed?"

"None but my brother knows I took you from Tremoral. Thus, unless you confessed your sins to Bernart, 'tis not likely he will look to me for you."

Was Gabriel right? What would Bernart think when he discovered her gone? Surely he would not believe she'd left Tremoral of her own will.

"Did you tell him?" Gabriel asked.

Tell Bernart of a sin he knew better than she?

"I thought not. So you see, there is no reason for him to seek you in France. He will simply believe you have run off."

Juliana shook her head. "Never would I leave without my sister. He knows that." Only after she said it was she struck by the full implication of what Gabriel had done. Alaiz was alone. None to protect her, to shield her from Bernart's wrath. Dear God, what was Alaiz feeling at this moment? Did she think herself abandoned? Juliana recalled the vow her sister had extracted months ago—if she were to leave Tremoral she would take Alaiz with her.

Desperate to make Gabriel see reason, to convince him to return her to Tremoral, Juliana touched his sleeve. "The last night . . ." It was so hard to speak of that night she had lain down for him in the glow of torchlight. "The last night I came to you, 'twas to ask you to leave Tremoral. I did so because I feared Bernart knew of us. Do you remember, Gabriel?"

He looked from her face to her hand upon him.

She lowered her arm to her side. "He will come."

As if a confrontation with Bernart was of little conse-quence, Gabriel shrugged. "Perhaps. But with the setting in of winter, it will likely be spring before he appears at my gates. By then the child will be born."

"And if you are wrong and Bernart comes a fortnight hence?"

"Then that much sooner will he know the truth of you and set you aside as he intended did you not provide him an heir."

The truth. How little Gabriel knew of it, but were she now to tell him of the circumstances under which she'd given herself to him, he would likely think it another lie. And even if she were believed, to reveal Bernart's secret would endanger Alaiz. She was powerless. Anger surged through her. *Damn Gabriel! Damn Bernart!* They played with others' lives, manipulated and pulled the strings of their victims. "If it is the truth you seek," she said, "why did you steal upon Tremoral whilst my husband and his knights were gone? Why did you not face Bernart there and make your accusations? Are you really such a coward, Gabriel De Vere?"

The darkness of his pupils engulfed the paleness of his eyes. "I had my reasons." As if to continue to look upon

161

her might snap the slender thread of his control, he turned to the railing.

Juliana stared at the bunched muscles of his neck, the tense set of his shoulders. As much as she longed to put distance between them, to return to the awning and close herself in, she tamped down her anger. "When the child is born, what do you intend?"

Though she did not doubt he heard her, it was several minutes until he responded. He turned and pinned her with cold eyes. "If Bernart does not want you back, and it seems unlikely he would, you may enter a convent."

Tossed aside, like the whore he believed her to be. "And the child?"

"The child will remain with me."

He meant to tear her newborn babe from her arms. Here was the man Juliana had so hated when he'd come to Tremoral four months past, the same whose touch had, for three nights, made her forget his heart was as black as pitch. "I hate you," she said.

He delved her face a long moment. Then, so swiftly she had no time to retreat, he stepped forward and dragged her hard against him. "Not when I am inside you."

Memories of the dark, her skin against his, slashed through her as if she had not banished the images months ago. Despising herself for the fluttering in her belly, the stir of treacherous emotions, she looked up. "I will not lie with you again, Gabriel De Vere."

Satisfaction glittered from his eyes. "If I wish you to, you will. But I do not."

He despised her, thought her foul. "Unhand me!" Juliana's voice was so constricted she hardly recognized it.

Abruptly, he released her. "Return to the shelter and rest. Once we reach France, we've a long ride before us."

Eager to be as far from him as possible, she started to

turn away, but there was one more question that begged an answer. "How did you steal me from Tremoral?"

A wry smile touched his mouth. "The ale."

"The ale?"

"A sleeping draft, Juliana."

Here, then, the reason she'd awakened on the ship without recollection of the long journey from Tremoral. "You drugged me."

"Aye, though 'twas not my intent. The ale was meant for the castle folk and garrison. As I knew you were not particularly fond of the brew, I did not expect you to partake of any."

And she would not have if the wine stores hadn't gone dry. "How did you do it?"

"How did I slip the sleeping draft into the ale? I did not." He looked toward the bow.

Juliana followed his gaze to one whom she'd not noticed. Her breath caught. Though the man stood in profile and was no longer garbed in the vestments of the holy Church, she recognized him as the one whose dark looks had reminded her of Gabriel on the night past. The same man who had requested a night's lodging at Tremoral and been so kind to assist in the preparation of the evening meal . . . Now she understood. She looked back at Gabriel.

"My brother, Blase," he said.

Not Hermanus, and certainly not a priest with that sword hanging at his side. Her anger surged anew. "You are despicable! To disguise one as a priest that you might gain entry—"

"Blase *is* a priest. Of course, only when it suits him."

A holy man who assumed a false name that he might enter Tremoral and sneak a sleeping draft into the ale? Who disregarded the sanctity of marriage to assist his brother in carrying away another man's wife?

" 'Tis true," Gabriel said. "He is fully vested."

Juliana could hear her own breathing, shallow and quick, and feel the blood coursing her veins. "Then he is even more despicable than you."

"And you are not, Juliana?" He looked again to her belly, his eyes feeling like hands upon her. "Do you soon forget, 'twas your guile that brought us to this day. Your deceit."

Nay, she could not forget, had lived these past months not only with fear of his return, but the terrible knowledge she'd wronged him. To save Alaiz, she had used him.

As she stared at him, the side-to-side movement of the clouds behind caused her stomach to pitch. Then, without warning, the ship ran up on a wave and heaved sideways. With a cry, she threw her arms out, but there was naught to hold on to. Grasping air, she fell backward.

Suddenly an arm came around her and dragged her against a solid chest. Her stomach threatening to spill, she looked up at Gabriel.

There was something unexpected in his expression—concern?—but before she could verify it, he hastened her to the railing. She grasped it and leaned forward. When the worst was over, she accepted the square of linen he thrust before her.

"Better?" he asked.

She nodded. Now if her heart would only quiet. It was beating so rapidly she feared it might burst. She took a deep breath, then another, and opened her eyes.

Below, the ocean rolled and tossed and broke upon the hull of the ship. The cool droplets of water that sprayed her were welcome, but not the view. "Dear God," she muttered, and pressed her brow to the railing.

Gabriel's hand, warm and strangely comforting, settled

on her back. "Look to the horizon. It does not move."

Even so, the ship moved.

"Trust me," he said.

Trust a man who hated her as he did? A man bent on hurting her? Still, if it calmed her insides . . .

Juliana lifted her head and looked to where the sky rested upon the ocean. As Gabriel said, it did not move. Shortly, her heart curbed its erratic beat and the nausea subsided. "I am fine now," she said, hoping he would remove his hand. Even so simple a touch was not without memories.

"You are certain?"

Why the sudden change? Why did he not simply leave her to her misery? Surely he thought it deserved. "I am certain," she said, "though I shall be most grateful when we reach France."

After a long silence, Gabriel said, "Will you?"

The tone of his voice brought her head around. "Only to be on land again," she clarified.

"Of course." He dropped his hand from her. "Get some rest, Juliana." He turned away.

Her stomach beginning to churn again, she returned her gaze to the thin, dark line between ocean and sky. Who had cried all the tears that made up this vast body of water? Was it possible their pain had been greater than hers? She sighed. It didn't matter. They were useless tears.

Gabriel tossed back the awning flap, spilling moonlight upon the still figure within.

Knees drawn to her chest, a fist curled beneath her chin, hair cast over her brow, Juliana slept. Finally. Though she had retreated to the awning shortly after Gabriel had left her this morn, throughout the day she had time and again returned to the railing to ease her nausea.

It was the babe he was concerned about, Gabriel had told himself, but watching Juliana grow paler as the day grew old had unexpectedly troubled him. Thinking food might ease her discomfort, he had thrice sent one of the crew with dry biscuits and salted meat, but each time she'd refused the fare.

Fortunately, the new day would see them on the shores of France, and by the evening of the following day they would be at Mergot—providing Juliana's illness did not persist and force them to delay their travel. Gabriel hoped not. He wanted to see color restored to her face, light to her eyes, for her to eat and nourish his child. Too, more than ever he wanted to return to the lands Sir Erec administered in his absence. Mergot was no Wyverly, and it was unlikely he would ever think of it as home, but it was all he had.

For the time being, he reminded himself. He did not need Juliana to tell him that stealing her from Bernart could result in the loss of his lands and title. He knew it well. But, as he'd told her, it was a risk he would take.

Juliana rolled onto her back, causing the blanket to slip. Gabriel's gaze was drawn to the swell that pressed against the material of her gown. During the ride from Tremoral to Southampton he had not allowed himself to touch her there, as if in doing so he might violate her— absurd, considering how the babe had been gotten.

The shifting wind lifted the hem of his mantle, reminded him of the cool night air. He ducked beneath the awning and drew the blanket over Juliana's shoulders. Though he had no intention of lingering, something held him there. He looked from the auburn tresses framing her face to her gently bowed mouth. How innocent she looked, as if she were the victim rather than the offender.

Not for the first time, he remembered their encounter

this morn, specifically her accusation. Once more she thought him a coward. Or perhaps she'd never stopped thinking him one, had said she believed he was not responsible for Bernart's failure at Acre only that she might keep Gabriel from revealing her adultery. And to gain his bed one last time.

A coward. There were many things Gabriel could be called, few of them flattering, but a coward was not among them. Upon learning that Juliana was pregnant, he had burned to bring an army of mercenaries against Tremoral, to expose her before Bernart. But Blase, with his abundance of wisdom, had made Gabriel see reason. He had pointed out that as great as Bernart's enmity was for Gabriel, his reaction to learning his enemy was the father of the child he believed to be his own could prove dire. Could endanger Juliana.

The thought that Bernart might harm her had turned Gabriel from his reckless quest, but only because of the babe. Thus he and Blase had devised the plan to steal Juliana in the night. If Bernart learned who had taken Juliana, it would be far safer for her beneath Gabriel's roof when Bernart was told of her faithlessness.

A faint sound brought Gabriel's head around. There, stark against the billowing mainsail, stood Blase. Watching. No doubt wondering.

As close as Gabriel had grown to his younger brother this past year, he resented being judged by him. True, Blase had played no small part in bringing Juliana out of Tremoral—could even be said to have relished it—but from his silence throughout the day, his priest's conscience tasked him.

Gabriel stepped from beneath the awning and lowered the flap. As he strode toward Blase, he saw his brother stroke the hilt of his sword, as he often did when something bothered him. Of course, when he was attired in priest's vestments it was his cross to which he applied himself.

Gabriel halted before him. As they were nearly the same height, they came eye to eye. For several minutes neither spoke, the only sounds that of the ship's movement through the water, the flutter of sailcloth, the occasional slither of rope and rattle of blocks.

"You are certain the babe is yours?" Blase finally asked.

"Ease your conscience, brother; the child is mine."

"She denies it?"

"As I knew she would."

Blase took a deep breath of the salted air. "But perhaps the babe is—"

"Mine, Blase. Be it son or daughter, the child Lady Juliana bears is of my loins."

Blase stared at him a long moment, then nodded. "Then 'tis right what we did."

Gabriel sighed. "Ah, froward priest, did your conscience prick you so when last you drunk yourself into a stupor? When you pocketed winnings from a wicked game of dice? When you went wenching a sennight past?"

Though Blase struggled to keep his expression sober, a smile tugged.

"Think no more on it," Gabriel said. "I have taken naught from Bernart Kinthorpe that does not belong to me." *Including Juliana.* As long as his child grew in her, she was his.

Blase nodded. "Then I am sure God will understand."

Would He? Gabriel shrugged off the question. "Good eve, Blase."

"Good eve." Blase stepped past and crossed to the awning the ship's crew had erected for him and Gabriel.

When he was gone from sight, Gabriel looked to the heavens. Though dense clouds had threatened a storm this afternoon, they'd moved inland, leaving the inky canopy pricked with starlight and the night waters relatively calm.

But how long would the calm last? How long before his prideful revenge brought war upon Mergot? Perhaps never, he told himself. *Perhaps a fortnight hence.* Juliana's words returned to him. He laid a hand to his sword. Either way, he was prepared.

Chapter Eleven

France

She would have to return to Alaiz, which meant escape. Juliana looked to where Gabriel and his false priest of a brother rode ahead. Not only must she escape them, but also the men-at-arms who'd awaited Gabriel when the ship put in at Bayeux. She glanced behind. Eight soldiers and Gabriel's squire, each an obstacle in her quest for freedom. And there were yet more. If she made good her escape, she had neither coin nor escort to return her to England. To be a pregnant and penniless woman alone in a strange land would be dangerous. But not as dangerous as it would be for Alaiz were Bernart to turn her out to wander the countryside. Somehow she must return to Tremoral. Then what? Would Gabriel follow?

"Resolve yourself to it, Juliana."

She jerked her head around and saw that Gabriel had

drawn his mount alongside hers. "Resolve?" she repeated, as if innocent of plotting.

A sardonic smile broke the hard line of his mouth. "Lest you forget, you are going to Mergot. Only after you have birthed my child may you leave. No sooner."

She put her chin up. "I do not need to be told again."

"Indeed. Consider it a reminder only."

She expected him to return to his brother's side, fervently wished for it that she might think more clearly on how she was to elude him, but he did not oblige her. Though he spoke not another word, his nearness over the next two hours distracted her again and again. Still, she used the time to familiarize herself with her surroundings in the event she passed this way again. And if she managed to escape, it was likely she would.

It was drawing late when Juliana glimpsed a distant castle rising against the sky. As it was yet another day's ride to Mergot, it was certain they would seek lodging there. She breathed a sigh of relief. Having been on a horse since late morn, she was sore. There was nothing she wanted more than to dismount and rest her weary body—except, of course, to return to her sister. She eyed the castle. Within those walls, might she find a means of escaping Gabriel? An ally?

It was not to be. Gabriel urged his mount ahead and veered east.

With his men at her back, Juliana had no choice but to follow. Could there be another castle within reach of what remained of daylight? It did not seem likely. She put heels to the tired mare, passed the false priest, overtook Gabriel.

He slowed as she came alongside. "What is it, Juliana?"

"Do you not intend to seek lodging at the castle?"

He swept his pale gaze over her. "I do not."

Thus her hope of an ally was for naught. "Why?"

He looked forward again. "As Baron Faison is not yet content with the restored rule of King Richard, 'tis not likely he would welcome an English baron within his walls."

Juliana had heard of the uneasy alliance between King Richard and the barons. The king of France had installed them upon his seizure of Richard's French dominions following the Crusade.

"And certainly he would not welcome me," Gabriel continued. "You see, 'twas his brother who held Mergot before me. Had he not refused King Richard his allegiance, still he would hold it."

Then Faison was Gabriel's enemy, or near enough. Though the French baron obviously had little liking for the English, might he aid her if she escaped and presented herself before him? She became so caught up in the possibility that it was a long moment before she realized Gabriel was watching her. Fearful of what her face might have revealed, she asked, "Is there another castle nearby?"

"There is not."

"Then where shall we pass the night?"

"In the wood."

The thought of another long, miserable night made her groan. Although the floor of the wood would be still beneath her, and not the ship's deck, her aching body longed for some comfort. "Surely there is an inn at which we could pause for the night."

"Aye, but we will not."

"For what reason?"

"The fewer who know you are at Mergot, the less likely Bernart will learn of your whereabouts." Gabriel's brow creased. "Which reminds me—henceforth you are to be known as Lady Isolde Waltham."

Juliana felt suddenly cold. Isolde—to remind her of her

sins. She averted her gaze and drew her mantle more closely around her. "And if I refuse to be called such?"

He was watching her, seeking to read her emotions. "Isolde Waltham has the freedom to move about my donjon. Juliana Kinthorpe does not."

Meaning he would lock her away if she refused. "I see."

"I expected you would."

She drew a steadying breath. "What of the castle folk? Do they know of my coming?"

"They do."

"What will they think of my presence?"

"What I have told them."

She met his gaze, dreading the answer to the question she must ask. "And what is that?"

"That Isolde Waltham carries my bastard seed." In response to Juliana's sharply indrawn breath, he said, " 'Twas unavoidable. One has but to look upon you to know you are pregnant and, as I intend to raise the child you bear, there was no other course."

Even so, she hated him all the more. "They know I do not come willingly? That you have stolen me from my home?"

"There was no need to tell them. Still, they have been warned that you are not to be trusted."

She gripped the reins tighter. "You are a cruel man, Gabriel De Vere."

He acceded with a nod. "As you made me, Isolde."

As Bernart made you, she longed to retort, but as much as she wished to absolve herself of wrongdoing, she could not. Unable to bear his nearness any longer, she slowed her mount. Once more, Gabriel took the lead.

Juliana stared at his broad back. God willing, she would not long suffer the name of the woman who'd lain down for him. Whenever an opportunity for escape presented itself—tomorrow, the following day, perhaps this night—she would be ready.

Out of the corner of her eye, she saw Gabriel's brother draw near. She looked around.

"Lady Juliana," he acknowledged.

She made no pretense of civility. " 'Tis Lady Isolde now, or did you not know?"

"Ah, that. A necessary falsehood."

"As it was for you to assume the name of Father Hermanus?"

To his credit, a slight flush crept over Blase De Vere's face.

"Is it your habit to disregard holy vows, false priest?" she pressed.

In an instant, the flush turned angry. "I no more wished bloodshed than would you, *Lady Isolde*. Had I not done what I did, my brother would have brought an army against Tremoral, and the ground would now run red with the lives of many."

Would Gabriel have laid siege to Tremoral? Juliana looked to where he rode, far enough ahead that he was unable to hear the conversation between her and his brother. Though anger had made her name him a coward for stealing her from Tremoral, she knew it was not so—just as she knew he'd not forsaken Bernart for fear of losing his own life.

"He did it for the babe you carry," Blase said. "I did it for those men whose lives would have been uselessly spent in the name of a woman's deception."

Juliana met his gaze.

" 'Tis true I am a sinner," he said, "but my reasons for breaking my priestly vows are more noble than yours for forsaking the marriage vows you exchanged with Bernart Kinthorpe."

His harsh words injured her nearly as much as Gabriel's. A priest Blase De Vere might be, false or otherwise, but he was not to be underestimated.

With a snap of the reins, he urged his mount forward, leaving her alone once more.

She drew a deep breath to counter the tears stinging her eyes, and swallowed the emotion tightening her throat. She would not cry. No matter what cruel words were spoken against her, she would keep her head up—and her eyes open, should Gabriel close his.

From the darkness of her tent, Juliana peered past the campfire to the larger tent Gabriel had erected for himself. No light shone from within. Was he inside? Though minutes earlier she'd heard him bid his men good eve, she had not made it to the tent opening soon enough to verify the large tent as his destination.

She swept her gaze back to the fire. Blase and a soldier sat before it talking quietly between themselves, while five others slept upon the ground—including Gabriel's squire, who snored before the entrance to his lord's tent. That meant Gabriel had set the other three to guard the camp.

She bit her lip. Was this the opportunity she hoped for? More important, if she did not take it, would there be another? Perhaps, but if not, she would have to get past far more than three men-at-arms once they arrived at Mergot.

Decided, she sat back and waited. A half hour later, there was still no sign of Gabriel. He was in the tent, then. Asleep. As for Blase and the other man, they had also put down for the night. It was time.

She moved to the back of the tent and began prying at a corner. It was firmly staked, but persistence finally loosened it. She lifted the canvas and looked ahead, left, right. All was still, but it was at least ten yards without cover to the wood. She could make it, providing she was careful not to rouse the men who slept around the fire. And of those who guarded the camp? Hopefully they were more heedful of those who might try to attack than of one trying to escape.

Juliana touched the pouch at her waist. As Gabriel had not objected when she'd told him she preferred to take her meal in the tent, she'd been able to hide away enough bread and cheese to satisfy her hunger a day or more. As for coin, if needed she would sell her jeweled girdle and wedding ring.

She crawled from beneath the canvas and, once outside, sat back on her heels and looked around. The night was still. She pulled the hood of her mantle over her head and cautiously rose to her feet. A few moments later, she gained the cover of the wood.

Her back to a tree, she searched the dark. Though there was enough moon to light her way, there was not enough to distinguish the figure of a man from that of the surrounding wood. Any one of the shadows could be Gabriel's men. She would have to proceed slowly.

She chose her footing carefully as she slipped from tree to tree. The snap of a twig caused her heart to speed, the crackle of fallen leaves snagged her breath, but she pressed on, assuring herself she would soon be out of range of Gabriel's men. Still, that would not be the end of it. Once she was discovered missing, Gabriel would give chase. She only prayed her absence would go unnoticed until the dawn, when she would be well away.

Gabriel peered closer. It was no woodland sprite come out to make mischief upon the night. It was Juliana.

GET YOUR 4 FREE* BOOKS NOW— A $21.96 VALUE!

Mail the Free* Book
Certificate
Today!

4 FREE* BOOKS ❧ A $21.96 VALUE

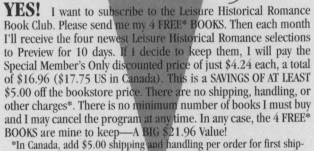

Free Books Certificate

YES! I want to subscribe to the Leisure Historical Romance Book Club. Please send me my 4 FREE* BOOKS. Then each month I'll receive the four newest Leisure Historical Romance selections to Preview for 10 days. If I decide to keep them, I will pay the Special Member's Only discounted price of just $4.24 each, a total of $16.96 ($17.75 US in Canada). This is a SAVINGS OF AT LEAST $5.00 off the bookstore price. There are no shipping, handling, or other charges*. There is no minimum number of books I must buy and I may cancel the program at any time. In any case, the 4 FREE* BOOKS are mine to keep—A BIG $21.96 Value!

*In Canada, add $5.00 shipping and handling per order for first shipment. For all subsequent shipments to Canada, the cost of membership is $17.75 US, which includes $7.75 shipping and handling per month.[All payments must be made in US dollars]

*Name*_____

*Address*_____

*City*_____

*State*_____ *Country*_____ *Zip*_____

*Telephone*_____

*Signature*_____

If under 18, Parent or Guardian must sign. Terms, prices and conditions subject to change. Subscription subject to acceptance. Leisure Books reserves the right to reject any order or cancel any subscription.

(Tear Here and Mail Your FREE* Book Card Today!)

Get Four Books Totally
F R E E* —
A $21.96 Value!

(Tear Here and Mail Your FREE* Book Card Today!)

PLEASE RUSH
MY FOUR FREE*
BOOKS TO ME
RIGHT AWAY!

Leisure Historical Romance Book Club
P.O. Box 6613
Edison, NJ 08818-6613

Hair escaping her hood, the skirts of her bliaut visible beneath her mantle, she darted amongst the trees. His anger rose. He had believed her wiser than to attempt such foolishness. After all, not only was she without resources in an unfamiliar land, but she was with child. His child. Cursing beneath his breath, he set after her. With his long-reaching stride, he quickly gained on her, but rather than overtake her from behind, he circled wide and placed himself in her path. "Seems you are not resolved to your fate, after all," he said.

With a choked gasp, she stumbled to a halt. Eyes wide, face pale, the foolish woman stared. Then she did something more foolish. She turned and ran.

Gabriel lunged after her and, moments later, caught her around the waist.

She cried out, flailed, somehow unbalanced him. Fortunately he had enough foresight to turn his shoulder and take the brunt of the fall. As he lay on his back struggling to control his anger, there was silence; then Juliana began to writhe. She pried at his arm around her, strained, but to no avail. When she finally stilled, Gabriel sat up. " 'Tis over," he said, and released her.

She scrambled off his lap and landed on all fours. As if intending to flee again, she started to rise.

"Do not!" he warned. "You have been foolish enough for one night."

She met his gaze through the hair flung across her face. It was a long moment before she accepted her fate, but when she did, it was not lightly. "A pox upon you!" she said in a hiss.

A pox. There were worse things with which to be cursed. He stood and brushed the debris from his tunic and hose. "You surprise me, Juliana."

She sat back and swept the hair from her eyes. "You

truly believed I would not try to escape a man who has stolen me from my home and husband?"

He braced his hands on his hips. "Truly, I did not expect you would put the babe at such risk. In the future I must not forget that the child you took from me is but a means of securing your place at Tremoral." It was too dark to be certain, but he thought pain flickered across her face.

She straightened. "I say it again: 'tis not your child. Hence he is at greater risk do I remain with you."

Gabriel narrowed his gaze on her. "You think it a boy?"

Her laughter was forced. "A boy . . . a girl . . . it does not matter. Either way, the child is Bernart's. His heir."

"No more." He reached to take her arm.

She drew back. "I *will* escape you."

"And I will bind you hand and foot for the duration of your pregnancy, if needs be. The choice is yours."

Though loathing shone from her eyes, her jaw quivered.

"Which is it to be?" he pressed. He felt her struggle as if it were his own.

"Very well," she acceded with a thrust of her chin, "no more attempts shall I make to escape."

"Your word, Juliana."

Her jaw clenched, and her mouth tightened. "I vow I shall do naught until my husband comes to free me."

Ignoring that last utterance, Gabriel stepped forward, gripped her arm, and parted her mantle. A pouch was suspended from her girdle. Doubtless there was food within, but no coin. "How did you intend to pay for passage to England?"

She stared past his shoulder.

As she would have it. Consideringly, he lifted the ends of her girdle. They were threaded with gold beads, several of which were set with small jewels. "Remove your girdle."

She moved her gaze to his. "For what reason?"

"Lest you forget our bargain and think to use it for trade."

She shook her head. "You have my word."

"Even so, I will also have the girdle—whether you surrender it or I take it from you."

Her pale cheeks darkened, but she didn't argue further. She wrenched her arm from his grasp, unfastened the girdle, and thrust it and the pouch of food at him.

He took them. "And your ring as well."

She opened her mouth to protest, but in the next instant began working the ring from her finger. It was tight, but finally slid free. She dropped it in his outstretched palm.

Gabriel closed his fingers around the symbol of her marriage to Bernart. Now she truly belonged to him. He spread the drawstring of his purse and dropped the gold band atop the coins.

"You are satisfied?" Juliana asked.

He looked back. Indignation was evident in the set of her face—more, in her sharply drawn breath that caused her breasts to rise and fall against the material of her bodice. As he stared at her, his loins stirred. For all her treachery, still she quickened his blood. The dark was a dangerous place to be with Juliana Kinthorpe. "I am satisfied," he said, and motioned her to precede him. "Come, 'tis late."

Head high, she stepped past him.

Less than a quarter hour later, Gabriel tossed back the flap of her tent. "Sleep well, Juliana. Tomorrow, Mergot."

Without a word, she bent and stepped inside.

Beneath the regard of Blase and the men who'd roused from their sleep, Gabriel strode to the back of the tent, pulled the loose corner taut, and restaked it. "Killen!" he called.

The burly soldier stepped from the fire. "My lord?"

"It seems Lady Isolde is in need of a keeper. You will stand watch over her for the remainder of the night."

"Aye, my lord."

Gabriel looked to his brother. "Blasc, you will guard the northern perimeter of the camp." That area which Gabriel had covered until Juliana had blundered into it.

Blase nodded, adjusted his sword belt, and turned away.

Gabriel strode to his tent, stepped past his bleary-eyed squire, and dropped the flap. Other than removing his sword belt, which he placed beside his bedding should it be needed, he did not undress. He lay down and stared at the darkened ceiling of the tent. It was a long while before he closed his eyes, but when he did, he was visited by visions of Juliana—her arms reaching for him, peaked breasts beckoning his mouth, fair skin flushed from lovemaking. Aching, he opened his eyes. *Damn the witch!* Damn her for affecting him so when all he wanted was his child! Naught else. The morn could not come soon enough.

Castle Mergot. Like a specter, it rose against the darkening sky, stinging Juliana with fear. She gripped the reins tighter as she stared at the prison that awaited her. As evidenced by the great number of torches set about the walls—within and without—they were expected. Still, in spite of the glow, it was difficult to determine much about the castle other than its immense size, but soon she would see for herself that which she had no desire to look upon.

As she urged her mount to keep pace with Gabriel's, her thoughts turned to Bernart. It was three days since she'd been stolen from Tremoral. Had word of her absence reached him in London? Providing he was still at court when the news was sent, that he had not ranged farther afield, it was likely he was now on the road to Tremoral. By tomorrow, or the day after, he would be home.

Juliana imagined his raging and prayed Alaiz would not fall prey to it. What would Bernart do? Where would he begin searching for her? Would he guess it was Gabriel who'd taken her? If so, in a fortnight or less he would speed his army over this same ground. Then there would be bloodshed. For the child that would prove his manhood, he would strike down all, and neither the Church nor King Richard would reprove him for making war upon one who'd stolen his wife.

Would Gabriel fight to the death for the seed planted in her womb? Would he denounce her for what she'd done to gain it? She was struck by that last thought. What she feared, Bernart might also fear, and more. Though he surely knew she would hold his secret for fear of retaliation against Alaiz, if Gabriel were to appeal to the king, Bernart might have to prove himself capable of fathering children. Would he risk the truth of his emasculation to reclaim her?

She returned her gaze to the looming castle. If Bernart did not ride on Mergot, it was likely she would not be coming out for a long time. Which would be best, really, for then there would be no bloodshed, and only she would be made to suffer. Beneath her mantle, she pressed a hand to her belly. Although she had not wanted to bear this child, the thought of losing it, of never holding it, tore her. Of course, once it was born she might return to her sister. Would Bernart accept her back? It did not matter. All that mattered was that no ill befall Alaiz during her absence. "Please, God," she whispered, "keep her safe."

181

A movement beneath her hand, little more than a flutter, made her catch her breath. It was the first she had felt. Emotion piercing her heart, pricking her eyes with tears, she pulled her hand away. Though it would be increasingly difficult over the next five months, she must distance herself from the life within. Otherwise the pain that awaited her would be tenfold greater when Gabriel took the babe from her.

She looked ahead to where he was silhouetted against the lit castle. Only a man of no heart could do what he intended. She squeezed her eyes closed. She was tired. Unable to sleep on the night past after Gabriel had thwarted her plans for escape, and since dawn forced to keep pace with him and his men, she felt near to collapsing. In fact, it would be so easy to fall asleep in the saddle. Fearing the fall that would result, she forced her eyes open. A short while later, she guided her horse onto the drawbridge behind Gabriel.

The outer wall of the castle looked solid. In fact, several sections had been recently repaired, as evidenced by the different shades of stone. It seemed Gabriel was prepared in the event Bernart came calling.

Upon entering the outer bailey, Juliana corrected herself. The outer wall would have to be strong, for the inner wall enclosing the donjon was badly damaged. Scaffolding was erected around it and restoration had begun, but it would be many months before the work was completed. In the interim, if attackers made it past the first bastion of defense, the donjon would be theirs. Of course, judging by the number of soldiers who manned the outer wall, such conquest would be hard-won.

A few moments later, Juliana passed over the inner drawbridge and got her first look at the donjon. It was imposing, but also in need of repair. Whoever had resisted

King Richard's return to rule had held out until the end. Had the man given his life for a lost cause? The lives of those who served him? Likely. A man's possessions, deserved or otherwise, were of far more import than human life.

Juliana reined in before the steps of the donjon. At the landing above, a dozen or more servants waited to receive their lord. Before them stood one whom Juliana recognized immediately—the handsome Sir Erec. Until that moment, she had not questioned the reason he hadn't accompanied Gabriel to Tremoral, but likely he had remained at Mergot to administer the barony in his friend's absence.

"Come."

Juliana looked beside her. Gabriel stood with arms raised to receive her from her mount. She drew a deep breath, then glanced at the donjon. Once inside, would she be allowed without? Or was she to be denied the out-of-doors for the duration of her pregnancy? She recalled Gabriel's words of yesterday. He had said Isolde Waltham had the freedom to move within the donjon, but naught about whether she was to be confined to it.

" 'Tis only five months," Gabriel said, as if inside her thoughts.

She turned her gaze to him. "Does the babe comes early. Otherwise six."

His lids narrowed. "Put away your lies, Juliana." His words were too dangerously soft for any but her to hear. "They have no place at Mergot."

"Nor do I."

So swiftly she did not have time to evade him, he gripped her arms and lifted her down beside him.

Juliana jerked her head back to meet his anger.

" 'Tis true you have no place here," he said between

183

his teeth, "but until you have returned that which belongs to me, we will have to suffer one another."

How she wished to lash out at him, to injure his pride, to pain him as he pained her.

He must have seen it in her eyes. "I warn you, Juliana, bedevil me and your days here will be long and not a little uncomfortable."

She quelled her anger, though not so much that he might think her defeated. "Lest you forget, the name is Isolde, and my prison awaits."

A mocking smile curved his mouth. "My lady." He slid a hand to her elbow and turned her toward the steps.

As much as Juliana resented his touch, it proved necessary. Not only were the stone steps pitted and, in places, missing rather large pieces, the deceptive shadows cast by the torches made the climb treacherous. On her own, it was not likely she would have made it to the landing without mishap.

Sir Erec was the first to step forward. "I welcome your return, Lord De Vere."

"All is well?"

"Aye, and quiet."

"Good." Gabriel drew Juliana forward. "Sir Erec Sinward, I present Lady Isolde Waltham. Lady Isolde, Sir Erec."

Not a flicker of surprise, as if he knew well the reason for Juliana's presence at Mergot. He inclined his head. "Lady Isolde."

Juliana looked past the knight to the household servants who regarded her with interest.

"Lady Isolde will be residing at Mergot for the next five months," Gabriel said.

Sir Erec smiled. "A pleasure, my lady."

He lied well, since he could not possibly find enjoyment in receiving the one who'd deceived his friend.

"It has been a long day," Gabriel said. "Let us go within."

Sir Erec stepped aside.

The servants murmured greetings to their lord as he ushered Juliana past them.

As she stepped over the threshold, she wrested her awareness from the man at her side and looked to the hall. Though it was nearly as large as Tremoral's and bore the signs of past grandeur, it was in a shabby state. Where tapestries must have once hung, the walls were scarred and, in several places, blackened as if by fire. The rushes were scarce underfoot, as were the tables, benches, and sideboards scattered around the great room. A canvas was stretched taut over what must be a hole in the far wall, but though it was surely meant to keep out the night air, it was less than effective. The resultant draft tugged at Juliana's hair, nipped at her ankles, caused the fire in the hearth to spark and sputter.

Would the castle rise again with Gabriel? Not if Bernart—

"Hardly Tremoral," Gabriel said, halting in the middle of the hall, "but it will suffice for the short time you are here."

She pulled her arm from his grasp. "My chamber is abovestairs?"

"It is."

"Then that is where I would like to withdraw for the night."

"After you have eaten."

The thought of spending another moment in his presence, of enduring the castle folk's scrutiny, of stomaching even a morsel was too much for her. So much she lowered

185

her pride. "Pray, Gabriel, allow me my rest. 'Twas a day long and hard."

From the set of his eyes, she feared he meant to refuse her, but he surprised her. "Very well. I will show you to your chamber." He strode to the stairs.

Juliana followed. Unlike the stone steps outside, the stairs were smooth and even, seemingly untouched by the siege. It was the same abovestairs, so different that she wondered if she'd imagined the shabbiness of the hall.

Gabriel strode down the corridor, retrieved a torch from a wall sconce, and threw open the first of three doors. He motioned Juliana to precede him.

She stepped within and was met by an unexpected sight. The chamber was of a good size, nearly as large as the lord's solar at Tremoral, but that was not as surprising as the rest of it. The ceiling was painted blue, like the sky, and the four corners of it embellished with intricately detailed flowers—so fanciful it reminded her of her youth, when she'd believed in such things as love.

Two of the walls were hung with finely worked tapestry. The right depicted a garden, in the midst of which a lady and her lover sat, the left a unicorn surrounded by white rosebushes. Positioned before the latter tapestry was a large, postered bed, its linen curtains drawn back to reveal plump pillows and a fur coverlet that beckoned to Juliana so strongly her lids grew heavy.

She stepped farther into the chamber. Not only were the rushes more plentiful here than belowstairs, they teased her nostrils with the scent of cowslip, hyssop, sweet fennel. More, they drew a sharp contrast between herself and the room. Having worn the same garments for the past four days, she smelled of dust and horses. What she wouldn't do for a long soak in a bath and a change of clothes.

She eyed the carved chest set between the shuttered windows against the far wall, fleetingly hoped that within she might find garments to fit her swelling figure.

"You approve?" Gabriel asked.

For those few moments, Juliana had forgotten she was not alone. She looked behind and saw that Gabriel leaned against the door frame. " 'Tis not what one would expect of a prison."

He swept his gaze over the chamber. " 'Tis not a prison at all, but a place for lovers."

Lovers. Suddenly wary, she clenched her hands in her skirts.

He returned his gaze to her, and saw the fear she should have kept hidden. "You think I intend to seduce you as you did me, Juliana?"

Did he? He had said he did not want her. Had he lied?

He smiled slowly. "As you see, the chamber is how it was when I took possession of Mergot. Were it not the only private room other than the lord's solar, I would put you elsewhere." He straightened from the doorway. "Be assured, I want only that which you carry."

And in five months he would take it from her.

He set the torch in a nearby wall sconce. "I shall send a tray of food to you." He started for the door.

"I would prefer a bath," Juliana called after him.

He turned, considering her. "You must give some in order to get, Juliana. Eat; then I will order you a bath."

Doubtless if she did not eat he would know of it. "Very well."

Gabriel pulled the door closed behind him.

Juliana listened to his receding footsteps. Only when they'd faded into nothingness did she surrender to the bed. She lay back upon the thick feather mattress. It welcomed her to its soothing depths, tempted her lids closed, deliv-

ered her into a dreamworld from which the serving girl
who appeared a short while later had difficulty rousing
her.

Somehow Juliana summoned the appetite to consume a
small portion of the viands. Fortunately it was enough to
satisfy Gabriel, for soon thereafter a tub was brought to
her chamber, along with twenty or more pails of steaming
water required to fill it.

"I shall help you disrobe, my lady," said the maid Gabriel had sent to tend her.

Juliana considered the lovely woman whose accent was
truer than her own. Though English nobles' first language
was that of the French, the years since Duke William had
conquered the island kingdom and the distance of the
channel had diluted the accent of the English such that it
lacked much of the musical quality of this soft-spoken
woman.

"Lady Isolde?"

Juliana blinked. "I am sorry, what is your name again?"

"Lissant, my lady."

Juliana nodded. "I thank you, Lissant, but I can manage
myself."

The maid's brow puckered.

Had Gabriel ordered that she was not to leave Juliana's
side?

"You are certain?" Lissant asked.

"I am."

Her gaze strayed to Juliana's belly. Then, as if she understood the reason for Juliana's reluctance to disrobe, she
nodded. "I will leave you, but should you need me I shall
be outside your door."

"You need not wait on me."

Lissant smiled. " 'Tis the task Lord De Vere has set
me, my lady."

And none dared disobey him. "Very well. I will call you should I need you."

Lissant inclined her head. Her bearing proud, almost noble, she turned and left the room.

Juliana removed her soiled garments and stepped into the tub. She sighed as warmth flowed over her. If not that the tub was too short for her to stretch her legs out, she would have dozed. Though weary, she set about bathing herself from her hair to the tips of her toes, and only when she had accomplished that did she rest her head against the rim. She soaked until the water grew tepid, then stepped out of the tub, dried herself, and crawled naked between the sheets.

This night she would not think about her troubles, nor dwell on what the morrow might bring. In the days to come there would be plenty of time to worry and wonder, to search for a way out of her predicament. Now she needed rest. Even so, her last thoughts before sleep were of Alaiz. Was she well? How great was her fear? Was she strong enough to endure whatever Bernart subjected her to? Somehow she must be strong.

Chapter Twelve

England

Alaiz rose from the hearth as the doors of the hall swung inward. There he stood, the man who wanted only one thing more than her absence—Juliana's child.

In an instant, Bernart's eyes fell upon her. "Where is she?" he demanded as he strode forward.

The captain of the guard and three of the knights who'd accompanied him to London entered the hall and paused inside the doorway.

"Where has your sister gone?" Bernart repeated.

Frantically, Alaiz tried to order her thoughts, tried not to feel the fear that breathed at her neck. "I-I do not know, my lord. When I awoke, she was gone from her . . ." What was the word? It was so simple; why could she not summon it? Finally she snatched it from the muddle. "She was gone from her bed."

Bernart halted before her. "Gone? With nary a trace?"

She could not remember him ever looking so directly at her, was accustomed to the embarrassment that always swept his gaze from her. "Aye, gone."

His nostrils flared, his face coloring brighter. "You are telling me you saw naught? Heard naught?"

His spit sprayed her face, made her blink. As much as she long to wipe it away, she quelled the urge. "I-I was tired."

"It is as I told you, my lord," the captain of the guard spoke from behind Bernart. " 'Twas as if we were drugged. Every one of us."

Bernart looked around. "What of the priest who stopped for the night—this Father Hermanus?"

"We have searched, but he is gone."

Bernart's jowls quivered. "Keep searching! Sir Hector, Sir Nigel, accompany him."

The two knights followed the captain of the guard from the hall. The remaining knight, Sir Randal, stared at Alaiz. His smile boded no good.

Bernart turned back to her. "I know this is difficult for one of your . . . intellect, but I need you to think hard. For your sister's sake—and yours."

Anger supplanted the unease Alaiz had felt a moment earlier. Though words did not come easily to her and she struggled to order her thoughts that she might be understood, she was not dull-witted. There were so many things she knew that Bernart would never know. Unfortunately, those things dwelt behind locked doors. Would she ever find the keys?

Bernart stepped closer, the sweat of his ride rank. "Tell me, who would steal Juliana away?"

She gathered up handfuls of her skirts, squeezed the material so tightly her short nails bent to the pressure. "I do not know, my lord." It was the first lie she'd told in years, though it really was not a lie. After all, she was not certain it was Gabriel De Vere who had taken her sister. What she did know was that Juliana would not have willingly left her behind, and that the child in her belly was Gabriel's—not that Juliana had confided in her. Nay, it went back to the night Bernart had approached Juliana and demanded she give him a child he was incapable of fathering. Then there was the night Gabriel De Vere had arrived at Tremoral and Bernart had later sought Juliana in the solar. He had thought Alaiz asleep, and she *had* been until he'd raised his voice. How she had ached to learn that her sister would have to surrender to a man she hated. Although Alaiz feared the answer, she questioned the reason for Juliana's sacrifice—why she had not refused her husband.

"Who?" Bernart shouted.

Alaiz started violently. Who? Who what? What did he ask? Her breath coming in gasps, she searched backward, grasped at their previous discourse.

Bernart gripped her upper arm and shook her. "Imbecile! I swear, do you give me one moment of grief, I shall turn you out." He thrust her from him and swung away.

If not for the chair behind her, Alaiz would have tumbled to the hearth. Shaking as if taken with chill, she stared at her brother-in-law's retreating back. A moment later, she remembered his question: Who would have stolen Juliana?

Ought she to reveal her suspicions? She considered doing so only a moment before deciding against it. As much as she longed for Juliana's return, and dreaded life at Tremoral without her, something told her it was best she said naught. Best Bernart believed her an imbecile.

"None to watch over you, Lady Alaiz?"

She looked up. Before her stood Sir Randal, his eyes bright with something Juliana would not have liked. Alaiz glanced past him and saw that Bernart had gone, leaving her alone with this knight whom her sister had not trusted, whose gaze Alaiz too often felt.

Show not fear, she counseled herself. *He would not dare bother you.* Would he? "Excuse me, I-I must rest until the n-nooning meal."

He was slow to stir from her path. Only after he'd slithered his gaze over her did he step aside. "Rest well, my lady."

She could not go from his sight quickly enough. Once inside her chamber, she barred the door. She was safe, but only for the moment. The question was how she was to remain safe while she dwelled in the home of a man who so disdained her. Bernart was her sister's husband, but he would not protect her as Juliana had done. As he'd warned, if she caused him difficulty he would turn her out. Which would be worse? To remain at Tremoral among men like Sir Randal who looked at her the way he did, or to be a woman wandering the countryside amid outcasts and thieves who would as surely take advantage of her? The latter, she concluded. Thus she must preserve her place here, must protect herself.

She wiped her moist palms down her skirts, straightened, crossed to the chest at the foot of her bed. She knelt and raised the lid. At the bottom she found what she was looking for: the jeweled dagger her father had given her before his death.

Who dared come into his home and steal his wife from his bed? It was the same question Bernart had repeatedly asked himself since word of Juliana's disappearance had reached him in London. And still he was no nearer the answer.

He wiped a forearm across his brow, wetting his sleeve with the excessive perspiration he owed more to his considerable weight gain these past months than the hard ride from London.

He was tired and badly wanted to seek his rest. As he longingly eyed the bed from which Juliana had been stolen three nights past, the question rushed at him again: Who had taken her? He imagined a dark figure entering the solar, standing over her, lifting her. Had she struggled? Cried out? Had ill befallen the child she carried, the son he had sacrificed all to gain?

He slammed a fist against the bedpost, grunting as pain exploded through his hand. Where was she? Whose bed was she in?

Nursing his hand to his chest, he dropped to the mattress edge and stared sightlessly at his surroundings. He had always prided himself on possessing a woman so desirable that any man who saw her instantly wanted her, but never had he believed any would dare steal her. Who would be so bold?

Without a doubt, the visiting priest had been part of the plan, but he had not done it alone. Who had engaged him? Bernart plodded backward through his wretched memory to the days of the tournament. Not one of the participating knights had been able to keep his eyes from Juliana— except, of course, Gabriel.

Gabriel. Once more he entertained the possibility that his enemy was responsible for her abduction. Had Gabriel discovered it was she who'd shared his bed, believed the child she carried was his? His brother *was* a priest.

Bernart shook his head, denying the impossible. Gabriel did not know who had come to him those nights. Juliana had assured him of it, had told him Gabriel had simply taken that which she'd offered and not asked her name. Nay, if he was to find Juliana, he must look elsewhere.

Could it be Sir Henry? The handsome Sir Morris? The lecherous Sir Arnold? One by one, Bernart considered the multitude of knights who'd come from near and far to gain the purse Gabriel had taken for himself. Any one of them could have done it, could this moment be spreading her thighs.

Bernart's stomach constricted, cramped, threatened to expel the ale he had recklessly quaffed a half hour earlier. He swallowed hard, and again. Finally the nausea subsided enough that he was able to gain his feet.

Now to begin his search. Regardless how long it took—a fortnight, a month, a year—he would have Juliana back. Would have the son owed him. He tightened his sword belt around his sagging waist, crossed the solar, and threw the door wide.

Chapter Thirteen

France

No daylight penetrated the shutters, but Juliana knew it was morn from the sound of activity ascending from the bailey. She pushed aside the covers, shivered as chill air swept her bare skin, and clenched her jaws to prevent them from chattering. Dragging the fur coverlet around her shoulders, she lowered her feet to the floor.

As she stepped toward the windows, she caught a movement out of the corner of her eye. She peered closer. Someone lay on a pallet at the foot of the bed. Though it was not light enough to make out who it was, she knew it must be Lissant.

A true lady's maid. Not only was it a long time since she'd had one, it was even longer since one had been so readily available. Lest the distance Bernart put between himself and Juliana in bed give credence to the rumors, or prying eyes discover the truth of him, he'd allowed neither male nor female servant to bed down in the solar. It was going to be odd, indeed, to be waited on as befitted a lady.

Juliana frowned. Of course, it was customary for a maid to rise in advance of her mistress. She looked to the shuttered windows. It must be early, likely not even dawn. Clutching the coverlet around her, she stepped to the nearest window and opened the shutters.

The breath of night, that would soon yield the dawn, nipped at her nose and cheeks. She huddled more deeply into the fur and looked out across the torchlit inner bailey. Her gaze settled to the right of the drawbridge, where workers had already begun their day's labor to restore the integrity of the inner wall.

Would it be needed? If so, when? As she stood there dreading what would happen if Bernart came, a familiar figure entered her vision. Gabriel. Even from on high he was imposing, shoulders beneath his mantle broader than any other man's, long legs quick to close the distance between himself and the workers. He halted before the scaffold, but though his voice carried to Juliana, she could not discern the orders he gave his men.

Her stomach rumbled. Having eaten little on the night past, she would have to go belowstairs and see if she could find something to fill this emptiness. However, she soon discovered her garments were missing. Likely Lissant had taken them to be laundered. So what was she to do? She could not venture from the chamber wrapped in naught but fur.

The chest. She knelt beside it and pushed the lid back. The contents were barely distinguishable in the bit of light cast by the torches outside, but they were women's clothing and, from the feel of them, of the finest material. She drew forth a bliaut and a chemise, then dug deeper and located hose and slippers. The latter were too small and narrow, but they were the least of her concerns.

She straightened and held the bliaut against her. Unlaced, it might accommodate her increasing girth, but it would reveal her ankles and lower calves. Whoever these clothes belonged to had been of smaller stature than she. Disappointed, Juliana turned to replace the garments. She paused. Gabriel had said Isolde Waltham had the freedom of the donjon, yet had not provided her with a means of leaving her chamber. Would he mind her roaming about in clothes that shamelessly bared her lower legs? He would. Dared she?

She dropped the coverlet and donned the garments of a lady who would have been fortunate to reach Juliana's nose. In tightly stockinged feet and a gown that strained its unlaced seams, she made her way to the hall. Not surprisingly, the household servants were still scattered upon their pallets and benches.

She crossed to the sideboard. Only ale and unappetizing scraps were left of last eve's supper. Guessing the kitchens were located down the corridor off the hall, she retrieved a torch and shortly entered the cavernous room. It was well-appointed, and as untouched by the siege as were the rooms abovestairs.

As expected, the pantry was locked. Juliana retrieved a stool, positioned it to the side of the pantry, and climbed atop. The key was beneath a pot. Within minutes she sat down to a meal of bread and cheese.

A stout man entered the kitchens. Hair tousled from recent awakening, circles beneath his eyes, clothes rumpled, he halted. "Who are you?" he demanded in an accent as thick as cold stew.

Juliana reminded herself of the name Gabriel had given her. "I am Lady Isolde Waltham."

He squinted, looking closer. Fortunately, the table concealed her undersize garments. Of course, eventually she would have to come out.

"So you are," he said. "What do you in my kitchens?"

Then he was the cook. "I am eating." She held up a crust of bread.

He glowered. "You could not wait an hour longer?"

She was not accustomed to being spoken to so rudely by a servant. Even Nesta, with all her impertinence, had never challenged her so. Was it because the child she carried was ill-gotten? That the only conclusion to be drawn from it was that she was a whore? It had to be. Would Gabriel allow such ill treatment of her? If so, her time at Mergot was going to be more wretched than she had anticipated. Denying the man an answer, she popped a piece of cheese into her mouth.

He turned on his heel and crossed to the hearth. It wasn't long before the glowing embers sprang to life and licked at the kettle suspended over it. Shortly, several kitchen maids entered the kitchens and set about their duties. Though curiosity carried their gaze to Juliana time and again, and they tittered and spoke behind their hands, none addressed her as the cook had done.

Juliana had barely satisfied her hunger when the kitchen door burst open.

A man-at-arms stood there. When his gaze lit upon her, relief lightened his expression. "She is here, my lord," he shouted over his shoulder.

Then Gabriel had discovered her missing and set the garrison searching for her.

Juliana pushed the remains of her meal aside and clasped her hands on the tabletop.

199

Heavy footsteps resounded in the corridor. A moment later Gabriel appeared. Head and shoulders filling the height and breadth of the doorway, he settled his eyes on her. He was vexed, as evidenced by the set of his jaw, the lowering of his brow. "Leave us," he ordered the servants.

They were quick to comply.

He stepped within and closed the door. "What do you here?"

Was he as dense as the cook? "Is it not obvious?" She nodded to the bread and cheese that remained. "You thought that perhaps I had escaped you again?"

If her words pricked, he did not show it. He strode forward. "I will not have you wandering the donjon."

His words pricked. She slipped off the stool. "You said Isolde Waltham had the freedom of the donjon. 'Twas the bargain we struck."

He halted before the table. "So it was, and it holds. However, at all times I will know where you are."

"That is your freedom? That I be ever under watch? Why do you not simply lock me away?"

He pressed his palms to the table. "If that is what you prefer, 'tis easily done."

Though she did not doubt his threat, she disregarded it. "You fear I might slip past your men? Is that it? You have no confidence in their ability to guard your walls?" Another thought struck. "Or is it their loyalty you question?"

His lids lowered, his eyes glittering through the narrow slits. "You will find no allies at Mergot, Juliana. The castle folk are loyal to me."

Were they? After all, most of them were likely of French descent and had served the previous baron, who'd fallen to King Richard's siege. Had they no loyalty to their fellow countrymen? No resentment toward the Englishman who had supplanted King Philip's baron? "If you are so confident of their fealty," Juliana said, "why do you deny me a measure of privacy?"

A bitter smile etched his mouth. "One cannot be too careful where women are concerned."

She remembered the last night she'd spent with him, when he had revealed far more than he had wished to. "I suppose I have your thieving mother to thank for the fetters put on me."

His eyes darkened. "You have only yourself to blame for that. *Your* deception."

How she hated the revenge he was set on regardless of who might be destroyed. Aching for her sister, she stepped around the table. "Should my jailer seek me, I shall be in my chamber."

Gabriel caught her arm, sweeping his frowning gaze from her straining bodice to skirts that came nowhere near the floor. "What manner of clothes are these?"

She pushed her shoulders back, lifting her chin. "My own garments were gone from my chamber when I awoke. Thus I borrowed these from the chest. You object?"

"Object that the mother of my child looks more a trollop than a lady?"

She cocked her head. "I thought you would find it fitting."

His fingers tightened around her arm. "I know what you are, Juliana, but I will not have my child raised with gossip that wanton displays such as this rouse."

"You do not think servants already talk? Come, Gabriel, I am Lady Isolde Waltham, not Isolde De Vere. Do you succeed in taking my babe, all will know it for what it is. A misbegotten child. A bastard."

His black heart shone from his eyes. " 'Tis a burden the child will have to bear, but all the more reason you do not weight its shoulders more heavily."

As if in clothing herself in the only garments available she'd sought to bring shame upon her child. She turned her nails into her palms. "What would you have had me do? Venture belowstairs wrapped in naught but a coverlet?"

"You could have sent Lissant for food."

"She was sleeping."

"You could not awaken her?"

"There was no need to rouse her when I could as easily come myself."

"As easily . . ." His eyes swept her with distaste. "I have given you a lady's maid for a reason. In future you will make use of her. Do you understand?"

She drew a deep breath. What good was it to argue with him, especially over so trifling a matter? "Of course. Now if you will unhand me I shall vex you no more."

"That I doubt." He released her. "Wear this." He removed his mantle and dropped it over her shoulders.

His warmth, trapped in the folds of the garment, rippled over her, reminded her of the man who had warmed her as no other had done. His fingers, brushing the rise of her breasts as he fastened the mantle, swept her with memories of the dark, a touch, a caress. Her undoing. She looked up, stared at his bent head, and struggled to draw a full breath.

Gabriel finished with the mantle and met her gaze.

Too late, she shuttered her emotions.

A faint smile touched his mouth. "Do not tempt me, Juliana. Though I do not want you, I have been long enough without a woman that I might take what you offer. And 'twill change naught."

Burned by the humiliation her traitorous body visited upon her, she took a step back, and another. Now she could breathe again. Though she had not touched him, her fingertips had prickled with the feel of him, her tongue with the salty taste of him, her nostrils with the masculine scent of him, and her ears had echoed the words he had long ago spoken against her skin. "You are wrong, Gabriel De Vere," she managed. "I would as soon lie with the devil as with you."

Though his eyes gainsaid her prideful declaration, he spared her from comment. "Return to your chamber. I shall have more appropriate attire brought to you."

Juliana skirted him. This time when she passed through the hall, the great room was awake with servants who positioned benches and tables for the morning meal.

Lissant was also there. She hastened to Juliana's side. "My lady, I was so worried."

Was it she who'd raised the hue? Juliana wondered with a twinge of resentment. She tamped it down. The woman was only doing her duty to her lord. "I am sorry to have frightened you," she said, and continued toward the stairs.

The maid followed.

Gabriel stared at the inner wall that, stone by painstaking stone, was being refortified. Slowly. He turned, looking to the smithy from which came the sound of the forging of arms. He had paid much for the steel needed to build up Mergot's stock of weaponry, but it was a necessity. No matter how solid the walls, they alone would not keep out an attacker. Not that Gabriel believed Bernart would come to Mergot. Simply, life had taught him to be prepared for the unexpected.

Once again his thoughts turned to the woman who was

responsible for much of the activity at Mergot. He ground his teeth. He was a liar. In spite of everything, he did want Juliana. Not because he had been without a woman for so long. Were that so, he could ease his need with one of the wenches in his hall. But he had not in more than four months.

Did Juliana ever relive their nights as he did? Was that what he'd seen in her eyes when he'd looked up from fastening the mantle? Or did she merely seek to gain his bed that she might turn him from his course? Aye, the woman he had so long wanted had never wanted him. She had come to him only to steal a child. That she had done exceedingly well.

Damn her! Damn her deceit! Damn her for not allowing him to forget those nights, especially the last, when she'd lain back for him in the light of the torch, when she had allowed him to drink from her sweet mouth, when he had revealed things about himself of which he had never before spoken.

In spite of his anger over her treachery, the memories of that night caused his loins to ache. If he took her one last time, used her as she had used him, *would* it change naught? Could he then so easily take the babe from her?

Cursing himself, he thrust a hand through his hair. Had he waited for the child to be born, then ventured to Tremoral and taken it from its cradle, the same result could have been achieved without submitting to the temptation of Juliana. Unfortunately, he'd been too impatient, his vengeance too strong. But what was done was done. In five months, all would be as it should.

Shortly after noon, two homespun bliauts and a chemise were delivered to Juliana's chamber. Doubtless they belonged to a heavy woman, for they were wide enough that she could easily wear them to the end of her pregnancy. She hoped she would not have to.

As Lissant secured an unadorned girdle around Juliana's waist, containing the garment's voluminous folds, Juliana scratched her upper thigh, her shoulder, her ribs. Not only was the chemise of poor quality, but it was worn too thin to keep the bliaut's wool fibers from chafing. Was it Gabriel's desire that she suffer discomfort until the babe was born? She set her jaw. She would endure it without complaint and, eventually, become accustomed to it, as did all women who were not of the privileged class.

Lissant sat back on her heels and sighed. "It will have to suffice until we can sew some new gowns for you, my lady, but I shall begin this evening."

Juliana blinked. "You have the cloth to do so?"

"*Oui*, Lord De Vere gave it to me. As it was to have been fashioned into tunics for him, I fear it is not so fine as that of Lady Clarisse's gowns, but it is of good quality."

Juliana felt a twinge of remorse. She had thought the worst of Gabriel. Of course, his consideration was surely due to how it might reflect on him were he to clothe the mother of his child as a servant.

Lissant stood and gathered the garments Juliana had worn belowstairs.

"What of my own clothes?" Juliana asked. Though they would not fit much longer, she might gain a few more weeks from them.

"They are being laundered, my lady. If they are dry by the morn, I will bring them to you." Lissant crossed to the chest, neatly folded the garments, and replaced them.

"The lady whose chamber this was must have been quite small," Juliana commented.

Lissant shook her head. "Merely young."

That would explain it. "How old?"

205

The maid lowered the chest lid. "Lady Clarisse was twelve years old when Baron Leon Faison wed her, fifteen when she died."

Juliana could not help but feel grief for one lost so soon. "How did she die?"

"During King Richard's siege, she was taken with a sudden illness. As there was no physician to tend her, she could not be saved."

"I am sorry."

Lissant nodded. "So grieved was the baron that, even when defeat was certain, he refused to yield to the English king." She breathed a heartfelt sigh. "Unable to bear the thought of living without his beloved, he longed to join her in death."

Though Juliana no longer believed in love, she was touched by this story that echoed those of the troubadours. She swept her gaze over the room. Though romance shone from every corner, it was that very thing that raised a question. "Why did Lady Clarisse not occupy the solar with her husband?"

"Ah, that. Lord Faison wished his wife to grow into a woman before he took her to his bed. Thus he surrounded her with beauty while he waited for her to come of age."

Juliana felt a pang in her chest. Unless a bride was quite young, few men willingly postponed their husbandly rights.

Lissant nodded to the tapestry behind the bed. "As you surely know, the unicorn is the symbol of chastity and purity. My lady was that."

And last eve she, Juliana Kinthorpe, pregnant with a child not her husband's, had lain beneath it. How sadly ironic. Nay, sacrilegious. Feeling the whore she had become in Gabriel's arms, she turned away. "You were her maid?"

"I was."

Yet Juliana sensed no hostility toward herself. "What of the baron? Did he die?"

"It is thought so, that he was among the dead brought out after the siege, but as some bodies could not be identified, it is not known for certain."

Could he still be alive, languishing over the loss of his lady? *Ah, sweet suffering. To have loved and been loved so deeply—*

Juliana halted her childish fantasizing. Far more likely, Baron Faison had not touched his child bride because he'd been impotent, aged rather than young and handsome as she envisioned. Only women knew how to love, and, as they were alone in that knowledge, none but the foolish believed their love returned. Though Juliana had once been among their ranks, Bernart and Gabriel had taught her well the truth of a man's heart.

"A romantic tale, *non*?" Lissant asked.

Juliana looked around. Aye, a tale. Doubtless one that grew more fanciful with each telling. "It is." No reason to hurt Lissant's feelings.

"Just like your name," Lissant said. "Isolde. So romantic."

Juliana had once thought so herself. "Do you miss your mistress?"

The maid's smile wavered. She hesitated before speaking. "She was beautiful and most elegant for one of so few years, but so spoiled and full of vainglory it was difficult to tend her. She could be charming, but I do not think she saw much beyond her nose. Even Lord Faison, who worshiped her, fell outside her sight. But for all that, I do miss her some."

Then this was not a tale the troubadours would embrace, after all. It would take much embellishment for it to find an audience, and greater exaggeration of the baron's immortal love than existed in this maid's heart.

As if remembering it was a lady to whom she spoke and not a servant, as Juliana looked in her new garments, Lissant's cheeks flushed with color. "Th-the nooning meal is soon to be served," she said.

Her stammer fleetingly reminded Juliana of Alaiz. How she missed her sister, her gentleness, the companionship they'd shared.

"My lady?"

Juliana met Lissant's questioning gaze and shook her head. It was not that she was embarrassed by her clothing. Rather, she declined so that she might avoid facing Gabriel so soon after her humiliating confrontation with him in the kitchens. "I would prefer to eat in my chamber."

Lissant looked momentarily disconcerted, but her brow smoothed. "Then I shall bring you a tray."

"Thank you."

The maid's hand was upon the door when Juliana called her back. "What of Baron Faison's brother whose lands lie west of here? Is it true he bears ill will for Lord De Vere?"

Wariness transformed Lissant's face. "Why do you ask, my lady?"

As the others had been warned Juliana was not to be trusted, so had she. "Curiosity. During the ride to Mergot, your lord spoke briefly of it."

"Did he?" Lissant considered her, shrugged. "It is true. But then, Dominic Faison is a dark one."

"A dark one?"

Lissant nodded. "Not only does he serve a king not of his choosing, he lost an arm during the crusade. He hates the world for it."

Juliana was swept with compassion for a man she did

not know. Though many had given their lives in taking up the church's call to rout the infidels from the Holy Land, there were those whose suffering went deeper, who bore scars to forever remind them of the horror to which they'd been subjected. Bernart was not alone. "I see," Juliana said.

Lissant opened the door. "I will return shortly with your meal." She bustled from the chamber.

Juliana lowered her gaze to the rushes. If she escaped Gabriel, would Faison help her return to England? Or was he too embittered to help anyone? More, would she be given the chance to find that out?

For her remaining minutes alone, Juliana turned her attention to her chamber, this time with the eyes of one who knew something of what had gone before. Was it true the frivolous Lady Clarisse had felt naught for her husband? Or had she yearned for the touch he denied her as Juliana had been denied Bernart's?

She looked to the garden tapestry that adorned the far wall. A lady and her lover sat among flowers, faces rapt with infatuation.

Juliana stepped forward and lightly ran her hand over the tight weave, touched the faces of love. If only life were different, if feelings such as these existed in reality as they so readily existed in the imagination.

She started to turn away, but paused. As wall passages were most often concealed behind such hangings, perhaps . . .

She was not disappointed—at least, until she discovered that the narrow, iron-banded door was locked. No doubt by Gabriel's hand.

In the shadow of the tapestry, she fingered the keyhole. Could another instrument be used to open the door? If so, what lay beyond? Escape from Mergot? She sank her teeth into her lower lip. She had given Gabriel her word she would make no more attempts to escape, but what of Alaiz? If an opportunity to return to her sister arose, could she turn from it? She could not.

Though Juliana's decision to seek a way past the locked door meant breaking her word, she reasoned that Gabriel was, himself, without honor. After all, he had stolen her from her home. Forget his reason for having done so, that he had more of a right to the child she carried than Bernart. Were he in her place, he would feel no twinge of conscience for what she intended.

A sound, slight, but telling, caught her ear. Lissant had returned.

Hurriedly she stepped from behind the tapestry. The door swung inward, but it was not the maid bearing a tray.

Gabriel's gaze swept her, shifted to the garden scene, returned to her.

Did he know? Out of the corner of her eye, she saw the tapestry sway slightly. Heart pounding, she stepped from it. "There is something you require?"

"Your presence at table."

She faltered. "I have sent Lissant for a tray."

"Aye, but you will take your meal belowstairs."

"I prefer to remain in my chamber."

"Even so, you will join me."

What did it matter where she ate? Considering what he believed of her, he ought to appreciate her absence. "For what purpose?"

As if settling in for a debate, he put a shoulder to the door frame. "Though your time at Mergot is short, I will not have you spend it sulking. You are a guest and will behave accordingly."

"A guest? What absurdity you speak. I have no freedom, little privacy—"

"If 'tis privacy you seek, the tower will more than meet your needs."

Imprisonment again. As suppressed as Juliana felt, undoubtedly the tower would be worse. She gritted her teeth, searching for a way around Gabriel.

"Come," he said, confident she would do as bidden. "Cook waits the meal on you."

She clenched her hands in the coarse material of her bliaut.

Gabriel's gaze caught the movement. " 'Tis not that you are ashamed of your appearance, is it?"

She looked down the garments. Ashamed? Nay, but so pricked with discomfort it was all she could do to keep from scratching the dozen or more places that vexed. Of course, perhaps it was her show of pregnancy Gabriel referred to. . . . Either way, she would not give him the satisfaction he sought. She lifted her chin, pressed her shoulders back, and walked forward.

He turned and strode the corridor ahead of her. With their arrival in the hall, the din of soldiers and servants subsided and all eyes turned to them.

Juliana stood taller, gathering her dignity to her as she followed Gabriel to the high table.

As told, Cook had waited the meal for her and, from the displeasure shining from the faces of those in the hall, none were pleased. And why should they be? After all, it was not as if she were of import. Not as if she were their lady and thus owed their respect and forbearance.

Only as Juliana ascended the dais did it occur to her it might be the lower tables at which Gabriel expected her to take her meal. Though it was known he was the father of her illegitimate child, her place was certainly not with

211

the baron of Mergot. Not in the chair that his wife would one day occupy. Still, she followed Gabriel around the table at which Sir Erec and the false priest sat.

Gabriel lowered himself into the high seat, gesturing for her to take the chair beside him.

Then he *did* intend her to sit at his side. She supposed she ought to be grateful, for it implied she was to be treated with more respect than the cook had afforded her. Unfortunately, it also meant she was flanked on one side by Gabriel, and on the other by his brother.

No sooner did she take the chair than serving wenches began filing into the hall bearing platters of the day's main meal.

Determinedly, Juliana ignored the men on either side of her and looked to the lower tables. It seemed all eyes were on her, but whereas resentment had shone from them moments ago, now there was confusion. The castle folk were at a loss as to her place at Mergot. She was a lady who held a chamber in the donjon, took meal at their lord's side, and was allowed to move freely about the donjon—even if under constant watch. In Gabriel's own words, a guest. Yet she carried his illegitimate child and he'd made it known she was not to be trusted. It was no wonder his people were confused. But perhaps she might use it to her advantage. . . .

Shortly, the noise in the hall resumed and the occupants turned their attention to the meal.

Juliana looked down and found a trencher before her, rather than between her and Gabriel, or her and his brother. Relieved that she did not have to share with either of them, she lifted her spoon and chased a piece of venison in the bowl.

"You will leave on the morrow?" Gabriel asked.

Juliana looked around and saw it was Sir Erec whom he addressed.

"If you have no further need of me, 'tis time I return to Fey."

Fey? A lesser castle of Mergot? It must be, and likely Gabriel had awarded it to his loyal tournament partner. She dipped her spoon again and turned her thoughts elsewhere. If she succeeded in escaping Gabriel and convincing his enemy to aid in her return to Tremoral, what then? She was not so much a fool as to believe Gabriel would not follow. And this time he would confront Bernart. Then the struggle to possess her would lead to bloodshed. But what if she were not there, nor Alaiz? What if she stole into Tremoral and brought her sister out? If neither man held her, there would be no reason for battle—other than that they were men and, thus, inclined to violence. Either way, if she were nowhere to be found there was less chance any would die. But where would she and Alaiz go? They could not return to their childhood home, for the nobleman who owned wardship of their mother and brother would either turn them away or hold them for Bernart.

What of the church? If they sought sanctuary at a convent distant from Tremoral, neither Gabriel nor Bernart might ever find them. And if they did, they would not be permitted within the walls. Though it was true Alaiz's infirmity had caused the church to reject her, if she and Juliana claimed sanctuary it would be granted. That was what they would do, Juliana decided. Even if she must live out the remainder of her days in a convent, it was preferable to what Alaiz might suffer at Bernart's hands, and what awaited Juliana when the babe was born.

Though it was not unusual for the noonday meal to linger well into the afternoon, Gabriel called an end to it an hour later. Obviously the work on the inner wall took precedence. Without a word to Juliana, he descended the dais. Sir Erec followed. Though the others in the hall were reluctant to abandon their meal, they also rose. Within minutes only Juliana, Gabriel's brother, and the serving wenches remained. The latter set about clearing the tables.

Feeling Blase's regard, Juliana considered ignoring it. After all, their last encounter had been less than friendly. In the end, she looked around.

He lifted his goblet, leaning back in his chair. "What think you of your first day at Mergot, Lady Isolde?"

She was going to have to become accustomed to being called that. "Methinks it far too long a day for one barely half done."

Blase smiled. "You have been made comfortable?"

She lifted her hands. "I am not in chains."

"Fortunate, indeed. Four months ago it would have been different."

Meaning Gabriel's anger had lessened in the intervening months.

Blase sighed. "But time has a way with such things."

Juliana knew she shouldn't argue with him, that she was more likely to be stung by his words than he hers, but her frustrations needed venting. "Does time also have a way with your conscience, false priest?"

Something flashed in his eyes, and for that brief moment it was as if it were Gabriel before her. How foolish she had been not to have heeded the resemblance this man bore his brother when he'd come to Tremoral. She had thought they shared only dark looks, but it went beyond that: the nose, the chin, the height and build. That which distinguished them was eye color, Blase's being a green so penetrating it was almost unholy. The length of their dark hair was different, Blase's barely skimming the neck of his tunic, and, though Blase was also plain of face, he was somehow more attractive. Too, there was his ability to smile and laugh, as he had done in the guise of Father Hermanus.

A moment later, his eyes cooled and a smile returned to his face. "The state of my conscience is between me and the Lord, Lady Isolde. I answer only to Him."

She inclined her head. "And so you shall."

He quaffed the remainder of his wine. "Now I must apply myself to the books." He stood.

Juliana frowned. "You keep Gabriel's accounts?"

"There is none other he trusts." From the slight twist of his lips, it was not a task he enjoyed. What would he rather be doing? Swinging that sword at his hip, which his hand was wont to rest upon?

"I know accounting," Juliana said. "If you would like, I will do some posting for you." It was not that she wished to do him favors; rather, time would pass more quickly if she had something to do.

"I will consider it," he said, and turned away.

Of course, her time would be better spent seeking her escape, Juliana thought as she followed Blase's withdrawal from the hall. She fingered her spoon. Would its slender handle fit the door lock? Grant her access to the hidden passageway? Not likely, but she had to try.

Chapter Fourteen

The steady beat of rain that had begun to fall moments earlier drew Juliana's gaze across the hall to the damaged wall. The canvas covering the hole was soaked, meaning it was only a matter of time until rain seeped in. A pity Gabriel had not seen fit to repair the wall. Not only would the rain mildew the rushes further, but the chill of autumn would give way to the frigid cold of winter. Then it would be intolerable here, unless one kept near the fire.

Restlessness weighting Juliana, she lowered her sewing to her lap and sighed. Always she'd had something with which to occupy herself, be it training in the art of love as a fanciful girl, or the keeping of Bernart's household as a disenchanted wife. Now she had only a needle and thread. Barely a sennight at Mergot and it felt a month. Unfortunately, as the spoon handle and a half dozen other items had proven worthless in her quest to open the door to the passageway, she was no nearer escape.

She looked about the hall. The only occupants other than herself and Lissant were Blase, who was seated at the lord's table with journals spread before him, the porter, who dozed alongside the door, and two women servants who were more concerned with idle chat than tending their duties.

She frowned. Though Mergot was in dire need of a lady to put order to the household, Gabriel seemed blind to all but fortification. Were she the lady of Mergot, she would put the women to work replacing the rancid rushes with fresh rushes scented with herbs, and gather a half dozen more servants to scrub the walls, the hearth, the tables and benches.

But she was not their lady, and never would she be. One day another would sit at Gabriel's side, share his bed, birth his children. The thought of it wrenched her heart, as did, even more deeply, the thought of another woman raising her child. Would Gabriel choose his bride wisely? In the next instant, she berated herself for such thinking. *She* would raise her child. No other. Her back aching from having sat too long, she laid aside the unfinished gown and stood.

Lissant looked up from the sleeve that could soon be set in the bodice. "My lady?"

"I am stiff and need to walk."

As Lissant started to stand to accompany her mistress, as she did from the moment Juliana rose in the morn to the moment she lay down at night, Juliana motioned her to remain seated. "I will not stray from the hall."

Though the maid appeared uncertain, she nodded.

Juliana stepped from the hearth, leaving its warmth behind. The coarse material of her borrowed garments chafed, but she was grateful for the thick weave and voluminous folds that retained her heat far better than her

217

own gowns would have done. As she walked the hall, she paused every so often to toe an unmentionable. Gabriel needed more dogs to keep the rushes clear of food tossed to the floor during meals.

Blase looked up from his journals as Juliana neared the dais. Judging by his grim mouth, he was displeased.

She halted. "What vexes you, Father Blase?"

He returned his attention to his work. "A mystery," he muttered.

"The entries do not sum?"

"They will." He dipped his quill.

Though Juliana knew he would likely refuse her help, the thought of applying herself to something other than sewing made her step up to the dais. "If you would like, I will see if I can find the error."

He shook his bowed head. "I do not need your assistance, Lady Isolde."

"As you would have it." She turned, and her gaze fell upon the women servants at the far end of the table. Though they made a show of wiping crumbs and drippings from the tabletop, their attempts were feeble.

Juliana itched to show them how it was done. And why shouldn't she? She was not their lady, but there was none more suited to the role. She traversed the dais, halting before them. "Do you not apply yourself, the filth will not come clean."

From their expressions, they did not know how to respond to her authority. They blinked, exchanging glances.

"We shall need buckets of hot water and more cloths," Juliana said.

Their eyes widened.

Juliana lifted her chin. "Be quick. There is much to be done."

The women looked to Blase.

Would he support her? Or give them more reason to speak behind their hands?

"Do as Lady Isolde says," he finally said.

Juliana released her breath.

Though the women were displeased, they stepped from the dais.

Juliana turned. "Bring brooms as well, and summon the others from the kitchens." As she had learned, it was there the servants gathered to engage in idle talk.

When the women were gone, Juliana looked to Blase.

"Gabriel will not like it," he said.

She didn't imagine he would. So why had Blase allowed it?

With a crooked smile, he bent his head and began scratching figures on a scrap of parchment.

Two hours later, working side by side with a half dozen servants, Juliana began to see a difference. It was slight, but a sennight of hard work would see it made right.

As she swept the rushes from the floor before the dais, she caught a glint of metal. Peering closer, she saw it was a meat dagger. Was its blade narrow enough to fit the lock? She glanced around. The servants were occupied with their tasks, and Blase with his journals. As casually as possible, she bent and swept the rushes from the dagger. Its blade was dull, but it need not be sharp. She lifted the hem of her skirt and slid the dagger into the top of her hose.

"Curse it!" Blase spat.

Fearing she was caught, Juliana looked up.

Color in his cheeks, nostrils flaring, he dropped the quill and thrust back in his chair. "Accursed accounting!"

Relief sagged Juliana's shoulders. Using the broom handle to assist her, she straightened and stepped forward. "Do you once again forget you are a priest, Father Blase?"

"A priest I would rather be than a steward," he grumbled.

Though tempted to let him suffer for his pride, she ascended the dais. "May I?"

He pushed the journal toward her. "You will find naught."

"Because you cannot yourself?"

His color deepened. "You are welcome to try."

Juliana leaned the broom against the table's edge and lowered herself into the chair beside Blase. She flipped through the pages to the last balancing of the books and began summing Mergot's income. A half hour later, she was no nearer to solving the mystery. She pushed the journal aside, reaching for the journal of expenditures.

"It is not there," Blase said.

"Perhaps." A short while later, she returned to the first journal and found what she looked for. She stood and pushed the books in front of Blase. "There 'tis." She tapped the entry. "You have posted income as an expenditure."

He leaned forward. When he looked up, a sheepish smile turned his lips. "So I have." He chuckled, reminding her of Father Hermanus. "Gabriel would do well not to underestimate you, Lady Ju—Isolde."

His words reminded her of the dagger. Gabriel *would* do well not to underestimate her, but she prayed he would.

"I thank you," Blase said.

She peered at him through the hair escaping her braid. Though she didn't wish to like this man who wore the robes of a priest for his own benefit, some of her anger dissolved.

He reached up and swept the hair from her eyes. "You are a shameful mess, Lady Isolde."

Juliana smoothed her hair back, glancing at her soiled

gown. "What think you your brother would say if he came upon me now?"

His eyebrows soared. "I do not wish to ponder it."

Nor did she. She tried to hold back the grin teasing her mouth, but it came forth.

Blase laughed, and she had to join him.

The scene that greeted Gabriel when he strode into the hall was so unexpected it drew him to a halt. Juliana leaned over Blase, a smile curving her mouth as Blase laughed at something they shared. What?

Although Gabriel would admit to none the emotion clenching his gut, he knew it was jealousy. He was thankful when it was quick to pass into anger. What had Juliana to smile about? What spell had she cast over Blase? He looked to the servants, of which there seemed an over-abundance. Their attention was also on the high table.

Forgetting he had returned to the donjon to change out of his drenched clothing, he strode forward. "Something amuses you, brother? Lady Isolde?"

Faces reflecting surprise, they turned their gazes to him.

Only as Gabriel drew near did he notice Juliana's disheveled state. Her gown was soiled, her hair barely confined, and there was dirt upon her cheek. He ascended the dais.

Blase broke the silence. "Lady Isolde has assisted me in finding an error in the books."

What did Juliana know of such matters? Though her training would have included some instruction in reading and writing, it was the idea of love upon which her mother had fixed. When had she learned accounting, and for what reason, when Bernart did not require it of his wife?

Juliana reached for the broom that leaned against the table. "I shall return to cleaning."

Of course. It accounted for her appearance. "You will not."

She stilled. "For what reason?"

He put his palms to the table. "Lest you forget, you are a lady."

"Am I? Considering what you believe of me, I am surprised you acknowledge it."

He leaned forward, speaking low so that none beyond her and Blase might hear. "I assure you, I speak only of that which noble birth affords you."

She pressed her lips together.

Gabriel looked to his brother. "You allowed this?"

Blase shrugged a shoulder. "There seemed no harm in it."

"No harm? She is not a servant!"

Blase swept his gaze over Gabriel. "Nor are you, my *lord*, but look at you."

Though the rain had washed away much of the evidence of Gabriel's work, enough remained to tell of that which would have been more fittingly performed by a laborer.

"Was it you who set the servants to cleaning the hall?" Gabriel asked.

" 'Twas I," Juliana answered for Blase.

Gabriel clenched his jaw. As if she were the lady of Mergot, Juliana ordered the servants. As if a servant, she worked alongside them. He met her defiant gaze. "No more." He looked back at his brother. "We will speak of this later."

Blase sighed.

"Attend to your grooming," Gabriel ordered Juliana, and turned away.

Heavy with resentment, she watched his long strides carry him across the hall.

"And I thought 'twas only the child he wanted," Blase murmured as his brother disappeared up the stairs.

Juliana looked around. "What speak you of?"

He motioned for the servants to resume their duties, then turned a smile on her. "That was jealousy, my lady. Though my brother professes to despise you, it seems he feels otherwise."

She shook her head. "You are mistaken."

"I am not. If he sends you away when the babe is born, he will not do so easily."

Wouldn't he? "Do you believe that, then you do not know the man I know. There is none more full of hate than Gabriel De Vere."

"Not even Bernart Kinthorpe?"

His question jolted her. What did he know of Bernart? Surely only what Gabriel told him. Juliana put her chin up. "Methinks I like you better when you affect to be a priest."

Blase was amused. "But I am a priest, my lady. From my own mouth did I speak the vows that doomed me to life in the church." He heaved a sigh. "Still, 'tis not as if the vows were spoken from my heart. But God knows that."

"Thus you believe yourself absolved of the sins you have committed in the name of God?"

The sparkle in his eyes extinguished. "End of truce, eh?"

Was that what they'd enjoyed these past hours? Juliana felt a pang of regret. Blase *had* allowed her to direct the servants, accepted her offer to assist in finding the error in the books, and defended her to Gabriel. She sighed and shook her head. "Forgive me. 'Tis Gabriel who deserves my anger."

Blase stared at her for a moment before speaking. "Then a truce it is."

She was relieved. "A truce. Now I must needs rest until the evening meal."

"Do not forget to tend to your grooming," he reminded her of Gabriel's command.

She almost smiled. She picked up the broom, walked around the table, and stepped from the dais.

Instantly Lissant was at her side. "My lady—"

"Here." Juliana passed the broom to her. "Finish clearing the rushes before the dais; then come to me."

The maid nodded.

Only when Juliana began her ascent of the stairs did she realize how hard she'd labored. Her muscles ached, especially those of her hips and lower back. Doubtless she would feel it even more come the morrow.

She stepped from the stairs into the corridor. No sooner did she put a hand to the door of her chamber than a rustling alerted her to another's presence. She looked to the lord's solar and saw the door was ajar.

Her bitter exchange with Gabriel returned to her. He wished her to behave as a titled lady, though only to the extent that she be idle in the confines of his donjon. Little freedom, no respect. Anger surging anew, she traversed the corridor, pushed the door open, and stepped inside.

Clad in naught but braies and hose that clung damply to his loins and legs, Gabriel stood over the chest at the foot of a very large bed.

Juliana's pulse quickened. *Retreat*, her mind warned. *Withdraw ere he notices you.* Though she wanted to obey, her eyes held her where she stood. There was no spare flesh on Gabriel, his arms, chest, and abdomen defined by the light and dark of converging muscles. Just as she remembered him.

224

She should not be here. She took a step back.

"Rather brazen of you to come to my chamber," Gabriel said, continuing to search the chest. "But then, that ought not to surprise me." He removed a tunic and turned.

She averted her gaze and, in so doing, noticed that the lord's solar was absent the lavish trappings of her own chamber. "I but wish to speak with you," she said.

"That is all?"

What did he think? That she came to him as she had done those nights at Tremoral? Of course, it was hardly proper for a lady to enter the chamber of a man to whom she was not wed, but her mistake could not be undone.

Juliana braved his gaze. "For no other reason."

He dropped the tunic atop the chest and advanced on her. "Then speak."

She drew a deep breath. "I am not accustomed to being idle. If you will not allow me to direct your servants in making your hall more habitable, how would you have me spend my time?"

He halted before her. "As a lady spends her time—with sewing and the like."

"You think that is all a lady does?"

" 'Tis all your mother trained you for. That and the art of love, of course."

At which she had failed . . . How she wished Gabriel would cover himself, that he would not stand so near. He made the simple act of breathing difficult. "Doubtless it will surprise you," she said, "but I kept Bernart's household and tended to his accounting."

Gabriel leaned his weight against the door frame. "Be it so, I will not have you acting the lady of Mergot."

She shook her head. "Are you so blind you do not see the state of your hall? 'Tis hardly fit for humans."

225

"The least of my concerns. Once the castle walls are strong again, the hall will be seen to."

"But it can be seen to now! You have the servants. All you require is someone to direct them."

"In time, Juliana."

"And till then, how many of your people will fall ill? Surely you know spoilage breeds sickness and disease?"

He considered her. "If 'tis so great a concern, Blase can oversee the servants."

" 'Tis woman's work, not that of a man who would prefer to be out-of-doors swinging a sword." She took a step toward him. "Allow me this, Gabriel."

His eyes narrowed. "What gain for you?"

" 'Twill make my days pass more quickly." What she said was true—had naught to do with the meat dagger in her hose that she hoped would *end* her days at Mergot.

"I see," he said. "Then you are eager to birth the child and surrender it."

The thought of her babe being torn from her arms sent unexpected tears pouring into her eyes. She looked down. "Of course not, but in that I've no say, have I?"

Gabriel lifted her chin, looking into her eyes. "Will it truly pain you to give up the child? Or are these tears for having failed to secure your place at Tremoral?"

She jerked her chin out of his hold. "What does this child matter to you? 'Tis no different from the dozen or more bastards you have doubtless scattered between here and England."

His brow lowered. "You know better than that, Juliana."

She opened her mouth to argue, but what he said was true. Never could she forget what she'd done to gain his seed.

"The child is mine," Gabriel said. "When 'tis born, I will be father to it."

"Then will your revenge be complete? Will you be satisfied?"

"I shall."

She stared at his hard-set face. There was no reaching Gabriel De Vere. No getting past that black heart of his. Still, something prompted her to try. "Do you know what pain is?" she asked softly.

His laughter was humorless. "I assure you, 'tis something with which I have a firm acquaintance."

Was it his treacherous mother to whom he referred—his loss of Wyverly? "Pain is living in fear of you these past months," Juliana continued. "Knowing you would return to take my child. Knowing you would hurt me. That is pain. Every moment of every day its vicious breath is at my neck."

A muscle in his jaw spasmed. " 'Tis pain you brought upon yourself."

"Did I?" She shook her head. "Like all men you prefer to think the worst of women than look beyond their perceived sins. Did you once consider that I might have had no choice in what I did?" No sooner did she speak than she wished she could snatch the words back. She had said more than she should have. But it mattered not. Gabriel heard only what he wanted to hear.

"What is it you wish to tell me?" he surprised her by saying.

It was as if some part of him longed to believe her innocent of wrongdoing. As if he had feelings for her, as Blase said. But as much as she yearned to defend herself, she could not. As long as Bernart held Alaiz, his secret was safe. "Naught," she said.

His hands fell to her shoulders. "If there is something you have to say, speak."

His touch was achingly familiar. "I cannot."

"Why?"

"I . . . cannot."

"You can."

She shook her head.

He stared at her, then pulled her against him. "Do you remember our last night together, Juliana?"

Though her body awakened to the feel of him, she put her hands to his chest and tried to push away. "Please, Gabriel, I should not be here."

"Do you remember?" Upon her upturned face, his breath quickened; against her breasts, his chest rose and fell; in the cradle of her thighs, his manhood stirred. Dear God, he did want her. Though he had denied it in the kitchens a sennight past, he wished to lay her back and have her as he'd had her all those months ago.

He lowered his head and lightly brushed his mouth across hers. "Do you remember this?"

She shuddered.

"I do," he said. "Every time I look at you, I remember the sweetness of your lips." Then his mouth covered hers.

She was drowning. Though she ought to struggle against these feelings, she was going under.

Gabriel lifted his head. "Then I remember your treachery."

She surfaced. Though it was loathing she expected to look upon, something else grooved his face. Pain? Regret? Could it be Blase was right? That he could not so easily take her child from her? "You do not hate me, do you, Gabriel?"

He released her, pushing a hand through his damp hair. "As God is my witness, I want to."

228

He looked so tortured, so different from the avenging man who'd brought her to Mergot. "But you do not hate me."

He swung away. "Go, Juliana. Go before I do something we shall both regret."

Nor did she hate him. The opposite, in fact. But those were emotions she dared not dwell on. She laid a beseeching hand to his arm. "Release me. Allow me to return to Tremoral."

He shook his head, stalked to the chest, and snatched up his tunic. "When you have birthed my child, then may you leave."

As he dragged the tunic over his head, Juliana stared. Though he might feel something for her, his revenge was more deeply felt. She turned.

"Juliana!"

She looked over her shoulder.

"Forget not what I have said about acting the lady of Mergot. 'Tis not your place."

Bitterness swept her. Very well, she would busy herself in ways that would further her own cause. She left the solar, closed herself in her chamber, and removed the dagger from her hose.

He should have allowed her to take her meals in her chamber—better, should have locked her in the tower and forgotten her for the next five months.

With a harsh sigh, Gabriel strode to the window and threw open the shutters. Rain lashed at his face, warning of the winter to come. A winter that would be made tenfold longer by Juliana's presence. Though he immersed himself in the affairs of the demesne and the repair of the wall, and would do so for as long as the weather permitted, eventually he would be spending more time in the hall with her. Then his desire—and that was all it was—would plague him more.

It was not supposed to have been this way. Her deceit should have sustained him well beyond five months. Instead his anger was slipping through his fingers and laying him open to what had nearly happened minutes ago.

He had not wanted to listen to anymore of her lies, yet had pressed for an explanation when she'd alluded to having had no choice in stealing a child from him. He had not wanted to touch her, yet had pulled her into his arms. He had not wanted to kiss her, yet had covered her mouth. He had not wanted to make love to her, yet had nearly done so. Though he had every reason to hate her and wanted to, he could not.

He slammed the shutters closed. *God's rood!* If only she would give him reason to send her to the tower.

Chapter Fifteen

October 1195

Were she caught, he would banish her to the tower.

Juliana eyed the mallet at the opposite end of the tool-strewn bench. Nay, the risk was too great. She would have to be content with the chisel alone.

Lissant drew alongside. "We ought to return to the donjon," she fretted as she'd done time and again this past half hour.

The maid had not wished to walk the inner bailey, had pressed for the gardens for fear of her lord's wrath when he returned from the hunt, but Gabriel's absence had been too great an opportunity for Juliana to yield. Though the porter had also protested, Juliana's reasoning that no ill could befall her while the workers broke to satisfy their hunger—and a smile—had worked him to her will. Of course, throughout the walk neither he nor the men-at-arms had let her from their sight. The commotion of the workers returning to their tasks had granted the only opportunity to take what she'd come for.

She clenched the chisel beneath her mantle. "Yes," she said, "I am suddenly quite tired."

Shortly, she closed the door of her chamber. With two hours of uninterrupted nap time ahead of her, she turned toward the room and swept the mantle from her shoulders. She crossed to the tapestry and stepped behind it. In the dimness, she fingered the chisel's hard, sharp edge.

It was nearly a month since she'd come to Mergot, and every day since she'd labored to gain entrance to the passageway. After the first week, which had been marked by numerous failures, she had determined to go around the lock by digging out the mortar and removing the block of stone into which it turned. Beneath cover of the din from work on the inner wall, the mortar gave, but not without effort and detriment to the various implements with which she worked upon it. And her hands. Though she wrapped her palms and fingers in linen each time she ventured behind the tapestry, they were callused, reddened, nicked. Were she not more mindful, Gabriel would catch sight of them. Of course, if he continued to pay her as little regard as he had these past weeks, she was safe. Though she sat beside him during meals, he rarely glanced her way, and few were the words he spoke to her. It was as if she were not even present.

Juliana sank to her knees alongside the rock she would use in place of a mallet, and the pouch she would fill with mortar dust and dispose of in the garden. She peered at the furrowed mortar. She'd removed as much as an inch deep on three sides of the stone, but it was yet many inches before the block came free. Now, however, she had a chisel. . . .

She set it to the furrow. God willing, the tool would see her gone from Mergot long before the babe was born.

"You enjoyed your walk?"

Juliana turned.

Gabriel was at the base of the stairs. Throughout the evening meal he had said naught of her venture outside the donjon, but she did not doubt he knew of it. Grateful for the dimly lit stairway, she clasped her hands beneath her swollen belly. "I did enjoy it. 'Twas a pleasant change from your garden of weeds."

He stared at her, then began his ascent. He halted a step below her. Even so, Juliana had to raise her gaze to meet his.

"What are you planning?" he asked.

She shook her head. " 'Twas only a walk. Why do you make more of it?"

"Because I know you, Juliana. You have been quiet too long, which can only mean you are scheming."

"Scheming? To escape you again?"

"Perhaps."

Her laughter was forced. "Not only have I given my word I will make no more attempts, but I am five months with child. You think I would—"

"Five?" Gabriel snapped up her blunder.

Struggling to hold her composure, she said, "Four is what I meant."

A smile curved his mouth. "Of course you did."

"It is late." She turned. "Good eve."

He pulled her back around. Though his grip was not cruel, it pained her. Those memories again.

"My men were foolish to allow you to leave the donjon," he said, "but I assure you they will not be so again."

What had he done to them? "They have been punished?"

"Not yet, but it will be seen to."

Should she plead for them? Would it do any good? "Do not forget, Gabriel, they are not to blame for their confusion over my place at Mergot, for you have made me a guest and a prisoner in the same breath. What are they to think?"

Anger flared his nostrils. "I care not what they think. I but require they follow my orders. And you will do the same, else forfeit the freedom I have allowed. Do you understand?"

How could she not? "Perfectly."

He released her.

Eager to distance herself, she turned and grasped the railing. On the third step up, a sharp kick landed to her side. She gasped and pressed a hand to her belly, but in the next instant pulled it away. She must not become too familiar with the babe lest she lose it to Gabriel.

Unfortunately her response did not escape him. "What is it?" he asked, gaining her side.

She looked up and found his anger supplanted by concern. "Naught," she said. Then, as if to make a liar of her, the babe thrust again, snagging her breath. But this time she withheld the instinct to put a hand to her belly.

"Tell me," Gabriel said sharply.

Though she wished him as far removed from her pregnancy as possible, she knew he would be satisfied with naught but the truth. " 'Tis only the babe."

His brow furrowed deeper. "Something is wrong?"

"Nay, he is simply making himself more comfortable."

Gabriel searched her face, then lowered his gaze to her belly.

In that moment, Juliana sensed he wished to put his

hand to her, to feel the evidence of his child, but that she could not bear. "I am tired," she said tightly. "Good eve." As quickly as her increasingly awkward figure allowed, she mounted the stairs and went from his sight.

Gabriel stared at his broad, tapered fingers, then curled them into a fist. He had nearly touched Juliana, had so badly wanted to put a hand to her that naught but her chill words could have prevented him from doing so. It was as if he truly wanted this child, though not for revenge. Did Juliana feel the same? In spite of her reasons for having conceived the child, did she feel anything for it? She did not rest a hand upon her belly as pregnant women were wont to do, did not curve an arm around it when she sat. In fact, this eve was the first time he had seen her touch herself there—and only for a moment. Could she be so cold? Or did she seek to suppress her feelings so that her impending loss would not be as deeply felt?

He closed his eyes. He shouldn't care. Even so, what he meant to do four months hence vexed a conscience he ought not to have. He looked to the stairs Juliana had ascended. Though he avoided her as much as possible and did his best to ignore her when they met, his traitorous emotions would not be put down. He felt for her, wanted to hold her again, wished things could be different. He was a fool. Silently, he cursed himself as he did more and more of late. If he was not careful, he would all the sooner find himself in hell.

Chapter Sixteen

England, December 1195

Safer this way, Alaiz told her groaning belly as she crept down the stairs. As hungry as she was from forgoing supper last eve, it was a small price to avoid Bernart and his terrible wrath. She paused on the bottom step and peered into the hall. There were only servants about.

She sighed. When would Bernart leave again? Soon, she hoped, though it was only two days since he'd returned from his latest search for Juliana. For the fourth time, he'd come back with empty hands. And angrier than ever.

Alaiz dragged her teeth across her bottom lip. Was Bernart mad, as it was whispered? Had his mind gone the way of everything else? Blessedly, she'd avoided that which his knights and servants could not escape. So completely, in fact, that it was as if he had forgotten her. Thus she left her chamber only to feed her hunger, and only when Bernart and his men were not present. Such as now.

She smoothed the tendrils that escaped her braid, squaring her shoulders. As she trod rushes grown putrid from her sister's absence, she fell under the servants' regard, but none approached her. It was hardly different from before Juliana had been stolen from Tremoral, with one exception: Nesta. As the wench had never hidden her contempt for Alaiz's infirmity, now that Juliana was gone, she'd become increasingly bold. She sought out Alaiz, spoke words meant to wound. And they did.

As Alaiz entered the corridor that led to the kitchens, she quickened her step.

"Ah, the elusive Lady Alaiz," a voice rasped near.

She swung around to face the one she'd blundered past.

Sir Randal Rievaulx stepped from the shadowed doorway of the storeroom. "I thought you might pass this way. Hungry?"

Of all of Bernart's men, she avoided him most. And her fear of him was now justified. Before he had accompanied Bernart on his most recent search, he'd pressed her into a corner and ran a hand up her breasts. Fortunately, the one scream she'd managed had brought an older knight to her aid.

She tensed for flight. "I am on my way to the . . . the . . ."

"Kitchens?" A smile bent his mouth as he slithered his gaze from her face to her breasts. "You look lovely, my lady. Of course, a bit unkempt." He cocked his head. "A pity your sister is not here to tend your grooming."

Half a dozen steps to the kitchens . . . She lunged—and fell two steps short of salvation.

Sir Randal caught her braid and wrenched her back against him. Before she could scream, he clapped a hand over her mouth. "Not this time," he said in a hiss.

She struggled as he pulled her backward, but he was too solid. He dragged her into the storeroom and kicked the door closed.

Fear coiled around Alaiz as she swept her gaze over the room, searching for something to aid her, but it was too dark. Though light from the lower level of the storeroom filtered up the stairway, it was not enough to make sense of the shadows.

"We are alone," Sir Randal said, mouth to her ear.

His moist breath made her spine quake, but she would not give in to him. She kicked a heel back and landed it to his shin.

"Bitch!" He wrenched her head to the side, gripped her face, and dug his nails into her flesh.

Alaiz cried into his hand, but the sound was too muffled for any to hear.

"Fight me and I will kill you," he rasped. He strained her neck further. "Do you understand?"

She did not want to die, but would she want to live when he was finished with her? *God, have mercy.*

"Do you understand?" At her nod, he removed his hand from her mouth, grasped her upper arm, and pulled her toward the stairs.

If she screamed, would any hear? Would any come to her aid? She suppressed a sob. Surely it was not hopeless.

As she began her descent, something pricked her memory. Desperate to unlock the door, she squeezed her eyes closed. And stumbled. If not for the knight's hold, she would have plunged to the bottom.

"I have warned you," he snapped, and hastened her down the remaining steps.

A single torch lit the lower storeroom, but it cast

enough light to show there was naught here that might aid her. Only casks and sacks of grain.

Sir Randal pulled her to the back of the room and drove her against a wall. "Be kind to me," he said, "and mayhap I shall be kind to you."

She scrabbled through her tangled mind for something to turn him from the heinous act. "Do not . . . do this." She spoke the only words to which she could lay her tongue.

He leaned into her, cupped a breast, and began kneading. "You will like it, I promise."

"I beseech you. . . ."

When his breath came upon hers, Alaiz jerked her head to the side. She could not bear his mouth upon hers.

He lowered his head and sank his teeth into the soft flesh between her neck and shoulder.

She cried out.

"Give in to me," he rumbled, and proceeded to nip and suck his way up her neck.

She shuddered when his tongue thrust into her ear, cringed when he groped her woman's place through her gown. Were not her belly empty, she would retch.

He began to drag her skirts up.

"Nay!" she cried, and thrust her hands to his chest.

He knocked them aside and struck her so hard across the face her head snapped back against the wall. Alaiz struggled between consciousness and that which would close her mind to ravishment, but as appealing as the latter was, she refused it.

"I'll warn you no more," he said, face contorted. "Yield or I shall kill you."

She raised her chin. "Kill me."

His brow lowered. "Then that I shall, my lady—after I finish with you." He yanked her from the wall.

She landed on her hands and knees. Blood thundering in her ears, she tried to rise.

He planted a booted foot to the middle of her back, sending her sprawling upon the dirt floor. "Patience," he murmured.

Alaiz glanced over her shoulder. He tugged at the ties of his braies. And in that moment, she remembered the dagger. Though each morn she donned it, it had become so much a part of her she'd forgotten the reason for carrying it. She reached, found the slit in the side of her gown, and closed her hand around the hilt. As she drew it forth, the thought struck her that it would be of no use in her present position.

Think! she ordered her cluttered mind. She saw again those knights on the tournament field who were beaten to the ground, heard their shouted surrender.

"I yield!" she cried. "Take me and be done with it."

A grunt of triumph issued from Sir Randal. He lifted his foot. "Remove your gown."

Slowly, she turned onto her back and looked up at where he stood with legs planted wide, unfastened braies visible beneath the hem of his tunic. *Not yet.* She curbed the desire to seize the dagger. She levered up.

"Be quick," he snapped.

She straightened, then took a step back. Making a pretense of reaching for her laces, she plunged her hand through the slit and captured the dagger. She swept it forward.

Astonishment flashed across the knight's face, followed by fury. He took a step toward her.

Alaiz shook her head. "Leave me be, else *I* shall kill *you*."

It gave him pause. "I believe you would," he murmured, "providing you had the skill and strength to match

240

a knight, *my lady*." He lunged, throwing his arm up to strike the dagger from her.

Guided by fleeting lucidity, Alaiz slashed the blade downward and caught his forearm.

He staggered, gaping at the blood seeping through his sleeve.

Alaiz wrenched free of her own disbelief and ran.

The devil followed.

She gripped the dagger with one hand, snatched up her skirts with the other, and took the steps two at a time. She'd spanned only half the stairs when he knocked her facedown.

"I shall kill you!" he bellowed where he spread upon her. He closed his hand around hers that held the dagger, pried a finger free and forced it back. It snapped.

Alaiz screamed and released the hilt.

He turned her and pressed the blade to her throat.

With gasping sobs, she tried to focus on him where he straddled her. Aye, he would kill her, but not before gaining what he'd come for.

Cool air swept Alaiz's legs as he lifted her skirts. Though she longed to resist, to do so would cause the blade to penetrate her throat. *Dear God, preserve me.*

A whisper of sound met her ears. Though she knew it was likely a rat, she rolled her eyes up—and stopped her breath at the blade's edge. Someone stood on the landing. But for what did they stand there? Surely they saw what Sir Randal did.

"Aye," he said softly.

Alaiz slid her gaze to him and saw that he lowered himself toward her. *Nay!* Uncaring whether the blade carved her neck, she brought her knee up and impacted with his groin.

He howled, clutched at himself, and collapsed atop her.

The dagger clattered to the step alongside Alaiz's head. With her throbbing hand, she closed three fingers and a thumb around it.

Spewing curses and saliva, Sir Randal also reached for it.

She slashed the air, straining left and right.

He jerked back and seized her flailing wrist. And lost his balance. He hit the stairs first, then Alaiz, over and over until they hit the bottom.

Pain bursting through her, she forced her lids to part. It was not the dirt floor beneath her, but Sir Randal, his eyes wide where he stared beyond her.

Why did he not move? As the question sank into her, she felt something at her breast. She put her hands to the dirt floor, and on trembling arms raised herself from the knight. The dagger was embedded in his chest, and all around it ran his life's blood.

Alaiz clapped a hand to her mouth and staggered to her feet. Trembling harder, she looked down her front. Her bodice was stained red. "Nay," she said under her breath.

The creak of the stairs spun her around.

"What have ye done, Lady Alaiz?"

Nesta.

"I . . . he . . ." Her mind was slipping away, jumbling, tossing.

Nesta descended the stairs, stepped past her, and bent beside the knight. "Ye have killed Sir Randal." She looked over her shoulder.

Alaiz shook her head. "I did not mean . . . It was a . . . You saw . . ."

Nesta straightened. "Murderer!"

Dear God! Alaiz looked from the wench to Sir Randal, back to the accusation that shone from hating eyes. With a sob, she grasped the railing and fled to her chamber.

She barred the door, then pressed herself against it and slid to the floor.

Cradling her injured hand to her chest, she stared at the room before her. Though Nesta had witnessed Sir Randal's assault and knew his death to have been an accident, she had named Alaiz a murderer. What if she were believed? What would Bernart do?

Alaiz buried her face in her hands. *I need you, Juliana.*

France

The stone moved.

Juliana gasped and lowered the rock she used in place of a mallet. Moments earlier, the chisel had worked freely in the furrowed mortar, but now it was wedged beneath the stone that had succumbed to her efforts.

She began to tremble. *Finally!* She slumped back onto her heels. The past three months of stealth, scraping, chipping, broken nails, and callused hands had not been for naught. Providing God did not now abandon her, within a fortnight she would be with her sister.

She pressed her linen-wrapped palms together. "Hear me, God; let no harm befall Alaiz before I return."

Knowing Lissant would soon come abovestairs to rouse her from her nap, she wiped her eyes on her dusty sleeve, then looked at the stone and touched it. *Patience.* She had come too far to risk being discovered. Tomorrow would be soon enough to work the stone free.

She quickly cleared the mortar dust and stowed it and the rock in her pouch. She eyed the chisel, deciding against attempting to free it. Wedged as it was, it could be used to pry the stone loose.

As she awkwardly gained her feet, she glanced at her protruding belly. In less than two months she would push forth Gabriel's child, but not here. Not at Mergot. Though the journey before her was daunting, she would make it back. Then Alaiz would be safe.

There was something different about Juliana: a glow that was not of the fire's heat, a light in eyes that had been dark these past months, and a nervousness that bespoke impatience.

Gabriel had first noticed it yestereve during supper. However, as with most things that had anything to do with her, he'd ignored it. It was better that way, though perhaps not in this instance.

He filled his tankard at the sideboard, took a swallow, and returned his gaze to where she sat before the hearth. The gown she altered to accommodate her increased girth lay untouched in her lap, while beside her Lissant plied her needle and chattered as if her mistress heard every word. Juliana did not. Her gaze was rooted across the hall, restless hands the only movement about her. She clasped and unclasped them, ground her palms together, plucked at her gown.

What was she thinking?

"Even with child, she is the most beautiful of women," Blase murmured as he halted alongside Gabriel.

Gabriel glanced sharply at his brother, resenting the familiar, contemplative look upon his face: lids narrowed, mouth pursed, head cocked. No doubt he wished to impart that holy wisdom he was expert at dispensing, but for which he, himself, had little regard.

" 'Tis increasingly difficult to believe she is capable of that which you accuse her," Blase continued.

"Because she has a lovely face?" Gabriel scoffed. "For as much time as you spend between a woman's thighs, still you have much to learn about the other sex, little brother."

Blase looked at him, arching an eyebrow. "Not so much as you have to learn about the heart and soul, big brother. From what I have observed these past months, Juliana is not one who easily deceives. In fact, there is something true about her."

True? If not that Blase's words struck jealousy in him, Gabriel would have laughed. Well he remembered the day three months past when he had come upon Juliana and his brother in the hall: Blase's laughter, Juliana's smile. For the hundredth time since, he questioned whether Blase had fallen victim to Juliana's beauty. He tensed. "Do you think yourself in love?"

Blase chuckled. "Do you?"

The question unsettled Gabriel. He, Gabriel De Vere, in love? With Juliana Kinthorpe? Impossible. He desired her, and that need would be quenched once he took a wench to bed. If not that he was occupied with the affairs of Mergot, he would have done so long ago. But he would do it—and soon. He shot his brother a thunderous look that should have withered him. It did not.

"As for me," Blase said, "do you forget, I am a priest. Hence I am forbidden such love. But 'tis not forbidden you, Gabriel."

Why did he tolerate such talk? Were it any other who spoke thus, he would quickly teach them their place. "Hatred is all I feel for her," Gabriel said, though he had long ago accepted it for a lie.

"Ah, but hatred and love entwine. What you hate deeply grows from having loved deeply."

"Is that what your Bible tells you?"

Blase shrugged. "If it does, I have not read it. But then, there is much I have not read in those exalted pages."

"No doubt." Gabriel quaffed the remainder of his ale and set his tankard atop the sideboard. "Be assured, brother, I want only the child Juliana carries."

"Do you? I am not blind, Gabriel. More, I know you as well as anyone can know you. Though you rarely glance her way, she is ever upon your thoughts. She sits at table and you speak not a word to her, but she might as well be on your lap for all the suffering you endure."

Gabriel clenched his hands into fists. "Were you not my brother, you would suffer for such foolish talk."

Blase smiled. "I am most fortunate."

Infuriating! "Even where you are concerned, there are limits to my patience. Thus I suggest you speak no more of this."

Blase nodded. "As you would have it."

Gabriel turned to go.

"I received a missive today."

Gabriel came back around. "From?"

"The bishop of Briarleigh. He has called me to England."

"And?"

"I leave on the morrow."

Gabriel frowned. "For what reason?"

Blase laughed. "The bishop is my master, Gabriel."

"Aye, yet rarely do you allow his summons to move you."

"True, but 'tis time I left Mergot."

"I have need of you here." Gabriel had come to depend upon him, especially as he, himself, was minimally learned in letters and numbers.

"You do not need me," Blase said. "Another can as easily keep your books. Perhaps Juliana."

"Juliana?"

"It would give her something to while away the hours."

246

Blase hoped to force them together. "Your scheme will not work, Blase."

He appeared unconcerned. "Even so, I leave on the morrow."

Was Juliana privy to his plan? Was this the reason for the change? He glanced across the hall. Her hand was on her belly, stroking it as he had not seen her do before, as if she were going to be a mother to the child. His chest tightened. Blase was a fool to believe she sought anything other than her release.

"You won't take the child from her," he said.

Wouldn't he? Gabriel turned his gaze to his brother, and found himself confronted with one he hardly recognized.

Blase looked older, his young face drawn with seriousness that, for once, matched his outspoken wisdom. "You will not," he affirmed. "You feel too much for her."

Gabriel had had enough. "Godspeed your journey," he said in a growl, and turned on his heel. It having been a long time since he'd found a good night's rest, he decided to seek his bed. Upon entering the solar, he dragged his clothes off, scooped them from the rushes, and threw open the chest at the foot of the bed. As he tossed the garments inside, something caught his eye. He reached for it, knowing what it was the moment he touched the fine weave. He drew it forth.

Juliana's chemise, the one she'd left behind on the second night she'd come to him. He rubbed the material between his fingers, stirred as he recalled it gliding over her silken flesh, the pleasure he had given and taken as if they were the truest of lovers. Far different from the first night, when he'd consumed too much drink. Though his memory of their initial joining was vague, he knew Juliana had not enjoyed it. In fact, more than once she'd reacted as if

247

he were hurting her. As if she were inexperienced in love-making. But that was not possible. As for the scant blood she'd left on his sheets, it had to have been her monthly flow.

He wadded the chemise, pushing it to the bottom of the chest, where Juliana's wedding ring and girdle lay atop a dozen or more unopened missives his father had sent him these past years. He dropped the lid, extinguished the torch, and climbed between the sheets. As chill as they were, they did naught to cool his loins. He groaned, turning onto his stomach to subdue his straining manhood. Blase was wrong. This was desire. Were he not so tired, he would send for a wench and take his relief.

An hour later, he awoke from a fitful sleep even more aware of his need for the woman who slept in the chamber beside his.

Juliana looked from the maid on her pallet to the flickering torch beside the door. Dared she risk it? Though she was not prepared to leave this night, she must know what lay beyond the tapestry—if, indeed, the passageway presented a means of escape. She had meant to venture into it this afternoon, and would have if the stone had not proved difficult to remove. By the time she worked it free, her two hours of nap time were nearly spent.

She drew her bottom lip between her teeth. If she explored the passageway this night, tomorrow afternoon could be spent surmounting any difficulties in her path. Of course, were she presented with another locked door, it could take months to get through, but she would not think about that.

Quietly, so as not to awaken Lissant—who luckily slept like the dead—she donned her mantle over her thin chemise and pushed her feet into slippers. Then she retrieved the torch and slipped behind the tapestry. Careful to keep the flame from catching the wall hanging, she put her hand to the door. Without so much as a squeak—owing to the hog fat she'd applied to the hinges—it opened inward. A cool draft lifted the hem of her mantle, breathed its chill upon her scantily clad limbs, and caused the torch flame to jump and glow more brightly. Shivering, she stepped through the doorway.

The torchlight illuminated narrow, rough-hewn walls, stairs that wended downward into darkness, silken threads of cobwebs upon cobwebs, and the glowing eyes of a rodent.

Juliana swallowed. It was a long time since the passageway had been used. However, as much as she dreaded her foray into its depths, especially considering her advanced pregnancy, she must brave it or resign herself to her fate. She pulled the hood of her mantle over her head, squared her shoulders, and eased the door closed behind her.

Supporting herself with a hand to the wall, she tested each step before putting her weight on it. The going was slow, but there was no way to hasten her journey without endangering herself and the babe. As she descended the winding stairway, she used the torch to sweep aside cobwebs, did her best to ignore the rodents that scurried left and right, and checked her progress each time her foot sent rubble skittering. Did any hear? Nay, the walls were too thick.

There were several twists and turns off the stairs, no doubt leading to other rooms in the donjon, but she was interested only in what lay at the bottom.

At last, she stepped onto level ground. In the dim light cast by her torch, the flame of which grew ever weaker, she peered at the shaft stretching before her. Where did it lead? To the gardens? To the rear of the donjon? Perhaps underground to an outlet beyond the castle walls? If the latter, her escape would be tenfold easier.

More quickly, she traversed the shaft. It ran straight for a time, turned right, spanned another straight course, turned again, and, at half the distance of the previous stretch, ended. A low door set in the wall drew her forward. She knelt beside it. No lock. All she needed to do was lift the bar and she'd be free of the donjon. She sighed. Though her hope of an underground passage was not to be realized, her prayers were answered. By this time tomorrow eve she would be gone from Mergot. Of course, she must make it past the walls, but it should be fairly easy. Villagers and workers came and went at the castle. Though scrutinized before allowed entrance, little attention was paid them upon departure. She would hide in her mantle and slip amongst a group of them.

Juliana pressed a hand to her belly, allowing herself a moment of the joy that she'd denied herself these past months. "Soon you will be safe, little one. Abide a bit longer."

As she straightened, something scampered over the back of the hand in which she held the torch. She cried out, jerking back. The creature took flight along with the torch. The latter struck the wall behind, fell to the dirt floor, sputtered, and rolled away. She scrambled after it, but had barely reclaimed it when its struggling flame lost the battle. With the glowing tip lighting little beyond her hands and face, she attempted to fan the flame back to life. To no avail.

She looked about her. It was as dark as pitch, not a sliver of light to return her to her chamber. But she knew the way. She knew the distance covered and the number of turns. Daunting as her return journey would be through this place of darkness, cobwebs, and creatures, she would make it.

The torch being of no more use to her, she left it. A hand to the wall, reaching the other out before her, she started back. Unfortunately, the sounds that she'd earlier done her best to ignore would no longer be quieted: scuttling, squeaks, the distant trickle of water, an intermittent creak and groan. And they grew louder as she neared the stairs.

Heart pounding, she reached a foot forward, found the first step, and put a palm on either side of the wall. A cobweb brushed her face. She shuddered and swatted it away, then began her climb.

Finally she reached the landing before her chamber. With a sigh, she stepped forward and searched a hand down the door. She pulled the handle. The door remained solid. She tried again. It was as if it were locked. It could not be. Unless . . .

She felt for the hole from which she'd removed the stone. The stone was in place, which could only mean this was not her chamber. She dropped her arms to her sides. She had turned wrong, but where? She'd kept to the stairs, had not taken any of the turns off of them just as when she'd first traversed them. Or perhaps she had.

Calm, she counseled. It was only a matter of returning to the bottom and beginning anew. Over the next hour, time and again she descended and ascended in search of her chamber, but the door she came before was always locked. And she was not certain it was the same one each time.

Once more at the bottom, she eased herself down upon the last step and huddled into her mantle. She was weary and cold, feet sore and palms grazed by the rough stone walls, and so very frustrated it would not take much for her to cry. She was not giving up, though. She just needed a moment to rest and think on how she was going to get out of here before the morn rose upon her empty bed.

What if she went through the barred door into the bailey? Nay. If she managed to slip past the guards, never would she make it into the hall unnoticed. She clasped her stiff hands before her face, breathing warmth upon them. Could there be other outlets into this passageway? She stilled. Though she did not recall passing any, that must be it. She had chosen the wrong one.

She stood, then turned right off the stairs and felt her hand over the wall. Naught. She must go back the way she had come. Shortly, her hand rounded a corner. It had to be the stairway she had numerous times searched. She continued on and, a few moments later, found the entrance to another.

"Pray, let this be the one." At that moment, wanting nothing more than her bed, she began her ascent. Shortly, she stepped onto the landing, found the handle, and pulled. With a soft click and a dissenting creak, the door yielded to the dark of her chamber.

Juliana hesitated, listening for Lissant's awakening. All was still.

She released her breath, stepped inside, and drew the door closed. It groaned softly on its hinges, but again she detected no movement in the chamber. She seated the door. Another faint click. And it was that which gave her pause.

The click . . . the creak . . . the groan . . . Due to the absence of the stone and her application of fat to the hinges, none of these sounds belonged. Meaning this was not her chamber. She'd been too tired and relieved to come upon an unlocked door to make certain it was hers. She squeezed her eyes closed and leaned back against the wall.

Where was she? The chapel, she hoped. Or could this be Gabriel's chamber? Nay, God would not be so cruel. Would He?

A moment later, the tapestry was swept aside and rough hands descended to her shoulders. As she had learned from her nights with Gabriel, he slept too lightly to allow any to sneak up on him. All was lost.

Chapter Seventeen

"Damn it, Juliana! You gave me your word." He dragged her into the solar and pushed her down onto his bed. "Do your lies know no bounds? Your deceit?"

She looked up at the dark figure alongside the bed. Although she could not discern the anger upon Gabriel's face, the cooling brazier cast a red glow around him, showed him to be unclothed. Though it was not unusual for a person to disrobe for bed, his nudity unnerved her.

He stood over her a moment longer, then reached to the bedpost and retrieved his robe. "Do not move." He turned and stalked from the solar. Shortly, she heard the door of her chamber slam against the inner wall, followed by Lissant's cry of surprise.

Juliana sat up. She knew what he sought, knew he would find it, but no longer cared. The damage was done and now he would banish her to the tower to remain until the babe was born. Alone. But it was for the best, really.

He reappeared a short while later, a torch in one hand, the tools of her escape in the other. His seething anger made visible, he shoved the torch into a wall sconce, strode to the bed, and dropped the chisel and pouch of debris beside her. "You have been most busy."

She held his cutting gaze. " 'Tis not as if I had anything else with which to occupy myself."

Jaw hardening further, he grabbed her hands, turned them palms up, and stared at the calluses she'd kept hidden. "For all your guile, you are a fool woman," he pronounced, and released her.

Juliana lifted her chin. "But one who nearly bested the mighty Gabriel De Vere."

His lids narrowed. "Nearly does not win the battle, Juliana. Either you are the victor or the vanquished. As you are the latter, there is naught of which to be proud."

True. Her mistake would cost her not only her child, but Alaiz's safety. She lowered her feet to the floor. "If I am not mistaken, the tower awaits me."

"It does." He motioned her to precede him from the solar.

She walked ahead of him down the corridor. As she neared her chamber, she saw that Lissant stood in the doorway, her pretty face drawn with worry and hurt. Gabriel was not the only one deceived. Juliana turned her gaze forward, descended the stairs, and entered the hall. Though it was yet night, most of the occupants had awakened, no doubt roused by the commotion abovestairs. They stared at Juliana as she passed through the hall, as did the men-at-arms when she stepped outside.

Gabriel took her arm and led her down the darkened steps, across the inner bailey, and over the drawbridge. Their destination proved the eastern tower of the outer bailey.

At their approach, a man-at-arms hurried forward. "My lord?"

"Henceforth, Lady Isolde resides in the tower," Gabriel said.

"Yes, my lord." He turned and led them inside.

Before she stepped over the threshold, Juliana stole a glance at the night sky. A thousand stars blinked at her, and the quarter moon slanted a grin. Two months ere she would be allowed out-of-doors again.

Gabriel ushered her inside. The first floor was a guard's station, but she was allowed only a glimpse of it ere she met the stairs. They spiraled upward, landings at each floor, but only when there were no more stairs to be trodden did her journey end. The man-at-arms set his torch in a sconce, then fit a key in the lock of the thick-planked door. He pushed the door inward.

Gabriel drew Juliana forward. "Lady Isolde will require a brazier, fresh blankets, towels, and a basin of water."

The man inclined his head. "My lord."

Gabriel retrieved the torch and pulled Juliana into the room.

As empty as she felt, she was not beneath noticing her surroundings. Though it was obviously some time since the room had last been utilized, it was the sort of prison reserved for captives of high rank—large, furnished, boasting three shuttered windows. Of course, the latter were no doubt barred. Nay, Gabriel did not hate her. If he did, he could more easily make her remaining days miserable.

He released her. "Your prison," he said. "Until the child is born, it is all you shall know. No companionship will you be afforded."

Juliana crossed to the narrow bed and trailed fingers over the mattress. It was not without its lumps. Still, it would be more comfortable than the pallet she'd thought awaited her. She crossed to one of the windows and drew the shutters open. Barred.

The chill night air caressed her face, whispered of the snows of winter that would not be long in coming. Would she have made it across the channel before the weather turned? Or been stranded in France?

"Why, Juliana?"

She closed the shutters and turned.

Gabriel stood inside the door. Though his face was grim, there was something else there, something not unlike what she'd seen on Lissant's face. As though he were wounded.

"Why?" he asked again.

She walked to the bed and lowered herself to the mattress. "I am surprised you would ask."

"I need none to tell me of your reason for wishing to return to Tremoral. What I question is why you risk our child to do so."

Our child. As these past months he'd referred to it only as his child, it surprised her. Still, he would take the babe from her.

He strode forward and came to stand over her. "Curse it, Juliana! Not only is it winter, but you are less than two months from birthing. Are you truly so selfish?"

Should she attempt to explain? Would it make any difference? Not likely, but she was weary of his believing ill of her. "You think I do not want this child? Though I try to forget it swells within me, hardly allow myself to touch it, the thought of you taking it from me is a blade to my heart. I want to be a mother to it, but not for the reason you believe. Not that I might remain the lady of Tremoral."

What was he thinking? "Had I escaped, I would have

returned to Tremoral, but only that I might deliver my sister to safety. 'Twas for Alaiz I labored three months on my knees, cut and scraped and hardened my hands." She laid beseeching fingers to his sleeve. "She cannot protect herself. She needs me."

He glanced at her hand upon him. "So long as she is under Bernart's roof, she will be safe."

"But Bernart hates her. Never would he have allowed her to live at Tremoral had I not pleaded and threatened—" She caught back the words. She could not tell him of Bernart's emasculation. It was all the protection afforded Alaiz.

"What did you threaten, Juliana?"

She lowered her gaze and shook her head.

He was quiet a long moment, then knelt before her.

She met his gaze, saw in his eyes an urgency she'd not seen before.

"Tell me," he said. "Give me reason to believe you, reason not to take this child from you."

Had she heard right? Did she tell him the truth, would he turn from his vengeful quest?

"Trust me," he urged.

She wanted to. Longed to seek comfort in his arms. But Alaiz would suffer for it. Juliana laid a hand to Gabriel's unshaven jaw. "Forgive me. Though I long to trust you, I cannot."

The urgency emptied from his eyes. "Then naught changes. I shall have your clothing delivered to you." He straightened and strode to the door.

Juliana watched him go. If only she could tell him. If it were not that Bernart held Alaiz, she would, and Bernart's secret be damned! A thought struck her then, a way to right the wrong. "Gabriel!"

He halted. It was a long moment before he turned.

"Bring my sister to me and I will tell all. I swear it."

He appeared unmoved. "Two more months and you may return to your beloved Alaiz."

"Gabriel—"

"Sleep well." He stepped onto the landing, closed the door, and turned the key.

Juliana listened to his receding footsteps, then lay back upon the mattress and squeezed her eyes closed. With a muffled sob, she turned onto her side and curved an arm around her belly.

Just as she could no longer deny her feelings for the life that grew within, no more could she deny that which she felt for Gabriel. She loved him, even when he affected to possess no feelings. Could it be he loved her as well? Was that the reason he sought the truth denied him? Though it was folly to entertain the idea, she longed to believe it.

Another sob escaped. She scooted farther up the bed, buried her face in a musty pillow, and loosed her weary emotions.

Although Blase surely knew what had transpired the night past, he said naught of it when he sat beside Gabriel at the morning meal. Even when they stood alone outside the stables an hour later, he maintained a silence so outspoken it was all Gabriel could do not to choke it from his throat.

"Will you return?" he asked tightly.

Blase looked up from cinching his saddle. "Perhaps."

Gabriel knew he ought to bid his brother farewell and get on with the day, but could not. "You think I am wrong."

"I do."

"After what happened last eve—what she has aspired

to these past months—still you think her one who does not easily deceive?"

Blase finished with his saddle and met Gabriel's gaze. "Nay, not easily, but in some things we have no choice. You see, Juliana does not know as I do that when the babe is born you will be unable to take it from her."

Would he not? Blade did not know him.

"Thus," he continued, "she but tried to preserve her motherhood."

As indicated on the night past, but there was more to it. There was Alaiz and the threat Juliana had made to Bernart did he not allow her sister at Tremoral. What?

"Do you continue to put our mother's sins upon her," Blase said, "you will lose her."

As if he had her. Gabriel clenched his hands. She was another man's wife.

"Think on it," Blase said. He grabbed the pommel, put a foot in the stirrup, and swung atop his horse. " 'Tis past time I began my journey."

As Gabriel stared up at Blase, he fought an internal battle. And lost. "You will be passing by Tremoral on your way to Briarleigh?"

"Of course."

"Providing it does not place you in danger, I would ask that you inquire at the villages for tidings of Lady Alaiz."

"For what reason?"

Though Gabriel hated admitting it, there was only the truth. "Juliana fears for her sister. 'Twas the reason she gave for attempting to escape."

Blase nodded. "I will send word, but what will you do with it?"

What would he do with it? Arrange to take Alaiz as he'd taken Juliana? Bring her to Mergot as Juliana asked?

Cursing himself for allowing Juliana to dictate his actions, he said, "I have not decided."

"Then do." Blase took up the reins and urged his mount around. "Farewell, brother."

Gabriel raised his hand. "Godspeed." As he watched Blase pass beneath the portcullis, he was washed with regret. He would miss his brother, even his unsolicited wisdom. He glanced at the prison tower. What would it be like when he sent Juliana away? He snatched the question back. As angry as he was, Blase was right. He did not want her to go. Hence, it was not when he would send her away, but rather when Bernart would come to claim her. And he would come. Though Gabriel was careful to keep Juliana's identity hidden, someone would recognize her—be it six months from now or six years.

He growled low in his throat. His plans to claim his child were folding, and all because of emotions he should never have allowed himself. *Damn it all!*

As he stared at the tower, he caught a movement in the uppermost window that overlooked the wall walk and gatehouse. It was Juliana. Had she seen Blase's departure? Likely. What she could not know was that his destination was other than one of Mergot's villages. Her champion was gone.

For a moment, Gabriel entertained releasing her, but only for a moment. Juliana was safer in the tower, where she'd be unable to make mischief that might endanger her or the babe. Too, Gabriel needed time to sort through his feelings and plan for the future, and that was too difficult to do with her present.

He turned on his heel, strode the outer bailey, and crossed the inner bridge that took him from Juliana's sight.

Chapter Eighteen

England, January 1196

Blase had but to listen to gain word of Lady Alaiz. His priest's robes exchanged for nondescript garments that none might recognize him from four months past, his mount tethered in the wood, he stood back as the village buzzed with news. Thus he learned of Sir Randal Rievaulx's death at Lady Alaiz's hands a fortnight gone, and of her escape from Tremoral that had been discovered this morn when she was to have been brought before the sheriff.

Clever girl. None had believed her capable of such. It made him smile. Though he did not condone murder, neither was he of the villagers' belief that the knight's death had come of a mad frenzy. True, he knew Lady Alaiz only from having helped Gabriel steal Juliana from Tremoral, but her behavior had not been that of one who was mad. Her head injury made her slow, that was all, meaning something had provoked the attack upon Sir Randal. He would not be surprised if she'd acted only to defend herself. Still, she'd be tried for murder and sentenced to death were she caught. If possible, he would see she was not.

Blase grimaced at the sight of his breath upon the air and pulled his mantle more closely around him. He hated winter. With a grumble, he pushed off the trough against which he'd leaned this past half hour. Ah, the things he did for Gabriel . . .

As he started for the wood, a hand fell upon his sleeve. He turned to a young woman whose loveliness was marred by a flush of angry red upon her right cheek and alongside her eye.

She tried to smile, but it was a false attempt in spite of the sweet bow it made of her mouth.

Who'd struck her? For what? Wrath coiled Blase's innards. "Aye?"

Her throat bobbed. "You would like me to . . . pleasure you?"

It took much control not to reveal his surprise. Naught subtle about her offer, but neither brazen. Someone had sent her to him with threat of more than a backhand.

A thousand nettles settling his back, Blase glanced beyond the golden-haired woman to the villagers. None looked to pay him and the woman any heed. Someone in the wood, then? Kinthorpe?

Beneath his mantle, Blase drew a hand up his scabbard and pressed the heel of his palm to his sword hilt.

"You would like?" the woman pressed, her gaze wavering in her fear.

Nay, it made no sense that Kinthorpe would send her to draw him out of the village. Like lightning to the ground, the lord of Tremoral and his men would ride upon the enemy wherever they found him. More likely it was one who thought to relieve him of his purse.

He slipped a smile for any who watched. "Aye, I would like. Where?"

Her beautiful eyes said she'd hoped he would decline. "The wood?"

Where he would be set upon. It would not be the first time he had dealt a swift blow to one who thought to take from him. Of course, there might be more than one. As the fire of combat was too often denied him, it would be a nice diversion. Too, it would warm him for the chill ride ahead.

"Aye, the wood." He laid a hand to her arm, turned, and drew her forward.

As her feet dragged, and since some degree of groping would be expected, Blase pulled her against his side and turned a familiar arm around her small waist. She tensed further.

"Where in the wood?" he asked low.

She glanced at him and choked, "Wherever thee would like."

"Nay, where waits the one who sent you?"

She stumbled and swept her fluttering gaze to him. "I-I do not know what—"

"Aye, you do." He tightened his arm around her, urging her on. "Now tell where he is."

Her eyes teared. "I did not wish to do it. Truly, I would not have had he—"

"I know." With the wood before them, he could not afford a lengthy explanation. "Where is he?"

Doing her best to hold his stride, she shook her head. "I do not know. I was but to approach you did you make to leave the village."

Alarm daggered Blase's spine. Not a thief, but Kinthorpe. Someone had recognized him as the priest come to Tremoral the night Juliana was taken and had gone for his lord. That realization tamped Blase's lust for swordplay. It would not be one on one, or one on two or three. More, did Bernart recognize him as the beardless youth he'd last laid eyes to eight years past, he would know it was Gabriel who held Juliana. It was time to leave Kinthorpe lands.

"He was astride?" Blase asked, hoping for a measure of how long he had until Kinthorpe descended.

"Aye."

"How long since he rode?"

"Mayhap a half hour. Mayhap more."

"I thank you." He halted inside the tree line, then loosed her. "You have done as you were bidden; now go." He would not have harm done her.

Her eyebrows gathered, and her mouth curved downward. "I am sorry. Pray, forgive me."

He nodded. "Go."

She ran. As did Blase.

Damnation! He ought not to have left his horse so deep in the wood. Of course, had he not it mightn't be waiting for him when he reached the ravine. As he chased a path through the wood, he kicked up mildewed leaves, vaulted fallen trees, ducked barren branches. Soon he would be mounted and away from here.

But another had other plans. At the sound of approaching horses, Blase glanced over his shoulder and expelled a curse. He was sighted. Naught to do but stand and fight those who outnumbered him a dozen to one.

He thrust his mantle back, reached for his sword, and spun around.

Then came a huff of air, followed by ripping, tearing,

burning. Fingers spasming around his sword, he was slammed hard against a tree trunk, grunting as the back of his head struck bark. Past constricted lids, he picked out those who approached at a more leisurely pace than moments earlier. And at their head was the bloated figure of a man who had to be Bernart Kinthorpe, though he no more resembled his former self than ugly did beautiful.

Blase tried again to pull his sword, but his hand refused to obey. He dropped his chin, and followed the hilt to his twitching fingers.

What had been done to him? His every breath loud in his ears, he looked to the bloody mess of his upper arm, then to his shoulder, from which an arrow protruded.

Heavenly Father! He was staked, his body pinned to the tree by that shot from a bow.

"Where is she?" demanded one whose voice bordered on a pitch nearer a woman's.

Strangely aware of the thud of his heart, Blase looked up to find Kinthorpe before him, his horse turned sideways. "Who speak you of?" Blase taunted the one responsible for crippling his sword arm. But it would not end at his arm—he saw it in the bastard's eyes a moment before he shifted his flab out of the saddle and clumsily made the ground.

" 'Tis my wife I speak of!" Kinthorpe spat as he took three labored strides to cover what Blase could in less than two.

Blase dropped his aching head back, giving Kinthorpe his full gaze. "A wife ought to be in her husband's bed. Have you looked there?"

Red burst upon the man's face. He growled, bared his teeth, and drew an arm back, but then came recognition. Veined eyes emerged from flaccid lids, and his lower jaw parted from the upper. "Blase De Vere," he said softly.

"Your brother's face I would know even had you and I never met."

Not even when Blase's father had set him aside, as he'd done Gabriel, had Blase regretted the resemblance. But then, never before had it boded such ill. Given another moment, Kinthorpe would realize who'd taken Juliana.

As if struck, the man stumbled back, eyes jerking, head bobbing. Then he went still, and remained so until he threw his head back and howled.

Blase looked beyond the pitiful figure to Kinthorpe's men. They stared at their lord with tangible unease. Though they could not possibly serve him with pride, they were his men and would not utter word against their lord did he gut his prey. He must save himself.

He reached up, snapped the feathered shaft where it entered his flesh, and wrenched forward. He came free, but not without such excruciating pain that his legs fell away. He landed hard on his knees and forced his uninjured arm to retrieve his sword. Awkwardly, he pulled it forth and swept it before him, but his vision wavered . . . receded. *God in heaven!* He would not lose consciousness. Would not!

The voices of Kinthorpe and his men indistinct, Blase drew a deep breath and began to see light. Unfortunately, not until the booted foot came at his face did he see it. It smashed his nose, knocked him backward, then slammed into his ribs and once more turned him to pained darkness. Still, he held to his sword, but the boot came down on his wrist, preventing him from raising it again.

"Pity"—Kinthorpe's voice fouled the air—"there appears to be naught for you but death, young De Vere."

Mouth pooled with blood running from his broken nose, Blase spat it out and clutched at the narrow ledge of consciousness onto which he must pull himself.

"Aye, death," Kinthorpe murmured, so near it was evident he'd dropped to his haunches. Still, his considerable weight paralyzed Blase's left arm, tested the strength of the bones and his resolve to not cry his pain. " 'Twould not do for you to send warning to your coward of a brother that I come to take back that which belongs to me."

Blase brought the man's fleshy face into focus. " 'Tis you who are the coward, Kinthorpe. As for Lady Juliana, she does not belong to you."

A tic started between Kinthorpe's mouth and nose. "Think you she belongs to Gabriel? She does not—nor the child she carries."

His mention of the babe could only mean he doubted it was of his loins. However, as much as Blase longed to put forth Gabriel's claim to the child, it was not for him to do. And it would only add to the threat Blase's capture put upon Gabriel.

Kinthorpe pounded a fist to his chest. "They belong to me!"

What had happened to Gabriel's friend to turn him into a man of childlike desperation? A man who would kill without cause? Blase tried to feel the fingers of his injured arm that he might command them to the dagger at his belt, but it was as if they were his no more. *Dear God, have mercy.*

Kinthorpe seized the sword from Blase's grip and heaved himself to his feet. "By thy own sword, then!" Face contorted, he put both hands to the hilt, raised the sword high over Blase's heart, and plunged.

Blase lunged opposite, but rather than his chest, the blade burned a hole through his side. He bellowed. The sounds around him dimming with the light, Kinthorpe's triumphant grunt like the buzz of an insect at his ear, he sank his gaze to the wood. It was imagined, he knew, but a moment ere he went into darkness he caught a glimpse of one with golden hair, wide, frightened eyes, and a bowed mouth. Blood thundering in his ears, his last thought was that his heart had been spared. Then his mind emptied.

Perspiration dripping into his eyes, Bernart stared at the still figure of Gabriel's brother. Death was his due. As it would be Gabriel's.

He stepped back and stared at his unsightly, bloated hands. They quaked. Rarely had he felt so cold an anger; more rarely had he directed it at himself. In fact, the last time had been at Acre, when he had watched those who'd followed him fall to the infidel's sword. But he had absolved himself of that, put it upon Gabriel, where it belonged. This, however, was different. Though for nearly four months he'd denied his own knowledge into believing it to be other than Gabriel who had stolen Juliana, in the depths of himself he had known. It was fear that had held him from examining his accursed enemy too closely. In everything, Gabriel prevailed. He was what Bernart could never be, had what Bernart could never have—Juliana.

Jealousy tightened his chest. Aye, he'd wanted a son, but Juliana had not done it for him. It was for her imbecile sister she'd broken her marital vows. That knowledge had pained him deeply, and he knew deeper pain when he again put a question to himself that begat others: Had Juliana lied? Told Gabriel of the plan to steal a son from him, plotted with him to take her from Tremoral? If so, what of Alaiz? Had Gabriel refused to take her and Juliana allowed it as she would never have allowed Bernart, placing Gabriel not only above her husband but her sister?

269

Bernart squeezed his hands closed, then splayed them. Nay, he would not believe it! Juliana had been stolen. As long as she believed he held Alaiz his secret was safe. And none would tell her different. He looked to Blase De Vere. Dead? If not, then soon.

He turned away. It was time to prepare for the journey to France.

"Pray, help me. I cannot do it alone." The woman's voice dragged Blase from the comfort of senselessness as it had done when he lay on the floor of the wood—how long ago? He slit an eye and looked to where she struggled beneath his arm over her shoulder. When he had lain at Bernart's feet, he had thought it mere imagining that he'd seen the village woman who'd offered herself to him. For some reason, she had risked her life to come to his aid.

Determinedly, he commanded his legs to take some of the weight from her. It was not much, but mayhap enough to see them to his mount.

"We are nearly there," she huffed.

The ravine. With effort, he opened his other eye and moved his gaze from side to side. "There," he croaked, catching sight of the horse.

"I see him."

Though he longed to close his eyes, he looked to his right shoulder, then his left side, from which the woman had drawn the sword. Too much blood. Only God's miracle would see him to the nearest abbey and heal him. And surely the Almighty was too busy for one so unworthy. But if He would only abide this undeserving life a bit longer, mayhap warning could be sent to Gabriel. God help him. . . .

Chapter Nineteen

France

As it would likely be all the time she had with her child, no more did Juliana squander. She touched her belly as she'd rarely allowed herself, curved an arm around it when she lay down, sang to it, loved the child within. Though the past three weeks had been spent in solitude, excepting brief visits by the guard who brought her food, drink, and coal for the brazier, it was only solitude in that she could not set eyes to the one who shared her quiet. He turned, flopped, stretched such that she could put a hand to his little foot until he pulled it back. Instinct told her the babe was a boy, that Gabriel's seed would bring forth a child who would one day stand as tall and wide as his father, whose eyes would be the same startling gray.

She caught her breath at the vision and shook her head to dispel Gabriel. It hurt too much to love a man who hated her so deeply. From his voice that carried to the tower, she knew he came often to the outer bailey to oversee work on the inner wall. At such times, she closed the shutters, sang more loudly to her little one, more vigorously applied needle to the disassembled bliaut from which she'd fashioned four garments to keep the winter and spring chill from the babe. So tiny were they, but the delight a mother ought to feel in handling them was not hers. Thus, she put them to the bottom of the chest.

She sighed, fingering the embroidery around the neck of the fifth garment. It was almost finished, but as with each time she neared completion of one of the tiny garments, she was loath to place the final stitches.

She pushed her awkward bulk off the bench, crossed to the chest, and raised the lid. She set the scissors aside and folded the tiny garment.

The scrape of metal on metal brought her head around. She frowned at the door. Supper already? Had time passed so quickly? Not that she wished it to, for the more it dragged the longer she had with her child.

She drew a deep breath, returned her attention to the chest, and lifted a blanket from atop the four tiny garments. Though all were of the same material, each was of a different cut. Her son would look handsome in green.

Behind, the door opened and the guard stepped within, but she ignored him. She and the man rarely spoke, the last time being a fortnight past when she'd entreated him to seek out Lissant to obtain her sewing implements. Grudgingly, he'd done so. Whether Gabriel had given his consent, she had not asked.

As she bent to place the fifth garment, she realized it was too quiet, no movement about the room as when a tray was brought her. She looked over her shoulder.

Gabriel. Head and shoulders barring the doorway, he stared at her.

Juliana could not prevent her start. Forgetting the reward of subtlety, she dropped the baby's garment atop the others, thrust the blanket over them, slammed the lid, and spun around.

Suspicion narrowed Gabriel's lids.

Lord, what fool was she? She clasped her hands beneath her belly. It was a mistake, for it emphasized the swell and drew his gaze. She crossed her arms over her chest. "For what do you come to my prison, Lord De Vere?"

He lingered upon the evidence of her advancing pregnancy, then stepped inside and closed the door. "What plan you now, Juliana?"

Unable to bear what would be revealed did he look upon the tiny garments, she shook her head. "Naught. What is it you wish?"

He crossed the room, then halted before her. "I wish to see what you hide."

It hurt to look upon him. "I hide naught." She lowered her gaze. "You surprised me, is all. I thought 'twas the guard who came."

Gabriel's hands settled onto her shoulders, his firm touch causing her to ache for those nights so long ago. If only the man who had come to her in the garden at Tremoral and told her he'd not easily surrendered his friendship with Bernart would show himself again. If she could tell him what Bernart demanded of her . . .

"Then you are resolved to it?" he asked.

She floundered before making sense of what he asked. She tilted her head back and drew a deep breath. "How can one be resolved to losing one's child?"

A muscle jerked at his right eye. "I could almost believe you, and I am more the fool for it, but you will forget this child as easily as you did your marriage vows."

She looked to her belly between them, trying to hold back her emotions. She could not. "I did not forget my marriage vows. That is where you err, Gabriel."

Silence, deep and moving.

"Then put me right, Juliana."

The strain in his voice returned her gaze to his. "If I could, do you not think I would?"

The softening swept from his face. "As you would have it." His hands tightened on her shoulders, then set her back from the chest. "I will see what deception you work."

As much as she longed to fling herself upon the chest, to keep hidden that within, she turned and crossed to the barred window. If not now, Gabriel would know when he sent her away.

She heard the creak of the lid and winced.

"Scissors, Juliana? What do you with such?"

Then he had not consented to their being provided her. She fixed her gaze upon the inner wall and the workers there. Soon the repairs would be complete.

Gabriel rustled the contents of the chest, but he would find naught for her to escape him. Only pieces of her heart.

Silence.

She tensed, waiting—though for what she could not say.

When he moved behind her, she stopped her breath. When he turned her to him, she shuddered.

"Why?" he asked.

She averted her gaze. "He—he comes into this world unclothed." Lord, how feeble, but she could not think clear with him so near. "Surely he ought to have—"

"Do you love this child?"

Aye. And his father. She braved Gabriel's gaze. "Knowing you would take him from me, I have tried to not love him"—she pressed a hand to her belly—"but he is all that is mine. Though you . . . take him, he will always be a part of me."

Emotion slipped past the armor in which Gabriel clothed it. He squeezed his eyes closed.

Try though Juliana did to not feel his pain, she reached up and laid hands to either side of his face. "Pray, forgive me for what I did. Never did I intend you harm."

His lids lifted. Were those tears? As he stared into her, his pupils slowly spread, turned gray to black. Too late, she realized she should not have touched him so.

She stepped back, but he caught her to him. Undeterred by her belly between them, he lowered his head.

Juliana gasped. "Pray, Gabriel, this is not—"

"Aye, 'tis." His eyes traveled downward and fastened on her mouth.

"Nay, you do not want—"

"I do." He leaned forward and opened his mouth onto hers.

She pressed hands to his chest to push him away, but the familiarity beneath her palms poured memory through her, brought longing to the surface, roused a sigh that parted her lips and let him in. *Oh, Mother Mary.* She ought not to allow this . . . ought to pull away . . . ought . . .

He thrust his tongue against hers, causing response to quiver the place between her thighs.

. . . ought to run . . . ought . . .

He curved a hand beneath her tender breast, and with his thumb brushed sweet ache to her nipple.

. . . ought to hide . . . ought . . .

He slid his mouth from hers, licked and nipped down her neck, lapped the base of her throat. "Touch me, Juliana." His voice filled her. "Let me know you again."

. . . ought . . . ought . . . ought . . . She gasped into him, slid her hands up over his shoulders and into his hair. She was utterly lost. Only he could help her find her way out.

When he lifted her, she did not protest. When he laid her upon the bed, she reached to him. When he dragged his braies down, his man's root sprang forth.

Her ache trebled. To feel him again, to be one with him . . .

He pulled her skirts up around her hips, stopping at the sight of the swell that surely reminded him of the last time they had come together. But it did not turn him from her. Gently he parted her thighs, knelt between them, and put his hand to her. Finding the sensitive bud, he began drawing circles over it.

Melting warmth hurdled through her. She wanted this. Wanted to hold this moment to her always. She closed her eyes and began to move her hips to his touch.

"Aye," he said, and slid a finger into her heat.

With a small cry, she arched, willing him inside.

His hand came away, and his hard length pressed against her woman's place, but then he stilled. "You would have me stop?" His voice was weighted. "Ask it and I shall."

Could he? She looked up at where he bent over her belly, met eyes of black. Though she knew she ought to preserve what was left of her, she shook her head. She needed to feel him inside her, to move with him, to don wings.

"I shall not ask it," she said softly. "Come unto me, Gabriel."

He stared at her, then levered up.

Ah, nay! It was his revenge upon her. She closed her eyes and sank her teeth into her bottom lip to prevent pain from issuing from her mouth.

Large hands turned her onto her side, but ere she could question what Gabriel did, his warm body came against her back, his hands to her hips, his straining warmth between her thighs.

Then he did not mean to leave her? Was it possible to make love in such a manner?

He entered, sank deep, and remained so until she thought she might scream with want; then he began to stroke.

Juliana felt awkward, unsure how to move—until she let instinct guide her to another shade of heaven. Moving with Gabriel—faster, deeper—seeking that which he sought, she reveled in the sensations spinning through her. Her arousal more intense than the last time their bodies had met, she suddenly found herself lifted to that place unlike any on earth.

Her cry split the room, but was muted by Gabriel's shout. Their joint convulsing quaked the bed, easing them deeper into the mattress. When all was still, their hearts kept time one with the other.

It was as if they were lovers, as if they might now kiss, might whisper sweet words, might fall asleep entwined. If only it could be.

Juliana opened her eyes and looked to the windows. How she wished the world outside would disappear, that she and Gabriel could remain untouched forever. Trying not to hurt any deeper for what five weeks would make of her, she sighed in concert with the babe's turning.

Gabriel must have felt it, for he tensed. A moment later, Juliana took the tension from him when his hand followed the movement to the other side of her belly.

"He is strong," he murmured, leaving his arm curved around her, though all grew still.

She nodded. What she longed to say was that the babe was as his father. But she didn't dare—not so long as Bernart held Alaiz. If only Gabriel would bring her sister out of Tremoral . . .

She sighed. How long until Gabriel realized the error of what he—they—had done? How long until his accusations claimed more of her heart? *Please, God,* she silently entreated, *let this last a while longer.* Though it was not likely the Almighty would agree to so sinful a request, Gabriel's breathing turned deep. Fatigue urged her to find rest as well, but she denied it, sensing that when Gabriel awakened all would be as before they had lain together.

Over the next several hours, shadows crept the walls, gathered night about the unlit room, turned it to pitch. Unwaveringly conscious of the man at her back, Juliana held herself awake until she could no longer keep her eyes open. Before she surrendered to sleep, she sent up one last prayer that the new day would not find Gabriel gone from her.

Dawn brought with it the unkind reality of what he had done. His body unto Juliana's had changed naught, only proven that, in spite of the reason she'd first come to his bed, she longed for their mating as much as he. Still, she had stolen from him. Or had she? He stared at the auburn hair he'd breathed through the night. Why this uncertainty that grew with each day?

Damning himself, he sat up.

Juliana murmured, shifted onto her back, and squeezed his fingers that curved her belly.

Until that moment, Gabriel had been too full of self-reproach to realize her hand was upon his—holding him to her as if to ensure he did not steal away. Why? He looked to her soft, fair-skinned fingers that contrasted with his callused and deeply tanned ones. Was it loneliness from these past weeks of confinement? Or did she truly wish him with her? She had not sent him away yesterday when he'd sought her consent. Indeed, she'd held naught from him—except that which she would tell only if he delivered Alaiz.

That last reminded him of the reason he'd come to her, though, in truth, it had been as much an excuse to see her again. He had sought her out to tell that which he'd been too angry to speak following her betrayal of weeks past— that Blase had returned to England and would inquire as to Alaiz's well-being. But though word had yet to arrive of her sister, he had not come to Juliana with the intention of laying her down. Not that it absolved him, for he'd known the temptation of being near her, especially with their child growing large in her—binding them as if man and wife. But they were not. Could never be.

He searched the swell beneath his hand, longed to see movement like that which he'd felt after they'd made love. He waited, but the babe was still. He frowned. Though he'd heard that lovemaking would do an unborn child no harm providing the mother was of good health, mayhap he'd heard wrong. He pulled his hand from beneath Juliana's and felt it across her silken flesh. No response.

Disquieted, he rose to his knees, laid hands to her belly, and put his ear to it. He heard the strong beat of a heart, but was it the child's? He searched to the side—naught. The other side—silence. Lower—he stopped his breathing, listening with eyes closed. There it was, rapid and steady. He let out his breath.

"Can you hear him?" Juliana asked softly.

Had he not years of masking his emotions, he would have revealed his surprise. How long had she watched? Looked upon his seeking? No matter. Had he made a fool of himself one minute or five, he remained a fool. He lifted his head and met her regard. "I heard him."

A smile touched her mouth. "Sometimes, when all the day is at rest, I can feel his beat beneath my hand."

He stared at her morning countenance—weighted lids, softly colored cheeks, bowed mouth, hair spread around her. It stirred him to new awakening. He ought not to have lingered. He dropped his feet to the floor and retrieved his braies and hose.

"You are leaving?"

Though he thought it regret in her voice, he did not pause in attaching his hose to his braies. "The morning's work has begun on the wall," he said as he reached for his boots.

"So it has," she murmured.

Sorrow, but he would not let it touch him. What had happened between them was done. It would not happen again.

He straightened and started across the chamber.

"For what did you come, Gabriel?"

That which was made more of a lie by his not having spoken it. Still, he did not break stride until he reached the door. He looked around and saw that she sat up, her belly gone beneath her skirts. "I came that you might know Blase has returned to England."

He was gone? Juliana blinked. "When?"

"Three weeks past."

That was the day she'd been sent to the tower and seen Blase depart the castle. She had thought he'd gone to a village from which he would soon return. Why had he left Mergot? Had it anything to do with her?

"Though he is to return to Briarleigh at his bishop's summons," Gabriel said, "I have given him instructions to first pass through Tremoral and make inquiry of your sister."

Though it was not what Juliana had asked in exchange for the truth she held from him, it was more than she'd hoped. "And what word has been brought you?" *Pray, let Alaiz be well.*

His brow lowered. "None yet, but methinks within the fortnight we shall hear."

Then to tell her of Blase's departure was not all for which he had come? Could it be he longed to see her as much as she to see him? Or had he come but for an ease of his loins? As much as she yearned to reject the latter, she feared that to do so would be pure fancy. She loved Gabriel, but he could not love her—unless, perhaps, she told him the truth of the child.

He opened the door.

She blinked, groping for words to hold him. "Gabriel?"

He looked over his shoulder.

"I thank you." It was all she could form.

He nodded, stepped without, and closed the door. The key turned in the lock. Naught had changed.

She pressed a hand to her belly. Five weeks—that was all she had. What would happen to her son once she was gone? Would he be loved? Would he know more laughter than tears? To whose arms would he run for comfort? Could Gabriel give him all he needed? Would Gabriel? Something told her he would endeavor to do so, but a child needed its mother. A nursemaid could never give him the love he deserved.

In that moment, Juliana knew what she must do—that

which her love for Alaiz and fear of Bernart's retaliation had too long held her from. She must trust Gabriel. But would he believe her, and if so, would he bring Alaiz out of Tremoral? She had to believe he would. And then? She was still Bernart's wife and could not remain hidden forever. She must speak to Gabriel.

She rose, crossed to the basin and washed herself in chill water, then waited for the guard to bring her morning meal.

Shortly, he appeared. Her request for him to send word to Gabriel was met with a frown, but he agreed. However, Gabriel did not come, nor the day after, nor the day after that.

Chapter Twenty

February 1196

The parchment crackled angrily as Gabriel put his fist around the words written by a monk of Briarleigh. Damn Kinthorpe to hell! A curse upon him and all come of his blood! Though Blase did not detail what had been done him, his injuries were serious enough that he'd been unable to inscribe the missive himself. Forget his assurance he would heal and soon return. It did naught for the fury that burned in Gabriel. Only one thing would cool it—Kinthorpe blood. But, according to the missive, he would not have to seek it out. It was coming to him. It could not come soon enough.

And what of Alaiz, accused of a murder she could not have committed? Was she in hiding? Or now, since her escape, had the dead man's family captured her? Likely. And the fault was Gabriel's. In truth, all of it was. If not

for his revenge upon Juliana, Blase would not lie infirm,
Alaiz would be safe under her sister's protection, and Bernart would not be bringing an army against Mergot to kill
and maim any who came between him and that which he
deemed his.

Gabriel thrust himself out of the lord's chair, staring at
the empty hall. Though he bore the blame, still he hungered for Kinthorpe, and would not be content with anything less than victory. Thus, there was a vast amount to
be done before the bastard came—weapons struck, completion of repairs to the inner wall, stores of food and
water brought in, intensified training for his men.

He strode from the hall into a day heavy with such cold
his breath billowed upon the air. For a moment, he entertained the idea that Kinthorpe might wait until the
spring to cross the channel, but rejected it. Juliana's husband came soon to claim a child not his, a wife who ought
not to be.

As Gabriel stepped into the outer bailey, he paused to
look up at the tower. How did Juliana fare? He wondered
often, listened intently to the guard's meager reports, but
had not gone to her since the morning he'd awakened in
the tower. Five times she had sent word, and each time
he'd disregarded her requests. As he could not be so near
her without wanting her, it was best he stayed away—
now even more so. Did he go to her, she would surely
inquire if word had come of her sister, and he would have
to lie. Regardless of whether or not Kinthorpe arrived before the babe was born, Gabriel would not tell her of the
missive. Its ill tidings presented too great a risk to her and
their child.

But there was something he could do. Though it might
prove in vain, he would send Sir Erec to England to root

out Alaiz and, if she yet eluded her pursuers, bring her to France. This day he would send for his vassal.

For two days it had been thus—the gaps in the inner wall filling twice as quickly as on the days past, workers darting bailey to bailey with an urgency not heretofore present, the clatter of wagons loaded with food stores, the ring of the forging of steel synchronous with the sound of men hard in training. And it frightened her. It could mean but one thing: siege was coming to Mergot.

Juliana closed her eyes against the scene in the bailey, pressing fingers to her brow. Though she prayed Gabriel's neighbor and enemy, Baron Faison, was responsible, she knew it was Bernart come in the yawn of winter.

She dragged a hand down her face, then closed it over the other that grasped the scissors and trailing material at her swollen waist. If only Gabriel would answer her summons. If only he had brought Alaiz out of Tremoral with her. But he gave her naught with which to fight Bernart's claim upon her and the child they had made. Thus there would be bloodshed.

A gush of warmth wet her thighs, calves, and feet, eliciting a gasp. She took a step back, looking to the pool of water that seeped from beneath her skirts. And knew.

The scissors clattered to the floor. The green material drifted down and settled atop the sharp blades.

Dear God, no. It was too early. Three weeks too soon. She pressed palms to her belly. Beneath her touch, it turned hard as it had done many times this past week. At first she had feared the tightening, but had calmed herself with the reminder that it was a normal part of those weeks preceding childbirth. Unfortunately, her knowledge of such things was limited to that overheard from serving women. But this she also knew: her waters had broken, meaning the babe would not be long in wailing from her body, its early arrival portending ill.

She nearly choked on a sob. Would her child be sickly, diseased, misshapen? Stillborn? Any or all of these as her punishment for the manner in which the babe was gotten? She would be deserving of such, but not this innocent who had naught to do with his getting.

She lifted her face heavenward. "Please, God, punish not this child. 'Twas I who sinned."

No answer but the easing of the hard ball of her belly.

She dropped her chin, gathered a quavering breath, then hugged her arms to her belly. No matter her child's infirmity, regardless of whether he was as befitted the heir Bernart came to steal from Gabriel, she would love him. Her next thought was bittersweet. Did Bernart deem the babe unworthy, he would have naught to do with him as he'd had naught to do with Alaiz—would gladly leave Gabriel his son. But would Gabriel accept such a child? Something told Juliana he would not turn away. She fought to hold her tears, but one after another brimmed over.

"Heavenly Father," she whispered, " 'tis not as I would have my prayers answered." Leaving the shutters open in spite of the chill that stole warmth from the room, she crossed to the bed. No sooner did she lower herself to the mattress edge than her womb hardened again, this time sending a shock of pain through her. She nearly cried out. The pain passed, but was not long in returning. After the fourth time it came and spent itself on her, she forced herself up from the bed. She needed a midwife to help her push her child into this cold, cold world. Months back Lissant had mentioned that Gabriel had arranged for one from a nearby village to come when the babe was due. God willing, the village was near.

Juliana made it to the door without further evidence of the babe's impending birth. She leaned against the planked wood and called to the guard. Minutes passed. Could he not hear her? She called louder, again without result. Cradling her belly, feeling it begin to harden, she opened her mouth a third time, but sudden pain turned her words to a cry. She slid down the door to her knees, would have tried to hold back the next cry if not that it might alert someone. But when the pain receded, she was still alone.

Trembling, more frightened than she could remember having ever been, she sat back on her heels. She looked to the unshuttered window. Though gaining her feet was awkward, she prevailed. Swaying, she touched a hand to her brow. It was damp with perspiration in contrast to a room grown increasingly chill.

A dozen steps, no more, she reassured herself, and put a foot forward. She nearly made it, would have gained the window if not that her belly cramped. She sank to the floor, sucking a breath against the pain. When she exhaled, it was on a wail that even God in his lofty heavens could not disregard.

After what seemed an eternity, she crested the pain and started down the other side. She squeezed her eyes closed, ground her jaws, curled onto her side amid the rushes, and began to pant away the ache coursing her womb. *Mother Mary!* Though she'd heard of the pain of childbirth, never would she have believed it to be so fierce. Mayhap she was dying. . . .

This time when the pain left her, she could not rise for reveling in those precious minutes of relief. It did not last long. She whimpered, sending up a fervent prayer that Gabriel would come to her. How she longed to feel his arms around her, to see their son cradled in those strong arms.

Through the delirium dragging her senses, she thought she heard his name cried high. Of her imagining, she told herself. Only her imagining.

"Gabriel!"

Her voice, a pitch above the clang of his blade against his opponents', caused him to falter. Imagined? He looked to the prison tower, and paid a price that might have meant his death were it true battle in which he engaged. Steel met wool, sliced through it, met flesh, drew blood.

He jumped back and glanced down his tunic to where crimson seeped from his ribs. A minor wound, though the knight's look of horror made it seem mortal.

"My lord," the man said with a gasp, "I did not—"

Gabriel silenced his words with a sweep of his hand, listening. And he heard her scream his name again. He raised his sword, ran from the training ground of the outer bailey to the inner drawbridge, and silently begged the Almighty to hold Juliana above harm. But would the Lord receive prayers from one who had not sent any heavenward for years?

It seemed forever until Gabriel reached the uppermost landing. The door stood wide, and when he charged into the room he saw that the guard knelt beside Juliana's writhing figure. Fortunately, his ability to quickly assess a situation held him from parting the guard's head from his neck. Juliana's time had come.

He dropped his sword, hastened forward, and nearly trod a tray of viands set to the floor.

The man looked up as Gabriel dropped to his knees beside him. "My lord, methinks she be birthing—"

"Take you to Tannon and bring back the midwife." Gabriel searched Juliana's pain-wrenched features. "Now!"

The man scrambled to his feet.

"And send for Lissant! Tell her the lady births."

"Aye, my lord." The guard ran.

Gabriel bent near Juliana. Her hair was tangled with rushes, her eyes closed, her brow furrowed, her face ruddy and moist. "Juliana!"

She shook her head, squeezed her eyes more tightly shut, and began to pant and rock her belly in the fold of her arms.

Gabriel's gut twisted. Would the midwife arrive in time? He ought to have sooner brought her to Mergot. But then, he had been certain the child was his, that it had yet three weeks—

Nay! It would not do to think on that now. Juliana's needs must come first. Putting the painful truth from him, he stroked the backs of his fingers down her wet cheek. " 'Tis I—Gabriel. Do you hear me, Juliana?"

He thought her lids cracked, but could not be certain. The scream that met his ears a moment later clawed his heart.

Though logic told him the guard could hardly have reached his station belowstairs, Gabriel questioned what caused Lissant to delay. *Damnation!* Where was the woman?

"Gabriel?"

He met Juliana's gaze that peeked from slit lids. "I am here." He ran a hand down her belly, covered her clenched fingers with his.

Her lids lifted further to reveal the brown of her eyes. " 'Tis truly you?"

"Aye."

A sob rent her throat. "You . . . came."

He tried to smile. "You called."

"For near a fortnight I have . . . sent word." She gasped, her chest heaving. "But only now you come."

"Only now do you need me."

She shook her head. "You are wrong."

Was he?

She turned her hands, gripping his fingers tightly as if she might never let go. "Promise you will not leave me again."

He did not wish to leave her; he would stay with her until the midwife arrived. Of course, the babe might deliver before the old woman put her rumpled face around the door. In that moment, he knew what he must do. Proscribed though it was for a man to be present during birthing—even were he a physician—for naught would he leave Juliana to inexperienced hands. Were it necessary, he would deliver the babe himself. However that was done . . .

He squeezed her fingers. "I shall stay as long as you need me."

Her shoulders slumped, her tension easing as if her suffering passed. "I need you."

Damn his revenge! Emotion making his hands quiver, he seized control of his anger and brushed damp tendrils from her brow. "The pain eases?"

She swallowed loudly. "Aye." Of a sudden, her eyes sharpened. "Know you the babe comes?"

It was as if she sought reassurance that at the end of her pain would come a child who lived. "I know." He bent his head and stirred his lips across hers. "I shall carry you to bed." He loosed his hand from hers and slid his arms beneath her.

She gasped. "Gabriel, you bleed."

He looked to where her gaze fell upon his rent tunic.

He'd forgotten about the injury, even now could not feel it. "But a little," he said. "Swordplay."

"You make ready for siege." New fear was in her voice. "Is it Ber—"

"Hush. 'Tis the babe you ought to put your mind to."

She stared at him, then nodded.

In spite of the added weight of her pregnancy, she lifted easily into his arms. He crossed to the bed and settled her atop the coverlet.

She shuddered into the pillows.

Gabriel strode to where the tray sat near the door. He bent, poured a goblet of honeyed milk, then returned to her. "You must drink." He slid an arm beneath her shoulders and raised her.

She allowed the rim to her lips, sipped, then shook her head. "Enough. I—" Her breath caught.

"The pain again?"

"Nay." She caught his hand and laid it to her belly. "Feel him."

He did, a wondrous ripple of shifting limbs beneath taut, silken skin. "I do."

She smiled weakly. "He is most impatient, your son."

His son? Now that it was proven that Bernart was the father, she relented? Once more, anger snapped at Gabriel, but he held it—washed it away when struck with another possibility. Mayhap the child *was* his, its early arrival a portent of miscarriage. Miscarriage that might claim Juliana as well. Miscarriage that his visit a fortnight past had likely put upon her.

Rushed with self-contempt, he stared at her hand atop his. *Sweet Jesus!* Was this his revenge? Death to her and the babe? Did he lose one or both he would himself deliver his soul to the bowels of hell.

Beneath his hand her belly grew suddenly hard, and an

291

instant later her hold on his fingers tightened. He jerked his gaze to her face, seeing her pain. Though she struggled to deny her cries, they came.

He was helpless! There was naught he could do but let her squeeze the feeling from his hand.

After the pain passed and ere the next, Lissant appeared. She bustled in, two women servants close behind—one's arms laden with blankets and towels, the other's with a large basin of water from which steam wafted.

"For what did you dawdle?" Gabriel barked.

Lissant faltered, but continued to the bed. "Pardon, my lord, I came as quickly as I could gather that needed to deliver the child." She looked to Juliana's fevered face. "I will see to Lady Isolde until the midwife arrives."

It was his dismissal from this, the domain of women. But he had promised Juliana he would stay as long as she needed him. Nay, he would not leave until the midwife arrived.

"My lord," Lissant said with apology, "go you to the hall and I shall send word as soon as the babe is come."

"Nay!" Juliana cried, frantically seeking Gabriel's gaze. "You gave me your word."

Why was she so desperate to keep him with her when he had naught to lend but his presence? A presence she ought to find repugnant? He inclined his head. "My word stays true, Juliana."

She released her breath.

"But my lord," Lissant protested, " 'tis not proper. A man should not—"

"I shall not leave!"

She nipped her bottom lip, struggled with an argument she could not win, then crossed to the brazier before which two chairs sat. She chose the nearest and pushed it across the rushes to his side. "It may be a long wait, my lord."

"I thank you." Gabriel lowered himself.

Throughout the next hour, Juliana's pain intensified. No more could Gabriel feel his fingers, so numb were they, but he stayed by her side and pressed cold towels to her brow, reassured her as best he could—while inside he raged at God for visiting such cruelty on her, then at the midwife for old legs that had yet to see her to Mergot. He ground his teeth. If only he could bear the pain for Juliana.

At last, the midwife arrived. Her wizened face glowered at the sight of Gabriel. "You must leave, my lord."

Though Gabriel had planned to withdraw, it was not easy to do. He looked to Juliana.

Eyes closed, she panted through her most recent travail.

"The midwife is here, Juliana," he said. "You would have me leave?"

She did not answer, causing him to believe she could no longer hear outside herself.

"My lord"—the midwife touched his shoulder—"there be much to do before she pushes forth her burden. You must go."

Must he? What if he did not see Juliana again? What if—

"Stay." It was no more than a whisper Juliana spoke, but it gripped him. "I shall remain, old woman," he said.

The midwife's lips puckered, but she yielded with a shrug to her lord's authority. "Then you will aid me." She looked to Lissant and the woman servants who stood opposite the bed. "And you. We have not much time."

Shortly, the room was alive with something other than the sounds of pain. As Lissant prepared a drink of vinegar and sugar to aid Juliana's labor, one of the women servants coaxed the brazier, while the second darted around the room opening windows, the chest, and anything else that could be opened.

That last snapped Gabriel's patience. "For what do you throw wide doors and windows when warmth is lacking?"

The midwife looked up from Juliana's bared belly. " 'Twill aid in the opening of the womb." Her voice was crusty as four-day-old bread.

Gabriel wanted to spit. Opening windows and doors while Juliana struggled to hold to her life and their child's! "What foolishness speak you?"

She probed a hand over Juliana's belly. "In all my years I have brought forth nearly three hundred babes, my lord. I know the ways of birthing. Do you let me do that for which I have been called, I shall birth your child."

Gabriel longed to argue the wasteful symbolism, but forced the argument down.

The old woman sighed. "A man's place be not the lying-in chamber."

Gabriel looked to Juliana. She rested, moist lashes laid upon the circles beneath her eyes, hair clinging to her brow, jaw, and neck.

"The babe is positioned correctly," the midwife pronounced. She creaked her body nearer Juliana's belly and put her ear to it. "A strong beat."

"And what of its mother?"

She considered Gabriel, then shook her head. "She is small and narrow, my lord."

He felt as if split down the middle.

"But she looks to be strong," the woman added.

Only to soothe him? "Will she live?"

Her mouth turned down. "I have not the answer you seek." She jutted her chin toward the ceiling. "You ought to confer with Him."

Gabriel resisted flaying her with angry words, and instead put his mind to a prayer he hoped would not go unanswered.

Lissant appeared at the old woman's side. "The drink is ready."

"My lord"—the midwife glanced at Gabriel—"raise your lady that she might swallow the draft."

He eyed the goblet Lissant held, conceding that though the mix of sugar and vinegar was likely of no more benefit than the opening of windows, it would moisten Juliana's mouth. He put an arm beneath her.

She grimaced at the trickle Lissant pressed upon her, but drank much of it until pain once more found her.

"Hot water and soap," the midwife instructed Lissant. "Move the chest aside," she commanded the women servants. "My lord, ease your lady down the bed that I can stand between her legs."

Gabriel did as told, aching for the discomfort he caused Juliana.

"Now pillows at her back." Having cleaned her hands up to her forearms, the old woman parted Juliana's quaking thighs and bent between them. A long minute passed ere she straightened. "The head is there and my lady is near full open." She raised four gnarled fingers to show measure. "God willing, 'twill not be long now. Lissant, go into my bag and bring out the oil for your lord."

Lissant unstoppered the vial and passed it to Gabriel. It was pressed of violets, its sweet perfume an unexpected balm to his emotions.

"Rub it into her abdomen and hips—with vigor," the midwife said.

No sooner did he do so than Juliana cried out and put her nails into his flesh.

"And my lord . . ." The old woman paused.

His breath coming hard as if he exerted himself, he looked to eyes that peered at him above Juliana's belly. "Aye?"

"Pray."

He did—with more fervor than ever he had. Lord, forgive him his sins, for Acre, for his tourncying, for his rejection of religion, most especially for his revenge upon Juliana.

She arched, threw her arms out, and gripped the coverlet on either side of her.

Gabriel slammed his gaze to the midwife's bowed head. "Can you do naught for her pain?"

Exasperation put sparkle in her aged eyes. "Henbane would ease her labor, my lord, but if I am to give a live babe into your arms, I shall need her help in pushing it forth."

A whimper parted Juliana's dry lips.

Gabriel bent and cupped her face between his hands. "I am here, Juliana. Hold to me."

She opened her eyes and searched his face. "Always . . . I shall," she whispered through chattering teeth.

Pain lanced Gabriel's breast, spilled something from him that he had too long denied. But before he could embrace it, Juliana gasped and threw her head back.

"I die! Surely I die!"

"Nay!" He shook her. "You do not! Now hold to me and 'twill soon be done—I swear it."

Breath shallow, she lowered her chin and searched his gaze, then reached up and gripped his shoulders. "Our son . . . is he . . . ?"

Their son. He pressed his lips to her brow. "He is well."

A scant smile touched her face, but in the next instant it was supplanted by yet more suffering.

"My lord?"

Gabriel looked to the midwife. "Aye?"

"Must I choose between mother and child, who would you have me spare?"

Gabriel felt as if run through with a sword, and nearly roared his pain and anger that it be spoken that Juliana might hear.

"My lord, I must know."

"Spare her," he said in a growl. "Spare Juliana."

She returned to the birthing.

"Nay," Juliana panted, "the babe."

Gabriel looked into her weary eyes and shook his head. "For naught will I lose you. Naught!"

"He is your heir. He—"

"He I do not yet love." He rushed the words to her before he could examine them.

Her lids lifted further. "Love?" That single word was more beautiful on her breath than ever he had heard it spoken.

He loosed his vised jaws and nodded. "Aye, love."

She closed her eyes as if to savor what he'd bared, for one moment looked serene, then sucked air.

"Push, child," the midwife commanded. "Now!"

Clutching Gabriel as if he were all there was in the world, Juliana obeyed with a strength he had not known she possessed. And a dozen times more. The setting sun cast its last rays through the open windows when the babe slid slippery and wailing from her womb.

"God has given you a son, my lord," the midwife said, "and he looks to be of good health." She cut the cord, tied it, then motioned Lissant forward.

A blanket over her arms, Lissant stepped to the old woman's side and the two swathed the babe.

"You are a father, my lord." A smile put a glimmer of

extinguished youth to the old woman's face as she lifted the bundled infant for Gabriel to see.

He stared at the little one who continued to fill the room with his cries. A father. His son? But the old woman said he was of good health when a child born three weeks early—

"I would hold him," Juliana croaked.

Gabriel looked at where her head rested in the curve of his arm. Never had one looked so weary, yet so beautiful.

"You are not done, my lady," the midwife said. "There is still the afterbirth."

"I shall hold him."

"Your son must needs be bathed, his palate rubbed with honey and—"

"Bring him to me!"

The old woman looked to Gabriel.

He nodded.

She snorted, but passed the babe to Lissant. "For a moment only."

As if the howling child were poured of the most fragile glass, Lissant bore him the scant distance to his mother. "Your son, my lady." She eased the bundle into the crook of Juliana's arm.

Juliana stared, so still he was certain she had stopped breathing. Then she smiled. "Oh," she crooned, and touched the babe's brow, nose, and lips. As if her touch were enchanted, he quieted. Juliana looked up, something very different about the eyes she laid to Gabriel. They were deeper, warmer. "Our son," she said softly as if to a beloved husband. "Ours, Gabriel."

He longed for it to be so, but it did not seem likely. Still, he reached forward and touched the tiny fist that rooted past the swaddling. It was soft. His heart leaped, but the midwife's impatience stole the moment.

"My lady, you must bear down one last time." She gestured for Lissant to take the babe. "Your maid shall tend him that he might return to your arms when the birthing is done."

Juliana's reluctance was as a great weight upon Gabriel, but she deferred to Lissant.

It took more than the midwife's "one last time" to expel the afterbirth, but finally it was done. A short while later, Juliana sank into a deep sleep, the babe suckling at her full breast.

Gabriel sat silent beside her, captivated by the sight. How had he believed he could take a child from its mother? His son or not, they belonged together. And when Bernart came? Finally he let himself go to that place he'd eschewed throughout Juliana's labor, and was torn by it.

"You would hold your son, my lord?"

He pulled his gaze to the midwife, who had come to stand beside his chair, entertained how like a witch she looked with torchlight flicking her sharp nose and chin, lighting her brittle gray hair. He had thought the same when she'd dressed his scored ribs a short while ago.

"He lies awake," she prompted.

Gabriel looked to the babe whose cheek was pressed to Juliana's breast and found his gray gaze upon him. Or was it? It was as if it went through him. "How fares Lady Juliana?" he asked, as he'd asked a dozen times since the delivery.

"Not as poorly as I believed she would, but come the dawn we will know better." Then, as if to reassure, "She is a strong one, my lord, and will likely bear you many more."

More children . . .

The midwife turned again to the babe. "He has the look of his mother—and you, my lord."

Gabriel sharpened his gaze on the old woman, then the child. Aye, hair like Juliana's, brown warmed through with red, but no other resemblance did Gabriel see—not even to Bernart.

He looked around the room. The women servants having withdrawn, Lissant was the only other occupant. She dozed in a chair near the brazier.

"The child was born early?" he asked the midwife.

Her eyes narrowed as if she considered her answer with care. It could not be the first time she'd been asked to assure a father a newborn babe was his get. "Mayhap. Though he is healthy and of good weight and length, he is somewhat small to be born of a man your size."

Bernart was not as tall or broad . . . "If early, how many weeks?"

Her brow rippled like puddled rain. "I cannot say, my lord."

"And if he had remained in the womb a fortnight or more?"

She pursed her lips, then gruffly conceded, "He could not have passed. But your lady is small. Sending the babe early is oft God's way of preserving mother and child." She broke gaze with him. "Now hold your son, my lord."

Bernart's son. The child had to be. *That* Gabriel's recently confessed love for Juliana could not overcome. Such unutterable pain, not only for his loss of the child and, thus, Juliana, but for his needless revenge—the pain he had caused her, Alaiz, and now Blase. He shook his head. "The child is content where he lies."

She heaved a sigh. "You are certain?"

He looked longingly at the infant. "Nay, I am not."

The midwife leaned near him and spoke so softly her old voice revealed a bit of the woman she must have been thirty years past. "All know 'tis good for a father to hold his child soon after birth—especially a son."

But he was not Bernart. "Aye"—he met her gaze—"I would wish it for him, but 'tis not for me to do."

Weariness settled deeper into her face, aged her beyond her years. "As you will, my lord." She turned away and hobbled toward the straw pallet the women servants had placed near the hearth for her. "I pray you shall not regret it."

Already he did. Since he had learned Juliana was with child he'd believed the babe to be of his seed, and in that belief had been made a father. He closed his eyes, finally granting admittance to that skulking in the back of his mind: he'd wanted this child for more than revenge, wanted it nearly as much as he wanted Juliana. Now there was naught to hold either to him.

He looked to Juliana. Though she was spent from labor, there was a radiance about her that made him touch her cheek, then the slightly turned corner of her mouth. This day she was changed. No longer was she simply a woman. She was a mother. Regardless whether or not she outlived her offspring, she would be a mother to the grave.

It was not so with fathers, as Gabriel knew well from his own sire's rejection of him nine years past. Lacking the certainty of parentage granted to women through the womb, it was easy for a man to deny a child, be he right or wrong.

Bitterness of old crept in, but ere it could settle, the babe snuffled.

Was he uncomfortable? Scared? Hungry? Gabriel glanced at Juliana. Should he awaken her? Nay, she needed sleep. The midwife? He looked over his shoulder.

The old woman lay on her pallet, back to him, narrow shoulders evidencing a steady rise and fall.

Gabriel fought himself, and would have fought longer

and harder if not for the babe's impatience that put a stronger whimper to the air. He stood, then gently lifted the bundle from Juliana's side. He held the babe out from him a long moment ere bringing him into the crook of his arm.

How strange it felt to hold him, to feel their bodies meet as if they were not one without the other. As if connected. Would that they were . . .

Juliana's son blinked and whimpered low.

What should he do? Walk him as he'd seen mothers do when an infant turned fretful? Gabriel crossed the room, then crossed back.

Shortly, the babe's whimpers turned to a gurgle, as if he grew content. Unfortunately, the sound was nearly as loud as the other.

"Shh," Gabriel breathed. "I am here, little one." He stroked the babe's small fist, and an instant later found his finger grasped tightly. Something inside him began to melt.

The babe yawned wide, showing pink gums and tongue, then closed his eyes and tucked his chin.

Gabriel grinned, turned at the door, and started back to the bed. But he did not return the infant to Juliana's arms. A few more times around the room, he told himself, just to be certain the babe was fully asleep.

The old woman smiled on her pallet. It was good for a father to hold his newborn child.

Chapter Twenty-one

A son, and with an appetite she would not have expected of one who ought to be sickly. Though he'd come three weeks early, the midwife said he was as healthy as if he had remained in the womb till due. Juliana smiled. God had blessed her.

She looked from the suckling babe to the chair Gabriel had filled throughout the birthing. The joy of holding her child dampened at the sight. The chair was empty, as it had been each time she'd awakened this new day. Would Gabriel return, or leave her summons unanswered as he'd done the past fortnight? She *must* speak with him, *must* tell him the truth of Bernart.

"Lissant," she addressed the maid, who bent to her needlework.

Lissant looked up. "My lady?"

"I would have you go again to Lord De Vere and tell him I must speak with him."

"My lord has said you are not to be alone, my lady."

Unfortunately, the midwife had departed a half hour past to tend a birthing in one of the villages. "Mayhap you could send the guard, then."

"I could, but word was brought Lord De Vere hardly an hour past." She smiled reassuringly. "Do you not worry, my lady, he will soon come."

Juliana was not so sure. Though Gabriel had professed his love for her—the words he'd spoken forever inscribed upon her mind—he likely regretted speaking them. But Lissant was right. She must give him time. An hour more, then, but that was all. If siege was to come to Mergot, Gabriel needed the weapon that only she could provide.

On that last, she considered Lissant, who had returned to her needlework. "The people of Mergot are made busy these past days," she probed.

"Aye." Lissant continued to concentrate on her needle.

"Think you Lord De Vere can hold against a siege?"

Lissant stilled, then raised her gaze. "We pray he shall do so."

Juliana ached for having guessed correctly. "Who comes against your lord? Baron Faison?"

She shook her head. "I know not his name, my lady, only that he soon crosses the channel to make war upon Mergot."

Bernart Kinthorpe was his name. No other. Juliana stared at the one Bernart thought to steal from Gabriel.

The babe suckled a moment longer, then loosed her breast with a loud smack.

She chuckled past her pained heart. "Full, little one?"

He blinked; a moment later he started at the creaking of the door.

Juliana looked around.

Gabriel hesitated on the threshold ere stepping within. "How fare you, Lady Juliana?"

Why did he no longer call her Isolde in Lissant's presence? Had he called her Juliana on the day past? Aye, when he'd told the midwife to spare her over their child, revealing his feelings for her ere he'd spoken them.

"I am sore and tired," she answered, venturing a smile that was not returned, "but the midwife says I shall recover fully."

He halted alongside the bed. " 'Tis as she told me. The child continues to do well?"

The child, not *my son*. Her misgivings lurched. Though the midwife had told her Gabriel had walked the babe last eve, had held him long into the night, he thought the child's early birth meant he was of Bernart. True, it was as Juliana had tried to convince him these past months, but no more could she lie to him. Once they were alone, he would know the truth. "*Your son*"—she emphasized the words—"is hale and satisfied, my lord. You would hold him again?"

From the darkening of his face, he either did not like the child to be named his, or had not wanted her to know he'd held him. Likely both. He leaned down and lifted the bundle from her. As he settled the babe close to his chest, he glanced at the little one. Though he looked quickly away, emotion struggled across his face, causing him to look again. Jaw softening, he drew a finger across the backs of their son's hands.

Relief eased Juliana against the pillows.

"Lissant," Gabriel summoned.

The maid dropped her needlework and hastened forward. "My lord?"

"Deliver the babe to the donjon."

Dread wended through Juliana. Regardless of his profession of love—mayhap she had only imagined it?—he would take their child from her as he'd vowed. Even though he might not believe he was the father.

Gabriel passed the infant to the maid. "A cradle has been placed in Lady Juliana's chamber."

"Nay!" Juliana labored up from the pillows and grasped Gabriel's sleeve. "Pray, do not—"

"Go," he ordered Lissant.

The maid passed a look of apprehension to Juliana, but turned to the door.

A hole opened up within Juliana. "Do not take him from me, Gabriel!"

He came back around and laid a hand over hers where she gripped his arm. "I do not." His voice was not unkind. "You shall be together again shortly."

Did he speak true? She searched his face, and found there only what looked to be sorrow.

"If you are ready," he said, "I shall carry you to your chamber."

He did love her. Though he might not speak it again, she was in his heart. She nodded. "I am ready."

He reached forward and tugged the bodice of her chemise over her exposed breast.

Strange, but she felt no embarrassment at having bared herself—as if she belonged to him. And in her heart, she did.

He pulled the coverlet up to her chin, then gently lifted her from the bed.

She winced at the discomfort between her thighs.

"I have hurt you?"

She shook her head and took a breath of his scent that she would recognize among a hundred men—nay, a thousand. "I am tender, 'tis all."

His gaze held hers, then drifted to her mouth, and for

a moment she thought he might kiss her. Instead he turned to the door.

Not until they ascended the steps of the donjon amid the soft flutter of snowflakes did Juliana break the oppressive silence. "Before Lissant you called me Juliana."

His gaze did not waver from their ascent. "I did."

"Why not Isolde?"

"Because you are no longer she." His jaw tensed. "You are Lady Juliana Kinthorpe . . . of Tremoral."

A chill swept her. Did he mean to return her to Bernart? And what of their son? Desperation gripped her. "I must speak to you about Bernart."

He stepped past the porter who held the door, then glanced at her. "What is there to speak of?"

"More than you can know."

"Not here." *

"Then my chamber."

As he carried her through the hall, Juliana was struck by the changes there. True, the great hall was not grand, but in her absence the blackened walls had been painted and the hole in the far wall repaired.

She smiled—until Gabriel started up the stairs that resounded with their son's cries.

No sooner did they step within the chamber than Lissant rushed forward. "He will not be quieted, my lord." She gestured to the cradle from which the cries issued. "Methinks he wishes his mother."

"Or his father," Juliana said.

Mouth pinched, Gabriel stepped past the cradle and lowered her to the bed.

"Bring me our son, Gabriel," she said as he straightened; then to Lissant, she added, "I must speak with Lord De Vere in private."

The maid nodded, backed out the door, and closed it.

Gabriel stared at her absence, then bent and lifted the babe from the cradle. Without pause, he passed the fitful bundle to Juliana.

"There," she crooned, but the babe would not be calmed.

Gabriel turned toward the door.

"Do not leave," Juliana called above the cries. "Stay and hear what I have to tell."

He held his back to her, but finally came around.

It took several minutes for the babe to calm, but at last he hiccuped, nestled against her breast, and lowered his lids.

Juliana looked up and found Gabriel's gaze upon their son. "You will sit beside me?"

He widened his stance. "I shall not stay long. What have you to tell, Lady Juliana?"

His purposeful use of *lady*, though they were now alone, further distanced him—as if they had not come together in the dark of night, cried aloud their passion, made a child of it. As if she did and ever would belong to Bernart. She struggled for words. In the end, it was the babe who gave her a means of revealing the truth. "What shall we name him, Gabriel?"

His nostrils flared. " 'Tis not for me to do."

Then he did believe the child was born of Bernart. "Very well, I shall name him." She looked to their son and kissed his smooth brow. "You shall be called Gabrien in honor of your father."

Gabriel drew a sharp breath. "Do you not mean Bernart?"

She met his fiery gaze. "Never could he be called such, for Bernart did not father him. 'Twas you, Gabriel."

He grunted, strode to the shuttered window, and stood darkly silent. Then he returned and put his menacing bulk over her. "These past months you have denied my fathering of this child. Why now that you are proven right do you claim otherwise? What games play you?"

She swallowed. "Upon my life, I play no games. Had you come to me these past weeks as I five times asked, I would have told you the truth."

"What truth?"

"The night you brought me to the tower, you asked that I trust you."

His brow lightened slightly. "I did—and you did not."

"I do now. I should have then." She closed her eyes, drew strength from the warm bundle pressed to her side, and opened her eyes to Gabriel's harsh gaze. " 'Twas Bernart who sent me to you at Tremoral. Bernart who so longed for a son he set his virgin wife to steal his enemy's seed."

Disbelief stormed Gabriel's face, but before he could vent it, she hastened to ask, "Did you not see maiden's blood upon the sheets the morning after the first night I came to you?"

Gabriel felt as if slammed into a wall. Bernart had sent her to his bed? Inconceivable. To steal a child from him? Outrageous. Juliana a virgin? Try though he had to forget his second and third nights with her, the first had been dimmed by too much drink. Still, the following morning there had been blood on himself and the sheets. " 'Twas surely your monthly flux."

She shook her head. " 'Tis as I prayed you would believe, but it was not."

A fire burned Gabriel's belly. "Such fantastic lies you weave, Juliana Kinthorpe. Why?"

Tears glistened in her eyes, and her lips trembled. "Did I leave blood the following nights?"

Her demand gave him pause. " 'Twas surely the end of your flux."

"God's mercy, think I could not have—"

Her raised voice caused the babe to whine.

Flushed with remorse, she patted him and put soothing words to his ears. When finally he quieted, she looked up. "Know you naught of a woman's cycle, Gabriel?"

He frowned.

"Had the blood been of my flux, I could not have been pregnant with this child by Bernart, as you believe. Had it been of my flux, 'twould have been at least another sennight until my time of breeding."

He was staggered, and had to step back to hold his balance. Though not ignorant of a woman's cycle, he'd not considered it.

"This child is yours." She touched the babe's head. "Ours."

He pinned his gaze to the one Juliana had named Gabrien, and could not breathe for the realization he was a father. This was his son. Theirs. And only moments before he had ached in the knowledge he must return mother and child to Bernart. If not for the rest of what Juliana had told, he would have reveled.

He met her waiting gaze. " 'Tis not to be believed that for three years you were wed to Bernart and he left you untouched. Why would a man who had you slake his thirst on another? On Nesta? More, why would he send one he prized above all to an enemy he hated to the devil?"

When finally Juliana spoke, it was so softly he had to strain to hear. "As Bernart had no knowledge of me these past three years, neither had he knowledge of any other, as he would have you believe. He could not have."

Something darkened Gabriel's soul, something he did not wish to acknowledge.

"It goes back to Acre when he went over the wall," she continued. Another silence. "He was set upon by Muslim soldiers, by their hand done an unspeakable injury." A tear slipped to her cheek. " 'Tis seen in his limp. What is not seen—what he lets none see—is the loss of his manhood."

Gabriel's soul went black. Bernart emasculated? He swung away. "It cannot be." But it was. It was! He knew it as surely as he breathed.

"He was the most beautiful of men," Juliana said, a sob in her voice. "Think you he would willingly allow himself to deteriorate so?"

"Enough!" Gabriel raised his fists, squeezing them so tight his arms trembled. Now he knew that which he had not fully understood—Bernart's bottomless hate. But was it deserved?

Behind him, he heard the babe fret, and Juliana's hushed words. He closed his eyes, seeing again that day at Acre, then the night. As he had asked himself a thousand times since, would it have been different had he not—

"Gabriel." A hand touched his shoulder.

He spun around. Juliana was before him, the babe laid in the cradle beyond. She swayed, the effort to rise draining her color.

"What do you out of bed?" he said with a growl, and swept her against his chest.

She wrapped her arms around his neck, holding tight as he carried her to the bed. "You are not to blame," she said, seeking the gaze he denied her. " 'Twould have been the same had you not convinced the others of their foolishness in joining him, the same had you gone after him."

He *had* gone after him, but to no end. He laid her down, but she gripped his shoulders.

311

It would take little to break her hold on him, but he would not risk harming her. "Loose me," he commanded.

"Only do you sit beside me that we might speak."

Though he knew there was more to tell, he longed to take leave of this chamber that he might battle the demons clambering for a foothold on his soul.

"I beseech you," she pleaded.

He met her velvet gaze so near his, yearned to go into her eyes and dwell there. But it would be short reprieve. Still there would be Bernart. "If 'tis what you wish," he said begrudgingly.

"I wish it." She loosed her hands, pulling them down his chest.

Aching where she touched him, he drew back. "I shall stand."

Mouth grimming, she nodded and settled back among the pillows. "Ask your questions." She folded her hands atop the soft mound that remained of her pregnancy. "I shall answer all."

He peered out of the darkness within. "Knowing Bernart could never be a husband to you, why did you wed him?"

Her lips compressed. "Not until after our vows were spoken did he tell of the injury done him. On our wedding night."

Anger surged over Gabriel's guilt, swept it under. *Curse Bernart's selfishness!* He had known Juliana would not shame him by annulling the marriage on the grounds that he could not consummate. How it must have pained her. How it must have shattered her illusions of love. How it must have hurt to know that never would she bear him children. On that last, he ground his jaw. " 'Tis true he sent you to steal a child from me?"

A breath shuddered from her. "Aye, to silence talk that

his lack of an heir proved he was as his brother."

Remembering Bernart's fervent hatred of his sibling, Gabriel could guess the desperation his old friend must have felt. But to steal a child from another? To claim as his own one born of the enemy? "Why me, Juliana? Why not another?"

Her smile was bitter. "Revenge twists men, makes of them what they were not intended to be. So it was with Bernart. He determined to take from you that which he believed you had stolen from him."

Gabriel could not conceive of such madness. Aye, madness! Regardless the loss of Bernart's manhood, what else could so ail his mind?

"Too," she whispered, "he chose you for the hate I bore you."

He frowned.

As if she grew cold, she dragged the coverlet up her chest. "Bernart believed 'twould hold me from you, that I would feel naught but revulsion. He could not bear that more than a child might come of our joining."

Had more come of it? In spite of the guilt and self-loathing that attempted to overcome his anger toward Bernart, he wondered if she felt for him what he felt for her. "Was it hate that caused you to do as he bade?"

"Nay."

"Love?"

A pained laugh parted her lips. "Love . . ." She rubbed a hand down the side of her face. "Even had my feelings for him not died long before, never could I love one who demanded such of me." She shook her head. "Nor did I come to your bed to secure my place at Tremoral. 'Twas for Alaiz I did it. Had I refused Bernart, he would have turned her out to wander the countryside. That I could not allow—no matter my sacrifice."

Gabriel swept back to Tremoral . . . the garden . . . the words Juliana had spoken: she would do anything for her sister. So much unexplained now explained, so much without sense given sense. Still, he felt as if someone had tied his entrails into a hundred writhing knots. He detested what Juliana had been made to do, the shame he had put upon her when he'd accused her of laying with him to assure her place. As for Bernart, regardless whether or not Gabriel was to blame for his infirmity, Juliana's husband was reprehensible. Depraved. Vile.

"Until now," she said, looking to the cradle, "Alaiz is all I have had, all who has needed me." She reached a hand from beneath the coverlet and touched Gabriel's sleeve. "Had I not feared for what Bernart would do to her, I would have revealed the truth long ago. I would have trusted you."

Gabriel's self-loathing stretched. If Alaiz were not yet caught, soon she would be. Unless Erec succeeded in finding her and bringing her out of England, in that direction lay her death. Then there was Blase. Despite the assurances he would recover, he had surely come near death himself.

Juliana caught his hand hanging at his side and squeezed it. "Bernart is no longer the one with whom you trained for knighthood, Gabriel. He is no longer the man I loved when I was a child making believe I was a woman. But know that you are not responsible. Never could Bernart take his wrongs upon himself. For every failing another was to blame."

As Gabriel knew, but did it absolve him of that day at Acre when he'd turned from one who'd called him friend? He thrust the question from him, lifting his gaze to the shuttered window. He ought not have a conscience where Bernart was concerned, needed no absolution from one such as him. Though what had been done to Bernart at Acre had surely made him what he'd become, it did not excuse the suffering to which he'd subjected Juliana and Blase. Still, Gabriel could not cleanse himself of the burden that had vexed him for nearly five years. Now, even more, it was a stain upon him.

Juliana squeezed his hand tighter. "Look at me, Gabriel."

He closed his eyes, then a moment later opened them on her sad, beautiful face.

She tried to smile. "At Tremoral you spoke of coming upon me when, as a girl, I wept over Bernart's faithlessness. Do you remember?"

In the garden. He could not forget. "Aye."

"It was the first time I truly looked at you. The first time I saw beyond the young man who scorned my notions of love, whose disdain of women put me on edge. That day, I nearly came into your arms."

Well he remembered.

She swallowed. "Though Bernart insisted 'twas you who sent the wench to him—tempted him—after those moments in the garden I could no longer believe you capable of such ill."

So that was what Bernart had told her. It would have made Gabriel laugh did it not sting so. Bernart had never needed any to tempt him to a woman's thighs. Had he not given Juliana his vow of continence for fear her doting father would not honor the betrothal, that night he would have had another wench.

"In truth," she continued, "though I hated you for your betrayal at Acre as Bernart wished me to, I do not think I ever really believed it. Whatever happened—and I do not ask that you speak of it—the man I know you to be could not have betrayed."

315

How he longed for his heart to be in agreement. Emotions warring, he pulled his hand from her. "I have much work to do."

She drew a deep breath, then clasped her cast-off hand with the other. "In preparation for the siege?"

Had Lissant spoken what she should not? "What know you of it?"

"Only that seen of the activity in the bailey." She nipped her bottom lip. " 'Tis Bernart who comes?"

She was no dolt. "He does." Would the new fall of snow delay his crossing of the channel had he not already crossed? Likely, and of certain benefit, for it would give Gabriel more time to examine himself and Juliana's terrible revelation—to better determine his course.

"No matter the guilt you wrongly put upon yourself," she said, "do you think to give me unto him, I shall not go."

Never would he do such, though what he ought to do he did not know. She was Bernart's wife. She could seek sanctuary within the walls of a convent, but there she would remain—far from Gabriel. They could leave Mergot, run with the babe, but it would be a lifetime of running. And of certain danger.

"Gabriel."

He pulled Juliana back to focus.

"My place is with you."

Was it love that brought such words from her, or the son between them? "Is it?" His tone was harsher than he had intended. Truly, it would be best for her if she ran as far from him and Bernart as her legs would carry her.

She tossed her chin up. " 'Tis what I wish."

"And what you cannot have. Do you forget, you are wed."

"Aye, to a man unable to consummate. In the eyes of

316

the Church, 'tis not a marriage—one dissolved without apology."

Of what did she speak? "Then you would reveal Bernart's infirmity? What you were made to do?"

He felt her struggle as if it were his own. "I do not wish it, but does he force me to it, I shall."

It was not something Gabriel had allowed himself to consider, though it seemed the only way they might truly be together. But such shame would fall upon her were it revealed what she had been made to do, and the unveiling of Bernart's terrible secret. . . .

"First, though," Juliana said. "I must be certain Alaiz is clear of his wrath. You will help me?"

What she did not know . . . "You ought to hate me, Juliana."

She shook her head. "One cannot hate what one loves deeply. And I love you, Gabriel."

Though part of him seized her avowal, set it to the beat of his heart, the other flung it from him. "After what I have done to you?" A bitter laugh pushed from his throat. "You are a fool to love what ought not to be loved."

She was undeterred. "Then we shall be fools together, for you also love me—and our son."

He looked to where the babe slept in the cradle, ached for the round cheek, the sweet breath, the tiny hand.

"Do you let yourself," Juliana said, "you will make a fine father. Do you forget how he was gotten, he will make you a fine son. Pray, Gabriel, do not reject him as your father did you."

Once more he was struck by something she should not know. His father's rejection of him as heir had been held close. Not even Bernart had known of it, only that no more would Gabriel be baron. "What did Blase tell you?"

Weariness bearing upon her, she returned to the pillows. "He did not. Though many speculate, none know why the third son will be Baron of Wyverly, as you ought to be. And if not you, then what of Blase? He may be of the clergy, but religion is not in his heart." She moistened her lips. "At Tremoral you said 'twas your mother who was responsible for your lost title and lands. How, Gabriel? For what were you and Blase set aside?"

That she did not need to be told. Or did she? Years of ache filled the spaces between the guilt he could not shed. "Very well," he conceded. "Throughout her marriage, our mother made of herself a whore. Upon her deathbed, she confessed all to a priest, and our father overheard. Though I am his son, as is Blase, our lack of De Vere looks made him question whose blood coursed through our veins. Thus we were set aside."

Juliana flinched. "I am sorry, Gabriel."

He did not want her pity. "I must leave."

"Gabriel." Her plea gave him pause. "If you could bring Alaiz out of Tremoral—"

"I cannot!" It was out before he could think better of it.

"Why?" There was a tremor in her voice.

Should he tell her the truth, that she might know what the man she professed to love had wrought? Was she recovered sufficiently to bear it? Aye. Not only was it best she knew, but the words he'd spoken could not be put back. "I fear your sister is no longer under Bernart's protection."

She came off the pillows. "Where is she?"

He filled his lungs. "Three days past a missive was delivered from Blase that told of her having fled Tremoral. None know where she has gone."

Juliana's breath rushed from her. It was a long moment

ere she recovered it. "But why would she leave? What could have happened?"

He longed to go to her, to comfort her for what had yet to be told, but soon enough the hate she ought to feel for him would give her cold comfort. "A household knight—Sir Randal Rievaulx—was murdered before Christmas. Alaiz is accused of having put the killing blade to him."

Juliana's heart fell out of her. "She would not . . . could not . . . Nay!" Tears floated in her eyes. "Surely you do not believe—"

"I do not."

She stared at Gabriel, then clasped her hands against her lips. "Sir Randal . . ."

"You know the knight?"

She saw again the man's cold, cruel eyes, saw him prowling the hall, his shadow too often creeping toward Alaiz's. "Aye, his half brother, Thierry Rievaulx, keeps Castle Soaring for Bernart."

"What can you tell me of him?"

"Only that I feared him, as did Alaiz."

"Why?"

"For the way he watched my sister, that he always came too near her, the things he said." She met Gabriel's gaze. "If she did this thing, it was surely in defense of her person."

"As I have concluded."

"Then you have bidden Blase to find her?"

Gabriel's hesitation boded ill. "I would have had he not been set upon at Tremoral."

"Set upon? But who—" She gasped. "Bernart."

He flexed his fists. "Methinks Blase was recognized as the priest come to the castle the night we took you. Bernart left him for dead."

Dear God, such evil, bearing no likeness at all to the one she had once loved. "He will recover?"

" 'Tis as his missive tells."

"I am sorry, Gabriel."

Bitterness pushed past his lips. "For what have you to be sorry? Of all who have suffered for Bernart's revenge, 'tis you—an innocent—who has borne the greatest burden. *I* ought to be sorry. And I am."

She shook her head. "You could not have known, and I did not tell you." She reached a hand to him, praying he would take it.

He did not take it. "Damn it, Juliana, hate me!"

She held his turbulent gaze, then dropped her hand to the coverlet. "Why? That you may more easily let me go? Nay, Gabriel, I now understand what love is and is not, and I shall let none—especially Bernart—steal it from me." She put her chin up. "Now, what are we to do about Alaiz?"

The bewilderment that swept his face reflected her own. Though she ought to be divided by fear for Alaiz, she was not. Why? The answer lay deep, but she dragged it to light. If Alaiz could devise her own escape and see it through, then perhaps she could survive outside Tremoral's walls. By that feat, she proved she was not as helpless as all believed.

Juliana pulled her lips inward. Perhaps her absence had been good for Alaiz—forced her to think for herself, as she had not had to do since the accident. But how long could Alaiz evade her pursuers, among them Sir Randal's kin, who were likely of the same ilk? That last touched chill fingers to her spine. "You will send someone to find her?"

Gabriel inclined his head. "Does the weather not turn

worse, Sir Erec should arrive at Mergot this eve or the morrow. 'Tis he I will send."

A cry issued from the cradle.

Juliana looked to Gabriel. His gaze was upon the babe.

"Mayhap he is hungry again," she said. "You will bring him to me?" She wanted to see again their child in his arms, father and son together.

Gabriel's hesitation made her fear he might disregard her request, but he stepped forward and bent to the cradle. The sight of one so large holding one so small warmed her through, and more when Gabriel did not hurriedly relinquish their child.

He stared at his son, who lay in his arms, and almost smiled. "Gabrien." He spoke low and touched a small, flailing fist.

Shortly, the crying subsided.

"Such sweet innocence," Gabriel murmured, "knowing naught of hate . . . revenge . . . deceit." He made a half dozen steps of what ought to have taken two strides, then lowered the babe to Juliana. "For naught shall I relinquish this child we have made. Our son."

She reached up and laid a hand to his jaw. "And of me, Gabriel?"

Though guilt weighted his eyes, he shook his head. "Bernart may bring all he has against me, but I shall die before allowing him to have you again."

Then she would remain with him at Mergot? Possible only if the truth were known of Bernart, and it seemed Gabriel's misplaced guilt opposed such revelation. But did he think to send her to a convent, he would soon learn the error of such thought. No more would she be Bernart's puppet. She had a child now, a child who needed his mother and father. As for Alaiz, they would find her and bring her to safety. She had to believe they would be together again. Somehow.

Chapter Twenty-two

He stayed away again. Two days now. Amid Lissant's protests, Juliana turned for the maid to pull the laces of her bliaut.

Lissant tied them, then stepped around to face her. "Pray, think on this again, my lady. You are not yet healed and the babe—"

"His belly is full, and he ought to sleep through dinner."

Lissant's pretty face soured. "If he does not?"

"I go to the hall, Lissant. Does Gabrien awaken and will not be consoled, you have but to send for me."

"But, my lady, what of you?"

Juliana laid a hand to the maid's shoulder. "I am sore—that is all. I shall be fine."

The maid clasped her hands this way and that, then swept them into the air. "Ah, my lady, Lord De Vere will be most—"

"Lissant, please!" Juliana dropped her hand from the woman and pushed her feet into slippers. "I am decided." She'd had enough of Gabriel's absence. And of equal import was the arrival of Sir Erec this morn. If they would not come to her, she would go to them.

"Forgive me, my lady. I am but concerned for you and the babe."

Juliana turned, staring at the maid, who was as near a friend as she had. She smiled. "Do not be. You shall take fine care of Gabrien, and I am fully capable of taking care of myself. As for Gabri—Lord De Vere—worry not. If his wrath comes upon any, 'twill be me, and I shall cool it."

Lissant nodded. "Very well, my lady." Her eyes drifted up Juliana's brow. "Come, I shall put order to your hair. It would not be seemly to sit at meal with it in such disarray, especially now that you are mother to our lord's heir."

But not wife. Never wife, if Bernart had his way. He would not, Juliana resolved. Gingerly, she lowered herself to the stool beside the cradle, staring at the miracle of her joining with Gabriel. Dressed in one of the many green gowns she'd fashioned in the tower room, the babe slept soundly.

A short while later, Lissant stepped back, surveying the plaits and coils she'd made of Juliana's hair. "You are ready, my lady."

Juliana fingered the coil over her right ear, then touched that over her left. "I thank you." She looked again to the babe, then reached forward and caressed his smooth cheek. "All will come right, little one. This promise I give you."

He made a faint sound, sucked in his bottom lip, but remained firmly in the arms of sleep.

Juliana stood and turned to the door. "Send for me if I am needed."

Before she reached the stairs, the din of those gathered in the hall to partake of the meal met her ears. She paused on the landing. As Lissant had said, this time when she entered the hall it was as the mother of Gabriel's son and heir, not a woman heavy with misbegotten seed. She smoothed her skirts, straightened her girdle, and put her chin up.

The hall quieted when she stepped from the stairs. Feeling all eyes upon her, she looked to the dais and met Gabriel's gaze. Was he angry? If so, she could not read the emotion across the distance.

He stood. "Lady Juliana," he acknowledged, his words tight.

He was not pleased, but it was upon him that she had come belowstairs. "My lord," she answered. As she stepped across the hall, she sought and found Sir Erec where he was seated to the right of the lord's chair. Her sister's champion—she prayed.

"Continue!" Gabriel ordered those at meal.

Conversations and the clink and clunk of eating resumed. Still, Juliana was watched. The people were curious about the woman who had birthed their lord's son and was no longer called Isolde.

Gabriel strode from behind the table and met her before the dais.

She was thankful it was not anger, but disapproval upon his brow.

He bent near. "What do you out of bed?"

She held his gaze. "Is not the question, 'For what do you keep yourself from your son?' And me?"

His lids flickered, and his lips thinned. "Come and sit at my side." He gripped her elbow.

324

Guilt—Juliana named that which kept him from her and Gabrien as he stepped her up to the dais. Though he knew Bernart was undeserving of it, he allowed it to weight him.

At their approach, the knight to the left of Gabriel's chair picked up his trencher and exchanged his seat for a vacant length of bench so that Juliana might sit beside Gabriel.

" 'Tis good to see you again, Sir Erec," Juliana said as they neared Gabriel's friend.

His lips pinched. "And you, my lady."

He was displeased. Was it her? Or the task Gabriel set him when he would prefer the defense of Mergot over a long journey to search out a frightened young woman?

Gabriel urged her past and handed her into the chair beside his.

Juliana nodded her gratitude to the knight who'd surrendered his place, then gently eased her soreness into it.

"You shall share my trencher," Gabriel said, then called to a serving wench, "Wine for Lady Juliana!"

Shortly, the wench returned and set a goblet before Juliana

Juliana tested it to her lips and was relieved to find the wine was watered. Her stomach was yet too wayward for anything stronger.

"Have you a meat dagger?" Gabriel asked.

She shook her head. "Do you forget, I was not allowed one in the tower room."

His face hardened.

Hoping to lighten the darkness that settled around him, she ventured a smile. " 'Twas thought I might use it to free myself." She shrugged. "And I cannot say I would not have."

He was not amused. "You shall share mine." He offered it.

With an inward sigh, she accepted the dagger.

Gabriel turned to Sir Erec, speaking in hushed tones that Juliana could not separate from the noise in the hall. She stabbed a chunk of meat from the trencher. Was it Alaiz of whom they spoke? She frowned. If so, she ought to be included in the discourse. Of course, it was not something easily discussed between three at meal. Afterward they would speak of it.

Afterward did not come for another hour, and by then she was fatigued.

"Join us in the lord's solar?" Gabriel asked, the first he had spoken to her since she'd come to table.

She looked around and saw he had risen with the others in the hall. "Aye." She pressed her palms to the table and levered up.

Gabriel took her elbow. With Sir Erec following, he steered her from the dais, across the hall, and up the stairs.

A fire was set in the solar, two chairs drawn before it. Gabriel guided Juliana to the first.

She shook her head. "I would stand."

An eyebrow arched, but then came realization of her discomfort. He nodded. "So shall we." He released her, stepped to the hearth, and stretched an arm across the mantel.

Sir Erec turned his back to the fire, his expression grim and impatient.

Gabriel was the first to speak. "Sir Erec and I have discussed at length that which he shall undertake in searching out your sister."

"And?"

"It could prove formidable. Know you where she might have fled?"

His query required no thought, for she had asked it of herself a hundred times. She shook her head. "She cannot return to our mother, for the lord who holds wardship over her and our brother would not tolerate Alaiz in what he now regards as his home. Too, did she try to return, he would surely give her into the sheriff's hands. Alaiz knows this."

"What of other family?" Gabriel asked.

"What other there is refused to take her into their homes following her accident." She swallowed, met his gaze. "Thus, though Bernart opposed it, I brought her to Tremoral."

"What of sanctuary?" Sir Erec asked.

She looked to him. "I have considered it, but as the church would not accept Alaiz without a goodly sum of money to maintain her, neither would she go there."

"Then where?" Gabriel asked.

Emotion thumped her chest. "I fear she has not anywhere to go. If Randal's kin have not yet captured her, she likely wanders . . . hides. . . ." *Is terrified.* Too late, Juliana looked away.

Surprisingly, her tears seemed to soften the brooding Sir Erec. He stepped before her and lightly touched her shoulder. "I shall do my utmost to find her, my lady."

She nodded. "I thank you."

He didn't quite smile, and one glance at Gabriel wiped away even that. Sir Erec took a vast step back.

Gabriel was jealous. A moment later he was before her. "On the morrow, Sir Erec departs for England," he said gruffly. "Once upon her shores, he shall go directly to Tremoral."

Fear coursed through Juliana. "But surely Alaiz is gone from there."

327

"Perhaps, but as it was there she was last, 'tis the place to begin."

Juliana looked beyond Gabriel to his friend. "Have you not thought what might happen if Sir Erec is recognized? His fate may be the same as your brother's. Mayhap worse."

The reminder of what had been done to Blase caused Gabriel's face to darken. " 'Tis likely Bernart is no longer at Tremoral. Has he not yet hazarded a passage of the channel, he surely awaits one—shall cross at the turning of the weather."

Meaning Sir Erec might also be delayed in setting sail. Might the two men cross paths?

A sharp rap on the door turned their heads, and sent Gabriel's and Sir Erec's hands to their sword hilts.

"Who goes?" Gabriel shouted.

"My lord," a voice sounded through the thick planks, "you must come!"

Gabriel strode past Juliana and wrenched the door open. "What say you?" he demanded of the man-at-arms.

"In the hall, my lord—a disagreement between knights. They prepare to shed blood."

Gabriel looked over his shoulder and wound his gaze around Juliana. "Our talk is concluded. I trust you shall return to your chamber forthwith."

Was it concluded? Perhaps for Gabriel . . . She inclined her head.

He swept his gaze to Sir Erec, then, leaving the door wide, stepped into the corridor and stretched his legs down its length.

Praying the knights in the hall would not come to blood, Juliana looked to Sir Erec.

He looked to her. "Good eve, my lady." He started to turn.

"Sir Erec!"

"My lady?"

"There is something you ought to know about my sister." In two steps, she covered the distance between them. "Alaiz is neither witless nor mad." She laid a hand to her chest. "Inside, she is as she was—intelligent, of good humor, kind. But though her injury closes doors on these things, she holds the keys to open them. Unfortunately, she cannot always find the right one to fit the lock." Emotion tightening her throat, she lowered her arm to her side. "Hence, I entreat you: do not mistake her for a fool."

He considered her. " 'Tis as I thought. Were it otherwise, it is not likely she would have escaped Kinthorpe." He crossed to the hearth. When he crossed back, his face was lined with thought. "Think you your sister donned disguise to escape Tremoral? That 'tis how she eludes capture?"

A jolt of memory put her in mind of the night of Gabriel's arrival at Tremoral. "Possible, indeed, and likely as a man."

"A man? What gives you to believe that?"

" 'Tis as she suggested the night you and Gabriel came to Tremoral." Did he know anything of what she'd revealed to Gabriel of the nights that had followed? Little, she decided, for though he was friend to Gabriel, Gabriel was not one to break confidences. "She knew we were in danger."

He nodded. "None would suspect it of a lady, especially one believed to be short on wits."

Fatigue more deeply settling in her bones, Juliana told herself it was time to return to her chamber. She offered the knight a smile of gratitude. "Though I know you do not gladly undertake the task, that you prefer to stand with

329

Gabriel against Bernart's coming, I am appreciative of your sacrifice."

He looked down, then back up. " 'Tis an honor to do the bidding of my friend and lord, but 'tis true I would be at Mergot when Kinthorpe pushes the gates, to stand at Gabriel's side, to die for him if need be."

Such fierce loyalty, but then, Gabriel was a man worthy of such—a good friend, though Bernart would deny it to his last breath. Curiosity made Juliana step nearer the knight. "How came you to know Gabriel?"

A muscle jumped in his jaw and brought darkness to his eyes. "We shared a cell at Acre."

Juliana nearly stumbled back. "At Acre? Gabriel was imprisoned?"

Realization made his eyes large a moment before he narrowed them. "I have spoken too much." He made to step around her. "Good eve, my lady."

Juliana caught his arm. "Pray, tell me."

He laid a hand over hers and pried her hold from his sleeve. "If he has not told of it, my lady, 'tis not for me to say."

Before he could put her hand from him, she turned it in his and gripped his fingers. "You must tell me!"

Anger slashed his face briefly. He searched her eyes, cocking his head. "Would it make you more kindly toward Gabriel did you know he did all he could for Bernart?"

"More kindly?" She shook her head. "Sir Erec, much has gone since last you were at Mergot." She loosed his hand and stepped back. "With all that I am and long to become"—she put her chin higher—"I love Gabriel. And have told him so."

The knight's gaze narrowed. "Love, Lady Juliana? You speak true?"

"I do. But though Gabriel returns my love, he holds himself from me and our son."

"Because of Kinthorpe?"

"Aye, his misplaced guilt grows walls betwixt us."

Sir Erec's chest puffed, and his hands snapped to fists at his sides. "Guilt!" he spat. " 'Tis Kinthorpe who ought to be awash in guilt for all those who died for his vainglory."

Then the knight would tell her how he and Gabriel had come to share a cell. "How know you that?"

Remembrance turned his handsome face nearly ugly. "I know because I am one of the fools Gabriel could not turn from your husband's quest—try though he did."

A chill crawled over her skin. "You followed Bernart?"

"Aye." He turned, crossed to the window embrasure, and held his back to her. "So confident were we that sixty men could take the city, especially as 'twas fairly easy to breach the wall." A bitter laugh clouded the cool air that slipped past the shutters. "No sooner did our feet touch ground than we were set upon by hundreds." He lowered his head. "Such slaughter. And it took only minutes."

Aching for those who had died, Juliana waited for the rest to be told, but the knight gave no more. Perhaps he could not. "Sir Erec?"

He turned. "My lady?"

"What of Gabriel? How did he come to be imprisoned?"

"He followed us over the wall—for a friendship of which Kinthorpe was undeserving."

Dear God. Years of allowing herself to believe Gabriel had betrayed, of hating him . . . Juliana stepped to a chair and put a hand to it to steady herself. "Never did Bernart tell me."

"Never did he know."

331

She started. "What?"

"Your husband fled—left those yet standing to fall beneath the infidels' swords. When Gabriel followed us over the wall, already Bernart was gone."

Juliana's stomach turned.

"Gabriel saved my life," Sir Erec said, "and if not that the infidels fell upon him and beat him bloody, he would have gone in search of Kinthorpe."

She shook her head. "I did not know."

"You could not have, my lady."

She clasped her hands at her waist and waited.

"For two months we nearly rotted in a cell too small to lie down in," Sir Erec continued. "We were taunted, beaten, oft made to go thirsty and hungry. And when there *was* food and drink . . ." His brow and mouth creased. "If not that Gabriel's tales of courtly love gave me hope, methinks I might have gone mad."

Juliana reeled. Gabriel had spilled tales he'd so despised? Recalled that which he'd scorned and ignored— or appeared to have ignored?

Sir Erec nodded. " 'Tis true, my lady. 'Twas in that cell I first heard your name—and many times, determined as he was to find Bernart and return him to you."

Pain lanced Juliana. How Gabriel had been wronged! Curse the guilt Bernart did not deserve!

"When we were loosed from our prison cell," Sir Erec continued, "Gabriel searched out the other cells in hopes of finding Bernart. It did not seem likely, but we found him in a cell distant from ours, the door thrown wide his shackles loosed by those of King Richard's army, who had released us." Sir Erec's gaze went past Juliana, then stuck on the fire. "Kinthorpe sat in a corner of his cell and stared at Gabriel. Dim though 'twas in that place, the hatred was so mortal one could hardly breathe for it."

Juliana knew it well, but neither Gabriel nor Sir Erec could have known whence it came.

"No words were spoken between them, my lady." Sir Erec traversed the chamber, halting before her. "None needed to be."

"Then 'tis true Bernart never learned Gabriel followed him over the wall?"

"Gabriel would not let it be told."

Juliana gripped her entwined hands to keep from throwing them into the air. "Why?"

"You would understand had you been there, my lady."

"But if Bernart had known—" Nay, no difference would it have made that Gabriel had nearly laid down his life to aid his friend. Still Bernart's manhood would be lost, and still he would put the blame anywhere but upon himself. For him, the deaths of those who had witlessly followed him and his resulting emasculation would ever be Gabriel's fault.

Juliana pried her fingers apart. "I do understand. What happened afterward?"

"Gabriel and I joined with King Richard's army and fought long beside our sovereign." Sir Erec pinned her with his gaze. "Know this, Lady Juliana: I have many times been in battle with Gabriel, and there is no coward in him. He fights with courage beyond my own and that of others, does ne'er run from danger, is ever loyal. 'Tis for this he earned the king's respect and was awarded this barony."

She needed no proof beyond that which she already knew of Gabriel. She inclined her head. "I thank you for telling me, Sir Erec." Not that there was anything she could do with the knowledge. Bernart would lay siege to Mergot, kill and plunder all for which Gabriel had worked so hard, would not be content with anything less than the drawing of his old friend's blood and the claiming of a son not his. None could stop him—except God, did He deign to dabble with common mortals. Or was there another? She blinked. How could she have been so blind?

She laid a hand on Sir Erec's shoulder. "I would ask that you help me."

His eyebrows bumped, suspicion glimmering from his eyes. "What say you?"

"I need you to deliver the king a message."

His mouth tightened. "For what, my lady?"

"If 'tis true he holds Gabriel in such high regard, he may intervene in Bernart's coming against Mergot."

The knight stepped from beneath her hand. " 'Tis not for me to summon him."

Juliana fought the impulse to seize hold of the knight. "Gabriel will not ask the king to intervene. And for that he may die—and others! Pray, Sir Erec, I do not ask that you betray him, only that you help me assure our son knows his father."

There was a struggle upon his face, but he put it from him with a shake of his head. "I am sorry, my lady. What you ask I cannot—"

"Come with me." She gripped his arm and started toward the door, but his resistance dragged her to a halt. She looked around. "There is something I must show you."

"What?"

"It cannot be told."

Grudgingly, he nodded. "Very well, but only this and that is all."

She led him from the solar to her chamber and slowly opened the door. The only sound within was that of sleep. She looked to where Lissant lay on her pallet at the foot of the bed, the flickering torchlight playing over her low-ered lids.

Juliana stepped within. Sir Erec hesitated, but came behind. She halted alongside the cradle. "Sir Erec, I would have you meet Gabrien."

The knight's face softened as he looked upon the sleeping infant. "Gabriel told me you were brought to bed of a fine boy." A smile slipped to his lips and he leaned down to look better upon Gabrien. "He is that, my lady."

"Aye, and does he not deserve a fine father, Sir Knight?"

He hardened again, then straightened. "Only if he be of Gabriel."

Her turn to speak secrets long held. She glanced at Lissant, assuring herself the woman slept. "After Acre," she began, "no amount of God's mercy would allow Bernart to father a child." She bit her lip. "That which has been taken cannot be given back." No more need be said, as evidenced by the knight's start.

"I speak true, Sir Erec."

Words eluded him, though they surely clambered through his mind.

"King Richard is still on the continent?" she pushed on.

A dry laugh parted his lips. "Where else would he be, my lady? Though he is king of all England, France is his home. 'Tis held by many that he will never return to England."

She had heard it said herself. "He is in Normandy?"

"At Rouen. He intends to build a castle on the Seine."

She could not ask for better. "You shall pass by there on your way to the coast, then."

"I shall."

"Then you will entreat the king to come to Mergot."

Displeasure unsettled his face. "Will I, my lady?"

335

His derision made her wince. She had pushed too hard. "I pray you will, for Gabrien . . . for Gabriel . . . for me."

His gaze wavered, and his nostrils flared. Then, with a grunt, he turned on his heel and strode toward the door.

Juliana squared her shoulders. It seemed she must go herself. Somehow she would slip free of Gabriel and find her way to Rouen. And the babe? She looked to him. Gabriel would provide—would find a wet nurse to feed Gabrien's hunger until she returned. But the ache! She pressed a hand to her breasts.

"What think you the king will do?" Sir Erec's voice cut through her pain.

She snapped her head around and saw he stood before the door. Would he do it, then? " 'Tis an annulment I seek, Sir Erec. King Richard's presence will not only stop senseless bloodshed, but assure I am heard."

"Then you will reveal your husband's . . . impotence?"

The word caught Juliana by surprise, and she darted her gaze to the maid on her pallet. The only movement about Lissant was the breath pushing her shoulders.

"Too long I have stayed at his side," Juliana said, "borne the weight of his hatred, done as he bade." She shook her head. "No more. This babe is not Bernart's, and he shall not steal him from Gabriel."

" 'Tis what he intends?"

"Aye." She swallowed. "As always he intended." There, it was said.

The air hung grave with his questions, but he did not ask them.

"I will do it," he said, "for Gabriel."

She loosed her breath and sent thanks heavenward.

"What message would you have me deliver to the king?"

"Tell him Bernart Kinthorpe comes to steal his loyal

vassal's son and the mother of that child—that he is needed at Mergot to put an end to the coming siege."

"And I should tell him who sends the message?"

Would King Richard come were he told? Stand for a man who had taken another's wife? "Only does he demand to know."

The knight nodded. " 'Twill be done." He turned and opened the door.

"Sir Erec."

He looked over his shoulder.

"Gabriel cannot know."

"This I know." He stepped into the corridor and pulled the door closed.

She stared at it until the sounds of Gabrien's awakening turned her to the cradle. She lifted him. "You are hungry, hmm?"

He yawned, stretched, and turned his face to her breast.

"Patience," she whispered. Gently she laid him upon the bed, loosed her laces, and pulled the bliaut over her head. Then, propped against the headboard, chemise dragged up, she put Gabrien to her breast. Though he was quick to satisfy his hunger, she was loath to return him to his cradle. Deciding it would do no harm to hold him a while longer, she lay on her side and stared into his half-hooded eyes.

"King Richard comes," she said, and touched his bottom lip. "He comes."

Gabrien gurgled, mouth twitching as if he might smile, his eyes closed.

She closed her own, but when she tried to lift her lids, she could not. She was very tired. . . .

Gabriel stared at mother and child as longing tugged through him. He should return to his solar as he had done the past two nights after first coming to Juliana's chamber. But something held him beside the bed. He fought it, but in the end removed his sword belt and stretched out beside his son and the woman who ought to be his wife. He stared at her shadowed face—rendered more beautiful in sleep. In all his life he had never wanted anything more. Not even the inheritance his father denied him. Juliana was all there was—and Gabrien. But how to hold onto them?

He closed his eyes, running through the castle's defenses he had put in place to withstand the coming siege. Was all provided for—food, water, weaponry? Were Mergot's people ready? He would prevail. Had to!

"You did not tell me," Juliana said.

He lifted his lids, meeting her gaze over Gabrien's small, round head. Though there was yet torchlight in the room, it struggled to put color to her warm brown eyes. Had he awakened her? He should not have lain down.

"Why?" she asked.

He frowned. "What?"

"Why did you not tell me you went into Acre to bring Bernart out? That you were also imprisoned?"

Damn Erec! Gabriel bunched his hands. He ought not to have left them alone. He pushed up onto an elbow.

Juliana reached over the babe and caught his arm. "Tell me."

In that moment, he wished he did not feel what he did when she touched him. It was too hard to go from her.

"Please, Gabriel."

"What is there to tell?" he said gruffly. "Other than that I failed? Think you there is redemption in that?"

She levered herself up. "You are wrong. You did all you could to stop him, but Bernart had to make his own way—as you have had to make yours. That you tried to turn him from his foolishness is unworthy of the guilt you let set upon your shoulders like a winter mantle." She touched his jaw. "You do not owe him a son—as I do not. You must believe that, must remember all he has done, must not forget Blase."

As if he could. What had been done to his brother demanded retribution, but what had been done to Bernart . . .

Gabriel remembered the day he had found his friend in a cell that reeked of death and excrement. He'd had but to look upon the man he'd grown up alongside to know that never again would they share a skin of wine, a laugh, good conversation.

"What would you have me do?" he asked. "Run? If so, know I will not. I shall fight Bernart and, God willing, arise the victor."

She shook her head. "I do not ask that you run, only that when Bernart comes against you, you not let the past darken your judgment."

"I shall do my duty, Juliana—to you, to Gabrien, to my people."

She drew her hand from his jaw and touched her fingers to his lips. "And when 'tis done? Will you let yourself love me, Gabriel? Without reservation? Without Bernart's shadow upon us?"

Her softly spoken words wrapped around his heart, pulled tight, and made him speak what he had not intended. "I do love you, Juliana, but I make no promises—not until it is done."

A sad smile turned her lips. She lowered her hand. "Mayhap if King Richard could be called upon to intervene, 'twould be done the sooner—without bloodshed."

He had considered it, but for a moment only. This was his battle—between him and Bernart. To bring the king into it would cause to be revealed Juliana's humiliation and Bernart's shame. "Nay, Juliana, I will not call on him. Bernart and I shall settle this."

She lay down. "I knew 'twas what you would do."

He sat up. "I shall leave you to your rest."

"Stay." She smoothed a hand over Gabrien's downy head. "You belong with your family."

His family. The war he waged was pitiful. He lowered himself to the mattress.

Juliana reached over Gabrien and curled her hand around Gabriel's shoulder. "I love you, Gabriel."

Her declaration was silk upon his jagged emotions. He relaxed more deeply into the mattress, lowering his lids. For the first time in a long time, his sleep was restful. For the first time in forever, he was where he belonged. Home.

Chapter Twenty-three

March 1196

War had come to Mergot. No words were yet exchanged, naught spoken between besieged and besieger, just the silence of waiting. But once the weather turned there would be siege. Soon.

Gabriel pulled his mantle closer, staring beyond his clouded breath to the bordering wood before which Bernart and his army of knights, men-at-arms, squires, and mercenaries had put down camp two days past. And more men were coming, as told by the wench Gabriel had sent into their camp. She had returned ere dawn, her pretty head filled with all she'd gleaned from her flirtations with Bernart's men. So it was told that Baron Faison, the vengeful brother of Mergot's former lord, would send reinforcements to aid Bernart's siege. Gabriel was not surprised. It was the opportunity Faison longed for, and

Bernart had never been short of cunning. *That* his injury had not altered. But Gabriel was prepared. Buckets of caltrops—many-pointed iron spikes that, when scattered before men and charging horses, caused appalling confusion—were placed around the wall walks. Great cauldrons to pour boiling water and hot sand upon the attackers were set at intervals between the battlements. Newly forged swords and pikes were in abundance, as were arrows and slings. Though quicklime and Greek fire were not as abundant, Gabriel knew when and where to place them so that they would have the effect of thrice as much. When the mining began—if it began—jars of water would be set upon the ground to detect underground movement. As for his people, those of the villages nearest Mergot had been brought into the castle, along with their food supplies and meager livestock. Though it made for crowded living, it would not only force Bernart to forage for his own supplies in the harsh of winter, but he would be unable to use the threat of harm to Gabriel's people.

All was provided for—or so Gabriel prayed, for no man could erect a defense another could not pull down. Which was true for Bernart as well. Beginning this night, Gabriel would lead a sortie out of the castle through the dusting of snow to destroy those siege weapons Bernart was building, the ultimate goal being to reverse roles so that the besiegers found no respite from harassing attacks.

Gabriel sighed, turned from his billow of breath, and strode to the steps. He ascended quickly, then slowed to weave a broken path through the displaced villagers who huddled against the cold. He stopped several times to speak to those whose eyes sought his, to reassure them, to thank them for their forbearance. The conditions were much the same in the inner bailey. As for the great hall, a mass of bodies fouled the air so that no amount of herb-strewn rushes could disguise the stench. And it would get no better. Henceforth, water was as gold, not to be wasted upon baths.

Finally he reached the stairs. He was halfway ascended when a hand curled around his upper arm. He knew the touch.

Though Juliana's smile was tentative, the chill of his unease warmed before it.

"All is well?" she asked.

"All is quiet." He could report no better.

"The weather?"

" 'Tis clearing."

Concern washed across her face.

Gabriel wiped a smudge from beneath her bottom lip. "For a lady and a woman who gave birth not three weeks past, you work too hard."

She glanced behind. "They must all be fed."

"Aye, though not by your hand."

She mounted the step beside him, the added inches permitting her to drop her chin from its strained tilt. "Gabrien is asleep and Lissant with him. I ought to be here."

He would not argue with her as he had done on the day past, when she'd insisted upon going among the people and tending their needs. She was too determined and too much in need of diversion from that which waited without the walls.

"At least they are warm," he said, sweeping his gaze to the hall. Some good would come of the rank press of bodies. But tomorrow these people would know cold again when they exchanged places with those in the outer bailey.

"Aye." Juliana pushed a damp tress off her brow. "There is that."

Gabriel stared at her and was reminded of the third

night at Tremoral, when they had come together and, for the first time, he'd seen her beneath him. She had looked much the same—dampened hair about her face, cheeks flushed, eyes wide. Feeling a rise between his thighs, he yanked his longing in. "I must make ready for the sortie."

Silence followed him to the top of the stairs, then her footsteps. She ran the length of corridor to overtake him before the lord's solar. "Must you, Gabriel?" Pleading and fear met in her eyes.

He stopped his hand on the door. "Better a battle beyond the walls than at the walls."

"But if you are captured—"

"I will not be. We will lay fire to whatever siege engines Bernart raises and return forthwith."

She took a step nearer and touched a hand to his jaw. "There is naught I can say to turn you?"

He nearly closed his eyes on the feel of her hand upon him. Three weeks since he had been so near her, three weeks of longing, three weeks of denying himself more than the fleeting contact when she passed Gabrien into his arms. But it was better this way. After the threat of Bernart was past—were it ever, a dissenting voice reminded him of his tenuous hold on Juliana—they could look to a future together.

"Naught you can say," he uttered, and drew her hand from him. He pushed the door open to the warm fire the chambermaid had kept stoked. If not for the heat of the hall that had chased all chill from him, it would have been welcome. He pushed his mantle back from his shoulders and stepped inside. Though he had not intended for Juliana to follow, she came behind him.

"Juliana, you should not—"

"I will help you ready for the sortie." She crossed to the chest and knelt before it.

He ought to send her away. It was not good to be in a place that held both bed and her.

"What shall you wear?" she asked, lifting the chest lid.

He stepped farther into the room. "White, that we shall not be seen against the snow." As Mergot was built upon raised ground, the snow would be at their backs. And all would be lit by a generous half-moon.

As she searched the chest's contents, Gabriel crossed to the bed. He freed the brooch that secured his mantle, swept the woolen garment to the mattress, and became aware of silence. Realization struck a moment before he set his gaze upon Juliana.

She sank back upon her heels, her eyes fixed on the fistful of white trailing from her hand.

Juliana's heart gripped as memories rolled across the months and put her back to that morn when she had tried to remove the chemise from beneath Gabriel's sleeping form, then later when she had gone to retrieve it. He had kept it. In spite of what he'd believed of her, he had taken it with him from Tremoral.

She looked up and found his gaze. " 'Twas more than the babe that returned you to Tremoral."

He breathed deeply. "It was."

Her insides fluttered as if they might fly. "And had you not been given rumor that Bernart intended to set me aside did I not bear an heir?"

His gaze went to the chemise. "I was searching you out that I might ask you to leave with me"—his eyes came back to hers—"when that wench, Nesta, caught me aside and told the lie."

Nesta, ever a bane. Determinedly, Juliana put the woman from her. Gabriel had felt for her even then—more than lust, perhaps the beginnings of love. Tears slid to her eyes. "I could not have gone with you. Alaiz—"

"I know."

She lowered the chemise. Where was Alaiz? Had Sir Randal's kin apprehended her? Had she been dragged before the sheriff? Did she yet live? She sent up a prayer that Sir Erec would find Alaiz soon.

"Juliana?"

She looked around and found Gabriel hunkered beside her. "I fear for her," she said.

"You shall see her again."

Such certainty with which he spoke! "Will I?"

He brushed the backs of his fingers across her cheek, then turned them around her jaw. "All that I can do I shall."

She closed her eyes. "I know." But if Alaiz was found and brought to Mergot, still there would be Bernart. *Dear God, send King Richard. Not a sennight hence, not a day. This moment.*

Gabriel's breath came against the side of her face, sweeping her ear. "All will soon be decided, and when 'tis, you shall be at my side."

She raised her lids.

They beheld one another, searched, let grow an awareness of their need to be near. When Gabriel bent his head, she welcomed the urgent press of his mouth, drew his tongue inside, gasped as he swept the sensitive tissue within. Then it was her turn. She drank from him, explored his hidden recesses, thrilled when his tongue came again to hers. How she needed him—to know that they would attain the age of the old together.

She turned into him and slid her arms around his neck.

Suddenly he pulled away. "We cannot."

Feeling light of head, Juliana put hands to the floor to

steady herself, steeling herself against the pain of his rejection. "Why?"

He gained his feet and turned. It took only a few moments of searching the chest for him to find what he looked for. "Because of this we cannot." He held her wedding ring, which he had taken along with her girdle when she'd tried to escape him en route to Mergot. She stared at it, hating what it represented of the past four years of her life.

"I want you, Juliana," Gabriel said. "I ache for it, but first I must finish with Bernart. This"—he turned the gold band in his fingers—"can no more be between us." His eyes swept back to her and he reached out a hand.

She looked to the long, tapered fingers that had touched her as she had never been touched. Would she know their touch again? She dragged her thoughts from that place. She pressed her shoulders back and put her hand in his.

He drew her to her feet. "When we come together again," he said, "it shall be as husband and wife."

Husband. Juliana turned herself around the word. *Wife. Let it not be a dream.* . . . "Aye, Gabriel De Vere, I will be your wife and you my husband. There is naught I want more."

His hand tightened on hers.

She looked to his other hand and lifted the ring from it. She stepped past Gabriel and hurled the band into the fire.

They stared at the covetous flames. A short while later, dressed all in white, he left her.

She stood before the empty doorway, listened to his retreating footsteps, and prayed he would return. A thought came to her a moment later. She bent, grasped the hem of her amber gown, and tore it.

She overtook Gabriel near the base of the stairs.

"Juliana?" Concern furrowed his face.

She pushed up his tunic sleeve and tied the material around his bare upper arm so that it would not be seen against the snow. "I am with you always," she said.

He touched the frayed favor, then laid a hand to his chest in a gesture meant to mirror her words.

As if spoken, they inscribed themselves upon her heart. She stepped back. "Godspeed, my love."

Gabriel turned at the postern gate, letting a grim smile bend his mouth as flames burned the night sky. In the light of those flames, Bernart's men rushed to douse the fire, shouting orders. The trebuchet would not be soon in coming to the castle walls. Just as heartening was that its destruction and the loosing of a score of the knights' destriers had been accomplished without a death on either side. It was good for the conscience, if naught else. None ought to die for Bernart's rapacious quest, though many would if the sorties proved unsuccessful. Tomorrow eve Gabriel would lead another, and again the following night. And each would become more dangerous. This night was a gift not likely to be given again.

He gave silent thanks, then stepped through the gate. It closed behind him and was secured by a man-at-arms.

Gabriel looked to the half dozen who'd accompanied him outside the walls. Also clothed in white, they were as ghosts in the dark of the bailey, but he caught the paleness of their smiles in their shadowed faces.

"Fine work," he commended. "Now get you to the hall and take your rest." He watched them go, then stretched his gaze to the donjon beyond the inner wall. From her chamber window Juliana would be watching. Waiting. He closed his eyes, pressed a hand to his opposite arm, and squeezed the knot of material she had tied beneath his sleeve. With him always. He lifted his lids and stared into the night. Always. Whatever the price.

Chapter Twenty-four

Now came Faison. One hundred strong.

A darkening in the middle of him, Gabriel put a hand to the embrasure and leaned forward to better see beyond the battlements to the morning mist before the wood. In the death of winter was the birth of spring, Faison brought siege engines—mangonels, trebuchets, ballistas, a battering ram—all of which the dark lord must have had ready for such an occasion. Revenge for his brother's loss and his own.

Gabriel thrust a hand through his hair and clawed at his aching scalp. For nearly a sennight, he and his men had night and again struck at Bernart's camp. Siege engines were destroyed, horses loosed, food supplies seized, tents brought down upon sleeping occupants. Then there were the injuries done to those of Bernart's men who had put themselves between Gabriel and his targets. Necessary, but not without a price. Fortunately, it did not yet go so high as to take the lives of any of Gabriel's men. But there would be no more sorties. This day Bernart had found his advantage. Ere the sun pushed the clouds overhead, siege would be at Mergot's walls.

" 'Tis the day?" A voice squeezed among the din.

Gabriel swept around and saw that Juliana stood on the step down from the wall walk. "What do you here?" he demanded too harshly.

Though her brow creased, she ascended the final step. "The hall is frantic with word that siege engines have come. They are of Baron Faison?"

Her scent teased the air between them. "Aye, the baron thinks to finally test his revenge."

She tried to hide her fear, but he saw it in her eyes, felt it, ached for it. He laid hands to her shoulders. "My vow is good, Juliana."

She nodded. "I do not doubt it."

"Then return to the donjon and keep with our son until I come to you."

She searched his face, glanced between the battlements. "At least he does not make pretense of bearing gifts." Her attempt at levity found no match in her voice.

Gabriel's grimness lifted enough to let slip a smile. "For that I am most grateful, my sweet Helen." He nudged her toward the stairs. "Now go."

Her hesitation was palpable. Thus he was not surprised when she thrust herself into his arms. She said naught, simply pressed herself to him as if it might be the last time.

Uncaring who might see, he slid his arms around her and put his lips to her hair. "You are mine," he murmured, "have always been mine."

She eased against him.

He made a memory of her body against his, set it deep

351

within that it might never pale. "And shall ever be mine."

She dropped her head back. "Ever," she whispered. "Ever."

Her mouth tilted, but before it could reach a full smile, a cry swept across the walls.

"My lord," a man-at-arms called, "they move!"

His announcement stirred the villagers in the outer bailey to gasps, whimpers, and frenzied speech.

Gabriel loosed Juliana and swung back to the embrasure.

The mist about their heads and shoulders, Bernart's army tramped the ground—numerous on foot, many astride, some upon siege engines pulled by horses and pushed by men. And there, at the fore, was the thick figure of the man Gabriel had once called friend. As for the one who rode alongside Bernart, there was no mistaking Dominic Faison, whose sword arm had been lost during the Crusade. A bitter man. An angry man. But this day he thought to smile again.

He would not, Gabriel silently vowed, and stepped from the embrasure. For a moment he met Juliana's gaze and was struck by the fear and pain she swept beneath her lashes. What he would not do to spare her this.

He looked beyond her to his men upon the walls and those in the bailey. They were still, poised for his orders. He inclined his head. "At arms!"

As if a great hand set them to motion, they dispersed. Shouting one to the other, they rushed to their posts amid the terrified villagers. According to plans laid to table a fortnight past, Gabriel's people were ushered toward the drawbridge that would see them to the relative safety of the inner bailey, men hastened to light fires beneath the cauldrons, archers took up bows, pikes were hefted. Soon blood would spill.

The approach of Bernart's army adding to the clamor within the walls, Gabriel looked again to Juliana.

Her shoulders were square, her gaze fixed upon her hands at her waist.

Quelling the desire to embrace her again, knowing it best that he distance himself so that he not be distracted, he said, "Go, Juliana."

The stillness of his voice moved Juliana's gaze to his. *Forget not the tournament,* she told herself. *None can best him.* But an army . . . And how many might die? It was the way of things, she knew, that by blood men held that which they laid claim to, but it did not make it right. What of the king? Though he had not answered her summons, might he answer Gabriel's?

"Gabriel," she ventured, "still you could send word to King—"

"This is how 'tis done, Juliana," he said sharply.

She compressed her lips, denying the stab of tears. Did a miracle bring the king to Mergot, Gabriel would surely be angered by her having summoned him. Unfortunately, it seemed she was to be spared his wrath. "Nay," she said, "it is how men do it."

Vexation touched Gabriel's brow, but then he sighed and said, "it is the only way I know."

She started to turn away, but stopped. Never could she turn from Gabriel. If this was to be his course, she would stay by his side. She pushed her stiff lips into what felt nothing like a smile. "God be with you, my love." She spoke so softly the words were little more than a breath.

But he heard. Emotion in his eyes, he nodded, then pivoted and strode opposite.

Juliana stared after him a long moment, but as she lifted her skirts to descend to the bailey, a sickly familiar voice breached the wall.

"Gabriel De Vere, you son of a sow, show yourself!"

Bernart, his words sure to torture Gabriel for his mother's cuckoldry.

A chill shot Juliana, pitching her innards. Dear God, had she never again heard his voice she would have been grateful to eternity. In the quieting of the bailey, she looked around, meeting Gabriel's gaze where he stood distant atop the gatehouse. Face expressionless, he jutted his chin, silently commanding her from the wall.

"Come, old friend," Bernart taunted, his voice strained from affecting a pitch to ensure it carried over the wall. "Surely you fear not this man with whom you were once as a brother."

Gabriel closed his hand over his sword hilt.

"I want naught that is not mine," Bernart sent to the walls.

A sickening feeling in her belly, Juliana continued to stare at Gabriel. In spite of the distance between them, she knew there was fire in his eyes, though more because of Bernart's mockery—his lie—than that she had yet to go from the inner bailey.

Suddenly he turned and strode to the battlements. He peered down upon the besieger, then came around. "Lower the drawbridge!" he shouted as he descended the gatehouse steps.

Juliana's breath fell from her. He would answer Bernart's summons?

"Archers at my back." He ordered his men to position themselves at the battlements.

Amid the screech and groan of the drawbridge, he came off the steps and called for the inner portcullis to be raised. It was three feet off the ground when he ducked beneath.

Juliana ran to the wall, put hands to an embrasure, and

peered at the ominous spectacle. Men everywhere. Fighting men. Killing men. And there, mounted upon his destrier twenty feet back from the descending drawbridge, was the one who led them. Appearing to have gained more weight, as evidenced by the roll of flesh between chin and chain mail that was as ruddy as his sagging cheeks, Bernart shifted his bulk. In response, the horse sidestepped.

With sudden remembrance of what he had once meant to her, Juliana dragged her nails over the stonework and sank them into her palms.

"Ah, Gabriel, old friend," Bernart mocked as the one he wrongfully called enemy ducked beneath the portcullis, "I did not think you would come out."

Juliana swept her gaze to Bernart, then back to Gabriel.

Sword in hand, Gabriel halted at the center of the drawbridge.

Her throat opened with a rattle. *Pray, send King Richard. Let truth decide this, not blood.*

"I am here, Kinthorpe," Gabriel answered. "For what do you come against me?"

Bernart chuckled, a gurgling sound that, to his obvious embarrassment, turned to a hacking cough.

Juliana lifted a hand and fumbled back the strands of hair the breeze coaxed from her braid. What now? What did Bernart plan? She looked to his men. The one who was absent an arm captured her gaze, likely due to the dark scowl he wore as easily as one might a girdle—slung low upon what appeared to be a handsome face, putting frame to his eyes, nose, and mouth. It had to be the Baron Faison of whom Lissant had spoken.

A moment later those eyes came to hers. She jerked back to Bernart, and could not suppress her flinch of sympathy for his indignity.

Mouth gone flat, he wiped it across his tunic sleeve. "You know for what I come," he heaved as if exerted. "I want that stolen from me—my wife and son."

Juliana swallowed. Though he would know the child was born by now, was it only a guess that she'd birthed a son? More likely word of Gabriel's heir had come to Faison, who had then passed it to Bernart. She looked to Gabriel. How she longed to see his face. Not that he would reveal anything he did not wish Bernart to see.

He braced his legs farther apart, raising his sword higher. "You can have neither. They are mine and ever shall be."

Though fear wore Juliana's shoulders, her heart surged against her ribs.

As for Bernart, he reddened like a cloud-laced sunset. "Then you choose death." His angry voice trembled in a pitch far higher than he normally allowed. A moment later, he pulled his sword from his scabbard. He raised it, but not to come alone against Gabriel. Rather, to call his men to attack.

"Bernart!" Gabriel bellowed. "Look thee to my walls."

Bernart's sword wavered, his eyes skittering to the archers whose arrows were nocked and sighted upon him and his army.

" 'Twill be honorable, this," Gabriel said, "else death shall be yours."

Too late, Juliana realized she should have stepped back from the embrasure.

Bernart's gaze found her, and his eyes widened. His lips formed her name, and for a moment pain came out from behind the vengeance he breathed—that great heaving ache that, for too long, had held her to his side. All she had ever wanted was to take it away, to ease it from his brow, his eyes, his heart. But *that* no mortal could do.

No peace would he find on earth—with or without her and the child he hoped would prove his masculinity. He was as if dead.

"Juliana!" Her name burst from him. "I come for you."

Movement pulled her regard to Gabriel as his head came around. She could look upon his eyes forever, she realized—even now with displeasure as their source of light.

"Juliana!" Bernart shouted. "You have heard all?"

Oh, Richard, why do you not come? She opened her hands on the embrasure. "I have," she raised her voice to make the distance.

"And what say you, *wife?*"

She put her chin up. "I say you ought to return to England without me."

Had her words been arrows, she could not have bled him more. He flushed, baring his teeth. "Whore!"

And he could not have bled her more.

"Return to the donjon, Juliana," Gabriel called.

She met his gaze and saw that his back was stiffer for the foul name Bernart had put to her.

"I warn you, Juliana," Bernart seethed, "many shall die, for I will not leave without my son."

One last time, she gave him her regard, searching for a piece of the man for whom she had once felt. Gone. She shook her head, then turned that she would not be made to witness the terrible contorting of his face as he spewed curses.

Now there would be war, and many would die.

Feeling more an old woman than her twenty years, Juliana descended to the bailey. Hardly had she stepped to the ground than the drawbridge sounded its creaking and tumbling of chains. A few moments later, Gabriel was at her side.

"Take you to the donjon," he said, wearing distance as if it were a mantle.

Realizing he was no longer the Gabriel who had taken her heart to his, that this day he was a warrior, ready to battle for his home and people, Juliana quelled the desire to be near him. Were he to stay alive, it was as it should be.

"I shall come to you at first opportunity," he assured her.

Which could be tomorrow, or the day after, or never . . . *Nay*. He *would* come to her. Her breasts twinged with ache, a reminder that her babe would soon be in need of suckling. "I shall await you," she said, and turned.

"Juliana?"

She looked over her shoulder.

"Ever," he said, for a brief moment coming out of his armor; then he swung toward the gatehouse and began shouting orders.

That single word swelled hope through Juliana. "Ever," she whispered, and pressed a hand to her chest. Not even when, as a young woman, she'd glorified love as being the end of all had she dreamed it could be like this—beyond the body, the heart, the mind . . . not only within herself, but without. No courtly love, this. And were she to lose it in Gabriel's death?

She refused to ponder that last. As she lifted her skirts and started toward the inner drawbridge, her thoughts turned again to the one who could end the siege with but his coming. *Where are you, King Richard?*

The walls were coming down again, the outer work crumbling beneath the barrage of boulders flung against the repaired stonework. There were fires as well, enough to warm the chill air and put sweat upon the brows of his men. But of all the ill wrought this first day, the worst of it was the shouts of pain that would not be put from Gabriel even after the injured were carried to the donjon for tending. As for the dead, there was one—at least until the wounded fell to infection, and it would happen if the siege did not soon end. Would it?

Gabriel peered through the arrow loop at the land before the castle. It was scarred and scattered with men and siege engines. Though Bernart's wounded were of greater number, partly owing to the vulnerability of battling on open land, and his army had suffered more deaths, still he sent men to the walls as if they were of no more consequence than the lifeless boulders culled from the wood. Most promising, though, was what appeared to be strife between Bernart and Faison. An hour earlier, Gabriel had witnessed across the distance the rebel baron's angry exchange with the man to whom he had offered aid. As there could only be one leader in any conflict and Bernart was not it, Faison was displeased. And he ought to be, for his losses included men, horses, and a trebuchet burned to the ground by a flaming arrow. For it all, he had bits of wall and a handful of the enemy fallen. It was not the revenge he sought.

Gabriel pushed his gaze to the horizon. Sunset was an hour away, but with the dark would come no respite. Of course, Bernart might not take advantage of the night to steal men over the wall to attack from within. But should he, those men would have to elude the light of torches Gabriel had directed to be set to the walls.

He turned into the gatehouse room, flexing his facial muscles in an attempt to ease the tension. He was tired, dirty, and smelled of the smoke of Bernart's fires. He closed his eyes and remembered the last that had leaped to the sky. It had taken a good portion of the stable roof before it was doused. As a result, a man-at-arms had been seriously burned and two horses lost. Of all that Mergot had endured this day, it was only the beginning.

Gabriel crossed to the stairs. As he began his descent, thunder sounded, rippling through the wood beneath his feet, but it was not of the clouded heavens. Another boulder had met its mark—a very large one. He took the last steps at a slide and surged into the bailey. "Damnation!"

The left face of the inner wall surrounding the donjon had taken a serious blow. Though it yet stood, four feet had been torn from its uppermost bounds.

Praying there were no injuries—especially to the villagers who huddled beyond—Gabriel ran past his men. Barely had he stepped to the inner drawbridge than a shout from atop the outer walls reached him.

"An army approaches, my lord!"

He faltered. An army. Yet more men Bernart brought against him? *God's rood!* Still, he did not turn back.

The mass of people were near frenzy when he strode into the bailey. The moment they caught sight of him, they surged forward.

"Any injuries?" Gabriel shouted above the babble of men and women and the cries of their children, the latter reminding him of Gabrien.

"Here, my lord!" A man's voice rose above the rest. "My boy's been struck on the arm and is bleeding."

Gabriel could not see beyond the others who crowded him. "Take him to the great hall," he shouted. "Any others?"

Two more answered. Fortunately, that seemed all, and the injuries were minor. Gabriel also directed them to the donjon, then instructed the villagers to keep back from the walls. They were hardly soothed, but there was naught else he could do. War awaited him. However, as he turned away he was struck by the sudden stillness—the absence of missiles striking stone and mortar. Who came to Mergot?

The riders came from out of the west, first putting fear to Bernart that they were hired by Gabriel to attack from without the walls, then foreboding when they drew near enough that the markings on their banners could be seen. It was no hireling army come to Mergot. It was King Richard.

Bernart quaked as he nudged his destrier around to face the one he dreaded. But was it coincidence that England's king took himself from the construction of his beloved castle, or had Gabriel called him to aid? Bernart would not have guessed the latter. Never had his friend-turned-enemy called upon others to do his battles, but men changed, as Bernart knew well. If Gabriel had, could this mean Juliana had revealed the truth of what had happened at Tremoral nearly a year past?

The dread possibility caused Bernart to sweat more profusely into his chain mail, and more so when he recalled her defiance this morn. A moment later, sharp pain shot through his groin. He grunted, squeezing his fists to keep from clutching himself. Would Juliana have risked her sister? With Gabriel's brother dead, she could not know that the meager-minded Alaiz was gone from Tremoral.

Bernart closed his eyes. Pray, let his secret be safe, let it be chance that placed King Richard at Mergot, or that Gabriel had turned coward. But if the latter, what hope had Gabriel that the king would allow him to hold another man's wife?

"What have you not told me?" the dark Faison quietly demanded as he drew alongside.

Bernart glanced sidelong at the irksome baron who

would suffer well to be put through with a sword. "I am as surprised as you, *friend*."

Faison pushed his barbed blue gaze to Bernart, flexing his armless shoulder as if his own thoughts ran with Bernart's. And perhaps they did, for his left arm came across his body and his hand turned around his sword hilt.

Bernart tensed, but reminded himself there was little to fear from one whose sword arm had long ago rotted upon infidel soil. Faison could pull the sword from its scabbard, but to swing it on an unbalanced body would be laughable. And the baron must have known it, for he carried his threat no further.

Bernart looked back at the approaching army, feeling a tic start at his eye, then his mouth as the one at the fore neared. Whatever Richard's reason for coming to Mergot, he would not be pleased that his vassal made war on another of his vassals. Bernart ought to have sought his permission, but though he could be forgiven for laying siege to one who'd stolen his wife, he'd feared that bringing the king into the fray might result in the question of who'd fathered Juliana's son.

A few moments later, the king halted his grand destrier less than ten feet from Bernart.

Bernart bowed his head. "Your Majesty."

The ensuing silence opened up rivulets of perspiration down Bernart's torso. Would his mail rust before the king gave response?

"Kinthorpe," Richard clipped.

Bernart swallowed, lifted his head, and met those fiery eyes a moment before they swung to Faison.

"Ah, Faison, we ought not to be surprised." The king spoke in the language of the French, so thickly accented Bernart had to strain to translate the words of England's king, who it was said knew not a word of English.

"It follows, hmm?" Richard taunted.

Faison inclined his head, but that was all. No other acknowledgment or respect did he give.

Surprisingly, the fiercely redheaded king grinned. "We will speak later, Faison." He looked to the castle walls. "Now we settle this matter between Kinthorpe and De Vere."

What knew he of it? Bernart wondered with a new rush of fear.

"Join us." Richard turned his destrier to the walls. Bernart and Faison followed, the former clutched with dread, the latter darkly silent.

The devil! Bernart silently cursed the man who was as if untouched by fear. Did he not care if he lived or died? Was his pain truly so raw? And what knew he of suffering? True, an arm he had lost, but still he had the get between his legs, still he could plow a woman's belly and grow it large with child.

The lowering of the drawbridge swept aside the clatterings of Bernart's mind, forced him to consider that which awaited him—Gabriel and Juliana. *Betrayers!* But the king would make good his claim. Come the morrow, Juliana and the babe would leave this place with him. All he must concern himself with was convincing the king that what Gabriel had done was so grievous as to warrant severe punishment. Death? Dared he hope? Unfortunately, from all he heard, Gabriel was among Richard's favorites.

Bernart pressed his sweat-soaked shoulders back and cocked his chin in terrible anticipation of again meeting Gabriel.

Chapter Twenty-five

Juliana sprang up from her knees, spinning around to face Lissant where she stood in the chapel doorway. "The king?"

"Aye, he comes."

Juliana listened, realizing the commotion without the walls had ceased. He had come!

"Lord De Vere would have you make ready for the king's arrival in the hall."

Juliana nodded. "A moment, please." She turned back to the altar before which she'd knelt until she could scarcely feel her knees, then clasped her hands before her. "Thank you, Father." She squeezed her eyes closed. "Pray, guide my tongue." She lowered her arms and swept around. "Gabrien sleeps?"

"He does, my lady."

"Then come." She hurried past the woman, traversed the corridor, and descended the stairs. Upon stepping into

364

the hall, she halted. Save for the servants who were dragging tables and benches from the walls and gathering debris from the rushes, the room was empty.

"Where are the villagers?" she asked.

Lissant came alongside. "Gone outside, my lady—'tis an audience of few the king seeks."

Of course. "And of the injured?"

"Moved to the storeroom, my lady."

Juliana nodded. "Good." She looked around and settled her gaze on a servant who yawned widely as she picked a bone from the rushes. "Ann! Prepare the sideboard." Juliana hoped the woman would not argue with her as a few continued to do, though she was now mother of Gabriel's heir. "Lay it with whatever cook can manage."

Ann inclined her head and bustled toward the kitchens.

"Cloths upon the tables," Juliana directed another servant. "And the salt cellar." She turned to Lissant. "Tend the fire."

The maid turned to the hearth.

Juliana looked around. All was provided for—or would be shortly. Now she must change her clothes.

Her hope that the babe would sleep through the coming of the king was doused when the creak of her chamber door brought forth a cry.

She hurried forward, lifted him from his cradle, and held him close.

He calmed and waved a fist as if to admonish her for awakening him.

She smiled past her worry. "King Richard is here, little one." She kissed his brow.

He gurgled, nuzzling her bodice.

It seemed the king would have to wait.

*   *   *

Who had sent for Richard? Gabriel wondered as, with a tightening of fists, he waited for the king to pass over the drawbridge. Bernart? Juliana? Blase? Nay, not his brother, and though Juliana had wanted to, she had no means of sending word. Bernart, then. What he could not take himself he had brought another to do. Though Gabriel had not denied the king entrance, as he'd momentarily considered, he would not surrender Juliana and his son. Be it by arms or a revelation he did not wish to make, he would hold them. *Damnation!* He ought to have taken them and fled France. But to leave his people to Bernart's wrath, to ever be running . . .

As the king passed beneath the raised portcullis, he thrust his gaze to Gabriel.

Gabriel swept beyond him to Bernart and Faison, then grew stiffer. The stink and filth of war upon him, he looked again to Richard and bowed.

The king reined in. "It has been long, De Vere."

Would that it could be longer, Gabriel straightened. "Your Majesty, you are welcome at Mergot."

"Hmm." He picked his gaze over the debris-strewn bailey, then lifted it to the holed walls. "We trust there is good reason for this, Kinthorpe."

Bernart sat taller in the saddle. "A good reason, Your Majesty. De Vere has stolen my—"

"We did not ask for an explanation," Richard snapped.

Gabriel watched the color rise in Bernart's face, embarrassment razing his smug expression.

"To the hall," the king commanded, and spurred his horse ahead.

Following, Bernart put hating eyes to Gabriel. "Mine," he said, loud enough that only Gabriel might hear his claim to Juliana and the babe.

Gabriel stared at Bernart until he was past.

As for Faison, the baron needed no words to express his feelings for the one who'd been awarded his brother's lands—but then, no words were needed for enmity so deep.

Bracing himself, Gabriel followed.

The villagers who crowded the inner bailey were silent as he strode past, watchful as if aware of the import of what was to be spoken in the hall, hopeful as if it would soon see them returned to their homes.

When Gabriel entered, the great hall was empty save for King Richard, who had taken the lord's high seat, as was his privilege; Bernart and Faison, who stood left of the dais; and four of the king's guards. No Juliana. Was it as the king wished? Gabriel wondered as he positioned himself to the right of the dais.

Richard flexed his shoulders, settled deeper into the chair, and looked to Gabriel. "Where is Lady Juliana?"

Then he had not sent her from the hall. Struggling to keep his face expressionless, Gabriel said, "Likely abovestairs, Your Majesty."

The king's brow gathered. "Summon her."

Gabriel hurled his gaze against Bernart and caught his old friend's smirk. *Damn Bernart for bringing it to this!* Such humiliation Juliana would suffer—and their son if the truth of his getting were revealed.

"Summon Lady Juliana," the king harshly repeated.

Gabriel started to turn.

"I am here, Your Majesty."

Gabriel sucked in his breath at the sight of Juliana as she stepped off the stairs—auburn hair dressed in luminous plaits and coils, brown eyes large and traced with thick lashes that caused shadows to flutter against her cheekbones, bowed lips parted to reveal straight, white teeth. A more beautiful woman there was not—would

367

never be again. And when she was old, she would be as captivating. Adding to the sight was her gown. Fashioned of profuse blue cloth that, in what seemed another life, was to have been made into a surcoat for him and trappings for his destrier, it embraced her figure as she crossed the hall with chin up and her gaze stuck to the king. Not once did her eyes waver toward Bernart. It was as if he were not even present. From Bernart's change of color, her slight struck center.

Juliana came to stand at Gabriel's side.

A longing to put an arm around her, that all would know she did not belong to Bernart, pulsed through him. But it was enough that she stood with him.

"Your Majesty," she said, and bowed.

Richard lifted an apple from the platter of viands set before him. "Arise."

She straightened, and for a moment met Gabriel's gaze. Though misgiving darkened her eyes, no more would she allow Bernart to manipulate her to his will.

The king looked from Juliana to Gabriel to Bernart, and twice more. Finally he took a bite of the apple and swung his feet to the table. One boot crossed over the other, he gave the appearance of having gathered his subjects to speak of hunting. "A siege in the winter of spring," he clipped. "A siege that has snatched us from an undertaking we hold most high." His eyes settled to Juliana. "Who will tell us what is of such import, hmm?"

Gabriel stepped forward. He would do the telling—all of it, if need be. Guilt for what he could not change had no place where he and Juliana and their child were concerned. "Your Majesty—"

"Nay," Richard barked, though still he held Juliana with his gaze. "We have not asked you, De Vere."

Bernart issued a derisive snort, causing Gabriel to jam

his fingers hard against his palms to keep them from his sword hilt.

"Speak!" King Richard demanded. "Surely there is another who might tell?"

Confidence expanding his chest, Bernart put a foot forward. "Allow me, Your Majesty. I—"

Richard slammed his hands to the chair arms, sending the apple bounding across the table and into the rushes. "Nor have we asked you, Kinthorpe!" For all his wrath, he kept his gaze upon Juliana.

Bernart's jowls worked, his eyelids fluttering. He slipped back to Faison's side.

Beneath the king's heavy regard, Juliana's mouth parched. Only she and the rebel baron remained to give answer. However, it was not Faison he called upon.

"We wait!" King Richard said scathingly.

She moistened her lips. "I would speak, Your Majesty."

Eyebrows jogging his brow, he said condescendingly, "That was not so difficult," and joined his hands upon his chest.

Not difficult? Only did one compare it to birthing. "Your Majesty, what I have to tell is but for you. Could you not send your men from the hall?"

"Naught that is told here shall leave," he said without consideration. "My men are trusted."

She glanced to the one beside Bernart. "The same is said for Baron Faison?"

Richard's eyebrows dipped. "Ah." He glanced at the rebel. "Indeed you have cause for concern, but surely the baron ought to know for what he gave men and machines to your husband's cause."

Battling the longing to put her shoulder to Gabriel's and slip her hand into his, Juliana said, "That I cannot argue, Your Majesty, but still I would ask it."

"Very well, this we shall grant you." The king's gaze went to Faison. "Await without."

The baron glowered, turned, and strode across the hall. A few moments later, Juliana, Gabriel, and Bernart were as alone as it was possible to be with England's truant king.

"Now tell, Lady Juliana," Richard said, "for what did you send Sir Erec to summon us to Mergot?"

Beside her, Gabriel went stiff. Now he would be angry. She only prayed he would forgive Sir Erec for carrying her message. She stepped forward. "As was told you, Your Majesty, Bernart Kinthorpe brings war to Mergot that he might steal the son of Gabriel De Vere."

As hard as Bernart's gaze was upon her, she ought to have been felled by it, but she refused to look to him, to see the threat in his eyes of what he would do to Alaiz.

"And to steal the mother of this child, as it was also told," the king reminded her.

Juliana pushed her hands into the folds of her skirts so that none would see her grip on them. "That is true, Your Majesty."

"But the child's mother would be you, Lady Juliana—*wife* to Bernart Kinthorpe."

She nearly flinched. "You are correct."

"Hmm." Richard shifted his lower jaw from side to side. "It is most serious what you tell, and yet if it be true, your husband comes to claim a child not his—a bastard."

Anger leaped at the foul name put to her innocent babe. "It is true, Your Majesty," she said tightly. "Gabriel De Vere is the father of my child."

She did not need to look to Bernart to know his fury. It coursed the hall as if lit by fire.

The king lifted a goblet of wine. "Do you speak of ravishment, Lady Juliana?"

She gasped and shook her head. "Nay, Your Majesty."

He pulled a long drink, then set the goblet back to the table. "Then De Vere seduced you?"

Were it not so dire, she would laugh. "He did not, Your Majesty."

Annoyance gathered Richard's brow. "Then willingly you went to him?"

Far from it, but could she tell of Bernart's infirmity? Speak the words that would dismiss his claim? After all he'd done, it ought to come easily. She gulped. "Nay, Your Majesty, willingly I did not go to Gabriel, but neither did he ravish me."

Richard's boots hit the dais with a resounding thud. He grasped the chair arms and leaned forward. "What riddles speak you, Lady Juliana?"

How shallow her breath. She must calm herself. "Not riddles, Your Majesty. The truth."

"And what is the truth?"

"That . . ." She looked to Bernart. There shone the threat, but also a glimmer of fear. Confident as he was that Alaiz would keep her from speaking the truth, a sliver of doubt festered.

His lids narrowed, his nostrils flaring. "The child is mine," he said.

The king's head snapped around. "How know you? By her own tongue she confesses to having made of you a cuckold—given herself to a man she chooses over you."

Bernart's face burst with crimson. As for Gabriel at Juliana's back, he was as a spring ready to snap.

"Cuckolded I may be," Bernart said, "but it was my seed that took."

The king swung his gaze to Gabriel. "What say you, De Vere?"

"He is my son, Your Majesty."

The tip of Richard's tongue pushed at the corner of his mouth, then disappeared. He came again to Juliana. "When was the child born?"

Dear God, not that.

"Do not think to lie," the king said menacingly. "I have but to ask of the household to know."

She pulled a long breath. "He was born a month past, but—"

"As due?"

Chill bumps swept her. "Three weeks early, Your Majesty."

"Ah." He looked again to Bernart.

Juliana followed his gaze.

Bernart's lips spread. He thought to have won. "There, Your Majesty, it is proven the child is mine, for De Vere was not at Tremoral those weeks before the tournament. Already a child grew in my wife's belly. My heir."

"The babe was born early!" Juliana protested.

Richard released a gust of breath. "Bring the child to the hall that we might see him, Lady Juliana."

There went her heart, twisting and grinding in her chest. She had no choice but to reveal Bernart's infirmity. "Your Majesty, there is something—"

"Now!"

She pressed her lips against argument, bowed, and turned. As she stepped past Gabriel, their eyes met. His were hard. Might he never forgive her for sending Sir Erec to the king? Prayers frantically coursing through her mind, she withdrew from the hall. Out of sight, she let her feet drag the stairs, then the corridor. Deny her though the king might, he would know the truth when she brought Gabrien to him. Never would Bernart hold Gabriel's son.

When she entered her chamber, Gabrien was gurgling his little sounds from the cradle of Lissant's arms.

The maid stood. "My lady?"

Juliana halted before her and looked upon her son. Aching for his innocence, she touched his cheek. "Sweet Gabrien," she murmured, then looked to Lissant. "I must take him to the king."

"For what, my lady?"

"Worry not." Juliana lifted the babe. "Gabrien will return shortly." Of course, though she revealed Bernart, the king might not believe her, might not demand evidence of Bernart's inability to sire children, might give Gabrien to him. What then? Blood?

When she returned to the hall, it was as if not a word were spoken in her absence. The king picked at the viands while the two men before him stood unmoving. Hating the lusty gaze Bernart put to the babe, Juliana pressed Gabrien nearer.

"Come," King Richard beckoned.

She accepted Gabriel's gaze as she approached the dais. Regardless of what the king determined, she knew he would not surrender their child. It could mean his death. . . .

Heart contracting, she passed near him and ascended the dais.

The king did not stand, but stretched up from his chair to look upon the babe.

Gabrien blinked at him.

"Hmm." Richard resettled himself. "They all look the same." He turned to Bernart. "How long have you been wed, Kinthorpe?"

Bernart shifted his weight. "Now four years, Your Majesty."

"Four years without an heir. A long time."

Bernart's larynx pitched. "My wife is not as fertile as I would wish her to be, Your Majesty."

Juliana gasped.

"Lady Juliana!" Richard bellowed. "Keep your tongue."

She bit it.

The king returned to Bernart. "Then you have been long in waiting for an heir."

"I have, Your Majesty. But now he is come."

"Hmm." Richard put a hand to the chair arm, swept it into a fist, and began beating out a rhythm.

On and on it went, thumping through Juliana like a lead ball. What was he thinking? When would he allow her to speak?

At last he met her gaze. "Lady Juliana, give the child unto your husband."

She stumbled back a step and shook her head. He had decided? No more to be said? As she searched for words, Richard lurched forward in his seat.

"De Vere," he thundered, a particle of food vaulting from his mouth, "for what do you put your hand to your sword?"

Juliana looked over her shoulder. Gabriel's hand was upon his hilt, his legs braced, his face as unmoving as stone, his eyes defiant. How large he looked—as if he could bring mountains to their knees. And the king's guards were prepared, did he think to try.

"Gabriel," Juliana entreated.

He was slow to drag his gaze from the king, but finally gave it to her.

She shook her head. "Do not."

She saw him swallow and knew he struggled, but he released the hilt.

"Wise," the king rumbled. "Now, Lady Juliana, we say again, deliver the child to his father."

That she could do. "As Your Majesty commands." She turned from the dais and crossed to Gabriel. "Hold your son, Gabriel," she said amid stunned silence. "Protect him." She passed the babe into his ready arms.

"Your Majesty!" Bernart protested, his voice squeaking as if a mouse sprang from his throat.

The high seat scraped loudly as Richard thrust to his feet. "You wish our wrath upon you, woman?"

Juliana turned. Was it the devil in him that caused his face to contort? She pushed past fear and clasped her hands at her waist. "Surely Your Majesty knows I would not be so foolish. As you can see, I have done exactly as bidden—delivered the child unto his father."

Richard slammed his palms to the table, causing the platter to clatter. "Lady Juliana!"

She hurried forward and stepped up to the dais. "Pray, Your Majesty, allow me to speak to . . . my husband. Do you, I vow all will be explained."

"You test us mightily," he said between his teeth.

"It is not my intention, Your Majesty," Juliana said, consciously softening her voice, "I but wish to right that made wrong."

His anger flickered.

She took a step nearer, smiling beseechingly. "Pray, allow me this." Though she was unaccustomed to using her woman's wiles, she prayed it would serve her.

The king looked closer upon her. "And if we allow it?"

She moistened her lips. "Then ever shall I be grateful, Your Majesty."

He considered her a moment longer, then inclined his

head. "Though it does not please us to grant your request, we shall."

Juliana nearly wilted.

"But we warn you"—he resumed his seat—"keep us not long."

She bowed. "I thank you, Your Majesty." With a glance at Gabriel, she stepped from the dais and crossed to Bernart.

The red gone from the king's face had found its way into his. "Juliana," he bit out.

"Bernart." She stepped past him.

He followed her to the far end of the hall and into an alcove curtained by shadows.

She turned to him. "You must stop this now—put an end to it before it puts an end to you."

Bernart took a step nearer her. "Your threat is without heart, Juliana."

She stared into his fleshy face, catching the shine of saliva he had yet to wipe from his chin. "*Is* it without heart, Bernart?"

He snorted. "If you could have told, already you would have. You cannot."

"But I can. And I have."

His lids snapped nearly closed. "What speak you?"

"Gabriel knows."

The air rushed from him and set his jaw to quivering. With a groan, he turned and clawed hands down his face.

The door Juliana had been so certain was closed against him creaked open. She lifted a hand, reached to him, and stopped. The past was done. She had not been able to reach him then, and could not reach him now.

He came around. "Whore!"

Laughter croaked from her throat. "Whore? And who made me such?"

"Who else have you told?"

As there was no reason to reveal Sir Erec, she said, "It need go no further. Withdraw your claim to Gabrien and your secret—"

"Gabrien? That is the name given the little bastard?"

She swung, and with the flat of her hand jerked Bernart's face hard right. "Do not speak so of him!"

He staggered back and pressed a fist to his seared cheek. "When I take him from Mergot," he heaved, "he shall be called by a name of my choosing."

Dear God, why did he persist? *Because for Alaiz you did for him what you would do for no other.* She shook her head. "Nay, Gabrien will not be leaving Mergot. It is his home, and one day, as Gabriel's heir, he will be baron."

Bernart stared at her.

She drew herself up. "Do you force me to it, I shall reveal all to the king."

"Then you have no regard for your sister?"

There it was. "You know I do, but through Alaiz you shall not have Gabriel's son."

His lips drew back. "Deny me, Juliana, and she will suffer. I swear it!"

It was time. "How fares my sister?"

He hesitated. "Well—for the moment."

Bitterness coated Juliana's tongue. "Such lies you tell. Alaiz is no longer at Tremoral, and can no longer make of me your puppet."

A sharp breath whistled through his teeth. "Who told you this?"

"Blase De Vere."

Bernart shook his head. "He is dead!"

"Though 'tis as you would have him, he lives, and is well enough to send word of that which befell my sister."

Bernart's confidence poured through his feet and puddled out from under him. He lurched to the alcove wall, braced a hand to it, and put his head down. "You love him," he whispered.

Clasping her hands to keep from reaching to him, silently commanding her tears to quiet, Juliana said, "I do."

"After what he did to me?" He turned and pressed his back to the wall. "His betrayal cost me my manhood!"

"It was not betrayal, Bernart. Though you may never admit it, twice as many men could have done no more than those who followed you. More spilled blood is all you would have gained."

He slammed his fists against the stone at his back. "Gabriel left me to die!"

She stepped forward and put a hand to his shoulder. "You are wrong. He followed you into Acre."

"What?"

"It is true, and for it he was beaten and imprisoned until the coming of King Richard."

"He told you this?"

"Nay, it was Sir Erec."

Bernart shook his head and scowled. "What knows he of it?"

"He was among those who could not be convinced to turn from your quest. Afterward, he and Gabriel shared a cell."

Clearly Bernart longed to cling to the bitterness and hostility that were more familiar to him than breath, but it was as if her words stirred a memory.

She squeezed his shoulder. "Believe it, Bernart. Believe it and turn from this wrong you seek to do Gabriel."

He stared at her hand upon him, then shuddered and dropped his chin to his chest. "I shall lose all."

His despair caused a tear to slip from her eye. "Nay,

Bernart, only that which you do not need." She drew her hand from his shoulder and cupped his cheek. "That which does not belong to you."

He squeezed his lids closed, drew a deep breath, and opened his eyes. Tears sparkled at her. "Once you belonged to me."

She fought the knot in her throat. "Once."

He knocked her hand aside. "Damn you, Juliana! Damn you and Gabriel." He pushed past her and stalked from the alcove, his limp more prominent than ever she had seen it.

Then he would not withdraw his claim upon Gabrien. Her chest burning with the cry she would not allow herself, Juliana followed. Bearing the king's impatient gaze, she crossed the hall.

Gabriel looked from Bernart, who trembled so violently the movement was visible across the distance, to Juliana. Sorrow grooved her mouth and brow. Had she convinced Bernart to leave Mergot with his secret intact? Or would hate destroy what remained of him?

Regaining Gabriel's side, Juliana looked to the babe, who contentedly sucked his fingers. "Bernart forces me to it," she murmured, and lifted her gaze to Gabriel's. "I am without choice."

In that moment, his anger at her for having summoned the king turned. He caught her hand and squeezed it. "I will tell it."

"Nay, 'tis for me to do." She turned to the king.

"And now all shall be explained, Lady Juliana?" Richard asked.

She nodded. "Your Majesty—"

"If it pleases you, Your Majesty," Bernart interrupted, "I shall explain."

Gabriel looked over Juliana's head to his old friend. More lies?

"Then speak," the king invited, "and be quick. We tire of this."

Bernart opened his mouth, closed it, and tried again. "It is . . . true what my wife tells."

Gabriel jerked; Juliana gasped.

The king cocked his head. "Then the child is not yours?"

Bernart could not meet his gaze. "He is not mine, Your Majesty."

Gabriel drew Juliana against his side, looking into the face she turned up to his. Her heart was in her eyes.

"You are certain?" the king pressed.

"I am."

"How?"

"I . . ." Bernart stared at the floor, struggled to get the words to his tongue. "I am impotent"—his voice broke—"Your Majesty."

It was as near the truth as he would give, but Gabriel would not argue it. It was enough.

The king fell to silence, the only movement about him the tapping of a finger. "Impotent . . . hmm. Was your marriage not consummated, then?"

Bernart's swallow could be heard to the opposite end of the dais. "It was not."

Richard pursed his lips. "Most curious, this. It begs the question of the circumstances of the child's conception."

Tension leaped through Gabriel, stiffened Juliana, staggered Bernart back a step. *Curse Richard's curiosity! No more need be told.*

"I have met your brother," the king said. "Osbern, is it not?"

Repugnance twisted Bernart's lips. " 'Tis the name my father gave his second born."

"Hmm." Richard stared long at him, then swept his gaze over Juliana and Gabriel. "Rumors are terrible things." He pushed back in the chair. "There is naught that can more quickly reduce the mightiest to worms."

Bernart's color deepened.

The king heaved a sigh. "But though we are certain it would make for lively tale, we shall speak on this matter no more." He swept a beckoning hand before him. "Come forth, Lady Juliana."

She looked to Gabriel, then reluctantly pulled her hand from his and stepped up to the dais. "Your Majesty."

"Seek you an annulment?"

"I do."

Richard looked beyond her to Gabriel. "You would wed the lady and give her and the child your name?"

"It is my greatest desire, Your Majesty."

Richard reached for a chunk of cheese and flattened it between thumb and forefinger. "You love her?"

Though the king but amused himself, Gabriel said, "I do, Your Majesty."

Richard popped the cheese into his mouth and spoke around it. "It is good we like you, De Vere."

Did he? It was hardly evident.

"Very well, an annulment the lady shall have."

His blood warming, Gabriel bowed. "I thank you, Your Majesty."

"However"—Richard drew him back in, once more put strain to Gabriel's muscles—"we do not think it necessary that annulment be awarded on grounds of impotence." He looked to Bernart. "Consanguinity. Aye, that would be better, do you not agree?"

Bernart's gratitude shone dim. "There is no blood between Juliana and I, Your Majesty."

"Ah, but there will be—third cousins, we think . . . or perhaps fourth."

"But how—"

"Illegitimacy makes kin of us all, Kinthorpe. It is but a matter of degree." He smiled. "As it can rarely be proven, neither can it be disproven."

"But the Church—"

"Will accept the word of the king of England."

How Richard loved his power, though it was granted him by an island kingdom he deemed unworthy. But in this Gabriel would not fault him.

Bernart bowed. "I am indebted, Your Majesty."

"This we know."

Bernart straightened.

"By first light you and your men will be gone from Mergot," the king said. "As for Faison, we shall deal with him." Richard tossed a hand up. "Your leave is granted—all of you."

"I thank you, Your Majesty," Bernart said. Withholding his gaze from Juliana and Gabriel, he started across the hall.

Gabriel turned, staring after Bernart. Something tugged at him. In spite of all, he felt no victory at having prevailed over Bernart. Indeed, sorrow settled within him.

Juliana gained Gabriel's side.

He looked down at her. There was a brightness to her eyes—a reflection of love and hope that made him long to take her in his arms, but at the moment those arms were filled with Gabrien. Too, there was something he must do. "Gabrien needs his mother," he said.

Smiling, she lifted him from Gabriel. "And his father," she said softly.

"Both," he agreed. "Take him abovestairs. I shall join you shortly."

Her gaze faltered. "You go to Bernart?"

"Aye, but I shall not be long."

She pressed a hand to his forearm. "Be of good care, Gabriel."

"I shall." Denying himself her mouth, he pivoted and traversed the hall.

"We shall require the lord's solar, Lady Juliana," he heard Richard call.

"Then you will stay the night, Your Majesty?"

"Perhaps."

"I shall see that the solar is made ready."

Gabriel halted at the doors, glancing behind to see Juliana begin her ascent of the stairs. When she was gone from sight, he stepped outside. Faison was there, staring out across the walls as if remembering when the castle and these lands were held by his family.

"Faison," Gabriel acknowledged as he stepped past.

Silence was the man's response.

As Gabriel descended the steps, he shouted for the villagers to ready themselves for their return home. A cheer went up as he made his way among the throng.

In the outer bailey, he overtook Bernart. "I would speak to you," he said as he drew alongside.

Bernart halted, then swung around. "You have what you want," he snarled. "What else is there?"

He has lost all, Gabriel reminded himself. "I but wish to say I would that it could have been different between us."

Bernart's lips twisted. "And I would that I had killed your brother."

Gabriel splayed a hand upon his sword, but stayed the desire to draw it. Nothing good would come of slaying him—though perhaps it was what he wished. . . .

"Pity I did not sink the blade deeper," Bernart mused with a flash of teeth. "Pity I did not gut him."

The sword hissed from Gabriel's scabbard. Breathing harshly, he swept the point to his old friend's throat.

Bernart merely smiled. "Ah, but there is yet that idiot sister of Juliana's, isn't there?"

The threat rushed blood through Gabriel's veins, demanded he drive the blade home. And the desire trebled with Bernart's next words.

"Be you assured, *friend*, I shall find her and make of her many gifts for that whore who bore your bastard."

The blood fled Gabriel's hand upon the hilt. In all his years, was there anything he had wanted more than to spill Bernart's life? He glanced at his men upon the walls. They watched, waited—as did the king's men. Anything at all?

His heart stirred. Aye, Juliana and his child he wanted more. Did he run Bernart through, he would likely lose them. Which was as Bernart wished it.

Gabriel lowered his sword. "God help you, Bernart Kinthorpe," he said and pivoted. Feeling Bernart's gaze across the rubble, he returned his blade to its scabbard.

"Soon, old friend," Bernart called.

Gabriel clenched his hands, but did not falter as he crossed the inner drawbridge. The villagers closed around him when he stepped into the inner bailey. There were questions, and he welcomed them, for they set his thoughts from Bernart. All he answered ere returning to the donjon where King Richard roared at an expressionless Faison.

Gabriel crossed the hall and started up the stairs. First his ablutions and a change of garments; then he would go to Juliana. However, he had first to send from his chamber the maids set to readying it for the king. He commanded them to await without and closed the door.

Though by basin and hand towel he bathed away much of the battle, his search for a suitable change of garments was thwarted by the unopened missives that lay at the bottom of his chest. He stared at them, at their unbroken seals. He knew what message they contained—the same as the first and only one he'd read six months following his departure from the barony of Wyverly. Though the third son would be baron, Arnault De Vere longed to see Gabriel again, to reconcile, to be at peace with him.

Gabriel closed his eyes, for the first time in what seemed forever opening feelings he'd locked away that day of revelation, when he had thought all lost. Deny though he had his love for the man who'd set him aside, it ached within him. He had Juliana, Gabrien, a God who answered prayers, the people of Mergot, and a place in the world. If he could but forgive his father he would be free of the lonely, barren places of his heart.

He lifted his lids. Once his son was of a suitable age for travel, he would take Juliana and Gabrien across the channel to England. They would pause at Wyverly and come to know better the man from whose seed Gabriel had sprung. Then mayhap he would be healed whole. Of course, there was still Blase, whose injuries were unknown, and Alaiz, who would know death did Sir Erec fail to locate her. Much to do in England, but it would be done.

He chose a red tunic and russet hose. A few minutes later, he stepped into the chamber Juliana shared with Gabrien.

Juliana heard the creak of the door, and reveled in his coming. All was changed, their destinies made one. She turned from Gabrien's cradle.

Gabriel stood with his back to the door, a smile in one corner of his mouth.

Juliana ran forward and thrust herself into his arms.

He closed them around her, putting his face to her neck. "Juliana," he murmured.

She dropped her head back and met his fiery gaze. "Gabriel."

The smile made it to the opposite corner of his mouth a moment before he fit it to her lips.

She pushed fingers through his hair, cupped his scalp, delved. She was flying, like a many-feathered bird whose wings knew no limits. As long as Gabriel soared with her, she needed no ground beneath her.

His tongue swept hers, lapped the underside, traced her teeth, circled her lips.

So sweet, so perfect. But then he loosed her mouth.

Hoping he would return to her, she held her eyes closed and levered to her toes.

"Juliana."

She groaned and opened her eyes.

His smile was absent, in its place a gravity that put her heels back to the floor.

"Gabriel?"

He sighed. "I thank you."

She shook her head. "For?"

"For you . . . for Gabrien . . . for doing what I could not."

"Then I am forgiven for sending Sir Erec to the king?"

There was the smile she missed. "Most assuredly—providing you no more trifle with Richard's affections."

She laughed. "You noticed."

He growled. "Who could not?"

She drew a deep breath. "Ah, Gabriel, I am to be your wife."

"Wife," he repeated as if all the world were in that one word. He inclined his head. "And I your husband."

Though it might take months, perhaps a year for her marriage to be annulled, a thrill went through Juliana. "It could not be sweeter."

His eyebrows arched. "Could it not?" He swept her into his arms, carried her to the bed, and laid her back. "On that I differ, my lady."

She reached to him, but no sooner did he draw near than the babe wailed.

Gabriel stilled, then eyed the cradle. "Our son wishes something?"

Juliana pushed up on an elbow and looked to the little fists that shook above the cradle. "He does."

Frustration at the poorly timed interruption lined Gabriel's brow. "He is hungry?"

"Nay, he has been fed. That is the cry he makes when he desires to be held."

Incredulity leaped from Gabriel's frustration. "You know this?"

"Of course I do. I am his mother. As his father, you must learn these things too."

He grunted, pushed off the bed, and crossed to the cradle.

After a few moments, Gabrien ceased wailing.

"So," Gabriel said, "you hold me to my vow that your mother and I will not come together again till we are wed, eh, Gabrien?"

"Goo," the babe affirmed.

Gabriel chuckled. "I will wait." He lifted his son from the cradle.

The sight of them sent shivers through Juliana. Father and son. Son and father. Naught could keep them apart.

Gabriel settled the babe to Juliana's side, and lay down opposite.

She met his gaze over their son's head. "Never have I known such happiness."

He grasped her hand, carried it to his chest, and pressed it to the beat that was only for her. "Beloved Juliana."

She sighed. "Beloved blackheart."

Epilogue

She was found. But not by Sir Erec. Though the missive was delivered of him, it told that Thierry Rievaulx held Alaiz. That news, though fearfully unwelcome, was somewhat lightened when it was related that Rievaulx had captured Alaiz two months earlier and that, though she was his prisoner, no ill had befallen her. Speculation put that the brooding baron was captivated by this one who was said to have murdered his brother. Could it be?

Hands trembling, Juliana set the missive on the table, smoothed it top to bottom, then read it again.

"She is well." Gabriel spoke from over her shoulder.

Juliana nodded. "At the time of this writing."

His hand touched her shoulder. "Sir Erec will keep near until we arrive in England."

A fortnight hence—providing summer did not abruptly

turn to fall. Juliana dropped her head back, looking up at Gabriel where he stood behind her chair. How was it that fourteen days could suddenly seem a year? This past month she'd been light as air with news that the church had granted the annulment, throwing wide the door to marriage with Gabriel. But now to learn that Alaiz was Rievaulx's captive . . .

Gabriel leaned down and caressed his mouth across hers. "She will endure," he murmured.

"How know you that?"

He drew slightly back, arching an eyebrow. "Is she not your sister?"

She was, wasn't she?

Gabriel smiled. "All will come right, Juliana. This I vow."

Juliana met his smile, then reached up and laid a hand to his jaw. "Aye, it will, won't it?" It had come right for her and Gabriel. Somehow it would come right for Alaiz. . . .

Pure Temptation
Connie Mason

Spirits can be so bloody unpredictable, and the specter of Lady Amelia is worst of all. Just when one of her ne'er-do-well descendants thinks he can go astray in peace, the phantom lady always appears to change his wicked ways. A rogue without peer, Jackson Graystoke wants to make gaming and carousing in London society his life's work. And the penniless baronet will gladly damn himself with wine and women—if Lady Amelia gives him the ghost of a chance. Fresh off the boat from Ireland, Moira O'Toole isn't fool enough to believe in legends or naive enough to trust a rake. Yet after an accident lands her in Graystoke Manor, she finds herself haunted, harried, and hopelessly charmed by Black Jack Graystoke and his exquisite promise of . . . Pure Temptation.

___4041-7 $5.99 US/$6.99 CAN

The OUTLAWS: Rafe

Connie Mason

He is going to hang. Rafe Gentry has committed plenty of sins, but not the robbery and murder that has landed him in jail. Now, with a lynch mob out for his blood, he is staring death in the face . . . until a blond beauty with the voice of an angel steps in to redeem him.

She is going to wed. There is only one way to rescue the dark and dangerous outlaw from the hanging tree—by claiming him as the fictitious fiancé she is to meet in Pueblo. But Sister Angela Abbot never anticipates that she will have to make good on her claim and actually marry the rogue. Railroaded into a hasty wedding, reeling from the raw, seductive power of Rafe's kiss, she wonders whether she has made the biggest mistake of her life, or the most exciting leap of faith.

___4702-0 $5.99 US/$6.99 CAN

Dorchester Publishing Co., Inc.
P.O. Box 6640
Wayne, PA 19087-8640

Please add $1.75 for shipping and handling for the first book and $.50 for each book thereafter. NY, NYC, and PA residents, please add appropriate sales tax. No cash, stamps, or C.O.D.s. All orders shipped within 6 weeks via postal service book rate. Canadian orders require $2.00 extra postage and must be paid in U.S. dollars through a U.S. banking facility.

Name_____
Address_____
City_____State_____Zip_____
I have enclosed $_____ in payment for the checked book(s).
Payment <u>must</u> accompany all orders. ❑ Please send a free catalog.

Taming Angelica

Alice Chambers

What is the point in having beauty and wealth if one can't do what one wants because of one's gender? Angelica doesn't know, but she plans on overcoming it. Suffragette and debutante, Angelica has nothing if not will. Lord William Claridge has a wont to gamble and enjoys training Thoroughbreds, but his older brother has tightened the family's purse strings. Strapped for cash, the handsome rake decides to resort to the unthinkable: Marry. For money. But when his mark turns out to be a more spirited filly than he has ever before saddled, he feels his heart bucking wildly. Suddenly, much more is on the line than his pocketbook. And the answer still comes down to . . . taming Angelica.

___4682-2 $4.99 US/$5.99 CAN

BEYOND *Forever*
DEBRA DIER

1999. He appears to her out of the swirling fog on the cliff's edge, a ghostly figure who seems somehow larger than life. Dark, handsome, blatantly male, he radiates the kind of confidence that leads men into battle and women into reckless choices. But independent-minded Julia Fairfield isn't about to be coerced into anything, especially not a jaunt across the centuries in search of a miracle.

1818. Abducted from her own time, Julia finds herself face-to-face with this flesh and blood incarnation. Gavin MacKinnon is as confounded as Julia about her place in his life, but after a night of passion, they learn that their destinies are inextricably bound together, no matter what the time or place.

___4623-7 $5.50 US/$6.50 CAN

MacLaren's Bride — Debra Dier

BESTSELLING AUTHOR OF *LORD SAVAGE*

She is a challenge to the gentlemen of the ton, for they say she can freeze a man with a single glance of her green eyes. Meg Drummond wants nothing to do with love—not when she has seen her own parents' marriage fall apart. And though she promises to marry an Englishman to spite her father, she has to find someone to win her stubborn heart. Then Alec MacLaren charges back into her life, unexpectedly awakening her deep-seated passions with his wicked Highland ways. He kidnaps and marries her out of loyalty to her father, but once he feels her tantalizing body against his, he aches to savor all of her. He knows he needs to break through the wall of ice around her heart, gain her trust, and awaken her desire to truly make her...MacLaren's Bride.

___4302-5 $5.50 US/$6.50 CAN

. . . and coming
May 2001
from. . .

THE OUTLAWS: SAM

CONNIE MASON

Down and out, his face on wanted posters across the West, Sam Gentry needs a job. And the foreman of the B & G ranch is hiring cowhands. But who is the behind-the-scenes owner the ramrod mentioned? Surely this Lacey isn't the same one who has haunted his dreams for the last five years. This Texas rancher can't possibly be the dyed-in-the-wool Yankee whose betrayal sent him to a Northern prison camp. Most unlikely of all, this widowed mother simply cannot be the hot-blooded wife who once warmed his bed. Yet one look in her emerald eyes tells him the impossible has happened. How can he take a paycheck from the golden-haired beauty when what he really wants to do is take her back in his arms?

___4865-5 $5.99 US/$6.99 CAN

DEBRA DIER

MACKENZIE'S MAGIC

Nothing can prepare Jane for her husband's abrupt about-face the morning after their arranged wedding. Suddenly the city's fashion plate is running about clad in only his silk robe, speaking in a strange Scottish accent, and claiming to have never seen a fork. Jane can't possibly believe what he says: that he is Colin MacKenzie, a Scottish earl who lived 300 years ago. Nor can she believe the spine-tingling attraction she feels for the man she has sworn to hate. But then, Jane never believed she could be bewitched, and suddenly she is at the mercy of....MacKenzie's magic.

___4866-3 $5.50 US/$6.50 CAN

Dorchester Publishing Co., Inc.
P.O. Box 6640
Wayne, PA 19087-8640

Please add $1.75 for shipping and handling for the first book and $.50 for each book thereafter. NY, NYC, and PA residents, please add appropriate sales tax. No cash, stamps, or C.O.D.s. All orders shipped within 6 weeks via postal service book rate. Canadian orders require $2.00 extra postage and must be paid in U.S. dollars through a U.S. banking facility.

Name_____

Address_____

City_____State_____Zip_____

I have enclosed $_____ in payment for the checked book(s).

Payment <u>must</u> accompany all orders. ❑ Please send a free catalog.

CHECK OUT OUR WEBSITE! www.dorchesterpub.com

Always a Princess

Alice Chambers

The woman is a fraud if ever Philip Rosemont has seen one. And not only is she masquerading as an aristocrat, the dark-haired beauty is posing as the Princess of Valdastok—a tiny country that has been a dukedom for years! Yet though this impostor can hardly be a noblewoman, Philip has good cause to believe he will find her anything but common.

Eve Stanhope despises the aristocracy: a gaggle of scoundrels that are noble in name alone. She has few scruples about stealing their jewels. But ripping off rubies is harder than she expected, especially when she is cornered by a man who knows too much. And if kisses are illicit, the viscount is an arch-criminal.

___4867-1 $4.99 US/$5.99 CAN

Dorchester Publishing Co., Inc.
P.O. Box 6640
Wayne, PA 19087-8640

Please add $1.75 for shipping and handling for the first book and $.50 for each book thereafter. NY, NYC, and PA residents, please add appropriate sales tax. No cash, stamps, or C.O.D.s. All orders shipped within 6 weeks via postal service book rate. Canadian orders require $2.00 extra postage and must be paid in U.S. dollars through a U.S. banking facility.

Name_____
Address_____
City_____State_____Zip_____
I have enclosed $ _____ in payment for the checked book(s).
Payment <u>must</u> accompany all orders. ❏ Please send a free catalog.
CHECK OUT OUR WEBSITE! www.dorchesterpub.com